A BUTE CRUCIFIXI

CW01551845

'Award-winning author William Scott explores the relationships in a small community with sensitivity and conviction and produces a superb novel of power and devastating consequences in a titanic struggle between good and evil.'

—David Torrie, an editor, DC Thomson Publications

'A riveting read I must say. A modern tragedy with the energy of Coronation Street, the passion of Dickens and the intellect of Carlyle.'

—Rev Jock Stein, Minister and Theology Publisher

'What a powerful book! Greek tragedy meets the Book of Job. I heartily recommend it to anyone who has at all pondered the questions of good and evil in the Christian context. It is also a wonderful exposé of life in a small Scots town.'

—Tom McCallum, MA Hons, St Andrews, Classicist

Other Books by William Scott

The Bannockburn Years

Bannockburn Revealed

Bannockburn Proved

The Bute Witches

Honour Killing in Argyll & Bute

A BUTE CRUCIFIXION

by

William Scott
BA,BSc,MEd,FIMA,FSAScot

ELENKUS

MMVIII

First published in Great Britain in March 2008 by

ELENKUS

PO BOX 9807,
Rothesay,
Isle of Bute,
PA20 9YA
Scotland,
United Kingdom

Email: elenkus@yahoo.com
Website: www.elenkus.com
Telephone: 01700505439
Mobile:07842 404268

© William Wallace Cunningham Scott

All rights reserved. No part of this publication may be copied or transmitted in any way without the permission of the author.

ISBN 9780952191063

The right of William Wallace Cunningham Scott to be identified as the author of this work has been asserted by him in accordance with the Copyright, Design and Patent Act 1988

DEDICATION

Lest this journey has not many more miles to run, in which case this might be my last publication, this work is dedicated to two very different people, John Patrick Crichton Stewart, VIth Marquis of Bute; and the Rev Dr JD Douglas, both deceased.

John Bute, as he called himself, would, I believe, have been delighted by this book which, was written, significantly, during his last year, around 1993, three years after I retired to the island of my birth to write full time. Giving up a career like that in teaching which had produced remarkable satisfaction and daily excitement as well as important results and even awards, was very difficult despite the compulsion to write which, after years of writing in The Times Educational Supplement, several journals and even national newspapers, had taken a grip upon my soul and demanded no less. It would, I knew, have been immoral to have ignored this vocation which I first knew of at the age of three and, though fiercely put off the idea by others, never left me at any time in my journey. Too many teachers have such ambitions and are thwarted by their commitments. Fortunately, I had become ill in a moral battle—an omnipresent factor in any decent life—was divorced because of the number and distress of such battles and was able to retire, though on a pittance. At that age (49) there was just time to work hard and try to develop the necessary skills before the ability to learn was irrevocably diminished by age. It was also a natural progression after so many years of teaching creativity to actively strive for it myself.

But the early years here, partly because of illness, poverty and isolation, were full of depression. John Bute was as helpful as any man could have been. I believe he (alone) understood the validity of my action in settling here to write and he offered a huge amount of assistance. Sadly, I decided that so long as I could remain independent I should do so. It meant I never got to know him and I regret this greatly. From my experience of his generosity I judge that he was one of the finest men of Bute ever, a worthy descendant of Robert the Bruce. Though my works have enjoyed no celebrity, he would, I believe, have understood their intrinsic value and rejoiced in them. His philosophy was that to be found in *The Leopard* by Giuseppe di Lampedusa in the life-purpose of the Duke. As applied to me by him it was phenomenal.

This work is also for the Rev Dr JD Douglas. Though metaphorical nowadays, every community has its share of crucifixions which occur from time to time. In Bute, around 1960, Dr JD Douglas was, in effect, 'crucified' here during his first ministry.

A lady sued him for breach of promise and it was found not proven. That is, she put it about that they were engaged yet he had never proposed. New to the place and by nature shy, quiet and introverted, he had few supporters: the Baptist minister, Borrowman, was the only one. I had gone to university by then. He left the ministry and became editor first of the *Dictionary of The New English Bible* [involving a fellowship at Selwyn College, Cambridge] and then of *Christianity Today*, a journal eventually taken over by the Billy Graham organisation which, when JD refused the command to report only forms of Christianity acceptable to the owners, was closed down with the loss of 12 jobs and then resurrected at a later date. [Billy G, I think, regrets this in his biography]

All his life, JD continued to correspond with me, often sending me copies of books and journals he had edited; always patiently listening to my objections to theology in the light of my studies of science in several forms. One of his 'jobs' for half of each year—a defining aspect of his fine character—was lecturing in the Bible College, Singapore where he taught journalism. For this he was paid 500S\$ a month [about £170], a pittance, partly redeemed by free accommodation, an allowance for air conditioning and an air ticket home which he became adept at swapping for many cheap flights which allowed him to call in at exotic locations, such as the eventual home of Tusitala, RL Stevenson, at Vailima, Samoa.

I remember, fondly, Jim's delight on learning that Encyclopaedia Britannica had paid him 3 pence a word for an article on Church History, my own at finding a copy of his 'The Light in the North' on arriving in Stornoway to head the maths department [for a brief period, the fact that I bought it and knew the author counted in my favour: it did not last!] and my discovery near the end of his life when I visited him in St Andrews that he was such a good friend of luminaries like Rev Eric Alexander [ex Tron Kirk, Glasgow, a most inspiring preacher] and Professor David Wright, Principal of New College. From the latter, I learned of Jim's prodigious and helpful correspondence with people all over the world. The fact that he should have been blessed by the friendship of two such outstanding men says much about his goodness, which, because of his short stay as a minister at St John's, Rothesay, never became clear to the town because it was so content to observe his oppression.

What must be recognised is that Jim's short stay on Bute killed his ministry and drove him from it. Given the effort he had put in to escape a tenement in Partick (a rare thing in 1950!) and acquire 4 university degrees it must have been terrible to find himself, in effect, declared, unjustly, unfit to preach after only a year or two in the job. That is what it amounted to. The lady was attractive, but past the age at which marriage was usual; she was known and he was not. That was enough. Maybe she had not married before because other men saw the flaws that JD was to come to know in court. He never married. Thereafter, students who would ask him: 'Are you married?' would receive the reply: 'Are you offering?' Always a conversation stopper.

William Scott, Rothesay, Isle of Bute, 2007

This is a novel. Any resemblance to any person, living or dead, is accidental.

In spite of everything, every community has its everyday crucifixion. What the world calls failure may be an inner triumph of the spirit, impossible, because untested, without it.

There is an island in a silver sea,
With sunlit meadows, woods and lochs,
And it gave life to me.

PREFACE

What is goodness? That is what this book is about. The question preoccupied philosophers for two and a half millennia until G.E. Moore[1] in 1903 showed that a satisfactory definition was never going to be possible[2].

Though it defies definition, then, the word goodness is important. To judge from the behaviour of the world at large, goodness is taken to be the quality observed in our role models, for these are the people who are looked up to. But who are they? Who are these celebrities? Sportsmen or women, film stars or pop stars, as often as not. Football players, Formula 1 drivers, even boxers—extraordinary that we should as a society celebrate the ability of one man to render another unconscious, to his peril, medically, as we have often seen.

Instead, it seems obvious, that goodness is to be found in quite different groups of people. One group, the most important, is the ministry: a group of men and women with an obvious commitment to being good in themselves as well as encouraging it in others. These are the people whom we should celebrate: the saints among us who steadily and quietly, with hardly a ripple of satisfaction for themselves, go about our local worlds doing good deeds.

---

[1] In *Principia Ethica*, 1903, Cambridge University Press. He called efforts to define 'good' examples of 'The Naturalistic Fallacy'. The impulse to the search for a definition was this. If you want to be good you need to begin by understanding exactly what this means. Thus the Platonic Dialogues are essentially efforts to answer this and similar questions, such as *what is justice*? If you wish to be a just person you need to begin by defining what you mean by it. So Plato et al believed.

[2] A summary of the proof is: If it is possible to define 'good', let us suppose that 'good' is identical to C. In that case, the statement 'C is good' is a tautology ie it is meaningless. However, it is a fact that statements of this kind are made every day with many different things standing in place of C; such as liberty, love, knowledge, justice etc. Eg 'Love is good' or 'Knowledge is good.' And all of these statements have meaning: they are not simply tautologies. This means that the statement 'C is good.' always has meaning. Finally, we see that it is never a tautology and therefore it never is the case that 'good' is identical to C, no matter what C is taken to be.

As a rule they are the last people to be aware of their own merit. That is a sign of it. They are self-transcendent: have their eyes not on their past good deeds but on the ones they are currently engaged in; determined to do their best right now; and unwilling to devote a particle of energy, still less seek any praise, for their former doings. Their goodness is a property which can be observed only in what they do. Sometimes it is not understood. When this happens, the saintly minister can even be turned on by those he seeks to help and has been helping at great cost to himself for years. That ultimately is what I was striving for herein: to show goodness in a man and yet that his goodness was not understood by enough people to save him from the machinations of another man who stood to lose by it. The moral value of this is to try to reveal what goodness really is and to celebrate it, for that is the kind of person who should be our role model.

When this novel was written it seemed best to try to distance the island from the reality. I called it Branden. I gave alternative names to certain parts of it and these are easily identified. This decision meant I had greater latitude to invent and need not trouble for utter consistency[3]. Some of the names are an advance upon the real ones. One housing scheme[4], for example, is known as *The Crimea*, and it is not hard to see which one is meant. I have decided to leave it this way. In so doing, I follow a long tradition, for George Eliot called Coventry, Middlemarch, Thomas Hardy's Wessex was Dorset and William McIlvanney wrote of Graithnock when he meant Kilmarnock.

I had no one in particular in mind when I devised the character of the minister who is the protagonist. I knew only that he was to be an especially fine person. What I wanted to show is that goodness can be subverted and disgraced by a self-interested evil person if he is sufficiently manipulative and I wanted to try to understand the process which I had seen in real life

---

[3] The ordinary reader invariably fails to understand that the novelist is obliged to invent from the outset [and will not be a novelist until he does so spontaneously], for once the reality of his experience is introduced, at least in a major way, it must be followed relentlessly. This means that nothing new can come from this procedure. Invention is the key to originality. Invention of character and action and even place, though there may be connexions between these and his reality. Even so, once the inventions are in play, human nature determines how things will turn out. The novelist's own experience is chiefly of value in reminding him what certain experiences feel like.

[4] I once lived there myself.

often enough. I wanted also to depict goodness, analyse and comprehend it, especially in relation to the opposite, without which it would hardly be noticed.

Since writing this book, I have become aware of the lives of both Rev Geoff Shaw[5] and Rev John Miller, people so outstanding that they deserve to be celebrated, though it is in the nature of such men that they would be embarrassed and reject any such effort. I even began to try to deal with this a few years ago in a separate book after I had read—with veneration and amazement—the text of a speech [shown me by my friend, the Rev Jock Stein] by John Miller to intending ministers. I now think after reading this book again 14 years after its construction, that I have already dealt with this after all. These great men, for that is what they are, are doubtless better men than the character created here. Yet, I hope he will be seen to have certain things in common.

The theology to be borne in mind is that within 'Honest to God' by John Robinson, Bishop of Suffolk, published at the beginning of the sixties. This book marked a sensational alteration in clerical opinion. Here, at last, God was identified not as a personal God but as 'the ground of being'. Even so, for some of them and most of the laity, God was still an old man with a white beard up in the sky.

For me, as the author, the best parts of this are the characters, all of them invented, some of them remarkable in interesting and attractive ways, and their interactions; the depiction of the love of knowledge and what it is really like, as distinct from what very many people believe it to be; and the ambition to achieve excellence and what it means. Two sorts of crimes make their appearance, one of which I have extraordinary knowledge of, having suffered at the sharp end of it. The other is original, yet likely to have been practised in small communities like this without discovery. There is also work on how to write poems for the first time; an effort to convey the love of classical music; rugby is part of it; and one character has an interesting medical condition. There is even a little mathematics in an appendix. Far from putting off some readers, it should be seen as a singular advance that, in

---

[5] Geoff Shaw was a minister in the Gorbals who operated an open door policy. That is, the door of his top flat in a tenement—his chosen manse—was forever open. It meant that he was often applied to for help at every time of day and night and by every kind of disreputable person. John Miller chose to live in a council house in Castlemilk since that was where he might best perform his vocation. Consequently, he suffered and his family, like everyone else, from the evildoers around him.

a novel, a Brandane should have thought it worth while to say something about the beauty and simplicity of beta and gamma functions, especially since nowadays they are often thought to lie outside the requirements of an honours degree in the subject. And yet, I had plenty of students who enjoyed them long before they left for university. Only a self-published work could achieve this. No publisher would have the insight to appreciate the deeper value of this inclusion. The writer should write to the limit of his ability, not the imagined level of the most backward reader. That is why so many of my students won so many national prizes and became successful mathematicians: they were brought up to appreciate the ecstasy of ideas and could understand honours-standard work while still at school. Limits were not placed upon them: what they might achieve was assumed and asserted to be limitless.

Above all, I am proud of the narrative: the drive of the story which describes the lives of people and how they affect each other, their failures and their triumphs, which are not always seen by the world at large. Reading it again, 14 years after I wrote it has done nothing to diminish its power. I wept over it, just as my daughter Rosalind had done all these years ago on a fleeting visit when everything else we planned had to be set aside while she devoured these pages.

William Scott, Rothesay, Isle of Bute, November, 2007

The Island of Branden c1962

The singular beauty of Branden, apart from her own sunlit meadows, woods and lochs, is that she nestles in a fork of the land, and is held there, by other islands. And so, across narrow seas, most days, the inhabitants look out over high wooded hills, and great fissures of sea lochs, cleaving the Argyll wilderness.

Of all the islands here, Branden is the strangest: a hybrid, with huge buttresses, mainly of red sandstone, which cast a rosy glow on warm summer evenings, and loamy hills providing views of several counties up and down the firth, which any world traveller will admit are matchless. And then, to the west, is the greatest glory of them all: the view to the towering peaks of Orrin, a wholly volcanic neighbour. There is no scene in the wide world to compare with this. Even in the worst drizzle, the discerning eye can still enjoy a thick line of fluorescent blue along her coast; but in winter, when the sharp-edged ridges stand out with snow, then the view to Orrin is Himalayan in its majesty.

In shape, Branden is roughly like a sleeping cat, all hills and hollows and silky smoothness, with here and there on the periphery, white beaches like tiny paws, though in the south they are pink because of the sandstone; and in the deep indentations, are villages and small towns, each with its harbour and sheltered anchorage. But the cat is not always asleep. She rouses easily and will seize and bite and kill any small animal in her vicinity. First, she will prick and prod it, as cats do; and only serve the coup de grace when all diversion is ended.

And so we find her, asleep, facing the snow-capped crags of Orrin that run up ridges to join the gods.

It was of a particular god, that afternoon, in Ottersay, the chief town of the island, that one of its citizens was speaking across his dining-room table. In looks, he was like other men, not taller or shorter, or stouter, though too many scones eaten with jam—unrefusable because made, so often, by the hostess—had increased his girth an inch or two. Fifty years of a fairly spartan life had aged the once dark hair to a grey furze; for, afoot in all weathers, in the nature of his work, he had little time and less inclination, to keep every strand in place. And for the same reason—the impulse of a high vocation zealously pursued—his dark-grey suit could always do with a pressing; and maybe a cleaning, where this or that crumb had fallen unnoticed, because he was too busy ministering to others. And yet he was not an ordinary man: the features were finer, the set of the head more noble, the eye more kindly, and lit by a quick intelligence. There was a sense of mission about him, of energy that might be yours for the asking, and when he smiled, which was often, there was an impression of goodness, and that form of love which is called, in the Greek, agape: the love of all people.

Concluding his argument—that not everything can be got out of books—which he loved—that some things must be thought out, and others experienced—even, that some books are worthless—he said, "'Take in our hand any volume of divinity or school metaphysics. Does it contain any abstract reasoning concerning quantity or number? No. Does it contain any experimental reasoning concerning matter of fact and existence? No. Commit it then to the flames, for it can contain nothing but sophistry and illusion!'"[1] The voice that spoke, rose exultantly, and the speaker's face flushed with pleasure, as he ended in a peal of laughter; but his chestnut-headed wife in her grey dress said, 'Hush, John! How *can* you, in front of the kids?' And then to the children—assembled over lunch, all in black blazers—'Off you go! The school-bell's about to ring.'

Alone of the children, Peter, tall, dark, bespectacled and pimply, with the last years of adolescence, stopped, and turned at the door, as if to protest, and then thought better of it. His mother had said it all.

Seated at the head of the table, John Manson grinned impishly, and when they had trooped out, unfastened his dog-collar above the shining blue stock. 'Well, thank God that's over, Jean. We have the whole afternoon to ourselves,' and he got up and took his wife by the hand: 'Bed!' he commanded.

But, as she was led into the hall, she was not done with him, and her lovely elfin face with the prominent cheekbones and pointed chin became anxious: 'I really think you should keep statements like that to yourself. What if the children mentioned it to anyone? What would they think?'

---

[1] David Hume: *An Enquiry Concerning Human Understanding*, Sec XII part III, para 132 et seq. 2nd edition edited by Selby-Bigge, Oxford, Clarendon Press. P165.

'At least *they can* think! That's the important thing.'

'But you should watch what you say.'

At the top of the stair he turned. 'Do you mean to tell me that something as finely put as that, should remain buried in books? It..it just cries out to be spoken.'

'But not by ministers of the Church of Scotland,' she said, shaking her brown hair out of its confinement, as she went ahead of him.

'Uch, away with ye, woman!' said John jeeringly. 'The ministry is not a straitjacket.' Already his hands were busy at her waist, still appealingly slender, unfastening the grey dress.

'If you go on like this,' said Jean, 'you might lose every jacket you have, and then where will we be?'

'Here with you, because I won't lose. This job's a sinecure. Who but a minister can spend every afternoon in bed, with his favourite girl?'

'You mean there are others?'

John laughed, as if that were impossible, helped her out of the dress, and started on the other things.

They were in the middle of it, when there was a noise downstairs. 'I wonder what that is?' said John.

'Don't stop.'

But there was a flurry of feet on the uncarpeted steps, and, a moment later, the creak of a door opening, further movement, and then a bang, as it slammed shut.

They lay in silence for a moment, until Jean called out: 'Who's there?'

'It's me, Mummy. I forgot my maths project,' said a young voice.

Silence. Two red faces considered each other from close range.

'What are you two up to, in bed at this time of day?'

'Having a wee rest, Roddy,' said John, 'what do you think?'

'Off you go to school now, or you'll be late,' said Jean, wondering why he had forgotten it again, but dismissing the question.

'Right. Bye.'

They lay together, for a moment, sadly contemplating a summit unattained, and then, without another word, got up and began to dress. As he did so, John Manson looked out of the window into the drizzle, down the brae to the seafront and the esplanade, with its palm trees and acres of lawns and rose-beds; and the Little Theatre, a Victorian rotunda of charm and quaintness; and beyond, the harbour—still, in the early autumn, full of vessels of various kinds: yachts and fishing boats, mainly. A peaceful scene, surely? And the steamer about to dock and exchange one cargo and collection of passengers for another. All the people, scurrying about their business, like so many ants in the distance, trading, transporting, coming or going from the office. And *they* were *his* business: the people themselves; his job, his vocation, to look after them, as a shepherd does. He sighed at the old image of himself; and suddenly, felt threatened by them, as they hurried to and fro on the distant pier, commanding taxis and queuing for buses—all movement, in a rustling tide of energy.

Indeed, they were like ants, or maybe cockroaches, except that they were different from each other; but in one way they were the same: intent upon their own affairs and devil take the other fellow, or anyone else who obstructed them. That was the source of the danger. And it had suddenly got worse at the start of the sixties, as if the bindings of society were loosening, as if 'dog eat dog' were becoming a fashionable philosophy, a kind of competition *uber alles*. And what struck him as especially ironic was that he, and others like him, had not so long before, at great cost, fought a war against a philosophy not less oppressive. How awful, then, that the new struggle for material and hedonistic well-being, a struggle conducted openly, at the expense of the poor and the weak, who were looked-down upon, their needs ignored, should have arisen within the borders of his own country, within the very party traditionally in control. And yet that was in the future; what he saw were the germinating seeds.

As he looked out, it began to rain properly, great gobbets of it falling on the windows, like musket-fire from the Gods above, and he shivered. What did this new hedonism mean to him? How would it affect his existence? Was his job *really* a sinecure? He had a sudden sense of foreboding, of dark doings in the future; that he would be tested again. And, as the awful images of war rose, like devils, from subterranean depths, into his mind, he clasped his temples and tried to shut out the thunder of the guns, the dead, lifeless splat-sounds, as this limb or that torso took its ration of lead or shrapnel, and the screams of the wounded and the tortured pleas of the dying. Would he never be free of it? Was there no end to struggle, no end to the battle of life, but death itself? And it seemed to him that his own death was not far off. For in a battle, it was only a matter of time; and he had been in it so long.

Later, downstairs, in the hall, Jean said, 'Do you want some tea?'

'No, I'm going out.'

'But you usually want tea.'

'I'll get some at Joe's.'

'You're not going there again, are you?'

'Of course.'

'But he's a dirty old man and a Catholic to boot. Can't you leave him to the priest?'

'No, I can't. None of the priests will go there.'

'Well, why must you go?'

'I don't have to. I just feel I should.'

'But there's been talk. You know what folk are like.'

'What kind a talk? That he's an old homo, and maybe I'm changing sides?' Forgetting his recent morbid thoughts, Manson laughed, as if all such talk were outrageous, and a fact of life, in which he took particular pleasure. Then, taking her by the arm, he said gently, 'He's an old man on his own. Nobody speaks to him. How could I not go and see him?'

She looked at John in silence, forced a smile through thin lips, and then helped him on with the coat, a black burberry he'd had for ten years. 'Hurry back then,' she said, finally, wondering whether that coat would last another winter of Ottersay's monsoon season, as she privately described it.

At the door, he turned and called out, 'The good fight cries out to be fought. What else is a man to do? Aye, and without counting the cost or watching his back.' He looked at her for a moment, intently, as if expecting a reply, and when none came, added, 'Even David Hume would have understood that.'

As she watched him through the glass door, striding down the path, she sighed. Her John would not be back until long after tea, for he would stay an hour at least, and go from there to every other isolated stray in the neighbourhood, no matter their religious persuasion, and cast innumerable crumbs of comfort, among the folk he chanced to meet on the way.

As she stood over the sink, washing up the dishes, she remembered him at college, at the end of the war. Dark-haired, with a high complexion and a figure like a three-quarter, strong and lean. A beautiful man, then. But it was the energy that attracted her. There was a dynamic presence about him and great initiative, which made her feel that you'd never know what this man was going to do—except it would be sudden, dramatic and extraordinary. At times, words flew from him like bullets, and at others, he could charm the birds off the trees. Always, he was exciting to be with. A dangerous, unpredictable man, never one to take a back seat, but always in there, with his sleeves rolled up, digging furiously or building whatever it was he had a mind to build, with demonic ambition and resource.

The trouble was—and she could not see it at the beginning—that there was no security, no certainty that life's comforts, the necessities in her case, for comforts were few on a stipend, would be there in the morning. One lived from hand to mouth, on a shoe-string and a prayer. Not even that! John was one who did not go in for that much. Like the great Lord George F. MacLeod, prayer had never done him much good. So it was something he did for other folk.

How he had changed! The Branden winter might be milder, because of the Gulf Stream that was supposed to affect the island, but it was wetter too. That old coat had taken a hammering, and its wearer had definitely aged. It was the grind of confronting, every day, so much poverty—actual as well as spiritual—that was taking its toll on him. A man could only give so much of himself, and her John had never stinted, never held back, never said: *I can't today. I have to put my feet up with my family.*

The family had never suffered really, so far. John had always performed some quick miracle, when a storm blew up and disaster loomed; but she sensed his strength was waning; that he would not always be able to bale the ship, and keep it on course. She kept the worry from him as much as possible, and he from her; but he was drinking more, and they both knew they could not afford it. One glass on a Sunday night, had become one every night of the week, and that one was now two, most nights.

Where would it end? What could she do? Talking had done no good. He just brushed her away; and there was no one, not one living soul she could confide in. A minister's wife confessed her husband's failings at her peril.

And then she wondered what his decline would mean. What were the consequences to one who never watched his back or counted the cost, who did the right thing all the time? It never occurred to her to question whether her perceptions were just; the result of too many years of close contiguity, to assess the real person, familiarity with the difficulties of such a life, having blinded her to the reasons for them. Missing from her calculations was his goodness and his constant ambition to promote it. Though she would defend him anywhere, the years had blinded her to this. Present, and something she had never understood, was the fierce intellectual honesty—the very cause of the quotation from David Hume. Why could he not just argue for his own position, she had often wondered? Keep his mouth shut about his doubts.

In truth, the theory of relativity applies not only to expanding galaxies but to people, any one of whom seems different through another's eye; all of whom literally, as well as metaphorically, mentally and spiritually, shrink and expand under changing circumstances. So that if Mrs A were to describe Mr B, C would not recognise him at all. Thus are we blinded to each other, forgetting the purpose, remembering only the consequences of supporting it, unless we are at the receiving end. Any description of anyone, is necessarily incomplete, for it is discerned from one point of view alone; and the situation of the observer governs all. As we float around each other, like objects in space, repelling, attracting, occasionally colliding—even coalescing—we are compelled to make judgements about each other, to make possible the business of living. Often these are false; often, because we are too limited by inadequate education—forensic dissection of ourselves in university tutorials, a sine qua non—to have developed the insight or the values necessary for an illuminating view.

Mindless of the rain, which tumbled down on that autumn day, John Manson halted outside the tenement, in Bridgeton Street, looking upwards at it. Like much of Ottersay, it was of red sandstone, quarried locally, but the pointing between the blocks was missing, which would explain why water was getting in. Some of the flats were empty, because of dry-rot. Looking up and down the street, he noticed other buildings in the same desperate condition. Everything was going to rack and ruin, because no one was looking after it.

The close was gloomy, and a rivulet of filthy water trickled along one side, by his feet, past an empty beer-bottle, which rolled back and forth in a corner, in the light breeze. The once-white ceiling was covered in a thick layer of grime, laid down over the years by smoke from chimneys, and the pre-war, pale-green, paint was peeling off the walls in many places.

As he set his foot on the stair, the smell of vomit assaulted his nostrils, so that he put his hand to his nose. He looked down, and saw dimly, that he had put his foot in it, and stopped momentarily, wondering: should I go on? Do I have to spend my time in places like this?

The door, when he reached it and rang the bell, opened slowly and the grey-headed figure, with the stick, moved back to allow his entry. 'It's yourself, Minister. Come away in.'

In the half-light of the dull day, dimmed by the unwashed windowpanes, Joe Gorman looked better than usual. The baggy black trousers were probably his best, and the roll-neck sweater, with holes in the elbows, concealed the lack of a shirt. Had Joe been making an effort on his behalf?

'Get me a cloth will you? I've stepped in vomit,' said John, waiting at the door.

'It'll no' matter. The place's a shambles anyway. Jist come in.' So John entered, and went into the parlour and sat down in a chair, that creaked under him.

'Ah'll make some tea. Make yerself at home,' said Joe, shuffling off to the sink to fill the kettle; but as John's eyes roamed the small garret under the leaking roof, with the wallpaper peeling off the walls, and the faded pictures of times past, when Joe Gorman had been a man of significance—not this shambling creature, half-destroyed by gossip—he wondered when the place had last been a home, and whether it could ever be again. Or would it be torn down by order of the council, and some concrete monstrosity erected by a developer, for a quick profit? It was just a matter of time, really. There wasn't the money to make good the building, as it was. There was money in selling off the land, as it stood, for new building.

As Gorman brought the tea—in cracked mugs—and sat down opposite, it flashed into Manson's mind, that Joe was like the building: beyond saving; fit only for the space occupied, to be made available for something altogether different. Angrily, he banished the thought, as unworthy.

'They should give you a caur, Minister,' said Joe, seeing the soaked raincoat. 'Do ye want to take it off and dry it?'

'No, it'll be all right,' said John, thinking of the dirt it would acquire if it were laid down on anything. 'It'll dry fine on me.'

'Ah don't suppose a stipend runs to taxis. Ah mind when a standard fare in Ottersay was a tanner. It's five bob now.'

'You used to drive a taxi, didn't you, Joe?'

'Aye, Ah worked for Buchanan's till ma..ma.. wee problem.'

Did Joe want to talk about it? Was that it? Doubting this conclusion, John said: 'I'm surprised there was ever a demand for taxis. Don't we all go by bus?'

'No' the hoi poloi. Them that hasnae caurs. Then there's no bus right up to the hospital. And then there's funerals. Ah wouldnay expect ye to forget that Minister.'

'And the services on Sundays. A lot of old folk come that way.'

'Aye, Buchanan was aye sharp. He used tae 'phone roon the auld folk tae make sure they had a taxi for Sundays.'

'That was very good of him.'

Joe laughed. 'No, it wasnae. It wis jist his way of keepin' in wi' them, so he could get tae do the funeral. There's a lotta money in funerals. Buchanan's a sharp lad, right enough.'

That's true, thought John, most of the funerals I go to are done by George Buchanan.

'Surely, the relatives decide who will be the undertaker?'

'No' always. Buchanan gets the auld wans tae sign a paper. Says it's as well tae get everything sorted out afore hand. He gies them forms for their will, if they havenay got wan. He's on hand tae be a witness. Ah've been wan masel', often enough. Ye need two, ye see.'

They sat in silence, sipping from the cracked mugs, until Joe said, 'Aye, the auld wans are right guid tae Buchanan. He aye gets left something. Wan hoose we went tae had a fine gran'fayther clock he admired, and, sure enough, when the auld yin died, Buchanan got left it. Hardly a funeral goes by but he gets left something.'

'So he gets the taxis every Sunday and the funerals when they die and something in the will as well?'

'Aye, Buchanan's a sharp lad.'

The silence filled the room, and the sight of Joe, seated under the single bare light-bulb, made John inwardly curse himself, for his own selfishness. He should be thinking about Joe, doing something for him. Maybe he wanted to talk about it. John decided to wait and see if he would say anything, but all he said was, 'Ah'm fine pleased that ye come up here jist tae see an auld man.'

'Don't you go to church, now, Joe?'

'No. No one speaks to me now. Even the priest's offish; willnay look me in the eye; and when the Canon sees me....Well, Ah jist know he'd like me un'nerground, as soon as possible.'

'But why? What happened to you?'

Joe put a hand to his forehead, and lifted it as if he'd been shot. Then he seemed to calm himself.

'It was boys.' Joe stopped, and looked up, as if he had just uttered the unmentionable, but, getting no reaction, he went on, 'Young boys. I just love the look of some young boys.' Joe sighed with pleasure, at the images flowing into his mind. 'Ah used tae follay them about the streets. They were slim and wiry and...and...beautiful.' A tear came to Joe's eye, which he banished with a finger.

'There was one boy in partic'lar. He was like a young god. Fair hair and blue-eyed. It was summer, and he went about wi' just a swim-suit and gutties on. Oh, Ah loved him! Ah jist loved him.'

'Well, there's nothing much wrong with love, Joe.'

'Aye, maybe, but ye need tae show love. Ye canny keep it tae yersel'. De ye ken what Ah mean?'

There was such a plaintive note to the entreaty, that John found himself saying in sympathy, 'I know, Joe. I know just what you mean.'

'Ah started givin' him money. No' much. Just a few shullins here and there for sweeties and the like.'

There was more, much more, but John would not break the silence to make the trite remark, that would take them forward. It was too intrusive, too curious for decency. So he waited for a while, trying and managing to look especially sympathetic. Joe, studying him, seemed encouraged.

'One day he came and asked for money. That was the day it started. Ah said Ah would gie him it, if he would let me touch him. Oh it was grand! He had thighs like.. like.. soft cheese; and buttocks like peaches—but Ah didnae get to see them that time.'

John waited, again, unwilling to interrupt the confession the man needed to make, but heard himself say involuntarily, 'You are a poet, Joe,' and thought, it has to be love to provoke such a response.

'Oh, Ah knew it was wrong—no' wrong tae do that, but wrong tae get that faur. Because it had tae go further. You know how it is? Ye dae somethin' that's innocent, and ye get the idea of goin' on tae something else, that's no' much different.

'One day, Ah started tae fondle him. He didnae have much at that age, he was jist startin' and Ah could see he liked it. He really liked it. He was a bit guilty about doin' it himself, Ah think. So it was better if somebody else did it fur him.

'Then, one day he saw that Ah was excited, and he reached out...'

Joe covered his face with his hands, blushing.

'And you enjoyed it, Joe?'

'Aye, Ah did,' said Joe, with wonder in his voice. He put his hands down, and his face took on an expression of amazement. 'You havenae said anything, Minister. Do ye no' think it was wrong?'

'No, I don't, Joe. It was just love.'

'But is that no' fornication?'

'I suppose it is, in a way, but it's no different from what a lot of people do in secret and alone. Why should it be wrong because one person helps another?'

'But that's no' all. Ah did it tae him, and he did it tae me too. Surely that was wrong?'

'You mean you made love to him, Joe, as a man does to a woman?'

'Aye, well.... aye.'

'And what did you do afterwards?'

'Ah let him do it tae me, and then Ah made him a cup a tea, and gave him hauf a croon.'

'What was the money for?'

'Just a present. Ah loved him and Ah was happy. Why would Ah no' give him money? Ah would have given him anything. Anything.' Joe's voice broke and he sobbed briefly.

At that moment, high up under the eaves, where the paper was peeling off, a spider ran down the web and began to take hold of a housefly, that had just succumbed there. And John saw it and wondered at the cruelty of life. What crimes are committed in the name of sex, because of the fixed ideas of idiots, most of whom bear their own share of burdens, which they manage to conceal?

'Ye must admit it wis wrong, a foul thing tae do tae a young boy?' said Joe. 'Oh, Ah prayed tae God after it, but Ah got no help. Every time the boy came, it happened again. Ah couldnay help maself. Oh, Ah loved him! And look what Ah did to him.'

'What happened to him?'

'Uch, it was the talk o' the town. The boy was ashamed. Scunnered o' me. The family left inside a month.'

'Did the father say anything to you?'

'No' much, he just belted me in the close, one night. That's when Ah lost the sight o' ma eye.'

'Did you lay a complaint?'

'No. Ah wouldnay say who it was, but the polis kent fine.'

'Did you do it with any other boys?'

'No. After that Ah couldnay. Ah canny hardly go out. Ah get ma messages at night, when it's dark, at the Paki shop.'

Joe leaned back in the chair for the first time, and John knew that was all there was. In a tremulous voice, on the brink of tears, Joe said, 'So ye see, minister, you're wasting your time on me. Ah'm just a miserable sinner, no' worth the trouble. Ah spoilt a young boy's life.' And his balding head fell back on the grimy antimacassar, and he seemed desolate, finished.

'Nothing of the kind, Joe. Nothing of the kind! You loved the boy and he liked you, or he wouldn't have gone so far. And if you gave him money, it was not for services rendered, but for the pleasure it gave you, to give to him. It was love, Joe. It was all just love.'

'But Ah'll go tae hell, Mr Manson!' said Joe, almost sobbing. 'Ah ken fine that's where Ah'm goin'.'

'No, you're not, Joe. People have made you think badly of yourself. That's all. A lot of the folk out there, never loved anybody but themselves, Joe.'

'So you think Ah didnae do wrong?' said Joe, with astonishment.

'I think it might have been better if you hadn't made love to the boy, but you did it out of love, and that's what makes it right. You weren't using him, you were expressing your love in the only way you knew—in the only way natural to you. Society might call it wrong, Joe, but I don't. The boy came back for more, didn't he?'

'Aye, he did,' sobbed Joe.

'And you didn't force him?'

'No! No' me! How could Ah, when Ah loved him?'

'Well then, Joe, you didn't do much wrong. You were just in love and you expressed it in the only way you could. I don't think you could have behaved any differently, Joe. We're all just flesh and blood, Joe, that's all.'

Joe wept and leaned forward in the chair, with his hands on his knees, and John put his hands on Joe's, and squeezed gently, comfortingly, and then drew him up out of the seat and embraced him, and felt Joe's tears run down his cheeks. Years had passed since Joe had known the comfort of human contact, all the years since that last time with the boy. What else could John Manson do but supply what a scarred soul had been crying out for, all these years? It was common decency, that was all.

While John Manson was inside, ministering to a poor man in need, outside, a green Mercedes drove up, and out of it stepped two men. One, the driver, was of average height and build with raven hair, which only the very discerning would realise was dyed black. In truth, it was quite grey, the result of an explosive temper and ruthless will, both of which, without him ever being aware of it, affected his health by raising his blood-pressure. This was George Buchanan, dressed in black morning coat and black trousers with a white pin-stripe, for he was attending a funeral that day, in his capacity as undertaker. Under the dark hair lay a pair of dark eyes, a large grey triangular nose that would have looked well on a rook, and a rather jowly shapeless face, the colour of concrete. It was about concrete that he had come, bringing an architect, visiting for the day from Glasgow.

'So this is what ye mean?' said George, moving onto the pavement without much co-ordination—like the rook, too, in that respect, as he cocked his head to look up, out of his black beady eyes, at the decaying building and its neighbours on either side.

'Not quite,' said Mackinnon-Smythe, holding an umbrella against the drizzle, which George disdained, as if it would spoil his appearance. 'I need the whole street and the one behind as well.' Mackinnon-Smythe was the archetypal professional: tall, slim, urbane, with gold cuff-links, Kelvinside tie, and a smart maroon waistcoat, beneath the superbly-tailored grey suit; everyone's idea of the trusted expert, well-paid and well-appointed.

George said, 'What do you plan to put up?'

'The works. A supermarket, arcade, shops, offices and flats—expensive ones. Up market, everything.'

'So this lot needs to be condemned, then?' said George, thoughtfully. 'That might be difficult.'

'Not for a man like you, though,' said Mackinnon-Smythe, smiling at him.

'No, it's not impossible, but it needs thinking about. Then there's the planning- permission for the new buildings. Ye'll need that too.'

'My principals are prepared for that,' said the architect, studying the building as if it were the Taj Mahal, with fees in proportion, for his expert professional survey.

'Do you mean, what I think you mean?' said George, turning to look at the man directly.

'Oh, yes. Definitely, Councillor Buchanan,' said Mackinnon-Smythe, deferentially, sensible of the need to pander to the vanity lurking not far below the surface of any unpaid elected official. 'No doubt about it. And before you say anything, I can promise you security. It will be absolute.'

'How do I know that?' said George, with a hint of aggression, turning his own eyes again to fix on the dismal prospect of the crumbling sandstone walls, and banks of unwashed windows.

'Because too much is hanging on it, if you see what I mean.'

George looked up and down the dull, damp street and saw no one within twenty yards. 'How much are we talking about here?'

The architect too, looked around him carefully, before replying. 'Thousands, Councillor. To you, about ten, when good progress is shown, and the same after.'

An hour later, after lunch at the Grand Hotel, the deal was finalised over Havana cigars and liqueurs, taken in the front lounge, facing out over the bay. They were sitting in the bow of a great oriel window, around an expensive antique table, and Mackinnon-Smythe, having gone over the details of the arrangement—what would be expected, how it would be managed—held out his hand. Ignoring it, George turned away to relight the cigar and, as he did so, looked out across the water to the far side, where, on the hill, was the great gothic school; above and to one side of it, the castellated Bannockburn Tower, with such a tremendous view of the town, and underneath, down the hill from the school, a large draughty detached villa, St Margaret's Manse, where Manson, the minister lived. Inhaling, for a moment or two, George contemplated the idea of John Manson, whether he might constitute any kind of threat; and then banished the thought with a puff of smoke. There was no one in Branden to be afraid of. Turning to Mackinnon-Smythe, he grasped the hand and shook it, a knowing smile filling the pasty face, as his fingers came in contact with a tight roll of banknotes.

'Just a sweetener, you understand, Councillor,' said the architect. 'Over and above the arrangements.'

George made no reply. As he sank back in the chair, transferring the money without examination to his pocket, he realised there would be no trouble. George Buchanan might not look much, but he was a match for anyone, for he had skills that few folk dreamed existed: the secrets of successful business, passed down from father to son, like a family of witch-doctors who retain among themselves the mysteries, cultivated and refined down the generations, of how to bamboozle their fellows.

Some months before, Roderick Manson had been called to see the Head of Mathematics in his room, at four o'clock.

Charles Braddock, M.A., had lately arrived on the island to take up the post, and had set about his work with characteristic energy, involving himself in all the doings of the community, from the Church to the Scouts and the rugby field. As an experiment, he had taught rugby to the 'quali'—

the senior class of the primary school—with a view to making some useful recruits for the third fifteen, when they graduated to the secondary, a stone's throw down the hill. And so, twice a week after school, the boys of the 'quali' were instructed in the arts, on the school playing-field at Otterhall, nearby.

In the final match, an eight a side, Roddy Manson had distinguished himself to the tune of five tries and three conversions—which Charlie considered a triumph. For how could a boy of eleven have the strength to kick the mud-encumbered ball over such an obstacle as the cross-bar, given the quantity of mud from which the act must take place?

But another issue raised itself. Why should not the 'quali' be matched against the first year of the secondary? Would not this be the ultimate test of Charlie's coaching?

Permission from Miss Mather, the headmistress of the primary school, was sought and found, and a team picked, and most important of all, from Charlie's point of view, a captain appointed. Astonishingly, Roddy was not elected, and Charlie was upset. Yet how could Roddy be elected when he had, under Charlie's encouragement, been knocking his opponents into the glaur with a natural hand-off anyone would be proud of? Too many of his classmates didn't like his harsh treatment of them.

'We must hold a meeting about it,' said Charlie. 'Come to my room at four Roddy, and you too Jimmy and Richard,' who had been elected respectively captain and secretary, with Roddy as vice.

Roddy was mystified. What was it all for? What was the point? 'I don't mind if I'm not the captain, sir. Jimmy can be the captain.'

But Charlie was adamant. A meeting must be held. And so it was, that three, eleven-year-old boys, still in the primary school, had to make the descent of the hill to the secondary, enter this larger world with its taller, heavier people and, suitably awed, line up outside the door of room 18, on the second landing of the great gothic building, with the clock-tower like Big Ben.

Richard, the fair-haired fat boy, went in first, and emerged with a hint of a blush, ten minutes later. 'You're next, Roddy. Watch yourself.'

A mystifying remark, surely? thought Roddy, as he made his first tentative entrance to room 18.

'Sit down, Roddy, sit down,' said Charlie, in black gown over blue suit with a white pin-stripe, white collar and Scripture Union tie; seating himself behind the imposing desk, piled with jotters, in the process of being marked. The sunbeams from the window behind him, fell on Charlie's large, domed, bald head surrounded by dark hair, so that it gleamed like a huge ostrich egg, and Roddy wondered at the quantity of marvellous intelligence that must be under it. As he looked at Charlie, in his majesty, and then around the room, at the symbols of his power—the rows of desks, where the ablest minds of the senior school would come to learn what Charlie knew; the book-cases stuffed full of the accumulated knowledge of centuries, all of it, at Charlie's command; and the blackboards, covered in neat handwriting, with mathematical symbols of extraordinary complexity and beauty—Roddy was filled with awe.

'So you don't mind Jimmy Taylor being the captain? That's very noble of you, Roddy. You're not in the cubs are you? Richard's already in the Scouts. What do you think? Would you like to join?'

'I think I would, sir. I've been thinking about it.... if I could.'

'Stand up against the desk, Roddy.'

Puzzled, Roddy stood up.

'Do you believe in God, Roddy?' said Charlie, rising.

'Yes, sir.'

'Do you believe in love?'

'I don't know. I suppose so.'

'You love your parents don't you?' said Charlie, coming around the desk to stand at one side.

'Yes, sir.'

'Do you have any girl friends?'

'No, sir.'

'Do you fancy any girls? I mean do you think about them lustfully?'

'Oh no, sir,' Roddy lied, blushing, and looked away out of the window to the grass that sloped up the hill to the primary school.

'Well, there's a different kind of love than either of these. It was often found among the Greeks. A man would love a boy and the boy would come to love the man. And the man would be a kind of protector, who would help the boy in all his troubles. How does that seem to you, Roddy?'

'O.K. I suppose.'

'It doesn't seem strange, then?'

'Not really. If a man can love a woman, I don't see why he can't love a boy as well,' said Roddy, trying hard to agree with the man of learning.

'What would be the sign of that kind of love, Roddy?'

'I don't know, sir.'

'What happens to you when you feel loving towards someone?'

'I don't know,' Roddy lied, blushing more than ever.

'Look out the window, Roddy,' said Charlie, coming behind him. And a moment later, 'Can you feel anything?' pressing himself against Roddy's backside.

Roddy could feel the short thing sticking into him, even though there were layers of clothing between them. 'No sir,' he said, reddening, as he had never been red before, like the ripest tomato ever seen. Fluorescent. The very heat of his face frightened him. The shock itself was horrific; the more so because of the awe with which he had approached this superior place. Confusion was utter, all initiative lost. Roddy felt as if he had been nailed to the desk, powerless to move, still less to complain. Anyway, it was a fundamental axiom of that world: one never complained.

'You don't feel anything?' said Charlie, with surprise. Then Charlie pressed harder. 'Do you feel anything now?'

Eyes apparently transfixed by the view from the window, across the grass of the field stretched out below, and compelled by the pain of the object sticking into him, as well as by the utter impossibility of further denial—for what might he do next?—Roddy croaked, 'Yes, sir,' and the sound that emerged was downright embarrassing, like an animal in distress.

'Well, you know how I feel now, eh?'

'Yes, sir.'

Charlie stood back silently for a moment, surveying the boy. Then he said, 'Will you promise to keep quiet about it? A lot of folk wouldn't understand. It would be very bad for both of us, if you said anything to anybody.'

'Yes, sir. I promise, sir.'

'Right, Roddy. Good boy. Off you go now and send in Jimmy.'

As he reached for the door-knob, Roddy felt as though all the blood which had, only minutes before, suffused and bloated his face, was now draining down his body into his legs. He felt giddy and stopped for a moment, trying to keep his balance. Then he recovered and left the room hurriedly, in case Charlie would notice and call him back.

Outside, Roddy was so shaken he could not speak the words necessary, and pointed to Jimmy and then to the door. When the door closed, he stood with his back to the wall next to Richard, who turned to look at him. 'Did he do something to you?'

'No,' lied Roddy, blushing.

'Are you sure?'

'Yes.'

'Are you sure you're all right?'

'Yes.'

'Well, I don't believe you. When you came out of there you were white as a sheet. Now you're bright scarlet.'

Roddy said nothing after that, and when Jimmy, who had a chest condition, came out coughing, he and Richard spoke in low tones for a moment, which Roddy determined not to hear, for surely it was about him? And so he shut it from himself and the two boys followed him down the stairs in silence, and soon went their separate ways. The happenings were too terrible for discussion by Roddy. The guilt he felt prevented it, for he imagined that he, and he alone, had been dominated and abused; turned, in an instant, from a thrusting boy into an empty vessel, to be filled at another's pleasure. And it was of course his own fault! Something about him had made this happen.

The others were not much different. It was inconceivable that any of them would talk about it. Who would listen? Who would believe it? And if anyone did, it was the calculation of a moment to recognise that the entire structure of the adult world on which they all depended would come tumbling down about their ears.

When Roddy reached home, he was still blushing from the shame, but, fortunately, he had a room of his own and escaped to it immediately, where, for an hour, he sat at his table over homework, but incapable at first, of the act of concentration necessary to do it properly. Then, somehow, he forced himself to read, and the work got done, very badly, much worse than ever before, but at least it occupied him and took his mind away from recent nameless horrors, which he never even took the trouble to state to himself, still less, try to resolve. It had happened and he was stuck with it, like a load of bricks he'd just been handed and told to carry forward, into a suddenly frightening future, without hope of relief.

'You're looking pleased with yourself, Peter,' said John Manson to his eldest son that evening at tea. For once, John had remembered to return at a sensible hour. They were all there. Himself in grey clericals and blue stock, at the head of the table, an old chipped table, but one of solid wood, which the last incumbent had left behind; Jean, in a beige tweed skirt and white blouse, at the other end. Then, on one side, Peter (17) with Jessica (16), next to her father, and on his other side Susan (11) and then Roddy (12) next to his mother; all the kids in school uniform of white shirts, black skirts or trousers, grey pullovers and grey and yellow striped ties with the Ottersay crest—the coat of arms of the royal burgh, a delicate design involving several colours: a gold ship of ancient design, some of the blue and white Branden markings, and a castle.

There was a clean, plain, white table-cloth, and white napkins, a bit ragged in places, on side-plates, dishes of butter and home-made jam, and plates full of bread and home-made scones and cakes—sponges with raisins in them and chocolate-coated rice-crispies. The one and only course was fish and chips, fried in lard, with a small portion of peas to give it colour. Tea there was, in a large tea-pot, covered over with the proverbial cosy, which, long ago, Jean had made herself. The bare beige walls were lit by one light bulb, to cut down on cost, which cast an eerie glow on the ancient faded red velvet curtains, frayed at the edges, which had been salvaged and cut down to size from a jumble sale. The only ornament in the room was a hand-painted plate, in black and red, of an Athenian warrior, which stood on the mantel against the wall.

'Big Charlie was showing us the Binomial Theorem,' said Peter, tall, thin, bespectacled Peter, with dark hair and spots. 'It was really complicated, but I understood it easily. And then he told us that e to the power (iπ) plus one equals zero.'

$$e^{i\pi} + 1 = 0$$

Peter stopped, said it again carefully, and looked around the group to assess the response, and when none was forthcoming said, 'Do you not see? It's fantastic!'

'But why is it fantastic?' said Jessica—tall, slim and red-haired, with features which reminded John of a thin version of the Mona Lisa.

'Because e and π are transcendental, i is complex—the square root of minus one—and one and zero are so important. It's very surprising, that's all.'

'And you think that's fantastic?' said Jessica.

'Yes, it's wonderful! I couldn't believe it.'

'Why *do* you believe it?' said John.

'Because Big Charlie said it's true.'

'Is that all?' said John.

'No. He promised to prove it to us, next time we get analysis.'

The meal over, without a word, Jessica rose and began to collect dishes and take them to the kitchen-sink next door, where her mother washed them. The table clear, she began to dry them. John had retired to his study for the customary glass of whisky.

'And what sort of day did you have, Jessica?' said Jean, evaluating the sounds as the other children scampered upstairs, and then looking up from the sink at this tall product of herself, with the dark red hair. Titian hair, she supposed it was, though she'd never seen enough Titians to know, but she'd noticed the word in a woman's magazine, and liked the idea of her fine daughter having a classical connexion.

Jessica did not reply, seemed abstracted.

'I asked you a question, Jessica.'

'Sorry, Mum. I was just thinking about Dad. He never mentions God much, does he? I sometimes wonder if he really believes in him.'

'Of course he does! How could you suggest such a thing?' But there was a strident note to her words. 'Don't you ever question your father on that.'

'Why not? What could be wrong about asking a simple question?'

'Some questions are improper, that's why. A minister is expected to believe in God. He has to believe in God to do the job. And if he doesn't, he'll lose the job. Where would we all be then? Just think about that, the next time you start asking such questions.'

'But Daddy thinks we can ask any questions we like. He's never stopped us; even encouraged us. Remember the time Roddy asked about Jesus? Whether he rose from the dead. Daddy was glad. It showed Roddy was using his brains.'

Jean did not like the way the discussion was going. Increasingly, the children were proving a handful, and she was less and less sure how to cope. 'Well, do you believe in God, yourself?'

'Of course, Mum. I know there's a God.'

'Well that's fine then. That's all you need to worry about, isn't it?'

'No, it's not. I worry about other people, Dad in particular. What if he doesn't really believe?'

'How do you know there's a God?'

'What a strange way of putting it, Mum. Anybody would think you weren't sure of him yourself.' Jessica folded the dishcloth and hung it on the rail at the end of the small work-surface. 'I know there's a God because I know him.'

Jean looked up from the sink as she pulled the plug. 'What do you mean you know him?'

'Just what I say. I have a relationship with him. I feel his presence every day, most of the time. He's never far away. Sometimes he's very close.'

Strange to say, this worried Jean almost as much as if her daughter had denied the existence of God altogether. She looked at Jessica in a fresh light, as the girl stood tall and straight like a willow, staring sightlessly out of the window into the garden. Later, as Jessica left to go upstairs and tackle homework, Jean thought about her future.

As she knew to her cost, the religious life was not one to enter into lightly. It was painful, and too often a life of suffering and poverty. It was the uncertainty of it that was killing. You never knew where the next crust would come from. It was a life of unremitting toil, housework and pastoral work, and, when every other person was able to relax at the week-end, you were expected to work harder than ever. And there were so few pleasures, so few excitements and delights. To Jean, it seemed as if, in marrying a minister, she had taken the very cross itself on her back. Could she allow her daughter to do the same? Even to get involved?

Upstairs in her room, an odd room for a child—devoid of ornaments or pictures on the bare white walls, and with black-painted floor-boards, for she preferred to do without a carpet—Jessica sat at a rough table with a few books on it, which served as a desk, on an old rickety chair, which she would not exchange because she liked it in spite of its creaky instability. She took out a plain, white sheet of paper from a drawer and a pen. Her one luxury: a fountain pen, hers because unrefusable: a birthday present.

In black ink, she began to write in an upright script, as if chiselling stone: slowly, tentatively even, at first, and then quicker, as insight guided her direction and the chips flew.

> My dear god who art all about me
> Please help my mum and dad.
> Many things they cannot see
> But they're more good than bad.
> Help them to find you, God above,
> And let them live within your love.
> Do this for me, who love you so
> But I will, whether you do or no.

It wasn't very good, she decided; but it was better than nothing. The bit about Mum and Dad being more good than bad, she recognised as false: chosen because it rhymed. At least the sentiments were mainly right, she judged.

With the instinctive good sense that governed all she did, she decided she would have to learn to write truly, no matter the rhyme. Time and effort would effect improvements. At least it was a start; every poet had to begin somewhere. And yet there was joy in it. One's first poem is a small miracle, even if it is slight. At least it is one's own, a precursor of greater things. Events would soon conspire to make of Jessica a poet in the fullest sense.

She got off the chair, knelt down by the desk, bowed her head, and closed her eyes. *Oh God,* she prayed, *let this family be good. Let it be noble and honourable, untainted by petty desires for worthless things. Keep my father safe and give my mother the strength she ought to have, and the eyes to see what she ought to see. Amen.*

''What are..are yo.ou doing?' The creak as the door opened, had gone unheard, and, emerging around it, was a mop of chestnut hair, rosy freckled cheeks and large brown eyes that studied her intently. Then, getting no answer, for Jessica was still in the grip of communion, Susan said, in her little slurring voice, 'Can I..I co.o.me in?'

'Yes, if you like,' and Jessica got up, sat on the bed, and was joined there by her little sister.

'I don't un'nerstan' this word and it's no.o.ot in the diction'ry.' A book was thrust under Jessica's nose, and a small, and not very clean, finger, pointed out a word on page one.

Jessica turned the book to look at the cover, and read: *The Sea Hawk* by Raphael Sabatini. Under a lurid sky, a turbaned warrior was carrying the body of a woman, followed by crossbowmen and swordsmen.

'What are you doing with this? Isn't it a bit violent?'

'You m.m.m.ean bloodshed? Yes, but it's ro.om.mantic too. At least Jenny Stew.ew.art say' so.o.'

Jessica reflected, not for the first time, that Susan's slur was much worse in the late afternoon—for it was not a stammer, it was want of energy, rather—and wondered whether it was a symptom of something more serious. 'What do you want with romance at your age?' she said, refusing to mention the impediment, out of kindness.

Ignoring this question as too obvious to merit discussion, Susan, flushing at the recognition that Jessica had noticed the handicap, pointed again to the word 'nable.'

'I don't know what it means,' said Jessica, and no progress was made by a search of her own dictionary, which she got from the table. 'It's just not here,' said Jessica, with surprise.

'Shou.ould I try Pe.eter?'

'No. Not just now. He'll be...occupied.'

'Would Daddy know?'

'I doubt it. He uses the same dictionary as me.'

'Well tha.at's not much goo.ood, is it?' said Susan with displeasure. 'How am I suppo.o.osed to un'nerstand a book when the words are invented?'

'Maybe it's a test. Maybe you have to work it out for yourself.' Jessica read out: '*There arose under the supervision of the gifted engineer, worthy associate of Messer Torrigiani, a nable two-storied mansion of mellow brick....* Well what do you think it means?'

'Beautiful? Goo.ood? I'm no.ot sure. What do you thin.ink?'

There it was again, thought Jessica, Susan's voice sounded lazy, not stressed. 'Maybe it's just a misprint. Maybe it should be 'notable', for that means 'memorable or distinguished.'

Susan laughed. 'That so.ound' right.'

'But maybe it doesn't mean that at all. Poetry is like that sometimes. The poet coins a new word. Maybe that's what this is.'

'How do we know which it is?'

'We could write and ask Mr Sabatini. He's the only one who might know.'

'But what if he's de.ead?'

'Then we'll just have to live with the problem.'

'But why? I want to know.' And there was something else, thought Jessica, Susan's passion for knowledge. There was something implacable about it. And she demanded rigour. Jessica thought carefully before saying: 'Well, there are some things that cannot be known.'

'I don't un'nerstan'. Why can't we find out?'

'Because no one can think of a way. Often there isn't a way. So we just have to go on living without knowing.'

The little girl looked around the bare walls, as she considered this profound statement, in the light of her burgeoning intelligence, and decided it was probably true. Then she said, 'Have you been pra.aying? Daddy doesn't pray much. Why do you do.o it, if he doesn't?'

'Because I like doing it.'

'Why do you like it? What's goo.ood about it? Nothing ever happens to me when I try.y it.'

'I like to talk to God. That's all it is. I always feel good afterwards.'

'Why doesn't Daddy do it the.en, if it makes you feel good?'

'I don't know.'

'Do you think I should ask him?'

'Yes, if you want to.' Then Jessica remembered what her mother had said and added, 'I expect he just doesn't like it as much. Maybe he just doesn't have the time. You know how much he has to do.'

In the room next door, with the key turned in the lock, Peter was thinking of Miss Morrison, the young science teacher; imagining taking her clothes off. She stood beside him with an alluring smile, and he was captivated by the look. He tried to imagine what it would feel like to circle her breasts with the palm of his hand, and then how he would kiss her, ever so gently, and she would kiss him back. And then, in his mind's eye, his other hand moved lower, inside her panties—a word that was itself enough to make him blush, whenever he heard it—and caress the hair beneath. And then....and then.....and then. And he shuddered under the pressure of the hand-movement and the wetness surged out of him.

As he bent down to wipe the last of it off his shoe, he sighed with relief, and wondered if he should bother to ask for a new pair of boots. The old ones were too tight now, but worse, they had lost some studs, and begun to split along one side. He knew, without asking, that the money for a new pair was not available. And yet, as the star second-row forward of the firsts, he had to get a good footing to make the jumps at the line-out. Then there was the goal-kicking. He did that too. But how was he to do well, if he couldn't stay upright for lack of studs?

Peter put Miss Morrison out of mind, and even the worry about his play being affected by the old boots, and soon lost himself in a textbook on vector calculus. Just before nine, he got up, went quietly downstairs, and made a pot of tea, set it on a tray with cups and plates of Jean's home-baking, and took it into the sitting-room, where Jean, in an armchair by the fireside, was sewing—patching worn elbows and frayed hems—and Jessica, on the sofa, was watching the end of a documentary on social deprivation.

'Where's Dad?' said Peter.

'It's the Kirk Session tonight,' said Jean, taking a cup from him without removing her eyes from the news, which had just started.

'I wish he didn't drive himself so hard,' said Peter, sitting on the sofa. 'He never seems to relax for very long. He's always out seeing somebody—or writing the sermon. What an age that takes. The whole of Friday and Saturday. You'd think he'd be able to polish it off with the amount of practice he's had.'

'They're good sermons,' said Jean. 'Not the kind of things you can just make up on the spur of the moment.'

'Well, I wouldn't like a job like that, where I had no time for my family.'

'There's no finer job for any man, and no finer man than your father.'

'I know Mum, but does it have to be so committing? I mean, he hardly has time to breathe. How can he do his job properly, when he does it so much?'

'Because there is so much for him to do. A minister can't shut the door at night and say, that's it for now. People's problems don't stop at five o'clock. They go on all the time.'

'Well, I don't think it's good for him, even if it is his job.'

'Some ministers read their sermons out of a book, and they see as few folk as possible—a visit here and there, mostly to the same place: the hospital, where all the really bad cases naturally collect together. Well, your father's not like that. I sometimes think he's too good for the folk in this parish.'

Jessica said quietly, 'I just wish he had somebody to go to, when he's in trouble.'

'He's got me,' said Jean.

'He wouldn't want to worry you, though.'

'There's always God, Jessica. You know that.'

'Yes, *I* know,' she said meaningfully, but her mother failed to catch the inflection.

Tom Henderson, convener of the roof fund, had just given his report on the work that should be carried out, the estimated cost and shortfall that would have to be found, for, in St Margaret's, the Congregational Board and the Kirk Session were one. They were sitting round the table in the vestry at the back of the church, four on one side of the minister and four on the other.

Tom was a fine-looking man with dark hair, in an expensive dark-blue suit.

John Manson suppressed a yawn with difficulty, but when 'any other business' was announced, he remembered there was something which had been nagging at him. 'I think efforts should be made to find people in the congregation, prepared to carry the old folk back and forth to the services. The ones who don't have cars or can't come on foot.'

Dr Telford—small, brown-haired, in a green tweed suit and white shirt, with half-moon specs and a crinkled forehead, as if the result of too much thought—said, 'What's the present system ?'

John Manson said nothing, waiting, content to listen to the hissing of the gas-fire and look around the bare walls of the room.

'They come in taxis, don't they?' said Bob Forsyth, the banker, tall and grey-headed, with red-veined cheeks, and a corporation under the waistcoat of his blue and white pin-striped suit.

The police sergeant, Jim Grant, already dressed for the backshift at ten pm, said, 'Who pays for the taxis?'

There was a silence, as the elders looked at each other, until Henderson said, 'There are no bills to the church for them. So *they* must pay for them, unless they're free.'

'Yes, it would be very good if they were free,' said Manson, 'but I don't think they are.'

'Are you implying that I should operate a free service?' said George Buchanan, in habitual black coat, white shirt and dark tie, which complemented his full head of jet-black hair.

'No,' said Manson. 'I don't expect you to do it for nothing.'

'Why have you raised this matter then?' said George, aggressively, jutting out the lower jaw of his dough-like face.

'I think a better system can be found. It would be better for the congregation if they took a hand in this. There are plenty of lonely folk in the congregation, with cars, who would welcome the opportunity to do a little a good in this way, and it would maybe draw them out of themselves. Make a few new relationships for a change, instead of moping off home on their own, as usual.'

'It's not necessary. A waste of time,' said Buchanan irritably, his jowls shaking.

'I think the minister has a point,' said Dr Telford, fingering his black and gold striped University tie. 'It's good psychology. Yes, I approve. A very good idea, I say.'

Henderson, who was an accountant, said, 'But what's it going to cost?'

'Nothing,' said Telford. 'Volunteers will simply run them here and back, in their own cars, at their own expense.'

'Well, I'm against it,' said Buchanan. 'I'm damned annoyed that the matter has been raised in this fashion. It's undemocratic, and unfair to attack my business in this way.'

'It's neither one or the other,' said Manson. 'It's just a small change which might have a good effect.'

'It will have a bad effect on my business. I won't have it!'

There was silence for a while, as the elders contemplated this reaction. Then Dick Souter, a little man in a brown sports jacket, white shirt and green woollen tie with dark, thinning hair and a thin black moustache, piped up, 'Maybe we should just leave it alone, then. The system works fine the way it is.'

'Aye, Ah don't want any bad-feeling,' said Calum Smith. 'We're supposed tae help each ither, no' cause trouble. We should jist forget the hale thing.' Calum was red- haired, shaped like a bull, like most blacksmiths, and looked incongruous in blazer and flannels.

A vote was taken at the chairman's suggestion, and the results counted and read out by him. 'Four votes each and one abstention,' said Bob Forsyth.

'Who abstained?' said Dr Telford. 'That was a funny thing to do?'

'I did,' said Ellen MacFadyean, bespectacled, in a brown skirt and jumper.

'But why? Can't you make up your mind?

Ellen pursed her pale-pink lips and lifted the fair-haired head. 'I just feel I don't know enough about it. The Minister's idea is a good one, but I don't know how much George would stand to lose in business.'

'Just a few taxi fares, that's all; but every little helps; you know how it is,' said George Buchanan, and some of the businessmen among them nodded sagely, for the problems of staying afloat on an island like Branden, with a limited population, were common.

'If it's just a few taxis, what's the difficulty?' said Telford. 'You're not short of a bob, George. You live in a fine house in the best part of town and you drive a Mercedes, for heavens sake. What's a few taxis to you?'

'It's the principle of the thing! I shouldn't be attacked in this way— not in my own church. I need to keep my business going like everyone else. It's help I want, not hindrance.'

Ellen took off her spectacles, and brushed the fair hair away from her face with her hands. 'Well, all right, I'll go along with the present system.'

'Wait a minute,' said Manson. 'It would seem best to find out all about the present system, before making up our minds.'

'What do you mean by that? What do you mean by that?' said Buchanan, reddening. 'Are you suggesting there's something untoward in my business?'

Manson said nothing and Telford said, 'I think you should answer that, Minister.'

Manson said, 'Well, I would rather not. I would rather you found out for yourselves by asking around, but if you insist, I would merely ask you to consider whether it is or is not the case that George here, does nearly all the funerals for this church. And whether there might be some connexion between that, and the fact that he also has a monopoly of the taxi service.'

'I object! There's no monopoly! Anybody can use any taxi rank he likes. If folk use mine, it's because they want to.'

'Maybe, George, but hold on,' said Telford, studying him over the top of the half-moon specs, as if he were a difficult patient. 'It is a fact that you do have nearly all the funerals and taxis. You must be making a fortune out of them all. What do you make on a funeral, a hundred? We have five or six a week. That's real money!'

'It's nothing like as much,' said George. 'But I earn every penny of it! I resent this discussion of my business affairs. There's no call for it! And I won't tolerate it!' George got up and stumped out, his cheeks red with fury and injured pride.

After speeding along the sea front for a couple of miles, and climbing the hill, George parked the green Mercedes in the drive of Silvertrees, a large detached villa, and crunched his way past the flower beds to the porch. Inside, he banged the door shut and, like a cloud carrying thunder and lighting, burst into the sitting-room, where Betty Buchanan, his wife, was watching television and, over in a corner, at a desk, Billy, his son, was writing a letter.

George stood in the doorway, livid of face and shaking with anger, pointing backwards the way he had come. 'That...that bastard Manson's trying to ruin the business!' Then he moved to the centre of the room, to dominate it more effectively, and stood, looking around at the red flock-wallpaper and the light-green, three-piece suite on the beige Chinese washed carpet.

The boy and the woman sat upright, and cast timorous looks at him. Betty had a small, regular face with fair hair in a perm, and wore a lovat-green twin-set, with a string of pearls down the front. Billy was a teenage version of his father, though more round-shouldered, still in the school uniform of black trousers, white shirt and grey and yellow striped tie with the town crest.

'Well, have you nothing to say?' said George, with amazement. And when there was still silence, 'Do ye not care about the business?'

'Of course we do, dear. You know we do,' said Betty, 'it's just the shock. What has he done?'

'He wants to stop the Sunday taxi service.'

'But why?'

'He says the lonely folk in the church should take the old ones in their cars. But I think he's found out what it means to us.'

'What can you do about it?'

'Persuade the minister to give it up.'

'But what if he won't?'

'Get rid of him.'

George crossed the room and stood with his back to the fire, warming himself, as the anger cooled, and the purple gradually drained out of his face.

'I'll make you some tea, shall I?' said Betty, and got up, never doubting for an instant that George would be capable of solving the problem.

'Yes,' said George, 'do that,' and then, sitting down in the chair opposite, from where he could see the boy, noticed that Billy was engrossed in other matters. 'Is that all the business means to you?' said George, but he said it too quietly for Billy to hear.

Curious, George rose and crossed the room with quick, splay-footed strides, on his heels, looked down on the desk for a moment, and then, in a huge talon-like grasp, seized the letter that Billy was writing. 'What's this?'

Betty re-entered the room and said, 'Would you like a piece of apple pie and ice-cream?' and when George failed to answer, stood near the doorway, uncertainly, nervously clutching her white pinafore.

'Dear Jessica,' read out George, 'You are very beautiful and I would like to go with you. I know I'm not up to much myself, but it would be a great blessing to me if you would.'

Billy stood up, blushed, and made to run out of the room, but George stopped him, with a talon clamped on the shoulder. 'What do you mean you're not up to much? You're my son! Of course you're up to much! Explain yourself!'

'Well, it's true. I'm not! I'm not! I'm not handsome and I'm not clever like her brother, and I'm not even good at games. I'm sixteen and I'm not even in the thirds regularly. Only when somebody can't play. I'm...I'm...just a failure.'

Betty stood still, shocked by the outburst, but made no move towards Billy, when his father was so close.

George said, 'None of that's true, son. None of it! You're as good-looking as anybody! And you are clever, and you do play rugby. Not everybody can do these things well, but you do them well enough.'

'But I'm not! I'm not, Dad! I'm smaller and weaker and uglier, and it wouldn't matter if I wasn't so stupid. Most of the folk in my class are much quicker than me. I get left behind all the time. And I don't like any of it!'

'Listen, son! None of that guff matters anyway. It's all kids stuff. In the real world, all that matters is power, and you get that by having money, and you've got plenty. You're the richest boy in that school, don't you know that?'

'Yes, but no one really cares.'

'One day, they will care. When they come to you for a job. When they depend on you to feed them and their kids. You'll see! One day you'll be the provost of this town. The folk will look up to you, the way they look up to me.'

Betty came over and smiled, now that George had sorted it out, as he always did. Any problem, her George could solve. Betty enfolded Billy in her arms, and kissed him. 'You've not to worry. We love you. To us you're the greatest. Believe it. It's true.'

Looking at the letter again, George said, 'Who's this Jessica, anyway?'

'Jessica Manson.'

'The minister's daughter?'

'Yes,' nodded Billy, wondering for an instant if his own problems would, after all, be seen as more pressing.

'Well, you've to stop thinking about her,' said George, tearing the letter across, crumpling it into a ball and throwing the paper into the fire. 'Just put her out of your mind. She's not for you.'

'But....but I love her!' said Billy, blushing.

'Well you can't have her. She's with the enemy, the man that's trying to ruin the business.'

Billy burst into tears and ran out of the room crying.

George looked at his watch, decided enough time had elapsed since the meeting, sat down in an armchair and picked up the phone from a table beside it. He would start with Ellen MacFadyean.

'I'm disappointed in you. Hurt and disappointed. I thought you and I were friends.'

'We are friends,' said Ellen. 'You've no reason to take it personally...'

'—Personally? How else could I take it? This is my livelihood we're talking about. Of course it's personal.'

Ellen was silenced.

'I want you on my side, the way you've always been. I can count on you, can't I, Ellen?'

'You know I'm your friend, George. I'll always be that, but I don't always have to agree with —'

'Anybody that would go against me on this, is no friend of mine. How could she be? I'm gonny lose a lot of business over this.'

'But it's a good idea, George.'

'It's no better than the system we have. The old folk get to the service, don't they? What could be better than that?'

'But the lonely ones might get involved.'

'Don't be daft! They're lonely because they want to be! If they wanted to take folk in their cars, they would be doing it already. Just you tell me where you stand. Come on now. Let's have it. Are you for me or against me? I want to know now. But if you're against me, that's it between you and me.'

There was a silence, while Ellen thought about the matter. Was it really worth the fuss? George was a dangerous man to make an enemy of, as a lot of folk had found to their cost. The worry of being at the receiving end of his enmity, was not something to take on lightly.

'Oh, all right,' said Ellen, finally. 'You can count on my support.'

At four-thirty, behind the cycle shed, Billy Buchanan waited for Jessica, who had agreed to meet him after her music lesson in the great gothic building, that was Branden Grammar School. The playground was silent and empty, until a swing-door slammed, and Jessica emerged with her cello.

As Jessica came up to him, Billy blushed, and stammered, 'He.. Hello.'

'Hello,' said Jessica, and then, like a pair of strangers, they stood looking at each other, in silence.

When Billy said nothing, Jessica saw that he was unable to do so.

'Thanks for the letter. It was very nice of you. I've never had a letter like that before.'

'Oh, it was nothing,' said Billy, blushing more than ever.

'But it can't be true, you know. I mean, you don't know me. So how could you really love me?'

'But I do! I think about you all the time.'

'You mean, you imagine me all the time. That's a different thing. If you got to know me, you probably wouldn't like me at all.'

'Oh no! No chance,' said Billy, shaking his head.

Jessica looked him over consideringly. 'I don't really want to have a boy friend. It's not something I'm ready for. I've got so much to do. My exams and all that.'

'But you don't do school-work all the time, do you? You must have some time to yourself.'

'Well, yes, I suppose so. I read a lot and I go for walks with the dog at night.'

'Maybe I could come with you on these walks. Maybe we could go out to the pictures the way a lot of kids do? Don't you go to the pictures?'

'No, I don't.'

'Why not? Everybody goes to the pictures, don't they?'

'My family don't. I wish we could, I suppose, but we're very poor. There isn't the money.'

'Oh, if that's all it is, that's no problem. I'll take you. I've got plenty money.'

'I'm not sure I could allow that.'

'Why not, for God's sake? The boy usually pays anyway. Go on, say you'll come. Please.'

And Jessica, who had come to tell him, in the nicest way possible, that she didn't need a boy-friend, and conceal the fact that Billy was not her type, saw the depth of his need, and would not say no.

Billy was overjoyed, and the pleasure she had given him was reason enough for doing it. They walked home to the Manse together in silence, and Jessica liked it, for she saw how she had lit up a rather dull life. Maybe making a friend of Billy would be worthwhile.

Half way there, Billy blushed again, and said, 'I'm awfully sorry. I should have asked. Can I carry your bag?'

Jessica grinned, 'What for? I can carry it myself.'

'Well, your violin, then? You've got too much.'

'I carry them all the time. I'm quite used to it. And it's a cello.'

'Please,' said Billy, and looked as if he would expire, if he were not accorded this small favour.

'All right, if it makes you happy,' said Jessica, transferring the musical-instrument case to him.

'I suppose it's an awful chore having to lug this thing around all the time.'

'No, it's a pleasure.'

'How?' said Billy, with shock. 'A lot of kids take music lessons, but none of them like it, do they?'

'I do. I'm very lucky to get lessons, and very lucky to be loaned this instrument.'

'I don't understand. It's just work, isn't it? Who wants to do that?'

'If it was only work, that would be a reason for doing it, but it isn't. It's a passion. I love the sound it makes, the tone; and I love music, so of course it's not work at all. It's pure delight.'

Billy stopped, and looked up at Jessica, who was slightly taller, and sighed, as if he'd just been made aware of a new world of experience.

'Do you mean to say, you play that for fun?'

'Yes. Well, no. It's more than fun. It's necessary to me. I would miss it terribly if I didn't.'

'But what good is it? What would you miss about it?'

Jessica walked on with her head bowed, thinking deeply, and then said, 'It makes me feel.....It helps me to expand myself by feeling. I would definitely feel less, be a shrunken version of myself, without it.'

'I don't understand,' said Billy, and then, as an afterthought, 'You know, I'd never admit that to anyone else,' and laughed. 'I can really talk to you, Jessica. You......you're wonderful!'

Jessica's eyes lit up. 'And you're a flatterer.' But, as Billy's head went down and he fell silent, she added, 'I'm sorry. I was wrong. Anyway, I wasn't serious. Forgive me.'

'O.K.' said Billy, managing to sound grudging.

They stood at the garden gate of the Manse, looking at each other, and Jessica knew that he wanted to kiss her, and that he wouldn't have the courage, and, being Jessica, she just had to help. She said, 'Well, thanks for walking me home. I'll have to go in now. They'll be waiting for me,' and she bent and kissed him on the pale cheek, and opened the gate, and walked up the path, between the lawns, turning half way to wave at the boy, who stood open-mouthed with wonder.

Jean Manson, who saw the pair from the window, said nothing until tea, when the family were all assembled. 'Jessica's got a boyfriend,' she told them, matter-of-factly.

Untypically, Peter laid down his knife and fork, without having cleared his plate first, and said, 'Who is it?'

Jessica, who never blushed, smiled. 'Billy Buchanan.'

'What? That little runt. I could get you the pick of the first fifteen.'

'I don't need your help, thanks very much. I'll do my own choosing.'

'But why him?'

'Because he asked me.'

'But you can't like him!'

'Who says I can't? Anyway, how can I know if I like him, until I get to know him?'

'Shouldn't she get your permission first, Dad?'

'No.'

'You don't mean to say you're going to allow her to go out with ...that?'

'Jessica can go with who she likes.'

Peter laughed. 'It's crazy. If you'd just waited a bit, somebody worthwhile would have come along.'

'Somebody worthwhile has come along,' said Jessica. 'He really likes me, and he needs me, and that'll do very nicely to be going on with.'

'Just don't let it interfere with your school-work,' said Jean.

'You know I won't, Mum.'

And sure enough, Jean knew. She looked up at John across the table, and saw the wisp of a smile, and wondered, not for the first time, what have we got here?

Before the meal was over, the phone rang, and Susan got up to answer it in the hall. She lifted the instrument and looked up at the picture of a bullfighter above the telephone table, listened, and then called out, 'It's some'dy's secret'ry. Someb'dy ca.alled Mrs Arbuthnott-Sne.ell for Da.addy.'

John went to the phone and picked it up. 'Would you come round and call on Mrs Arbuthnott-Snell this evening, Minister? Oh, you would? Splendid! In a quarter of an hour?'

'Well, I'm having my tea. I could be there in an hour.'

'But Mrs Arbuthnott-Snell is going out this evening, and she particularly wanted to see you beforehand.'

'All right, I'll come as soon as I can.'

'It would need to be then, I'm afraid, or she will have left.'

Curious, John agreed to go.

Tall maples, in red and golden livery, lined the avenue, which curled around acres of lawn, towards the three-storied house, ending in a great swathe of raked gravel, which crunched underfoot as John approached. He rang the bell and waited. Several minutes later, the door was opened by the secretary, Miss Semple, a short, dumpy woman, with grey hair.

'John Manson,' he said, holding out his hand. 'Sorry I'm a little late. It's a long walk up here.'

'It's half an hour since I phoned, Minister,' said Miss Semple, ignoring his hand. 'I'm not sure Mrs Arbuthnott-Snell will see you now. Oh, you'd better come in, I suppose.'

John was shown into a reception room on the right of the hall. The carpet seemed to envelop his feet as he crossed the floor. Persian, he decided, as he studied the ornate design, in beige and browns, which had clearly been created with this particular room in mind, for it fitted its dimensions perfectly. The walls were painted light-green, which matched the fireplace of green and white marble, intricately carved, and were of the same tone as the carpet, upon which rested a ten piece suite of furniture in various combinations, and a desk, and various occasional tables, laden with women's fashion magazines. Pictures in heavy gold frames hung around the walls, each with its own light.

For ten minutes, John stood looking out at the broad acres of garden, and the trees, which swayed back and forth in the rising wind, and, even as he watched, began to shed their bright plumage.

The door opened and a lady entered. She was tall and graceful and dressed in a full-length silver gown. She crossed the room like a galleon in full sail, under a fantastic creation of golden hair, swept up like royals, to extract every last inch of advantage, from the prevailing wind.

'Mr Manson. As you see, I am going out—to dine with Lord and Lady Branden. And you have made me late.'

When John said nothing, she seemed out of countenance.

'Oh, do sit down, there's a good fellow,' she added, with a trace of irritation. 'The fact is, I wanted to do something for the church.'

John said nothing for a moment, as he sat down and considered her. 'What is it you'd like to do?' he said, finally.

'I'm not sure. I thought you might help with that.'

'I take it a sum of money is involved?'

'Yes, shall we say, £50?'

'That would be very useful.'

'But what could it be used for?'

'Well, to buy something for the church, or it could be used in the same way as ordinary donations.'

'I wouldn't want it to be considered ordinary.'

'Oh, there's nothing wrong with the ordinary use, Mrs Arbuthnott-Snell. Some goes to the mission field, where it is much needed. It buys bibles and medicines; and food and shelter, even, for poor people in Africa and other places. And some are very poor. It would make your heart bleed to see them. A lot of them die every day, for lack of medical care or nourishment. But you know all this. It's well-publicised.'

'Yes, that's rather old-hat. I don't want to do anything ordinary. Some of that money goes to pay for the upkeep of buildings, and salaries, for people like yourself, does it not?' When John agreed, she added, 'I wouldn't want to contribute to that.'

As John looked around the great state-room, and compared its opulence with his own spartan establishment, there was a pang of regret at this woman's lack of sensitivity, but he said nothing.

'I would prefer some object, something to occupy a leading place in the church.'

'You mean a memorial of some kind? A stained-glass window, commemorating your late husband, maybe?'

'Good God, no! My husband wouldn't want to be remembered. What about a crucifix or a madonna, or something like that?'

'We don't go in for that kind of thing in the Church of Scotland. That's more the style of the Roman Catholics.'

'Well, that's what I would like, and I'm not a Catholic!'

'If that's what your heart is set on, there's nothing more to be said, then,' said John, rising.

'Hush! Of course, there's more to be said! I haven't finished with you! Sit down!'

John considered her flushed cheeks for a moment, and decided he'd had enough for one night. 'No, thank you, Mrs Arbuthnott-Snell. Duty calls. I will see myself out.'

'You'll do no such thing!' said that lady, ringing the bell for the maid, but John went to the door, opened it, and just before closing it behind him, turned and said, politely, 'I hope you enjoy your dinner with Lord Branden, and that I did not keep you too late. Good night.'

The maid crossed the hall as he was making for the front door, and he smiled at her before leaving. Outside, the wind had risen, the maples were creaking under the strain of staying upright, and the air was full of red and gold leaves, that swirled around him, as his feet crunched down the drive towards the sea front. All gone, he thought, the glory of autumn gone. All that lay ahead was winter.

The sea burst across the road, for the tide was high, and before long, the old black coat was soaked with flying salt-spray. Then, in one terrific gust, the hat was blown clear off his head and it rolled and cavorted like a wild thing, in front of him, defying every effort to catch it. Every time he caught up and stooped, to reach out, the hat would rise off the ground and run off like a hare, twitching this way and then the other, until at last, he gave up the futile pursuit, and resolved to do without a hat in future. A hundred yards away, it performed a final frolic, and disappeared over a cliff into the Clyde.

That evening, Moira Semple informed her sister Agnes, who worked in the savings bank, about the minister's rude behaviour; turning up late, refusing to apologise, and even refusing to accept a donation from Mrs Arbuthnott-Snell. And the next morning, at work, Agnes told Bob Forsyth, the bank manager, who promptly told Dick Souter, when that small worthy came cap in hand, to ask for an extension of his loan. And, over lunch, Dick told his wife Betsy, who told her friend Mary Smith, the blacksmith's wife, and somehow, between Moira Semple and Mary Smith, the sum offered had increased to thousands of pounds, so that it was being whispered that the number with a five in it, was actually a five figure amount.

Light streamed into the class-room and lit Jessica's hair as if it were on fire, and, as she flung the bow across the bridge, a tress fell across her forehead, almost blinding her; but she played on, mindless of what, Miss Carmichael judged, would be a huge distraction; and the room sang with sound which resonated everywhere, even out into the corridor and down the stairs.

Hearing another kind of sound, grey-haired, bespectacled Miss Carmichael, seated at her desk in her white blouse and black gown, turned and smiled as the Headmaster, Phil Mulholland, nicknamed Napoleon, because of his vanity and stature, followed by the much larger figure of Charlie Braddock, both in gowns, tip-toed into the room and, unseen by the soloist, who faced the window, sat quietly at front desks.

Fingers prodded and plucked, the bow cut into the strings with a power that was palpable; sweat glistened on Jessica's forehead and her eyes shone. The brilliant cadenza was completed in a blistering exhibition of manual dexterity, from which every note, as accurate and as clear as ever intended and as quick, swelling together in warm waves, suffused the room with deep, mellow tones that spoke symphonies of the performer's passion for the music; and when it was over, there was, at first, a dead silence. And then the sound of choked throats, releasing what had been surging within, and applause, rising breakers of clapping, as the three adults stood.

'That was wonderful Jessica.'

'Terrific! Oh, terrific!'

'Splendid, simply splendid!'

'What about that music scholarship at the Royal Scottish?' said Charlie, who was always up on the matter of prizes and distinctions.

'I couldn't agree more,' said Phil, who in contrast to Charlie, had a full head of dark curly hair. 'What do you say, Miss Carmichael? Does Branden Grammar have a winner here?'

Miss Carmichael ran a hand over her long grey hair thoughtfully, but said finally, 'Yes, I think Jessica should enter. If she continues to progress like this, she will have a very good chance.'

The adults talked among themselves, while Jessica prepared to leave, and then Miss Carmichael said, 'What do you think, Jessica? Do you want to try for it?'

'Would it cost any money? I won't be able to do it if it does.'

'We'll see that it doesn't,' said Phil. 'Just your fare up to Glasgow.'

'But she would have to stay overnight,' said Miss Carmichael. 'The competition takes several days.'

'Have you any relatives in Glasgow?' said Phil.

'No. All my relatives are abroad or dead.'

But Charlie was not to be beaten. 'Well, if you're stuck, you could always stay with me. I still have a flat there.'

And so it was agreed that on top of a full load of 5 Highers, taken young, Jessica was to work every afternoon, after four o'clock, at her music, under Miss Carmichael.

'Mind, you'll have to practice every day at home,' said that lady. 'At least two hours at home and one every day here.'

Once Jessica had left, Phil took Miss Carmichael by the arm and led her downstairs. 'What do you think Margaret? Should she wait till next year, maybe?'

'She might not do a sixth year. You know how poor her parents are. They might make her leave at the end of the fifth. I know they only just allowed Peter to stay on for a sixth year.'

'I see. Well, she'll definitely get her highers. That means she'll get into university.'

Margaret Carmichael stood politely, looking down at the diminutive Mr Mulholland, while he considered the situation. 'Well, there's nothing else for it,' he decided. 'She'll have to win it for us this year, just in case we lose her.' A critical decision.

At the next meeting of the Rotary Club, in the dining room of the Victoria and Albert Hotel, the speaker was George Buchanan. His topic: the ethics of business, one he had not chosen but agreed to speak on, when invited.

It is a truth universally acknowledged that business is enhanced by the possession and promotion of any skill, for everyone made aware of it is a potential customer who would rather buy from the better endowed person than his lowly competitor. And that there are two species of rogues in business is well-known. The bumbler, only half aware that his activities are immoral, and maybe illegal, and, in spite of vague feelings of uneasiness, continues as before, treading a delicate line between bankruptcy and prison, because he can do no other. His more advanced associate has no illusions and expects everyone to act illegally and immorally on every possible opportunity; and, if queried, will say with genuine surprise: *but this is the law of life*, citing Adam Smith as authority for the view that 'dog eat dog' is an empirical fact, impossible to challenge. There is, however, a rarer class of rogue yet, who, aware of the fact, presents himself as a pillar of moral rectitude, while seeking on every occasion to take advantage of the blindness of his fellows. Thus, he is an exception to the rule: his skills, his real skills, have to remain hidden. Success depends upon his appearing to be what he is not.

Mindful of the forthcoming election for provost, as well as his various projects, George stood, in the familiar black topcoat and trousers with the thin white stripe, as he had been taught years before, half of one hand elegantly in pocket, the other available for gestures, mostly palm up, conveying openness and honesty, to the assembly of well-dressed men, seated around long tables after a heavy lunch.

He spoke with glowing eyes and reddened cheeks, of the achievements and importance of business—how the country depends upon it for its wealth and the improvement of the lives of the people, through better services of every kind. Business, said George, 'is the heart of the nation; would be nothing without it,' provides jobs for millions, and a standard of living the envy of the rest of the world. And much of the profits are ploughed back in new machinery and new ideas and even funnelled into charities which do much good in so many ways, to so many deserving people. Business, in short, for George, was the finest thing in existence; itself responsible for what society called ethics. 'What are these?' asked George, a question beyond his usual intellectual summit, because seen fleetingly on a newspaper headline of the type he never tried to read because of the effort required. 'Nothing but common sense procedures for producing, buying and selling', he replied. If a producer makes sub-standard goods, it is right and proper that he should go out of business; if he provided a good service, it was right that he should live well on the profits. This was the method of business and of life. Finally, he revealed that he thought business men the natural leaders of society.

He gave an impression of the statesman, the avuncular man of maturity and experience, who had seen it all and done it all—and with utmost moral rectitude. And was successful, the applause showed it, for few present had ever experienced forensic examination of their heads in university tutorials; and too many years of lotus island life had dulled the intellects of those who had, to the point that a speech was judged on the presentation and not the wisdom, content being confused with the statement of half-baked ideas most were glad to share.

At the end, it was Bob Forsyth, the banker, who challenged him. 'Would you not agree that the community has many leaders, some of them not business men? Isn't the Headmaster of the local school a leader? And more important, the Minister? Perhaps the Minister would care to say a few words?'

John, who had spent the time wondering whether to resign because the cost of lunch was now beyond his pocket, got up and said, 'Yes, the community has many leaders from many walks of life, ministers among them. The minister is required to set a good example, which is both a burden and a privilege. It is not easy, but it has its rewards.' For a moment or two,

John contemplated the ceiling, as if thinking deeply. Then, looking at them again, he continued, 'What is leadership about?'

He stopped and surveyed them, one by one, wondering about them as men. Then he said, 'The first thing, is to see clearly what other men cannot, or not so quickly, the next is to persuade them to follow. It is the last part that is so very difficult. In business, I don't suppose there's much of a problem. The workforce must either follow or be sacked. In life, it's not so easy. Mr Buchanan talks about business as if it were real life, the tough life out there, that none of the rest of us know anything about, because we're insulated against it. He couldn't be more wrong. Business is a protected life, because the boss and the worker need each other. Outside business, it's less certain. People don't have incentives to help each other in the community at large, where men and women are free to commit every kind of sin of omission and commission, and may not realise they are doing it. That is the burden the minister shoulders and must bear.'

When he had taken his seat, Mulholland stood up to reply. 'What the Minister says may be true, but there are no risks in the ministry. It may be underpaid but it's secure, and there's always a berth in heaven at the end of it.'

Once the general laughter subsided, John stood to say, 'I fear our speaker is mistaken. The ministry is the riskiest business there is. It's very easy to step on someone's toe by accident, but ministers never get forgiven. Then there are the folk whose toes *should* be stepped on: they never understand.'

'But what about the ticket to heaven?' called out Phil Mulholland.

'I sometimes think it's harder for a minister than for any other man,' said John.

'Why would that be?' said Mulholland. 'Is it the temptations?' and then grinned at the laughter he had provoked.

'There are not too many of these. Ministers don't get to handle the money. No, the risks are in not being understood. In seeing the way, but not being able to convince the flock that it is.'

He was wrong about that; but as he made to sit down, he decided he had a duty to reply properly to George's speech. He stood up again and said, 'I must say that I am surprised that Councillor Buchanan should identify ethics with business procedures, as if they were the source. The fact is, that ethics is the philosophy of morals—the study of the reasons behind our moral judgements—and it does not derive from business, but from the highest productions of the mind and spirit. From books like *The Bible* and thousands of years of concentrated study of the principles to be found there. We must all hope that business procedures are morally conducted, but, it seems to me, there is something inimical in business which tends to make it immoral. The very profit motive—the be-all and end-all of business—too often takes precedence over moral concerns. It is even inevitable that it should. To that extent, business is a suspect activity, one we should all be wary of.'

George, who neither understood the meaning of the word 'inimical' or why it might be desirable to investigate the basis of moral judgements, as he never had any dealings with these companies, was angry. He had been attacked. Purple with rage, he stood up again. 'Are you implying that business is some sort of crime? I think it's disgraceful that the honest business men here should be insulted like this.' And so, even George could not be perfect: he had a temper, which occasionally interfered with the performance of the skills he most admired.

John said, 'Nothing in what I said insults anyone. I was speaking generally. Of course there are many honest businessmen, but there are also many rogues.' And George took it that he was one of the latter, but then he had reason to.

As they trooped down the stairs afterwards, some of the Rotarians, remembering the trouble over the taxi service at the Kirk, decided that a feud was in progress between George and his minister; and in the nature of bystanders, viewed one party as bad as the other. And those who saw John try to engage George in conversation without success, took the brush-off as probably deserved. Yes, they agreed, George had given a good talk, no matter what the minister said.

Late one afternoon, in the Manse, John settled himself down with a cup of tea and surveyed Jessica, who had just left Billy Buchanan at the door, and was sitting thoughtfully on the window-seat, looking out, while stroking the white cat.

'You must ask that boy in, some time, so that we can meet him.' A natural suggestion from a good man, but like issuing a passport to a fifth column.

'Yes, I will one of these days.'

Jean, who was knitting in the chair opposite John, on one side of the fireplace, said, 'I think you're too young for that sort of thing. You've got so much work to do.'

'Well, I've got some more now. Miss Carmichael's giving me extra lessons, so I can compete for the music scholarship.'

'Oh, that's wonderful, Jessica!' said Jean, her eyes lighting up, 'Just think if you won it! Oh, we'd all be so proud of you. Wouldn't we John?'

'Yes, we would, but do you want to do this, Jessica?'

'Yes, I do, but I'm not sure about a career in music.'

'What do you mean?' said her mother. 'You love music. You play all the time.'

'I know but I have a feeling I've been designed for something else.'

'Like what?' said Peter, entering the room. 'What's my wee sister going to be when she grows up?' Jessica smiled, and threw a cushion at him, and he feigned injury.

'Well, what are you going to do, if not music?' said Jean.

'I don't know for sure. I just know that music isn't enough.'

Peter laughed, 'Don't be daft! It pays well and the hours are short. You could have a fancy car, designer-clothes and a penthouse in London. And eat in the Savoy Grille instead of Margaroni's fish and chip shop—oh, I saw you last night, walking the dog with that wee runt you call a boy friend. I hope he paid. He's got plenty money, I'll say that.'

'You mean you sat inside?' said Jean, shocked.

'Where did you leave the dog?' said John.

'I took him in, too. He was very good.'

'What got into you, Jessica,' said Jean, 'eating chips in a dive like that, late at night? What will people think?'

'I don't mind what they think. I was invited, and I went. I'd do it again if I felt like it.'

'Don't you do anything of the kind! Speak to her John!'

'What for? It's harmless enough. She might learn something useful in a chip-shop with Billy Buchanan.'

'Are you going to do this scholarship, then?' said Jean.

'Yes, why not! I love music, so it's not work. I'll do my very best.'

Henceforth, Jean made sure that nothing stood in the way of Jessica's practice. So the house reverberated with the sound of the cello from 5.30 a.m., which was the time she chose, but it was not two hours, but three she put in.

After a fortnight of this relentless effort, by her daughter, Jean turned over at seven, and saw that John, too, was awake, and that there were tears in his eyes. 'Do you think she's doing too much?' she said.

'No. She's young and strong. She'll take the strain, you'll see.'

'But will she succeed?'

'I don't know.'

'But what if she fails? It would be a terrible disappointment after all this work. I couldn't bear it.'

John put his hand on hers and clasped it. 'Winning is not the most important thing, you know. It's trying to win.'

There was a full attendance at the next meeting of the Kirk Session. George Buchanan entered the vestry in the company of five of them, all of whom had been his guests for drinks beforehand, others having been unable or unwilling to attend.

Tom Henderson took the chair, and several matters on the agenda were dealt with; but there was an atmosphere of battle being joined, and all felt it. The issue of the taxis had been deliberately left off the list of topics, but, at the end, it was raised by George. 'I would like to know, what is to happen about that scandalous proposal last time, to interfere with my business.'

Tom Henderson, who had been trying to avoid a confrontation, cleared his throat and said, 'Yes, well, nothing was decided.'

'So can we consider the matter dropped, then?' said George.

There was a silence, during which George sat tall in his seat, in black coat, his eye covering every other around the table. There was an impression of force about him.

Tom Henderson sighed, 'Well then, since nobody has anything to say, maybe we should forget the whole idea.'

'I have something to say,' said Jack Bowman, bald-headed, with wire-rimmed spectacles like Mr Pickwick. 'I wasn't here last week but I heard about it, and I think it should be tried.'

'It's no use, Jack,' said Tom. 'It'll just cause dissension, and a Kirk Session can't have that.'

Again there was silence.

'Well, are you satisfied, Jack?' said George.

'No, I'm not. I think it should go to a vote.'

'What's the need of that?' demanded George. 'Nobody wants this. It's an offence. And I won't have it!' The words had a depth and determination about them, that none could fail to understand.

'Shall we drop it, then?' said Tom, nervously, looking about him, anxious as ever to avoid conflict—this very characteristic the reason for his lack of grey hair: he was not one to involve himself in battles.

John Manson looked hard at George and said, 'No. This is too important an issue to drop. I have no doubt it will damage George's business. That is exactly why George is so incensed. It is also necessary that George withdraw from this meeting, while the matter is decided: because he has a vested interest in the outcome.'

Dr Telford looked over the top of the half-moon specs and said, 'I move that George withdraw, and that votes be taken on it, if he won't go voluntarily.'

'Seconded,' said Bob Forsyth, purple of face, one of those who had come in with George.

'Look here,' said Terry MacLeod, in his Skye syllables, white-haired and dressed in the kilt as usual, 'I don't think George needs to go. He's one of us isn't he? A good Christian? We can trust him to be fair about this.'

Votes were cast and George lost by six votes to five. When Tom announced the count, George said, 'Let me see! I don't believe this,' and got up and took the slips of paper and counted them out on the table.

'Well I'm damned!' he concluded, red-faced. 'I've never been so affronted in my life! And by my own friends too.'

'There's no need for this outburst,' said John. 'You should leave now.'

'Damn you, Minister, damn you!' said George, and stumped out, slamming the door.

Without George, matters proceeded speedily. A sub-committee was given the task of drawing up a list of likely volunteer taxi-drivers, and John was authorised to announce the new scheme from the pulpit on Sunday.

George and his family were in their usual pews, and when John explained the new system, he watched George visibly stiffen and his grey doughball of a face redden, until it was purple.

John was moved, engulfed by feelings of compassion, and the spirit took hold of him. Ignoring the notes on the lectern, he said, 'Though I speak with the tongues of men and of angels, and have not charity, I am become as sounding brass, or a tinkling cymbal.

'And though I have the gift of prophecy, and understand all mysteries, and all knowledge; and though I have all faith, so that I could remove mountains, and have not charity, I am nothing.......'

'We see through a glass darkly, and then face to face.....'

On and on through the chapter, John's voice sang the words, savouring the music of the language, reciting from memory. And he was so moved by it himself, that a tear rolled down his cheek and finally, his voice broke, and faltered for a moment, until, smiling, he stopped and said. 'Yes, some words are too deep for ordinary response. Every time I play this passage to myself, I find I am overcome by it. Truly, Paul was a genius to write this. I can't tell you how much I admire it. To me, there is nothing finer in the entire world of language. But Paul was a genius inspired by God. I sometimes think the very existence of this passage is the best argument that God does exist. How could something so immeasurably beautiful arise from a false premise?

'Do you see how improbable that is? How could something so magnificent—this letter to the Corinthians—come from a man who believed in something which wasn't there at all? It's...it's just not possible, you see. Paul has to be right—there must really be a God, our God, because Paul couldn't have written this otherwise.' John's sincerity washed over them like a warm wave, and almost everyone present felt touched by it, cleansed by it, and the conviction was reinforced in some and took root for the first time in others, that God IS. 'Hallelujah!' said John, finally, with a face full of joy and delight. 'Hallelujah! God exists!' And many there, were moved and said the same thing.

'But the message is that charity is above everything; and what charity is, is love. Can you see what an insight that was? There cannot have been a more important recognition in the history of the world. For what it means is that men and women should treat each other like this all the time. And if they do, the world will be a place very far different from what it is. —I don't say there will be an end to misery. That disease and starvation will not always be a problem. That natural disasters will not occur. Like fires and pestilence and landslides, and car or plane crashes when lives will be lost. But at least, there would be no strife, and one man would not abuse his brother for his own profit; the thief will no longer lie in wait for his fellow, to attack and rob him, because he knows he has only to ask to be given unto him. Everyone would be a Samaritan to everyone else.'

And down in the congregation, George Buchanan heard and hated it, for he saw himself as abusing his brother for his own profit. Wasn't that the nature of business? To get as much profit for as little outlay as possible? That's what men called good business!

George frowned suddenly, as if he had missed something, and then set his heart against the enemy.

After the benediction, John sat on a while at the back of the pulpit, and then got up and slowly descended the red-carpeted stairs to the aisle and, with great dignity and humility, walked the length of it and waited at the door of the church to shake the hand of all who had come.

There was Jack Dickson, faced etched with lines of worry, whose wife had multiple sclerosis, was confined at home, and could not make it to church now. What could he offer Jack but sympathy and warmth for the travails he was under, the worry and the loss and the increasing fear of both? How did people cope with it? And yet they did, somehow. They met it bravely because there was no alternative. John did what he could, said it, and meant it and Jack smiled ruefully, and was glad of the comfort.

And May Webster, grey of head before her time. She was only forty and looked sixty. Why was this? And as John looked at her, looked very carefully, he saw the bruises on her cheek and jaw, and the efforts made to conceal them with powder and paint. This was a fine-looking woman. Or had been, until a few years ago, when her husband began to drink really heavily. Why did some men have to take out their frustrations on their womenfolk? Was it impotence? Sexual desire incapable of fulfilment? Or the irritation of being *measured* up by the wife's unerring eye, and losing her respect. And so one recovered it by *beating* her up!

But there was joy too, in the little old woman of ninety who made it every Sunday on legs like matchsticks, whose eyes still shone with life, and who always had a quotation for him, which he was sure she prepared specially, with him in mind. Mrs Merryman, was her name, he remembered. How was it that names had their own inner significance? Was that the secret of her near-eternal life?

'You were inspired today, Mr Manson. I enjoyed it! You know, I sometimes think you don't give God his due but, there. You did it today and I'm satisfied. Thank you. Oh, thank you.'

'And how have you been keeping?' said John. 'Are you getting everything you need?'

'Don't you waste your time worrying about me, Minister. I'm managing fine. Just you concern yourself with those that do need help. I know you do that really well. And look after yourself, too. Don't forget, now, will you?' John smiled at her. 'No man is an island, Mr Manson, just you remember that. Every man is a piece of the continent a part of the main.' And then with a wave of the stick-like hand, she was tripping down the steps like a robin in a red coat and hat, with a white feather curling out of it. And as John looked after her, the thought flew into his mind, that perhaps, after all, every man was an island, particularly those people who try to do the right thing; and received instant confirmation of it; for just then, behind Mrs Merryman, George strode past, without so much as a good morning, closely followed by his wife and the boy with lowered head. John thought: so that was it. War. Would some people never learn?

Jessica, further back, saw it and when she came up, shook his hand and said, 'That was great, Daddy. I'm surprised and proud too. I didn't know you had it in you to be a spell-binder.' John laughed, and felt suffused by a strange joy. What power had people to help each other, to make the long day's journey into night easier and happier than it otherwise might be. And he said a silent prayer for Jessica, she of the shining eyes and wholesome heart. How she could come onto you! Some folk were worth their weight in gold.

Outside, near the railings, he caught sight of her as he spoke to others. She was looking around—for Billy, no doubt. But that young man was further down the street, pulled by a force stronger than gravity, into the back of a green Mercedes.

Christmas came and went, as so often in Branden, without snow or anything but a slight frost. John conducted the watch-night service with his usual attempt to unite people by encouraging them to shake hands with everyone close by. But, as he surveyed them from the pulpit and later at the door of the kirk, there was a sense of distance he'd never felt before, as if some of them had drawn away from him, or been drawn away. It was nothing tangible, a certain lack of warmth, as if some dark force had intervened among them, recruiting them to its side. Peter was not present, which depressed him.

A week later, John left the Manse with the dog at five to twelve, carrying a whisky bottle in one hand, a thick slice of black-bun in his pocket and the dog's lead and a lump of coal in a paper bag in the other. Along the terrace in front of the school, he strolled, looking out between the houses at the bay and the harbour below, with ships of every kind at anchor. At midnight, there was a sudden tremendous, joyous racket as the hooter from every vessel at anchor sounded off. Well almost every one, for several were too slow to be on time, the hands that set off the whistles being less well-coordinated than usual, owing to the quantity of drink taken on board as a kind of preliminary.

And so it was time to return to the house for his customary first-foot. The coal in its paper bag was set on the fire, lit for the occasion, the black-bun shared out, Jean and he had a whisky; and the children, who had all stayed up, lemonade. After an hour watching the annual recitation of the 'Wee Cock Sparra', some singing, dancing and jokes on the tele, they went to bed.

George Buchanan looked at the list of planning applications and his eyes lit up. There was always something. They were seated at a big table in an office at the council chambers, with the applications laid out, and a young brown-haired female clerk, Lisbeth Morrison, beside them, in white blouse and black skirt, taking notes.

The Burgh surveyor, Adrian Brown, a tall, lean, man in a yellow sports jacket, cleared his throat and said, 'Just the usual crop. Nothing exceptional. A new garage in the garden of a detached house. A new house at Ambrisbeg. Change of use of a workshop into a house. Then there's the contract for the pier. A greenhouse. A couple of porches and an extension to kitchen premises.'

As Councillor in charge of planning, George said, 'So what are your recommendations?'

'There's no particular trouble with any of them,' said Adrian. 'The house at Ambrisbeg will stand out from the existing site lines and should be moved back a couple of feet. And the sewage pipes are drawn in the wrong place. I suggest we ask them to redraw the plans and then pass it.'

'What about the contract for the pier?'

'Advertise the job and put it to tender.'

'Right, do that,' said George, and the girl wrote the decision in her record book. 'Now, this matter of the extension to the kitchens of the Branden Hotel. Show me the plans.'

Adrian unrolled the paper, spread it out on the table, and laid some paper-weights on the corners. 'That's it. Nothing special.'

George studied it carefully. 'I don't like the way it encroaches into the garden. That's a fine green space it's occupying.'

'Well, they're lucky. At least they have the space to extend. Others don't.'

'Why do they want this?'

'Because the existing kitchen's too cramped. They want to install a big fridge-freezer and other equipment. They also need extra sinks for washing up. They say they may be contravening health regulations unless they get them.'

'Well, I'm failing this.'

'On what grounds?'

'Taking away a green belt in the middle of town.'

'But they won't accept that. Besides, it's nothing to do with green belts. That only applies to cities. This is a wee town on a spacious island.'

'Well, I won't have it. So you can forget it.'

'But you can't do this. They need this extension for the operation of their business. They could appeal to the Scottish Office.'

'Let them appeal if they like. They're not having it.'

'I don't understand your attitude,' said Adrian, and then his eye fell on the name of the applicant. Jack Bowman. 'Isn't he one of your Kirk Session?'

'What if he is?'

'He might think this is personal.'

'I can't make decisions for personal reasons,' said George. 'The one class of folk I can't do things for are my friends. Now, let's see the greenhouse plan.'

It was an ordinary greenhouse in the garden of a semi-detached.

'Isn't this a police house?'

'Yes. Sergeant Grant is the applicant.'

'But the house is owned by the local authority and he rents it?'

'Yes.'

'I'm turning it down, then. I don't want greenhouses in local authority properties.'

'But there's nothing against it in the planning acts.'

'I don't care. I know what's best for this town. That's what I'm elected for.'

And so plans submitted by two members of St Margaret's Kirk Session were turned down. George did not even examine the other plans, passing them on the Burgh Surveyor's recommendation.

By evening, the story was circulating about the streets and public houses of Ottersay, and the next morning, when it was official, for the decision was posted outside the Council Chambers, Jack Bowman went to see Donnachie, the lawyer.

The office was conveniently near the Court and the Council Chambers which occupied the same building. 'You can appeal against it, Jack,' said Donnachie, 'and that's what I advise, if it means that much.'

'How long will it take?'

'At least six months. A case will have to be assembled and sent off and then they'll sit on it for a while doing nothing, until it goes through the system.'

'That means I won't have the kitchen this summer. I could get had up by the health board before then. It's just not fair.'

'Maybe you should have a word with Councillor Buchanan and see what he says.'

'It's pure spite, so it is.'

'I don't say you're wrong but you would have difficulty proving it. Buchanan has full discretion to act in the interests of the town.'

'But this is blatant!'

'Well, you must never say so, or he will sue you, and you won't have a leg to stand on.'

They met in the funeral parlour in Duke Street. George was at his desk in the shop when Jack, dressed in an old brown trench-coat, walked in and stood before him. 'I want to know your reason for rejecting my kitchen-extension.'

George's face became livid. 'I don't have to give you reasons. Who do you think you are coming in here, like this? Just you take yourself off.'

'I want to know what I can do about it.'

'If you see a lawyer, he'll tell you. Appeal.'

'What if I don't want to appeal?'

'I suppose you could always resubmit,' said George, calming down.

'Would it do any good?'

'Depends on you, doesn't it?'

'What do you mean?'

'You know very well what I mean.'

'Are you saying I need to change my mind about a certain matter to get my plans passed?'

'I don't know what you're talking about.'

'You know fine, so you do!' Jack looked down in distress, put a hand to his bald pate, and began to move his foot inconsequentially in a circle on the floor, and George knew he had beaten him.

'I think you'd better leave.'

'I'm not leaving without knowing how to get my plans through.'

'Well, I can't say more than I have. You know where you stand.' George began to work on his invoices again, leaving Jack to shrivel in impotence.

'I could give you a doing!'

Laughing, at the Pickwickian figure offering fisticuffs, George looked up from his papers again, 'A good Christian like you? What kind a talk's that?'

Uncertain and unsure of himself, Jack walked out in dismay.

The people of the town were fascinated by the conflict. George's behaviour was so outrageous that it attracted a certain admiration in some. Only the very moral, and there are few enough of these in any town, were irritated to the point of action, but the more they thought of it, the less they could think of to do. In the nature of things, action would have to be postponed until the next council election; and experience had shown that, by that time, the matter would have been forgotten by enough people to make George's position secure.

Power is an attractive quality. Women love it; all weak men envy it, and, since the number of men strong enough to combat it is few, it is like a snowball which gathers size imperceptibly, in the course of moving about the locality.

Everything is in the demeanour. Is there a smile? The easy grace of the social aristocrat? The man of humblest birth can have this. All it needs are the signs of going forward confidently and, preferably, a few marks of having passed that way.

One such was Jim Grant, sergeant of police, who was found dead in his car in a disused quarry on an isolated stretch of road by the sea.

A hose-pipe had been connected to the exhaust, the other end shoved in through the window, the inside of the doors taped and the gap stuffed with a travelling rug. For a day and a half he was missing, before anyone thought to look in the quarry.

Madeline Grant was interviewed, but said little. The marriage was not going well but it was not on the rocks. She knew of no other woman and, on an island like Branden, where nothing moves without being reported, his colleagues would have expected to know for themselves. As far as Madeline knew, there were no money worries. The bank accounts were in the black and a holiday had been booked for the spring. He had even been on leave at the time—had seemed chirpy—as he went about, arranging this and that small matter, during the time off.

There were no children, and for a while they thought it must be the disappointment of this, until Madeline assured them Jim had not wanted kids, though she had. If only Jim had left a note. Why had he not? It was usual. It seemed callous not to do so.

And then someone connected it to the refusal of the plans. Jim Grant had been against George, hadn't he? Maybe George had got at him. How could he? Jim was such a big strong fellow, not the type to be frightened by George. But then someone else had a bright idea: maybe George had something on Jim. Was that it? And he had threatened to expose it. Maybe Jim had been worried about this all the time.

Soon, this theory was circulating; and enough foolish folk believed it, in lieu of anything better, for it to add to George's standing. The truth was somewhat different, but it took a long time to emerge and only after a remarkable chapter of events.

John Manson officiated at the funeral, of course, once the body was released, and every day he could after that, he made a point of calling at the house to see how she was. Other people, too, were encouraged to call to keep her occupied, and some did.

But it was on one of John's visits that matters took an unfortunate direction.   They were sitting opposite each other by the fireplace, with a log burning in the grate, when Madeline burst into tears and covered her head in her hands. 'No, I'm not really all right. I've been lying to you all.'

'I know,' said John, thinking how lovely she looked in the black and red striped dress with white ruffles at the neck, which matched her dark hair and red lipstick. 'But don't fash yourself. It's quite natural. We all cover up our hurts.'

'I feel so rotten. As if I brought it on! It must have been me. Maybe if I'd not kept after him about kids, it would have been different. Did you think it would? Maybe I drove him to it.'

'No, no. It's not that. Whatever it was. It's natural to want kids. He would have wanted them too. Maybe not right now, but later, he would. No, I don't think it's that.'

'But there must be something. A reason. He didn't do that for nothing.'

'Maybe he was just unhappy. Some people are, you know. People take their lives every day for no reason at all that we can fathom. I expect that's it.'

Madeline wept and wept, tears of remorse and regret, and John was suffused with love and compassion. Why did human beings do the things they did to each other?

He leaned across and grasped her two hands and squeezed gently and suddenly she reached across the space and kissed him. 'Oh, you're so kind. I feel I can talk to you the way I can't talk to anyone else. What a blessing it is to have someone like you to talk to.'

And John said nothing, waiting. What would it be?

Madeline seemed to rub her thighs together and shivered. 'I really miss it, you know. I'm almost demented. I never thought it would mean so much.' She looked up at him, furtively, wondering what he would say, what he would think of her. And when he smiled sadly, and patted her black-stockinged knee, she felt that it was all right.

'Oh, I knew I could tell you. That you would understand. Thank God for you!' She sat back and sighed with relief. Then she said, 'You do understand, don't you? You know what it means?'

'Yes, I know what it means. Of course I'm not like you. I haven't lost my loved one, but I can easily imagine how difficult it would be.'

'Maybe it's different for a man. He can always go somewhere and find someone. But for a woman there's nobody. Where could I go? Everybody in Branden knows about this. There's nowhere I could get help.'

The silence lay between them like a dark tunnel and she looked at him as if afraid. 'I've done some terrible things, terrible.' And John could hear the scream stifled inside and waited calmly, compassionately.

And when nothing came, he knew he had to release the horrors, or she would continue to be in hell. He said, 'I'm sure you've done nothing terrible, Madeline. Nothing you could do would ever be terrible.' And months later, he was to remember this, ruefully.

'But you don't know me! I'm really dreadful! And since this happened....'

'You're not dreadful, Madeline. Believe me! I know what you're going through.'

'I used. I used.....I used....' and she burst into tears again. 'I can't say it. I just can't. I feel so awful! Such a... such a strumpet!'

Where had she got the word? Out of the pages of Georgette Heyer, maybe. It seemed, out of context, faintly funny, but he retained control of his expression.

'A candle,' she said suddenly, and leaned back in the seat, as if surprised at herself. 'How could I do such a thing? How? It's...it's fornication, isn't it? Or is it worse?'

'No, no, Madeline. It's nothing of the kind. It's just natural. That's all. The main thing is that it helped.'

'Oh, yes! It helped, but,' leaning earnestly forward, 'are you sure? Is it really all right?'

'Of course, it is. Where's the harm? It's innocent enough. The only trouble is that you should feel guilty about it. No, no. It's nothing, nothing at all.'

'But isn't it a sin? It must be a terrible sin.'

'Well, it's not,' and John squeezed her hands gently and smiled compassionately. 'So just you do what you have to do and think nothing of it.' Madeline was astonished, but relief showed in her, for her mood lifted. 'Would you like me to say a prayer before I go?'

'Yes, please. Oh, would you?'

John bowed his head, 'Dear God, who understands all things, look upon us with compassion, and make us well, and bring us over these troubles, so that we are renewed in strength and love. Amen.'

Madeline stood up and John embraced her, for he knew it was what she needed above all: the feeling of human contact, the feeling of not being a pariah, but of being whole and noble and attractive, and when he released her, she said, 'Thank you, Oh, thank you! You can't know what it's like to be held by a man again, a loving man. I'll never forget you, never,' she declared.

'Just you get well, that's all. And don't worry. Do what you have to do and God will understand. God is love, you see. Just love. Nothing else.'

Power in a small community depends upon many things. A track record of getting your own way, and some of them had better be what other folk want too; but on know-how—knowing how best to get things done, and that comes with experience; and information—you can never have enough of that.

If George was uncultivated in the arts and sciences of academics, like John Manson, he was still an avid reader: he read every government report with the least bearing on his own affairs. So that anyone who wanted to know what his chances were of planning permission, could be told, off the cuff, in the street, how he stood, or what he would have to do, in addition to what he wanted, to qualify. But more, George was an encyclopaedia of information on the current thinking at District Council and Scottish Office Level. So any grants that might be applied for, and the procedure for doing so, was knowledge that George could provide. And provide it he did, judiciously, so that he alone retained it and others he spoke to gained only knowledge of their own case.

But there are other kinds of information, and George left no stone unturned in his search for these. One source was 'Sniffy' Johnstone, so called because of his habit of sniffing and even, when that failed, of wiping the trickle inside his nose on his sleeve. A short, balding, mousey-haired creature with a shuffling gait, dressed—day or night, some said—in a black leather jerkin with fur lapels, masquerading as having been designed for pilots, acquired through the columns of *The Exchange and Mart*. A pair of 'gutties'—gym shoes—and a navy blue boiler suit much in need of a wash, completed his attire.

They met during George's round of several pubs, a task he repeated like a painter on the Forth Bridge, ever ready to stand a round but always leaving some of his ration behind, for George knew the perils of intoxication and would have been abstemious if it had not curtailed his quest for information. In a town like Ottersay, it was mandatory to take a drink, and he had to be seen to be one of those who did. His liberality was simply political. If a vote or a favour could be won that cheaply, only a fool would not buy it.

'See what you can get on Manson, the minister,' said George, having first made sure that no one could overhear. They were sitting in the snug at the back of MacTavish's Bar, across from the castle, just the two of them. George had gone there on his own, apparently to read the evening paper in peace, and Sniffy, sensing business, had seen him at the bar and soon followed. At George's suggestion, they had adjourned to the privacy of the back snug.

George took his wallet from an inside pocket, extracted a fiver and laid it on the table, covering it with his hand.

Sniffy eyed it with interest. 'Hoo much is in it?'

'Depends what you find.'

'Ah mean, de ye wahnt me tae go aw' oot?'

There was such an expression of alertness and willingness on Sniffy's face that George had an impulse to laugh, but years of experience in man-management held him back. 'Yes,' said George, 'I want ye to get all ye can.'

Sniffy contemplated the fiver and wondered uncertainly. Then he took a noisy sough at his pint while he decided how to put it. 'Whit a mean is, de ye wahnt the hale jingbang? A list o' aw' he's movements. Am' Ah te follay him an' keek in through windaes, an' sich?'

George was surprised for a moment. An operation of that kind was not quite what he had in mind. More of a scouring of pubs for gossip; that was usually enough. There were pubs he could not go to himself. As an elder of St Margaret's, it would have been de trop to patronise The Carlton or The Antiquary and a score of others, all of them owned and frequented by Catholics. But maybe this was a time to step up the scale of operations. Manson had cost the business a bundle already, and it could only get worse.

'Yes,' said George decisively. 'Yes, just you do that. I'll see you right.'

'Well, I wid need mair'na a fiver. Ten wid be O.K. the noo, coonsellor.'

Impulsively, George almost lost his cool but control asserted itself. There were high stakes to be played for. Poker-faced, he reached for the wallet and found another fiver.

Sniffy pocketed the banknotes, sniffed, and then smiled knowingly. 'So ye've goat an inside man?'

'Come again?' said George.

'Ye mean ye dinnae ken aboot it?'

'Don't play games with me,' said George, grabbing the furry lapel of Sniffy's jacket in his large talon.

'Haud oan, haud oan! Ah thocht ye wid ken.'

Distastefully, George released the jacket, as if it were the fur of a ferret. 'What should I know?'

'Bully—your Bully's gawn wi' Manson's dochter. So ye've an inside man'll gie ye inside infurmation.'

George's dark face face purpled and he grabbed Sniffy again. 'Are you sure?'

'Aye, Ah'm sure. Ah thocht ye kenned.'

'Just you keep it to yourself, do you hear?'

'The hale toon kens about Bully and Jessica Manson.'

So that was it! He was being made a fool of, and everyone knew but himself! That was the price of power: you were the last to hear bad news. No one wanted to bear bad tidings.

But that night, as George walked down to the cab rank at the pier with more drink swilling in his bilges than usual, he was struck by Sniffy's reaction: instead of blowing a fuse and knocking the stuffing out of Billy, maybe he should hold fire. Later, in the living room at Silvertrees, however, restraint was beyond him. 'You've been seen with Jessica Manson. What have you got to say for yourself?'

Billy blushed and stood up, falteringly. 'I..I...don..know.'

'You admit it, then?'

'Y.Yes.'

Mother and son waited for the thunderclap to fall from the beetling brows.

'Well, you can go on seeing her for now.'

There was a hush in the room, as if, even yet, the storm would break; and then, gradually, the mood lifted, as mother and son realised that a transformation had occurred.

'Oh, thanks Daddy! Thanks!' And Billy skipped from the room in a whirl of delight.

Tremulously, Betty Buchanan rose from her chair and crossed to George and kissed him on the cheek. 'That was a fine thing you did, George. I never knew you had it in you. You've made Billy's day. He loves that girl.'

'Did you know about it?'

'Only that he felt that way about her. How could I not know that?'

'But you guessed? When has he been seeing her?'

'I don't know. He gets in later than he used to. Maybe he walks her home after school, like so many of them.'

'Well, don't count on it lasting for ever. It's just politics. That's all it is.'

But Betty wisely said nothing to Billy about that. How could she spoil his happiness?

Scotland is known the world over for its lad o' pairts and the source of these remarkables who have taken the best of the country to every corner of the planet, where they have exerted a profound influence, is, apart from the school, the local learned society. In the Ayrshire of Burns it was the Bachelors Club, where young sparks, lit up with usquebeatha, fired verses, arguments and epigrams at each other. In other towns it is the literary club or the history society. In Branden, it was the Philosophical Society, set up originally in the eighteenth century, by a Brandonian with a passion for natural philosophy, who undertook to explain to his fellows, the mysteries of Newton's new System of the World. The fact that he failed utterly to make sense of it at all, even a full century after its production, should not diminish the achievement of the effort to do so. For was it not written in Latin and, even then, made deliberately obscure to put off 'little smatterers' who might have disturbed the great man's solitary studies, harassing him with elementary questions?

Though the name had been retained, over the years, the interests of the society had changed with its members, becoming successively a natural history society, a Scottish history society, a society of antiquaries, an institution of chemistry [and some say, alchemy], an astronomical society, closely followed by a spiritualist society—though that lasted only a few years, till the leading light expired and was never heard from again—a political debating club—to which it was always likely to revert at election times—and, because of the prevalence of ministers of religion among its members, a society for the propagation of religious knowledge.

Latterly, the tide of science had strengthened and, accompanied by a coterie of free thinkers, the society was at about the most cosmopolitan in its history, which is to say, it had a rare collection of contrary beliefs and interests in its midst, all at the same time.

The programme that year had been: J. T. Smyth, M.A. on 'Fossil discoveries in South Branden'. A.J. Heron, B.Sc(hons), Phd: 'Habits of the Atlantic Salmon in Branden waters.' T. Horner, M.A.: 'An Archaeological Site in East Lebanon.' Fr F.X Gregory: 'The Woolwich Doctrine, a refutation.' Robert Grayson, BSc.: 'The Chemical Production and Biproducts of Coal Gas.' H.L.R. Bramble, B.A. M.Litt.: 'Poetry and Painting in Maori Society.'

The latest of these talks was entitled: 'Argument in Theology,' and the speaker, was Rev J. Manson, M.A., B.Sc., B.D.

John looked around the room and felt at home. It was lined with book-cases full of writings about the island, and its human, animal, vegetable and mineral contents—the intellectual detritus of centuries of Brandonian enquiry, knowledge and thought. The chairs set out in lines in front of him, old and wooden and delightfully solid, were occupied by the worthies of the place: two doctors, four lawyers, several teachers, a few men of the cloth, several hoteliers and sundry others: men and women in trades and small business, a librarian or two, bankers and bakers, farmers and postmen and clerks and master mariners, fishermen and seamen.

'Aristotle, it was, first made much of the rationality of man,' John said, 'though other Greeks like Parmenides, Pythagoras and Plato would have been as aware of it. But Aristotle was the first to systematise logic, discovering all the elementary forms of argument which were true.

'Since then, the use of logic to convince men of opinions they do not presently hold, has spread and become the norm of human discourse, so much so, that now, if we hear a man recommend something to our notice, we feel he has failed if he has not given reasons for doing so. These reasons are what is meant by 'argument' and some progress has been made over the centuries in the forms of argument.

'For a long while, there was an insistence on 'proving', as if that were what should be done. An example of a proof is the celebrated one by Aristotle: Socrates is a Greek. All Greeks are men. Therefore, Socrates is a man. Here, something is proved. Socrates is a man because he is a Greek; and the class of all Greeks lies within the class of all men.

'One is bound to say that although we have here a proof—a compelling argument—it is not very interesting, because we learn nothing new by it. Except in mathematics, it is difficult to learn anything new by proofs. Science, on the other hand, proceeds more by proofs of what is not rather than proofs of what is. And, according to Karl Popper, the thrust of science is hypothesis, testing and falsification, followed by construction of a fresh hypothesis to be tested. And the more easily falsified the hypothesis, the better it is, for it is soon got rid of.

'The situation is worse in domains like history, where the facts can often only be conjectured due to the lack of sufficient evidence and, worse still, in religion, where faith is a primary constituent. Yet, efforts have been made continually to prove things or at least convince us that they are likely.

'Medieval religious folk were very interested in the question of how to prove that God exists. One of the first was Thomas Aquinas, who gave five proofs of God's existence, known ever since, as the five ways. The first of these is that in the world, some things are in motion; and it is impossible that a thing be both moved and be the mover ie that it move itself. So whatever is moved must be moved by another; and that one by another and that one by another, and so on and on. But the process cannot continue to infinity. Therefore, it is necessary to arrive at a first mover and this everyone understands to be God.

'Many criticisms have been made of this argument and the other four. By the time of Newton, it was realised that the normal state is motion; and by Einstein's day, that everything is in motion, for the simple reason that there is no standard reference point in the universe. So it makes no sense to speak of bodies being at rest, though they may be at rest relative to each other. Indeed, as anyone can see, the argument seems to fail, if humans are the moved bodies, for they move themselves. Finally the fact that one thing is moved by another and so on, has no tendency to show that the process must ever stop. Why should it not continue infinitely, as so many other things do?

'Another argument is the ontological argument. Ontological means 'being'. The author of this is St Anselm, but many others have tried to improve upon it, including Descartes. One form of the argument goes:- God is a perfect being. A perfect being, if it really is perfect, must exist. For if it did not exist it could not be perfect. It follows that God exists.

'It was Kant who pointed to the flaw in this. Namely, that existence is not a predicate. That is, existence is not a property of objects. Thus one may imagine anything one likes, but there is no guarantee that it exists.

'Another argument is the argument from design. It goes like this. If you were out walking and you stumbled upon a pocket watch and had never seen one before, you would notice its complexity and intricateness and beauty, and so forth, and you would conclude that somebody must have made it. The watch could not have happened by chance. Well, then, the world with its hills, trees, plants and human beings is like the watch. It is complicated and intricate and beautiful and could not have been made by chance. So somebody must have made it.

'Against this, it may be argued that though life, as we know it, is very complicated, it may have arisen naturally by evolution. Also, though many things in nature are made and it is our experience that everything on earth has a source, this may not be true in the universe. Conceivably, the universe has always existed; maybe, the rules that apply there are different from those that we have discovered on earth. Relativity Theory is a good example—in reverse. It doesn't matter much in the context of our planet; but it does in the context of the universe as a whole.

'A contemporary of Descartes, Blaise Pascal, also produced an argument, though not a proof, that one should believe in God. He said: If I believe in God I will experience eternal life, and all the pleasures of heaven, when I die, and the terrors of hell if I do not. Since there is so much to gain by belief and nothing to lose, I ought to believe. This is known as Pascal's wager.

'Pascal's wager, it has been said, is a bad bet. For if you applied the argument elsewhere to horse-racing, for example, it might be like betting on a horse that wasn't running.

'It would seem that arguments to prove or disprove God's existence are not very helpful. And yet argument is important in religion in other places. In helping us to decide what happened at the cave just after the Crucifixion. The Gospels give us the story as it was told at the time, or near the time. We believe it or not depending upon how convincing it seems to us. The same is true for the whole story of Jesus and the lives of his apostles thereafter.

'The best argument I know, for the truth of all these events, is something like this. A lot of men worked very hard to write all this down at a time when writing was difficult; and many copies were made and carefully preserved. It seems to follow that something very unusual took place. Is Jesus a figment of the imagination? I think not. It isn't likely that all this fuss, ever since, has been the result of an imagined life. No. There has to be something in it. Just how much there is in it that is true is, however, a matter for each individual. For there are no compelling arguments. In the end, each man believes what he chooses.'

Seated in the front row was a short, square figure of a man with a red face, blue eyes and short, fair hair. His ears stuck out from his cropped-head like jug-handles. He wore a shiny black suit, black shoes and a black shirt with a bright yellow tie. During the lecture, though John had noticed one or two of the more geriatric members drop off to sleep, he was pleased by the level of attention this man was showing.

After continuing for a while and concluding, John sat down to polite applause and waited for questions. Two he fielded easily enough. Then the man in black with the yellow tie stood up, revealing himself to be no more than five feet six, and John suddenly realised who this must be. Bucephalus MacSween.

So called, as he was the first to point out to strangers, because his father had mistakenly supposed Bucephalus to be the tutor of Alexander the Great and not his horse. The joke had another dimension as men who shared the loo with Buce soon discovered between pints, for the horse had been named because of its beautiful penis. Alas, in Buce's case, the organ was too small to permit adequate investigation of the issue.

'If God canny be proved te exist, how dae ye know that he does?' said Buce.

'I don't know that he does,' said John. 'I believe he does.'

'But why dae ye believe?'

'It's not easy to say. I suppose because I was brought up that way and I always have. I know that isn't a very convincing reason, but the idea of God is part of my vocabulary and I use it every day. Perhaps the best way to put it, is to say that if I didn't have the word, if I didn't believe God exists, I would find living a lot more difficult all of a sudden.'

'What dae ye mean by God?'

'That's a very hard question. I don't mean a person. An old man with a white beard who lives up in the sky. I suppose I mean a presence, a kind of force for good.'

'Wid ye no' agree that there is no sich thing as a force fur good? That everythin' happens by the acciden'al conjunction of many forces, which are morally neu'ral? That whit happens in life is mainly a matter o' chance? We're able tae influence events, o' course, most o' the time, but we oorselves are often deeply affectit by the influence o' others?'

There was a significance to these words, and something about them made John catch his breath. He looked the idea over and grew increasingly attracted by it and, as he did so, he felt his position, standing on the dais, somehow undermined. 'I think what you have said is very profound and I thank you for it. I suppose life must often look like that, but that isn't how Christians view it.'

'Could ye mibbee explain the difference?'

'Well, Christians see everything in terms of Christ who is taken to be among us all the time and, whether we appear to suffer ill or good, it is always taken to be for good ultimately, in some deeper sense that we can't see.'

'So you ac'ually believe that Christ died on the cross and came tae life again and now lives eternally, daein' good?'

'I think it is a fact that Jesus lives in the sense that the idea of him is prevalent, a living reality if you like, and that it causes much good in the world because of our adherence to his ideas about how life should be lived.'

'But ye think he died and came te life again?'

'Not really. I'm sure there is an explanation. Either he wasn't dead in the first place or someone else was mistaken for him on the Emmaus Road and elsewhere.' There was a hush in the room, and then a collective sigh as everyone there sensed a coming disaster. John stood erect, seemingly unaware of it. 'I think the Resurrection is symbolic, the awakening of an idea—the new ideas of Christ. That is the important thing, not the physical rebirth or renewal of Christ. You don't need to believe in the Resurrection and the Virgin Birth to be a Christian. All you need to do is approach the world with love. That's all Jesus is about anyway. Just Love.'

'But how kin Jesus be the son o' God?'

'Metaphorically. Jesus is the embodiment of what we mean by God.'

'Ye mean thur really the same?'

'Yes.'

'Why didnae Jesus save himsel' then? Why doesnae he save the next man wha's gonny die in this toon, mibbee this very night?'

'Jesus had to die to show us—the world—about love, goodness and so on. But he's not all powerful in the sense that a human might think. His power lies in influencing men's minds, not in causing cracks of thunder. The most accurate view of God is the retired carpenter, not the omnipotent potentate; the man who suffered on the cross, not the warlord who slew the Egyptians.'

The questions had come quickly under the heat of a questioning mind, and the answers had been given honestly, calmly, and without concern for the consequences. The chairman had been as interested as any person present, at the statement of beliefs so very different from those expected. Now he stood up and thanked John and soon the room began to clear.

The Reverend Rob McCall looked at John thoughtfully, as if he should say a word to him, but, seeing his attention taken up with Buce MacSween, he decided to leave.

Buce was excited and stimulated. 'Mibbee Ah could join your church,' he said animatedly, 'Ah've always waanted tae belong tae a church, but Ah niver thought Ah wid be able. What would Ah have tae dae?'

'You would have to come along and take first communicants classes. Then, if you wanted to, you would have to take an oath in church to abide by the rules, and declare that you believed in the main articles of faith—that you accept God and Jesus into your life.'

'Wid Ah have tae say Ah believe God exists?'

'Yes, but what you mean by God is a matter for you. You would also have to affirm belief in the Resurrection and there again you have the option of believing the literal truth or a symbolic truth of the kind I mentioned.'

This conversation took place as they walked out of the Museum together. It pleased John to think that he'd done some good, so when Buce, evidently excited, suggested a drink in MacTavish's Bar, on the other side of the castle, he accepted because it would have seemed churlish to refuse.

The walk on the road around the castle, with the dark waters of the moat glinting in the moonlight, between the sloping lawns, was a time of pleasure, shared by men of very different backgrounds, but who seemed to be kindred spirits; and, before long, they were standing at the bar of MacTavish's, among a lot of young farmers quaffing pints, and Buce was in his element. Laughing, he said, 'Ah kin hardly believe it, ye know. Ah've always been an atheist since Ah wis knee-high tae a grasshopper and Ah thought Ah'd always be that. Now you tell me Ah kin join. Ah'm amazed. How kin this be?'

'Christianity doesn't require you to believe in things that are impossible. Mind you, there are a lot of folk in the kirk who believe it all literally, but that's changing. All these so-called literal truths don't matter. I sometimes think they were swallowed by people in the past because it helped the faith to seem a bit special. As if they wouldn't pay any attention without a lot of miracles to impress the peasants. We've got beyond that now. We don't need any of that. We're free to concentrate on the essentials. Like how we should treat each other. That's the most important thing.'

Buce was an engaging fellow and good company, with an underlying goodness, John felt, and it was pleasant to while away an hour or so in a hostelry, for a change. Somewhere into the second pint, Buce announced he was a communist, and John expressed sympathy for the idea that men should be regarded as equal, even if in many ways they were not.

The barman looked at Buce as he ordered whiskies, 'Do you not think you've had enough?' he said, quietly.

'No' at all, no' at all. Are ye tryin' tae embarrass me, or what? Here Ah am wi' a new freend and you say things like that. No' the best way tae keep a pub.'

But the second swallow put Buce on his back on the floor. 'He's always like this,' said the barman, coming around to prop him up. 'He can't hold it. Hardly a night goes by...'

'Where does he live? I'll take him home.'

'Don't trouble yourself, Minister. We have a routine for this. We phone a taxi and pour him in—a particular taxi. The driver's used to him and knows what to do.'

But John just had to lend a hand. The driver and he had just got the corpse into the vehicle, and were making sure no arms or legs were sticking out, when Sadie Forsyth came along the street and saw everything. Saw John leaning against the door of the taxi as if the worse for wear himself.

'Is he married?' said John, to the driver. 'Should I come with you and help?'

'No, no need. I put him on a couch in the back kitchen and leave him there till morning.'

As the car drove off, John stood contemplating it and then noticed Sadie, who had crossed the street to be on the castle-side opposite the pub. 'A fine night,' John called across to her, but there was no reply, only the click-clack of her high heels scuttling along under the street lights, as if he were a threat of some kind, she was anxious to get away from.

That night, as John was breathing alcoholic fumes on Peter, whom he'd met in the hall-way of the Manse, pretending to be drunk, Sadie told her husband, the banker, that the minister had staggered out of the door of MacTavish's Bar with a drunken friend, too far gone to manage on his own two legs. 'And it was only ten o'clock! Must have been at it for hours.'

Peter came into the sitting-room where, in an armchair by the unlit fire, Jean was knitting, and announced: 'Dad's sozzled!' and stood with an arm on the mantelpiece.

Having divested himself of his coat on the hall-stand, John, who overheard, entered, and stood in the middle of the room. 'Two pints and a half doesn't make a man drunk.'

'Shame on you, John! What made you do it?'

'I was invited by a man I met at the lecture. Name of Buce MacSween.'

'The Harbourmaster?'

'Yes.'

'They say he's drunk every night. His wife's just about to throw him out in the street.'

'Well, he looks like being a convert from atheism. We had a good talk before he took too much for his own good.'

'So he was drunk?' said Peter, sitting down on the front edge of an armchair.

'Oh yes! Two pints and a half is too much for him. It's the small size, you see. There's not the room inside to absorb the alcohol.'

'Well, I think it's disgusting,' said Peter. 'To get intoxicated like that. Did you have to carry him home?'

'No. He went in a taxi.'

'And did anyone see you?' said Peter.

'I suppose they did,' said John. 'What of it?'

'Ministers shouldn't be seen in pubs. And certainly not with folk that are known drunkards.'

'Away with you, Peter,' said John, sitting down on the sofa. 'We were having a friendly drink or two after a lecture. There's nothing wrong with that.'

'But what will people say?' said Peter, looking aghast.

'It doesn't matter what they say. Look, I didn't have to go and drink in the pub. I have drink here if I want it. But I was asked to go, and I went. It was a kindness. Besides, I was flattered. It's not every night a minister gets invited to have a drink in a bar. No, it would have been quite wrong to refuse.'

'But my friends won't understand that. What am I to say to them if it gets around that my dad goes drinking with drunks?'

'If they don't understand, they're not worth having as friends.'

'Well, I think you should be more careful, John,' said Jean. 'We have a standard to live up to. People might not understand and you can't blame them.'

'Look, you can't live your life worrying about what stupid, narrow-minded folk will think.'

'It's the way people are, John. You should know that by now.'

'What's all the fuss about?' said Jessica, entering the room in a white dressing-gown which contrasted with her long red hair. 'Anyone would think there was a battle going on.'

'Dad's been drinking with drunks in a pub. He's had a skinful. What will people say?'

Jessica grinned. 'I've never seen our father drunk,' she said. 'This should be interesting.' Crossing the floor to John, she sat on the arm of the sofa and sniffed. 'Well, maybe he's had a drink, but he's not like a brewery, if that's what you mean. Can you walk a straight line, Daddy?' Jessica rose and took her father by the hand. 'See that line there on the rug? Try walking along that.'

John got up, rolled his eyes, and began to walk along the line on the rug as if it were the plank on a pirate ship in a heavy sea. Then he caught Peter's shoulder, fell to one side onto Jean's chair and tipped her out onto the rug. Amid peals of laughter from Jessica, all three were soon lying on the floor, Jean annoyed and protesting, Peter insulted that anyone should touch him, let alone that he should suffer the indignity of being pushed onto the floor. John, who had if anything made the heap worse by rolling about, now lay back and laughed and Jessica joined in again.

'I'm going to bed,' Peter announced. 'This house has gone mad.'

News began to circulate like waves, every so often blending with each other to create bigger and bigger breakers. One faction, friends and acquaintances of Sadie Forsyth, heard about the minister's drunken spree with 'that... that... incorrigible wee drunk, MacSween'; another had the story of how thousands of pounds had been lost to the church because of John Manson's rudeness; and several people independently, among them the Rev Rob McCall, were transmitting the news of Manson's heresy, as it soon became known. 'A minister that doesn't believe what he preaches! How can you be a minister and not believe in Jesus being the literal son of God, raised from the dead? Isn't that what Christianity is about? The man's gone mad.' Others added: 'He spends his time with the likes of the drunken harbourmaster, when he should be keeping in with the hoi poloi, to make sure any money that's going comes to St Margaret's.' And the Catholic fraternity added their piece about him currying favour with their down-and-out homosexuals. As if he hadn't enough down-and-out homosexual Protestants of his own to be going on with—among all his other sinners.

And it is a well-known fact of oceanography that many waves acting together can easily make a storm of irrepressible violence.

Maybe it was the weather-warnings he had seen, maybe he was just glad to be able to add his own small stock of discomfort to the enemy camp, but the Roman Catholic Canon, informed his underling, Father Gregory, that it was time something was done about Manson's visits to Joe Gorman.

'I've come to see Mr Manson,' said Gregory, one day, taking down his umbrella and shaking it all over the porch of the Manse.

'Come into the parlour, and I'll get him,' said Jean, worried about the state of her hair and the presence of the apron; and what would he think of her old stockings with the holes in them, which she hadn't had time to mend, and the dowdy old black dress?

John, straight from the potting shed with hands filthy from gardening, said: 'Oh, it's yourself, Father. I didn't realise. Could you wait until I wash my hands? I've been doing my seeds.'

'No need, no need. I won't detain you long. I just wanted to have a quick word, en passant.'

'Sit down then, Father,' and John motioned him to a seat at the fire-side, though there was no fire at that time on a November afternoon, as they were trying to conserve fuel until the evening when it would get really cold.

John sat down opposite. 'Jean'll bring us some tea presently.'

'No need, no need. I won't be long. I'll come straight to the point. It's about Joe Gorman. The Canon feels that it isn't right that you should be paying him visits the way you do. Twice a week, isn't it? Yes, I thought so. Someone told us. Walls have ears, eh?'

Gregory, in clerical black, with black curly hair and a square face, was developing a considerable pot belly, thought John. Must be all the grub provided by the army of Catholic women helpers. 'Have you been to see him yourself, Father?'

'Not in the last few days.'

'But you intend to see him?'

'Oh yes. We can't have Catholics being got at by Protestant ministers.' Gregory seemed to radiate sunshine, at this riposte, as if he had just been very clever.

'I wouldn't say "got at" was the right way to put it,' said John. 'He's a lonely old man and I simply visit him to keep him company. That's all. I'm not trying to convert him if that's what you mean.'

'Well, it doesn't look good, and the Canon would like it to stop.'

John leaned back in the chair and thought for a moment. 'I'm afraid I can't do that. Of course, if he tells me not to visit him, I'll stop, but I think my visits help. In fact I know they do. He sees no one else, as far as I know. He told me himself that none of the members of his church have ever been to see him, since he was in court with what he calls his wee problem.'

'Not true. Not true at all. Why I know for a fact that several visits have been made.'

'By whom, Father?'

'Well, by me and others.'

'What would he have to gain by telling a lie about it? I find that very hard to believe, Father. In fact, I would be very surprised to learn that anybody but me and him had been in that house for years. Have you seen the house?'

'I can't quite remember. But I expect it's rather unkempt.'

'That's just it, Father. If any Catholic women had seen it, they'd surely have given it a good clean. You couldn't get anyone to go into that house. That's how I know for a fact that no Catholic's been to visit him.'

Father Gregory had grown red in the face. 'Are you saying I'm a liar?'

'No Father, I'm just saying that I find it very hard to believe that anyone but me has been in that house for years. There is a difference.'

'Not much!'

'Look Father, no one would be happier than me if people went to visit Joe, and I don't mind what denomination they are. I would like him to feel that people care about him. If someone would give him a hand to clear up, I'd be delighted. Maybe you could arrange that?'

'Yes, I'll do it. Directly. Directly. Consider it done,' and he got up to go. At the door he said, 'So I can take it that you won't be visiting him any more? Leave it to us, eh? His own folk.'

'No, Father, I don't think you can. But if there comes a time when I think he has enough visitors of the right sort, then maybe I'll turn my attentions elsewhere.'

'The Canon will not be best pleased.'

'If the Canon looked after his flock properly, they wouldn't need folk like me.'

As Gregory, stumped down the path, with a red face, Jean came into the hall and said, 'That wasn't very tactful.'

'No, but it wasn't a time for tact. They could have done a lot for old Joe. Instead, they've shut him out in the cold, made him suffer. The worst of it is, it's not really his fault.'

'What do you mean? He's a dirty old man. A homosexual. You can't blame them.'

'Well, I do. They've sent him to Coventry; made him feel like a pariah, so that he's afraid to go out except at night. No, they've treated him badly, and I'm not going to stop helping him, whatever they say.'

But two days later, when John knocked on Joe Gorman's door, there was no reply. Again he knocked, and when there was no response, he lifted the letter-box and shouted, without avail. John waited five minutes before trying again, then gave up and went away.

May Webster came to the door, as soon as he knocked. It was a flat in a rabbit-warren of a building, made of sandstone, with a central courtyard dominated by ancient wash-houses, overflowing litter-bins, criss-crossed with washing lines; one of the worst places on the island, known, actually because of its height, and ironically, because it was like a sardine tin, as The Grand Canyon.

May was in curlers and dressing gown, and blushed. 'Ah'm afraid Ah'm no' very decent,' she said. The bruises had receded, John was glad to see.

'Well, if it's not convenient, I could call some other time,' he said, but May was so pleased to see him, that she insisted he come in, and take them as he found them. And it was there in the sitting-room of the two-room flat, that he met Byron Webster, an unshaven, dark-haired, muscular lout, in a vest and pyjama trousers. Byron had a can of beer up to his lips and was slurping it, when John entered.

'Sit down, sit down, Minister, and Ah'll make ye a cup a tea,' said May, after introducing them.

Byron said nothing and carried on drinking, and for while John sat in silence, listening to the sounds of the kettle being filled and cups being got out. Then, there being little point in delay, John said, 'Why is that you beat May? She's your wife and she's good to you. I don't think there's any doubt about that. Is there?'

Byron looked at him sullenly and said, 'What is it tae you? If Ah want tae gie hur a doin', Ah'm entitilt. She's ma wife, i'n't she?'

'That doesn't give you the right. Why do you do it?'

'Ah dae it because Ah feel like it. Why should a no'?'

'But you're making her life a misery, Byron. Can't you see that?'

'Uch away! Jist mind yer ain business, wull ye?

May brought the tea, with a plate of biscuits, and began to pour out, blushing, with the embarrassment of the visit and its purpose.

'Well, May, the next time Byron hits you, I want you to walk out immediately. Just leave everything, and come to the Manse. You'll be safe there. Will you do that, May?'

'I..I don't know.'

'She'll dae nae sich thing!' said Byron. 'All jist come efter hur, if she does.'

John got up. He said, 'You won't get into my house, Byron, so you can forget any idea of taking her back. So that's it then, May? If he hits you again. Just once, mind, you come to the Manse as soon as you can; and you'll be safe there and you can stay as long as you like.'

It was at Madeline's house that the trouble really started. She was welcoming as ever.

'My, you're looking well,' he told her and it was true. Her hair was freshly dyed—a fair, flecked colour, shining in rolling waves from all the attention of Ottersay's best hairdresser; and she wore a bright red skirt with a matching jumper and shiny black shoes with tall heels which lent her an air of elegance he had never seen in her before. The face was thin, but very feminine and well-shaped, with a straight nose.

The words seemed to infuse her with warmth, for her face, made up expertly, flushed, and her hazel eyes sparkled, like many-faceted gemstones, as she stood looking at him. He stood, startled by the transformation, and she said, quickly, 'I'm so glad you came. You don't mind, do you?' And she gave him a little peck, like a bird, on the cheek. 'It's all the fashion in London, they say, to kiss friends when you meet them.'

'So how have you been?' said John, moving into the sitting-room and taking a seat.

'Pretty good, really. I decided to try and make something of myself. So I got myself done over. I hope you like it.'

'Yes, it's very pleasing. I should try it too, maybe,' said John, laughing. 'Yes, you're a very attractive lady. No doubt of it. You'll soon be thinking of some other new chap.'

'You don't think it's too soon?'

'No, not at all. If it's what you want, where's the harm in it? Best thing to start rebuilding your life right away. Finding a new fella's just the ticket, I'd say.'

'I'm still very lonely at night. Very. But what you said helped. You'll never know how much.'

'I'm glad.'

She sat opposite and he could not but see just how attractive she was, the sleek, nyloned legs disappearing into the short skirt. Then she looked at him warmly and said, 'I'll just make some tea,' and got up revealing, as she did so, more than she should have. She stood looking down at him assessingly.

Surprised, and attracted too, he said, 'You don't need to make tea, you know. I'll have to go soon.'

'It's no trouble.'

Conscious of the difficulty of the situation, he stood up. 'Look, now that you're so well, I needn't stay. I can see you're fine now. So I'll just get on without tea.'

Madeline's face fell, the bright eyes dulled, and a tear rolled down her cheek. 'Don't go. Please don't go yet. I was really looking forward to having tea with you.'

'I don't think I should stay.'

Madeline burst into tears and, taken by surprise, John remained rooted to the spot.

'I think I'm falling in love with you,' she blurted out, tearfully. 'I've thought of nothing but you since you left. I dream about you, during the day as well as at night.'

'Come and sit down,' said John, taking her hand and steering her back to the chair where they sat down again. 'It's just the bereavement, you know. That's all it is. I'm the first man that offered comfort, so naturally you turn to me. It'll pass in time, you'll see.'

'No it won't! I don't want it to.'

'It's just temporary. I've seen this before. The person who's suffered the loss turns their affection to the one who's offering help and sympathy.'

'You don't like me, do you? I'm not really attractive am I? You were just saying it.' She dabbed at the tears with a handkerchief, taken from her sleeve.

'I do like you and you are attractive. That's the trouble. Look, it will pass. In time, you'll find some fine chap your own age and then you'll see what I mean. That would be the right thing to do.'

'But I want you now. I don't want anybody else.'

'Well, I'm married to someone else, and I love her. I don't love you,' he added, gently, quietly, 'and I'm your minister. I couldn't take advantage of you.'

'You wouldn't be doing that. It's what I want. Don't you see? I want you, now. Inside me. Oh God! I get wet just thinking about it.'

She moved her legs and he saw, because he could not avoid seeing, that she was not exaggerating. John bent his head and took his forehead in his hands. Then he looked up. 'I'm going to have to leave.'

'Why? I need you here with me now. I've been looking forward to it all week. Please stay.'

'I can't Madeline. It's not possible.'

'It is! You just don't like me. You think I'm common—a...a strumpet!'

'I don't think anything of the kind,' said John, rising and heading for the door. She grasped his arm and said, 'No. Please stay! Please!'

There was something in the entreaty that bit into him. She needed him. That was the simple truth of the matter, and he could not leave her in spite of the danger to them both.

'All right. Go and make the tea. I'll stay a wee while longer, but then I'll have to go.'

Madeline took his arm and led him into the kitchen. 'I'm not letting you go. You might change your mind. Besides, you can keep me company in here while I'm getting ready.'

But, as John could easily see, everything was ready. Plates of sandwiches and freshly-baked pancakes and cream-cakes were laid out on a tray, with butter and strawberry jam. Somehow, this added to his worry.

'How did you know I like strawberry jam?' he said, jokingly, not expecting an answer.

'I asked somebody,' she said, and this was as worrying as anything; for if she were asking people about him, they would begin to wonder.

She took cutlery from a drawer, laid it down on the tray, and stood looking at him, with big eyes, sparkling with warmth, ignoring the kettle, when it began to sing. Then, impulsively, she moved across, suddenly, so that he would be unable to resist, and embraced him and kissed him and he was too dumbfounded to do anything about it. And the kettle's song became a scream, but she ignored it still. 'There, I've been dying to do that again,' she said, then, seeing he had not drawn off, but stood, irresolute, because astonished, she did it once more and he shook himself, as if out of a dream, and protested.

'No, Madeline,' he shouted above the noise, 'control yourself. This won't do.'

Not till then, did she reach back and switch off the kettle. Then she burst into tears. 'I'm not attractive, am I? You were just saying it. I'll never have a man again. I see it now. It's a punishment for not being a good wife.' There was a look of utter desolation on her face, as the tears rolled down, cutting fissures in the make-up. And she went to fill the teapot.

John crossed the room, took her from behind by the shoulders and hugged her tight. 'No, no, no! You're lovely, Madeline. Any man would love to have you. Believe it. It's true. And just remember that you *were* a good wife. There's no punishment. You'll find happiness, don't worry.'

She could feel the stirring in his loins and he knew it and disengaged and went to stand with his back to the wall. Without a word, she poured a cup of tea and turned to face him and went to him and handed it over. Grateful for something to do, anything to break the tension, he took the saucer in his left hand and the cup in his right and began to drink.

As he did so, she reached down with her hand and felt his arousal and then, while he was powerless to resist, unzipped and grasped him. He blushed and stepped back against the wall, still holding the teacup and saucer in separate hands, speechless with amazement and desperate to lay them down somewhere, anywhere. Frantically, he looked about for a place to put them.

'Let's do it here,' she said, huskily, urgently. 'Right now. Come on!'

Still holding him in one hand, in case he drew away, which he was now unable to do, she drew him, still holding saucer in one hand and cup in the other, to the table behind her and to one side of her, then rucked up her dress and pulled off knickers and suspender belt all in one smooth fierce continuous tug. Then she sat on the table and began to pull him towards her.

'No!' he cried, crimson with embarrassment, shoved the cup onto the saucer and, with the other hand, roughly, tore her hand off him. Then he frantically covered himself and zipped up; sat down at the table and bowed his head. 'I'm sorry. I should have stopped it before. I hope you'll forgive me.' The look he gave her was one of utter bewilderment, and yet, the sensation of her hand on him lingered, and his arousal, if anything, increased.

Madeline's cheeks were flushed with desire and frustration but, like someone in slow motion, she pulled up and adjusted her clothing, and sat down, and took his hands in hers. John looked at her and then got up. 'I'm going this time.'

'What about the tea? You've not had any. It'll only take a moment.'

John laughed ruefully. 'Never mind the tea. If I stay here any longer, I'll forget who I am. That's how attractive you are Madeline, just you remember that. You know it for a fact now, so you should feel better about yourself.'

'But why don't you....Please. Oh, Please!'

'You know I can't. It wouldn't be right.'

'Why not? Why is a candle all right and not a man? You like me, don't you? You said you did. I know you do!'

'Then let that be enough. I have a wife already. I promised to be faithful to her. It's a question of loyalty.'

'But just once. Please.'

'I can't. If I did, I'd hate myself. It would permanently damage me. Can't you see that? Do you want to destroy me? Do you?'

'No, but...'

'Then help me by not enticing me. I'm only flesh and blood, for God's sake!'

'Will you come and see me again?'

John stopped at the front door and turned. 'Yes, I'll come again. Depend on it.'

But as he walked down the High Street, John's mind was in a turmoil. Everything told him not to go back. The danger was intense. But another side of him defied such cowardice, accused himself of being a boyish fool, unable to withstand a pretty woman, who threw herself at him, and who had to be helped because she had no one else to turn to. And then, worst of all, by the time he reached the sea front, yet another side had presented itself. What if he went? What if he did it? What would it be like?

That evening, before George reached MacTavish's Bar, the story had begun, for Sniffy Johnstone had not been able to contain himself. Buce MacSween stood impassively listening, as Sniffy told the young farmer standing at his elbow. 'So you saw the minister shaggin' Madeline Grant, on her kitchen table?' said Buce.

'Aye, Ah did,' said Sniffy, brown thinning hair gleaming with Brill-Cream, sleeked back like a seal.

'Yer a liar! How could ye see? Where were ye at the time?'

'Ootside.'

'Well, how could ye see?'

'Ah keeked in the kitchen windae.'

'And how was it ye werenae chased off by other folks? It's a housin' scheme,' fur Christ's sake. They widnae let ye look in windaes.'

'Wull, Ah saw them.'

'What exac'ly did ye see?'

'Ah saw her haun' on he's prick and she took aff her knickers, still haudin' on tae it.'

'Uch away, with ye, ya wee fraud!' said Buce. 'Ah don't believe ye. How could a wumman get her un'nerclaes aff wi' one haun? There's stockin's and suspen'ers.'

'Wull she did it, all in a onener.'

There was a silence, and Buce waited to see what would be said next, but Sniffy took a deep slug of the pint and stood over it, staring at the array of bottles ahead of him, without seeing them, as if the images of the scene in the kitchen still flooded his mind.

Buce smiled at the farmer and waited some more. Then Buce said, 'Ye didnae see John Manson shaggin' Madeline Grant!'

'Ah did so, tae.'

'No ye didnae! Ye told us what ye saw and that's all ye saw. If there had been any more ye would've told us straight off. No,' Buce concluded with conviction, 'all you saw was what you described.'

'No, Ah didnae.'

Buce took Sniffy by the long, greasy hair and shook him. 'Admit it, ya wee bastard! Ye saw no sich thing.'

'Take yer hauns aff. Whit de you know? And yer no sae big yoursel'.'

'Ah'm big enough for you, ya wee sleekit cratur, ye, creepin' up on folks. Ye should be locked up! Yer a peepin' Tom.'

'Nuthin' of the kind! Nuthin' of the kind! It's ma joab. Ah'm a private detective. Ah'm supposed tae keep tabs on folk.'

The farmer and Buce and the barman met this with guffaws of laughter. Then Buce brought his face close up to Sniffy's, and said, 'Ah might no' be much but I'm big enough to take you and give ye a doin'. So just watch yer step and watch what ye say. If I hear o' you spreadin' malicious gossip about John Manson, Ah'll report ye tae the polis.'

'I'll just tell them ah wis oan a joab.'

'Who'll believe ye? They'll see ye for what ye are. A peepin' Tom.'

Eventually, George showed up, as Sniffy expected and, Buce having been already poured into a taxi by then, the pair were free to talk in the privacy of the back snug, the walls of which were hung with faded photos of old football teams of Branden Athletic and Ottersay Royal Victoria, which competed in the Scottish Junior League. 'What colour were the knickers?' said George, disbelieving such good luck, having set down a double whisky for his employee, who began on it thirstily.

'White.'

'You're, sure?'

'Course Ah'm sure.'

'And you say they were doing it? You saw them doing it?'

Sniffy looked away to the door, in case the young farmer or any of his mates came in. When he made no reply, George said, 'You never actually saw them, did you?'

'No, Ah didnae, but they must have. What else were they on aboot?'

'And the woman had nothing on below the waist and he had his whatsit out?'

'Aye, nae doot aboot it. Ah near fell ower. Ah wis that taken aback.'

'And who took Manson's whatsit out? Was it himself? No, dammit! I don't believe that,' and George's head went up, and he tried to picture it. 'No,' he concluded, 'it's not possible. It must have been the woman. It was her, wasn't it?'

'Ah'm no sure. It was that quick. She was comin' on tae him awfy strang, right enough.'

George sat and considered the situation calmly, trying to decide what use to make of this, how to use it for best effect, and was uncertain of anything except that it was dynamite. No, he decided, the best thing to do was leave things as they were and look for more. If he let it out immediately, Manson would stop visiting her. The wise course was to let them continue and watch and wait.

'Have you got a camera?'

'Oh aye.'

'Well, why didn't you use it?'

'It was so unexpectit. Ah wisnae ready.'

'You mean you were eaten up with curiosity. You were slavering over her yourself, is that it?'

'Ah couldnay very well help it.'

'Be ready next time. I'll give you fifty quid for a good photo of them together.'

For form's sake, George took a swig of the half pint. 'Anything else?'

'Bully's seein' a lot o' the gurl. They've been at the pictur's. Has he come up wi' onything?'

George was surprised. The idea that Billy should have so much initiative was a shock. He'd have to exercise more control over him. 'Never you mind. His turn will come,' he said, finally.

That was the night Billy Buchanan went for tea at the Manse. At John's suggestion, he was invited during the week. So, at five o'clock, after Jessica's music lesson, he met her at the school and accompanied her home as usual, but on this occasion went inside with her.

John met him in the hall. 'So it's yourself, Billy? Come away in. You're very welcome. Tea will be in a wee while. I would offer you a drink but I don't suppose you're up to that yet.'

Billy blushed and Jessica laughed and said, 'That's enough, Dad. Come on upstairs, Billy, and I'll show you where I live.'

Half an hour later, a gong sounded and the family assembled in the dining room, with their guest, a very embarrassed, boyish figure.

'And how did it go today, Roddy?' said John, seeking to divert attention from Billy.

'All right, I suppose.'

'Is that all you can say? How's the rugby going these days?'

'He scored two tries today,' said Peter. 'I heard Charlie talking about it. He might get a game for the seconds on Saturday, if Spud's not fit. He sprained an ankle last week.'

'Do you play rugby, Billy?'

'Yes, but I'm not very good,' said the pasty-faced, rather jowly youth. And John thought how ill-favoured he was. Somehow, the dark hair showed up the face, which was like a shapeless pudding; and the round shoulders did not look as if they would be much good in a scrum.

'Ah well, you're probably better than you think. Anyway, rugby's not everything. Though to hear these two you'd think it was.'

'I wish I was good at it,' said Billy. 'I'm not really good at much.'

'You need to practise,' said Jessica. 'If you really worked hard you could do it.'

'Right, Jessica,' said John. 'You need to learn, and to do that you need to work hard at improving.'

'I have tried,' said Billy. 'Maybe I'm too small. I'm not sure what to do.'

'Maybe you just need a little of the right sort of help,' said John. 'Have you asked Charlie Braddock to help you? He might be able to give you a few pointers.'

'No, I'm not one of his favourites.'

'But you're in the Scouts, aren't you?'

'Yes, but he doesn't bother about me.'

'Peter, you must have some ideas. What would it take to make Billy, here, a rugby player?'

'Guts and training, just like the rest of us.'

'What do you mean?' said John.

'The reason Roddy's good is that he's not afraid. And he's fast off the mark and he's got an eye for an opening. That's what a good scrum-half needs to be.'

'Billy could be that if he wanted,' said Jessica.

Roddy stopped champing long enough to say, 'You need to be good at passing the ball.'

'You have to take the knocks, though,' said Peter.

'I'm sure Billy can take it,' said John. 'What do you say, Billy?'

'I don't know. I never thought about it. I'm going to try though.'

'That's the spirit!' said John. 'I have a book on rugby that might interest you.'

The meal over, John took Billy into his study, picked up a book off his desk and handed it over. 'See what you can make of that.'

Outside in the hall, Peter was passing and saw the book. 'I didn't know you had a copy of that?'

'Got it last week in the library.'

'You might have said. I wouldn't mind reading it.'

'A big rugby star like you doesn't need it.'

Next morning, Susan did not get out of bed. 'Go and see what's up, Jessica,' said Jean. 'She's not usually late like this.'

Jessica found her weeping silently, still in her bed, rather woe-begone and red-eyed.

'I don't feel very well,' was all she could be got to say.

Doctor Telford was called and he seemed unsure. 'Maybe it's just a bug. There's a lot going around. Keep her at home for a few days and see how she does. I'll give you something to make her sleep.'

But three days later, there was no improvement. Indeed, if anything, Susan was worse. Telford examined her at length and questioned Jean. At length, he said, 'She'll have to go into hospital for tests. I'll make the arrangements. Be ready at two o'clock. The ambulance will take her over on the ferry to the Western.'

A week went by, a week of wondering and phoning up every day for news. On the Saturday, John and Jean went up to Glasgow by train to see her, and meet the consultant.

'She has Motor Neurone Disease,' he told them. 'It's a wasting disease of the limbs.'

'Oh no!' said Jean, and John laid a comforting arm around her shoulders.

'There's not much we can do about it, unfortunately. It's very rare. But a lot of people survive for quite a long time.'

'You mean there's no medicine?'

'No, nothing. We don't know much about it. Not much work has been done, you see. It's just not as important as some of the others like heart disease and cancer. They're the ones that get all the money spent on them.'

'Is there nothing we can do, then?' said John, with a horrified expression, and sobs in his voice.

'What you must do is get used to the idea that she will gradually get weaker. She might not be able to talk eventually. It depends which muscles get affected. In some folk it's very slow to develop. So it's not all gloom. But it will get worse, of course.'

Jean was shocked and started to cry. 'There, there now,' said John. 'At least she's going to live. We'll still have her.'

As they were about to leave, the consultant said, 'I don't suppose it will do much good since you're in the ministry. I know how it is, you see. My father was a minister...'

'Yes?' said John.

'Well, there is just a remote chance that something could be done in America. There is a new clinic in Baltimore which specialises in this disease.'

'How do I get in touch with them?'

'You would have to be referred by me.'

'Will you do that for us?'

'I'm not sure I can. You see, it's a question of money. There is the cost of travel and the medical fees. Then there's the nursing care. I'm afraid it would cost a great deal.'

'How much?' said John

'Off-hand, about five thousand sterling.'

'Leave it with me,' said John. 'I don't know how I can lay my hands on that kind of money but I can try. There's really nothing else?'

'No, I'm afraid not. It's the only hope.'

'What difference would it make?'

'I can't be sure. Every case is different. But I think it might make a difference to her. Really good care usually does.'

In Branden the next day, Susan having returned home by train and boat with her parents, John went to see about borrowing the money from the banker.

Bob Forsyth was sympathetic but firmly unhelpful. 'It's just not possible, John. You've no collateral, no security. Most folk have a house they own but you live in a rented Manse. And, if you don't mind my saying so, your income is nothing much. The wonder is that you can live on it at all. You wouldn't be able to pay it off in the sort of time available. The interest alone would be nearly a thousand a year and you only have two thousand a year all told. And that doesn't include the repayment of capital. You would need to pay about two thousand a year and you can't afford it because you can't live on what you've got.'

'There's no way, then?'

'No, I'm sorry. I understand how you must feel. The other banks will tell you the same only quicker, because you're not one of their customers.'

'I could take a job,' said Jean, that evening in the sitting room, when failure was reported.

'No. You're overstretched as it is. Besides, minister's wives never take jobs. They already have a job.'

'The house chores could be shared out among the rest of you. That would leave me free to work in a shop or something.'

'It won't work. You would only earn five bob an hour, maybe less. That's just ten quid a week—then there's deductions. No, it wouldn't do. We need at least forty a week clear. Even then I'm not sure the bank would agree. We have no collateral.'

'Could the children get jobs? If they all worked maybe we could make up the rest?'

'It's a lot to ask. Jessica would have to give up the music scholarship and they all have exams. You know how hard they all work already.'

The matter was left to be resolved by discussion once the actual cost was known for sure.

That afternoon, John went again to Joe Gorman's house. Again there was no reply; only an ominous stillness about the place and John was worried. After waiting a few minutes and hearing no signs of life, John rattled the letter-box. Joe should be there. He only went out at night, John remembered; unless Gregory had been along and taken him away. 'Are you in, Joe?' John shouted through the flap. Then, in the silence he heard a faint sound, like an animal. Was it a rat or a mouse? Could be either.

'Come on Joe! Let's hear you!' John shouted, and then stood wondering whether he should break down the door. He should really get the police, but they were a long way off. The difficulty was what to do if he found the flat empty. The door would be unsecured when he left.

Stooped with his ear to the letter-box, which he held open, John listened intently. Suddenly there was a sound. Like something sliding along the floor. Then it stopped. That was no rat. John straightened and stepped back from the door and then gave it a violent shove.

The weak door-frame gave and the door flew open. Inside, in the back kitchen, John found Joe lying on the rug. 'What've you been doing to yourself? Dear me!' John felt his cheek and found him cold and comatose but otherwise all right. 'Let me help you up,' he said, and soon Joe was sitting in a chair and the gas-fire was lit, a shilling having been found for the meter from John's own pocket. Hands and cheeks were rubbed and signs of life began to return.

'I'll make you a cup of tea, shall I?' and John busied himself among the debris of Joe's kitchen sink. 'How long have you been lying there?'

'Ah don't know,' said Joe, slowly, like a man awakening from a dream.

'What were you doing down there on the floor?'

'Ah'm no sure. Ah just got fair fed up.'

'But it's cold. You're cold, man. When did you last eat?'

'Ah'm no hungry.'

'You look famished. Is there anything here to eat?' John rummaged about in cupboards, but found nothing. 'Have you not done your messages then?'

'Ah wis feart tae go out.'

'But why? You must eat! You need to go out every day.'

'The priest wis here. He telt me no' tae see ye any more.'

'Is that why you didn't answer the door?'

'No. I wanted you te come.'

'But you must have heard me?'

'Aye, but ah jist couldnay get up aff the flair. Ah wanted ye tae come. Yer the only wan that cares.'

'What else did the priest say? Is he going to come and see you?'

'Uch, he wouldnay come ower the door-step. He said he wid come but he said that afore. Ah know he wullnay. If he wouldnay come in, he'll no' come again.'

'Will you come out with me and get some messages.'

'Ah don't feel like goin' out.'

'Well, I'll go and get them. You just sit there till I get back.'

Half an hour later, John returned with a newspaper, which he handed to Joe, and a bag with tea, sugar, milk, butter, jam, bread, ham, eggs, potatoes, fruit, tins of beans and stew, and a few new empty paper sacks. Ten minutes later, Joe was sitting down to a hearty breakfast.

When he had finished, John said, 'Did Father Gregory tell you to go back to the chapel?'

'No.'

'But you haven't confessed for a while, have you?'

'No' for years and years.'

'Well, shouldn't you go back? Maybe you'd feel better.'

'They don't want me back. They make me feel terrible. That's why I didnae get up aff the flair. Ah'm that depressed.' Tears started to roll down Joe's cheeks creating clean rivulets amid the dirt and stubble.

'I think you should get cleaned up. Have a good wash and shave. A bath would be better.'

The boiler—an old gas version—was lit with difficulty, and, an hour later, a cleaner variety of Joe stepped out of the bathroom. By then, John had set to work with a scrubbing brush and made a start at cleaning the kitchen. Windows were thrown open and rugs banged against the stairhead, outside. Sacks full of rubbish were taken down to the bins at the back of the derelict building.

Finally, five hours later, John left a rather spruced-up version of Joe sitting in his chair, absorbed in the newspaper, in a room that was just about fit for human habitation. The front door frame had been temporarily fixed with a few nails and a piece of wood to enable the door to lock shut.

He met Jessica and Billy at the garden-gate to the Manse. 'What happened to you at lunchtime, Daddy?' said she. And John had to explain all that had delayed him.

'And does nobody visit this man?'

'No, I don't think so. Not for years. He'd been lying on the floor for a few days in the cold. Had nothing to eat or drink. He just couldn't be bothered any more.'

'What will happen now?'

'I can tell the district nurses and the social work department. Maybe they can do something.'

'But you don't think they will?'

'Not much, no. When an old man has no friends or relatives or money, people don't go out of their way to help. It's the way the world is. Uncaring, uninterested.'

'What he needs are people to visit him, then?'

'Yes. I've thought about asking some in the congregation, but he's a Catholic, and I know most would be offended. Besides, the priest might actually make things difficult for anyone who did anything for him.'

'Could I help? I mean, I could be introduced to him and go and see him once a week.'

'Have you got time, with all your work and socialising?'

'I hope so. If I can't make time for things like this, there's something wrong with my priorities.'

John thought about it for a moment. 'You don't mind the fact that he's a homo? That's what his trouble is.'

Jessica laughed. 'I should be quite safe, then. I can always take Billy along for protection. In fact, we can protect each other.'

John said, 'It would be best if you always went with somebody. What would you do?'

'Talk to him. Tell him the news. If he never goes out, he won't know what's happening in the town. I could clean up for him. And maybe play chess or something.'

And so it was agreed that John would take Jessica along on his next visit.

They were sitting in the dining room having tea, when Peter said, 'I know we're hard up, folks, but could I have a new pair of rugby boots? The ones I have are worn out. The studs are worn right down and I can't get a grip in the mud. And you know what Otterhall's like. The water just runs down from one end to the other.'

Jean looked at John and said, 'I haven't a spare penny this week. You had four pounds this morning.'

John looked guilty. 'I'm afraid I'm skint.'

'Oh, John. What did you do with it? You weren't with the harbourmaster again at lunchtime?'

John laughed. 'You have the wrong idea about that wee man. He's no danger to me or anybody but himself. He can't hold his liquor.'

'Well, where did it go, then?'

'I bought groceries for Joe. He was starving himself. I found him lying on the floor unconscious. He'd been there for days.'

'But he has money doesn't he?'

'I suppose so. But it didn't seem very Christian to ask for any when he was just recovering. You don't ask that kind of thing of a man who looks like a corpse.'

'Maybe when he's better, you can ask him.'

'I don't think I could, even then.'

'So I can't get my boots?' said Peter.

'I'm sorry son. Not this week.'

Peter ate the rest of his meal in silence, and then went off to work in his room. As he watched him go, Billy reflected that he had enough pocket money in a week to buy what this this family could not.

In Jessica's room upstairs, he said, 'How would it be, if I paid for Peter's new boots?'

'He wouldn't allow that and I don't think Daddy would either. But it's good of you to offer. I appreciate it.'

'You mean I'm not allowed to help? That's crazy! A couple of quid is nothing to me. It's not because of my father—because it's really his money—is it?'

'No. That doesn't come into it. It wouldn't matter whose money it was. It wouldn't be ours.'

'But why can't you lot accept help when you give so much to other people? I mean, the reason you don't have the money, is that your dad gave it away to somebody in need?'

Jessica looked at Billy with new respect. 'That's quite an argument, as Daddy would say. I don't know how to answer it. I just know that even if there is no answer, this family will never accept charity.'

'You're crazy then, all of you. But I love you just the same.' Then a moment later, when both had sat wondering what to do, Billy added, 'Suppose I gave you the money, as a present. Would Peter take it from you?'

'It would depend on how I got it. If he knew it came from you, he would never accept it.'

'Well, can't we do it some other way? What if you said you'd won a competition, and you didn't need the money and you gave it to him?'

'I would have to tell a lie.'

'Is that so bad? It's only a white lie. To make it possible to do a bit of good.'

'I don't know,' said Jessica. 'I'll have to think it over. Maybe talk to Daddy about it.'

That evening, the phone rang and John answered.

The voice said, 'Jim Stewart, the lawyer, here. I'm acting for a client who prefers to remain anonymous. I understand you're in need of a large sum of money, to pay for medical treatment for your daughter. Is that so?'

John agreed.

'Well, my client would in certain circumstances be willing to pay a contribution towards this.'

'That's very kind,' said John, saying a silent prayer that this was the miracle he needed. 'What are the circumstances?'

'You would need to forget about the new system you introduced, for ferrying old people back and forth to church. You don't have to come out against it. Just take a neutral position. My client thinks that left to itself, it will die a death. There's nothing untoward in that, is there?'

'So you're acting for George Buchanan, then?'

'No, for someone who cares about his business. George knows nothing about this. Another condition is that you don't tell him.'

'I see. So to get this money, I need to do an about-face in the Kirk Session about this matter?'

'Not even that. Just let it alone. If others bring it up, say nothing. Let them push it if they like. My client isn't against that. She feels the matter will peter out if left to itself. That's all. Your support is the wedge that's separating George from his normal business. The fact is, George has suffered very badly and is very upset about it. That's why my client's so concerned about him. There's certainly nothing immoral in what you're being asked to do. It should be easy to satisfy her.'

'It sounds easy enough, but I'm not sure. I'll have to think about it. When would the money be available?'

'Immediately. Your word would be good enough.'

'I see. That's very generous. And would it be the whole sum needed or just some of it?'

'I think if it was five thousand, that entire sum would be found.'

'Well, thank you for the offer. I'm very interested and I'll think it over.'

'Just, don't take too long, will you? Shall we say a week from today? I'll phone you then.'

An hour later, John was sitting in his study in the chair at his desk with a book open in front of him, and a glass of whisky at his elbow—the fourth glass since dinner, he thought, sorrowfully.

He would rather have got up and taken the easy chair by the fire-side, even though it was unlit, but he was afraid to do that, in case one of the kids or Jean came in and saw him. How he was.

He had been like that since dinner, since he fled there to think. Only the phone call had interrupted. He was thankful for it, for more than just the offer. He had been so obsessed he hadn't even told Jean. Anyway, he rationalised, he'd have to think it out clearly first.

No, it was Madeline. He'd been strolling about the world as usual, as if nothing had happened, and all the time he'd been imprisoned in his head, with images of her flashing across the windscreen of his mind—that once bright instrument he used to keep well-polished, for the work of Jesus, of love and goodness. And now it was gone, lost in a whirlwind of chance circumstances outwith his control, which had covered it in filth, so that he could no longer see clearly, and which enclosed him.

His 'hellos' and 'good-mornings' had been distant, pale imitations of his former careful solicitude, for every person he came across, especially the strays without means of support, emotional or spiritual, and the down-and-outs, them most of all. Now, for the first time in his life, he was unable to take the time to reach them.

He was obsessed, possessed—it was just like that.

Images of Madeline seemed to float before his mind's eye. The shapely legs soaring upwards to supple, slender thighs and the gasp, every time, as he saw, half way, the pristine suspenders; and then the crotch, covered with the white briefs; that delightful place, with dark hair protruding from either side, in curls and tufts. And the way the flesh curled around the pelvis to the waist, a waist as firm as a woman who had never had children could be. And then.....and then ...and then the image of her seated on the table, naked from the waist down, revealing that dark venusian mound bearing the deep cleft, which he remembered for its pale pink lips, with just a hint of red inside. Oh God! Oh god. Oh god! oh god! ohhhh!

'I want her so! I want to mount her and penetrate that lovely secret beautiful succulent place. And ride and ride and ride for ever. And I know that when I come nothing will stop me. I'll want to do it again without stopping. I'll not be finished until I've ridden her for an hour at least.

'And that was what it was, would be: riding, horse-riding, by God. Stuffing myself into her, as far as possible and... Oh just to do it! To do it! It was lust. Lust, pure and simple. Not an iota of love. Not a bit of it. I just want to ride this woman. And I know, if I do, it will destroy me.'

At ten to nine, realising that the children would assemble soon, and expect him to join them, he got up quickly, and went directly to the hallstand, where he grabbed the coat, and swiftly put it on to hide himself from eyes that might chance to look in the wrong place. Then he stood in the hall, swithering; wondering how easily he could get out of the house.

Forcing himself, he went to the sitting-room door, opened it, and put his head round. 'I'm going out for a walk. Be back in a wee while,' and, as he closed it quickly, he heard the sound of protest, as Jean put down her knitting, prior to coming to get dressed and accompany him. It was the kind of thing she liked; the one activity they could do together. She wouldn't understand this behaviour. What was he going to tell her? The front door shut firmly, he strode down the path as if pursued by the four horsemen.

But he had to be alone. How could he walk the streets with his wife, when all he wanted to do was think about a far younger, more attractive woman, with the effortless power to induce rigidity of a kind he thought he had lost in youth? It was delightful, this sudden access of virility, and it seemed to last forever, fuelled by an inexhaustible store of images, remembered touchings and faint whiffs of scent and other aromas too mysterious to name. But it showed! By heaven it sat up and begged for fulfilment, relentless in its pursuit of favour. It was so embarrassing! What if he were seen like this? All the accumulated efforts of years wasted, for it would take only one eye to notice how he was, and one voice to spread the news, the bad tidings of utter destruction.

Once, days ago, he had rolled over and taken Jean with unaccustomed roughness, and ridden her the way he wanted to ride Madeline. A rough, fast, bucking-bronco of a ride, which left him evacuated but unsatisfied, and he felt the pain in her, the knowledge that she had been the victim of lust and not love, physically used without the least semblance of love, and he had rolled over again and grieved and expected Jean to say something, to notice his distress, and she did not. And it dawned upon him that she knew. She must guess, must see his preoccupation. And he had turned over to comfort her, and she did not move, lay with closed eyes, pretending sleep because she, no more than he, was incapable of discussing such things as love outside the marriage, still less, a demon-lust of this rampant, raging type.

And every night since, after she had put the light out, he had gone to bed quickly and lain in the darkness for hours, stiff with desire, nourishing the lust like a flame that needs kindling, with the sights and scenes of that day in Madeline Grant's house, every one embellished and extended by acts of his own that never occurred but he, by wishing, heightened and intensified.

Was this hell, truly? No furnace of Dante's could be worse than this formed in his own imagination.

His walk took him along the promenade, empty at night, and with the sound of the waves thud, thud, thudding against the sea-wall just beyond and below the railing; but at the pier, he stood for an instant and turned to look inland and uphill, and then he strode off up the High Street, with giant strides, stiffly, like one supporting a great weight between, in the direction of Madeline's house.

Madeline! Madeline! The name sang in his head like the prelude of some symphony yet to be written. It was as if she were the sea, the beautiful, stormy sea and he was about to dip his oar and propel them both on some mysterious voyage to uncharted islands filled with great treasure.

But put there by pirates, he reflected grimly. I will be a renegade, a traitor to my children and my wife. Did they deserve it? No. Well then, what must he do to exorcise the demon? Exercise it, he told himself, smiling. Go and knock on her door and she will open to him and he will go inside and inside and inside. He knew just how it would be. She in housecoat—no, a negligee, rather—and as she comes to the door, knowing who it is, the light shines through the flimsy cloth and reveals the fount of liberty, the empyrean, the hairy diadem, Oh my America! My Promised Land! And in an instant he would be in place, fused, fixed together for eternity. And they would stand and stand and savour the union. And.....And....And....

As he approached the short garden fence with the hedge starting between the posts, he began to slow down, the more to savour the moment. Behind drawn curtains were chinks of light and he looked about him to see if there were prying eyes, and saw none. Everyone watching the end of the television news. And then at the gate, at her gate, Madeline's gate, the opening, the entrance, he stopped and stared at the door, expecting it to open, to see her magically appear, because she might know, ought to know, by some feat of telepathy that he was come, he was here. IT was there, just beyond the door, waiting, dripping with desire for him. Oh, to be wanted is very heaven! And to want it too, paradise, paradise!

The gate opened silently under his hand, which caressed it as if it were she, and he stepped into the garden, with its green lawns and the shrubs waving in the rising breeze, and stopped, and listened to the wind rustling the hedge, and then heard his footsteps, as his legs took him forward, nearer and nearer to the door, her door, the door to paradise, and he slowed, and slowed, but still moved closer by degrees, like an automaton, until, at last, he stood below the step, and his hand clenched to knock, and moved to the door itself, and paused there, and he took in the name Grant, on the letter-box, and the hand unclenched, and the finger-tips gently touched the painted wood and caressed it at eye level.

Like a dream it was, under a spell, and then a gust of wind blew a twig into the air and it passed him, like a bat in crazy flight, and hit the window. The noise startled him into full consciousness. His head flew up, and he recoiled in horror, and then he turned right-about, and walked down the path, and opened the gate, and without a backward glance strode off down the street.

Behind him, standing now by the open door, brought there by the unaccustomed rap on the windowpane, was Madeline, in a pink night-dress, calling, calling. Aware she had a visitor, but uncertain of his identity.

Eighty yards away, glistening eyes hidden by the dark, stood Jean, wrapped up against the cold in old blue coat and scarf.

Still stiff with desire, but half-humiliated, half-frustrated, John walked with earthy tread, like a countryman, leaden-footed and purposeful, mindless of the world and its concerns, doomed to drudgery and dullness.

At the street corner, a voice said, 'John! Are ye aw right?' and an arm took his elbow and turned him. It was Buce, little Buce MacSween, fair hair blowing in the breeze. 'Ye look as if you've had bad news. Maybe Ah kin help. Let me see you hame. Or maybe you'd like a dram? The pubs are still open. What do you say? Are you game, man?'

John was beyond speech. He nodded with relief, and together they went off in the direction of the High Street, and, somehow, on the journey to the nearest pub, *The Gala*, his desire cooled and died within him, and at last, for the first time in two hours, he was at peace with himself.

The place was half-empty, and he stood at the bar while Buce hustled up pints and halfs, John merely nodding at the suggestion. Soon, he was quaffing the fiery spirit and then slurping down a great draught of beer, listening to Buce bleetering on in half-Scots, half-English about the pleasures of philosophy. And then, gradually, what was being said began to get through to him and have meaning and significance.

'Ah'm a Kantian masel',' said Buce, earnestly. 'Ah believe in the power o' the ca'egorical impera'ive: so act as if ye wid make it a universal law.'

Buce looked at him in a kindly way. 'But it was easy fur Kant—a wee skelf of a cratur, a bit like me. No' like a real man, aw cock and balls. Aye, the temptations you ministers must be under is terrible. I don't know how ye keep it up.'

The image hit like John a right-cross, and, for a moment, he thought he was being got at, but the expression on Buce's face was one of simple friendliness and kindness.

'You're quiet the night, John. Aye, but you've had a shock, anybody can see that. But ye did the right thing.'

'How do you know that?'

'I know you.'

'How can you? I don't know myself.'

'So ye did get a fright? Well, we're all flesh and blood, when ye get right doon tae it. We get attractit and sometimes we get offered things that turn our heids, like. Och, I know all aboot it. The passion o' the blood, the way yur imagination seems tae take over.'

'But I would have done it....I very nearly did,' said John, recoiling with horror at the revelation he had provided. What was he doing to himself?

'Aye, but you didnae, did ye? You couldnae take that last step? You thought ye could, that it would be easy—easier than daein' withoot.'

'But it was just the wind,' John protested, with a red face, waving a hand in the air above the drink, compelled to explain himself, 'if it hadn't been for the wind, I would have...'

'Would it really have made any difference if ye had? Would it no' jist have showed ye were human? No' a plaster saint but a man o' flesh and blood?'

'No, not at all! It would have destroyed me! I'm not sure it hasn't.'

'How can ye be destroyed, when ye jist make the same mistake every human makes?'

'How do you know about this? You seem to know.'

'A fairy telt me about Madeline Grant last week, when ye called tae see her in her hoose.'

'Oh, God! Then I am done for. Everyone will know.'

'Don't worry, I made sure they got the truth. That ye didnae dae anything. Ye were sore-tested, but ye did naething.'

The conversation was impossible. John could handle other people's weaknesses but not his own, especially not here in a public house, with a man he hardly knew. At this rate, he would soon be attracting a lot more opprobrium than for pouring Buce into his taxi again. He decided he had had enough and, making his excuses, he took his leave.

An hour later, having walked the length of the harbour, watching the boats at anchor, he slunk back into the Manse. Only the hall-light was on, and, as he began to make himself some cocoa in the kitchen, he looked upward at the ceiling, and pictured Jean lying there in their bed above. What was she thinking? What would she say? What could he say? Should he try and make love to her, to assuage the demon? But he knew it would not, and doubted his capacity to perform the act with the loving kindness necessary for it to be appreciated.

He read for a while, desultorily browsing through the newspaper, and then, an hour later, went upstairs, where he undressed quietly, slid between the sheets, and turned with his back to Jean, for he knew, without seeing, that she was awake and he had nothing to say.

She said, suddenly, 'You've been drinking.'

'Since when was that a crime?'

'In this house it's a crime to waste money by pouring it down your throat.'

'I was invited.'

'You didn't have to go.'

'It was the best thing.'

'I don't understand you. I just don't..... Why couldn't....' She burst out sobbing and John's heart melted, and he turned and fondled her flanks, lying stiffly beside him, and then cuddled up behind her and caressed the breasts, and gradually she relaxed and turned to him with tears in her eyes. She said, 'Do you want me?'

'Yes,' said John, kissing her,

'Are you sure? Do you mean it?'

'Yes,' he said, and then gently and quietly, so as not to wake anybody in the house, he made love to her, and, if it was not as it had been, missing the trust and ordinary familiarity of an act often accomplished together with mutual satisfaction, it was at least beneficial, helping to heal wounds and bring them together, by shortening the distance between them.

Next morning, there was a letter for Jessica, who opened it at the breakfast table and read it with excitement. 'It's for the music scholarship,' she announced, passing it to John and looking up at her mother with alarm. 'I'm to send five pounds for the administration fee, and they want to know whether I need accommodation.'

'When must it be paid?' said Jean.

'By the end of the month.'

'Well, I don't see where the money is to be found by then,' said Jean, looking at John, who looked down at his plate.

'I'll ask Miss Carmichael about it. Maybe the school will help.'

'What about the boots I need?' said Peter. 'And the next game's in Glasgow—against St Aloysius. We're playing their firsts and Charlie says a Scottish selector is going to be there. He thinks I've got a chance of a cap for the Scottish Schools against England.'

Every eye turned to John, and for once he seemed overburdened, as if the lack of money were, after all, his fault. If only he had not bought that bottle to help him put Madeline out of mind. Or was it the other way round? Had he bought it as pure indulgence to make it easier? And then the round he had bought in *The Gala* last night. Was it necessary, when he had these demands round his neck?

'I don't have the money, Peter. Look, I'll give you all I've got,' and emptying first his pockets and then his wallet, he produced two half crowns and nine pence in coppers, followed by a single one pound note. 'How much does a pair of boots cost?'

'Two pound fifty and I need the fare to Glasgow. That's another quid.'

It was then that chestnut-haired Susan, smart in her school-uniform, lifted a glass of water, and it shook in her hand and rattled against her teeth, making such a noise that everyone stopped suddenly, and looked at her. Susan, becoming distressed, put out the other hand to try and stop the rattling and succeeded only in making it rattle more than ever. Then the glass fell and smashed on the floor, and everyone stood up at once.

Tears fell down Susan's freckled face, great gobs of silent tears, in a deathly hush of quiet, and then, suddenly, she screamed. 'Mummmmmy, Ddddaddy, I'm not well. I'm.m.m.m n.n.o.o.ot well.el.el.el. And the slurred speech had become so pronounced that no one now could see it for anything other than what it was. She stood up straight, bewildered, lost, and crying her little eyes out, and everyone was shocked. In a moment, Jean grabbed her, 'Hush now, Susan, don't fret. It will all be right. It's just a passing thing.'

But John said, 'No, Susan, that's not right.' Then to Jean, 'She must be told the truth. She's a big brave clever girl and she deserves to know what's wrong with her.' And John knelt down in front of her and took her hands in his and said, gently, 'You have a disease. Motor Neurone Disease, which causes the muscles to fail. That's why your speech is slurred and why you have difficulty holding things. And it will get worse, much worse.' Then, almost on the point of tears himself, he stood up, still with both of Susan's hands in his, and said to all of them. 'We ought to face it, all of us. It will get worse. And it's a great and terrible shame and I can't tell you how sorry I am or how much I wish I could do something really constructive to help, but I can't. This disease has no cure.'

'But.ut Da.add.ady, why me? Why me.e?'

Taking her from Jean, John cuddled her and lifted her up. 'I don't know, Susan. I wish I did. Nobody knows. Nobody at all. It's one of the mysteries. I wish I could explain it but I can't. The only thing I can do is hope, and hold your hand, and keep you company, and do as much as I can to help you adjust to it,' and John wept, and, one by one, the others came and cuddled in to the two figures standing in the middle of the room.

All except Peter, who said, 'Well I think this is crazy! How can there be a God that allows this sort of thing? I don't believe in this God any more. It's a load of crap. That's what it is,' and he left the room and soon the house, slamming the door.

'I'll take you to school, will I?' said Jean, for Jessica would be stopping off at the big gothic Secondary School whose Primary was situated at the top of the hill above.

Susan looked at them with large eyes and said, firmly, 'Nno, mmmummy. I'll juust go with Jessica as usuual,' and there was such a look of determination that everyone else was on the point of tears all over again.

'Are you sure?' said Jessica. 'I could walk you up to the Primary.'

'But y.you'd beee la.ate, Jessica. Youuu'd get into troub.ble. No,' she concluded, straightening her small shoulders, 'I'll maanage it myself.' And as the children walked down the path to the gate, their parents drew together and their hands clasped as they watched them.

'Isn't it amazing?' said John, presently. 'Just when you think it's blown, everything falling to pieces, something happens to make you believe in life again.'

Jean said, 'There's not much wrong with life, it's people that are the trouble.'

When Susan returned home that afternoon, she went immediately to her room. There was no crying, no hysterics. Standing in the kitchen, Jean could hear the little feet tread purposely up the stairs and then silence. Ten minutes later, Jean went upstairs to look. The door opened on a child curled on her bed, reading.

She said, 'How was school this afternoon, then?' but, as there was no reply, Jean shut the door and went down stairs.

That evening, John was in his study at the unlit fire-side, with a glass of whisky, brooding over the lack of money and what might be done, when Jessica appeared. 'Are you busy?' she said. John shook his head and signalled her to take a chair.

'Billy Buchanan has offered the money to buy boots for Peter. I know Peter won't accept it from him. So he suggests that I should say I won the money in a competition.'

'That would be a lie,' said John, frowning.

'I know that, but a white lie, surely?'

'Yes, but still a lie. Would you do that? Tell Peter a lie? What would you be doing it for?'

'Because it's the only way he would take it.'

'To save him from his own pride, you mean?'

'You don't think I should, then?'

'It's up to you what you do, Jessica, but that's what it would be. Don't get me wrong. I don't condemn telling lies out of hand. No. There are circumstances when you *should* tell them. To save life. To give people comfort—especially when they're dying; but, even if they're not, if it would help them. But this is not one of those times.'

'Why not?'

'Because Peter could take the money without a lie. If the boots meant more to him than his pride, he would do that. He's too proud, though.'

'You're right, I suppose, but what about Peter? What's to be done?'

'I'll take the boots to the cobbler tomorrow. Maybe they can be repaired. If not, Peter will just to have deal with it himself. He can always try and get a job after school. It would mean less time for his studies, but it's up to him. The priorities are his. It's just unfortunate he's a son of the manse with no money. None of us can do anything about that.'

But when Jessica left to get on with her homework, John thought sadly that Peter was the least of his worries. Susan was the one that mattered, for she was wasting away before their very eyes. The slurred speech was only a symptom of something far worse. The 'not feeling well' had probably been an effect on the stomach muscle itself, causing nausea and the inability to hold up a glass of water, even with two hands to help. It was deeply worrying, for it signalled the start of a decline into a muscular collapse, which would make the poor wee girl increasingly dependent on those around her. Was this a punishment for Madeline Grant, he asked himself? But he remembered he had done no wrong—yet!

The time given him to consider the offer was nearly up and he must decide what to do. Jean he would not discuss it with, for he knew what she would say. Her duty as a mother over-rode every other, in her mind. No, if he took the money, he was the one who would have to pay the price. And what a price! His integrity shattered. And yet it might help Susan—must help her, for the NHS could, apparently, do nothing.

Was this just a white lie? No, this was far worse. He would be allowing George Buchanan to continue in his immoral business practices. The old folk in the congregation were being used. George's taxis were doing a regular amount of business, but that was nothing to the profits from funerals and legacies he continually received. Now that he thought of it, George always took a close interest in the old, but it was not from a spirit of altruism. From what Joe had said, John saw that it was a carefully calculated procedure, involving time spent, with the hope of money accruing. George was a specialist in the old. To him they were commodities. And because they were soon to die, a lot of money would be left lying around, some of which could always find its way into his pockets. The writing of wills for them was one of the most insidious aspects. What if they couldn't see very well? George could write down anything he wanted and, trusting him, they would sign anything. George's success depended on establishing trust, something he would be very good at. Being a local Councillor and a Justice of the Peace would help. They would trust him more easily.

Could John condone this activity? Act as if there was nothing wrong with it? No, it was against reason. And yet, when the phone call came, he was hesitant, knowing what a terrible difference it might make to Susan.

'I'm afraid I can't go along with you,' said John.

'I think you should reconsider,' said the voice. 'My client is a very determined person and may resort to other methods to achieve her ends.'

'What would they be?'

'There is the matter of Madeline Grant. You've been seen in her house in a compromising situation. In fact, I would say that it compromises your ministry here. You may have to leave Branden.'

There was a long silence.

John said: 'My behaviour with Madeline Grant has been above reproach.'

'That is a surprise. Many people will not think so when they hear about it.'

'There is a redress at law for that sort of thing. I can find out who spread the story.'

'I wouldn't try that if I were you, Mr Manson. Reputations have a habit of coming to grief in courts.'

As a relief from so many other preoccupations and not from any particular interest in the subject, John attended the meeting of the Philosophical Society that evening. The hall was almost full, and John, who was late, found himself in the front seat next to Buce MacSween, who smiled at his arrival, there, as if he had been accorded an honour.

The speaker was Sheriff Jamie Gorse, a tall thin man, with a head like a rugby ball, yellowed with age, as if too long in the sun; and ornamented about its periphery, by close-cut white hair. He was dressed in a kilt of Branden tartan of the hunting variety, green and black, mostly, with a large white sporran and red velvet jacket. But, if Sheriff Gorse was skin and bone, with a head that would have looked at home in a crypt, he still had the heart of a lion and had roared with such terrible effect, so often, in so many larger places, that his reputation had come to life at an early age.

In youth, a mere novice at the bar, it was no less a person than Sheriff Gorse who had been chosen, before a hundred other advocates, to defend a man who was expected to be put to death for his crime—terrorism, which is to say, setting off bombs in Princes Street, to bring about an Independent Scotland, an ambition that Gorse himself, and more than half that small country's citizens, desired with all their hearts. But the larger nation's government in Westminster took a different view, and had laid down, as a condition of such a change, that there should be a two-thirds majority, before such a dissolution of the United Kingdom would be permitted. Gorse had acquitted the man —and himself— with distinction, in an address which had left hardly a dry-eye in the court.

Tiring of the effort necessary to win his cases, which kept him up half the night, he opted for a quieter life on the Branden bench, there to pursue antiquarian interests: all things Scottish and the writing of Sir Walter Scott, in particular. It is an odd fact that so many intelligent Scots are apt to devote excessive energy and time to the great writers of their own country, almost as if there were no others. The talk that evening was entitled: 'Waverley, the author, the novels and the man.'

Paeans of praise fell from Gorse, himself an author of books on various aspects of his native country, including the food and drink. Scott was portrayed as a Sheriff like himself, with a great love of country, gallantry, history and poetry. Gorse quoted from several works, ending with the words from, *Lay of the Last Minstrel* ,

> 'Breathes there the man, with soul so dead,
> Who never to himself hath said,
> This is my own, my native land!'

It was a feat of eloquence and received cheers as well as applause, and when questions were invited, there were few, and all respectful, and inclined to grovel before the literary lion. Until John stood up, opened a volume of the poet's works, which he had brought, and read, 'The lines you quote are very good, none doubt it, but he does go on so. He continues: This is my own my native land!
Whose heart hath ne'er within him burned,
As home his footsteps he hath turned,
From wandering on a foreign strand!
If such there breathe, go mark him well,
For him no Minstrel raptures swell;
High though his titles, proud his name,

Boundless his wealth as wish can claim;
Despite those titles, power, and pelf,
The wretch concentrated all in self,
Living, shall forfeit fair renown,
And doubly dying, shall go down
To the vile dust, from whence he sprung,
Unwept, unhonoured and unsung.

'It is rather pointless, is it not? All these rather boring rhymes and this small content of meaning, expanded for the sake of the rhyme. Worse, some of his phrases are plagiarised from Coleridge—poems like *Christabel*, for example. Scott did a great service by devising the short story and the romantic, historical, novel when it hardly existed before, but we should not commit the error of over-estimating his achievement. Best of *our* writers he may be, but has he not been surpassed by others and should we not rather pay more attention to these, instead of wallowing in nostalgia for things past, that were good in their day, when that day is long gone? Scotland's history is not improved by the mythical bloodbath of the Battle of the Clans. Is not a too great worship of Scott a descent into a kilted twilight where Scots were all brawn and no brain? And isn't that what we ought to forget, or at least allow to rest in peace? Isn't Scott a far inferior poet to Burns, the best of whose work contains the ongoing connected force of a powerful narrative, which Scott's cannot?'

The Sheriff did not agree. His gaunt cheeks swelled with redness, like a cockerel challenged to fight, and he roundly condemned John for his lack of patriotism. 'Who needs Shakespeare and Tolstoy and George Eliot when we have Scott? We should revere him, not pull him down'. But there was little in the way of argument. Sheriff Gorse, for all his undoubted intellect, was like a blind man where things Scottish were concerned. But he was not blind when it came to finding an opponent's weakness. There was always something to hand that could be used. So when John replied, 'There is no requirement to worship false gods under the impulse of patriotism,' the Sheriff retorted: 'You are one to speak of such things. Did you not admit, in this very room, some weeks ago, that you do not believe in the very god you are supposed to worship?'

'No, Mr Gorse, I did not. I simply explained what I meant by God. And I do worship him.'

The Sheriff was unsatisfied. His sense of injury at being opposed on a matter of such importance to him, and in a place as lowly as this, was too much to bear. 'You said you didn't believe in a personal God! So how can you worship him? It isn't a 'him', you believe in!'

John said, 'It's a poor sort of man who will defend his case by attacking the man who opposes him, on different grounds altogether. There is no contradiction in my believing in a God that is not personal, yet speaking as if there is. How any man deals with religion is a matter for him alone.'

But there was a general feeling that John's position had been exposed. No one remembered that the Sheriff had been seen to take up a stance that was outmoded and unrealistic. All they would take away from the encounter, was that John didn't believe in God, but acted as if he did.

One evening, just before tea, John looked into Susan's room and found her engrossed. 'What's this you're reading?' he said, but there was no reply, and he had to lay his hand on the book to attract her attention. Picking it up, he said, 'Thucydides, The History of the Peloponnesian War,' big stuff for a wee girl of twelve. How did you come by this?'

'I go.o.ot it on your shelves.'

'But what made you start reading it?'

'I like hist'ry and I like the Greeks and I do.on't know much about them. So.o I thought I would ju.ust start here.'

'And do you like it? Isn't it difficult?'

'Oh, no! It's lovely. It's so clear and simple.'

'But why do you like it?' said John with surprise.

'I like the peeeople. Alcibiades is my faaavourite. And then Pericles. But I'm just d.d.dying to find out who wins. I want the Athenians to win but I'm not sure they will.'

'And why do you think they might not?'

'Because they're a democracy and the mob rules sometimes, and makes the wrong decisions.'

Humbled by this sign of erudition and pleased and proud too, John smiled, gave her a kiss, and then went downstairs, where he met Jean and embraced her, standing at the sink though she was, preparing the dinner. 'We have a scholar upstairs. There can't be too many twelve-year olds who read Thucydides for fun.'

'I wonder why she does it?' said Jean.

Jessica, who came in at that moment, said, 'I think it's the illness. Ever since she knew she was going to get worse she's been devouring books at a great rate. Maybe she thinks her eyesight will go. Maybe she just wants to cram as much as possible into her life, while there's still time.'

'Well, perhaps I should speak to her,' said Jean. 'She might be doing herself harm, reading to all hours of the night.'

'No,' said Jessica. 'Don't do that. Let her do what she wants. It can't do her harm to read. And if that's how she wants to spend the time she has left, why should she be stopped?'

John said: 'I agree. It's wonderful, that's all. Maybe that's the bonus, the good that's come out of this awful trouble.'

In the weeks that lay ahead, Susan's illness became progressively worse, though there were days when some improvement showed, but through it all, the little girl read and read—everything that interested her: history—of her own and other countries, novels galore, and even science. Her curiosity was boundless. She wanted to know everything, and bombarded everyone she met with questions most were hard put to answer. The Encyclopaedia Britannica was well thumbed and she would be found, at all hours of the day and night, huddled over its various tomes laid out on the floor of John's study, so that he began to wonder whose study it was. The mystery of how, at barely twelve, she could cope with the academic discourse, was insoluble. Partly, it was the fact that she had read already, several deep books written with a pure delight in intellectual rigour and clarity of thought. She had discovered a love of language so intense, that she hungered for new words and became adept at working out their meanings from the context, using the dictionary only when necessary. As some adults collect chateaux wines or stamps, Susan actively collected words, so that, before long, her vocabulary was equivalent to an educated adult's.

There was more, of course. Susan had an exceptional memory. Anything she saw or read or heard—anything whatever—immediately registered, was stored, and could be called up at will. Above all, anything *interesting* was instantly absorbed and automatically, as if without the necessity for actions to accomplish the fact, organised and associated with the existing contents. The importance of memory is often under-rated; and its richness, accuracy and speed of availability, is crucial, even to the highest creative functioning of the mind, which scans all its prehistory stochastically, in its search for unexpected connexions and auxiliary problems.

Her first memory was of an experience in the womb. Contrary to most medical opinion, that was where she first became conscious. Jean was in the eighth month of her pregnancy then, and what awakened the embryonic Susan was motion, surging motion around her, and especially below her. The event was annoying, worrying, frightening, because the thing—whatever it was—threatened to invade the small space in which she then lived, until that moment, secure from the invisible world outside. From the sounds of the speakers—her mother's voice, even she, protesting at the vigour of the exercise in which the other was engaged—Susan knew of the conflict, of the threat posed by her father, of his irresistible need, his powerful rhythmic intrusions, and yet how much it conflicted with her own needs, as an unborn child. Inside her little sac, she protested by kicking and, somehow, in a very short time, the threat was removed.

The fear of her father lay deep within her thereafter, so that there was always a distance, a kind of psychic obstacle, to the most complete relationship between them. That first memory of her father, months later, would have its important effect.

But there were other memories, soon after birth. Rich memories of rooms in which she lay as a baby, of being uncomfortable, of being changed, of being fed at the breast, and even of being denied it, because her appetite was, on occasion, too aggressive. Memories of seeing her parents make love, watching with large-eyed intelligence out of the cot or the pram and knowing all, registering and understanding and feeling jealous too, even then. And even feeling annoyance when her parents would laugh, assuming she could not possibly understand, which of course she did. And the memories were burnt on her brain, in full technicolour, so that, had she wished, she could have described the entire scene as if it were a moving picture and quoted the statements of the speakers. There were even memories of being threatened by the adults who stooped too much into her tiny territory of the pram, blotting out the blessed light of day and stifling her, often with bad breath or the hint of alcohol or tobacco smoke. Of the black rook, that perched on the pram-handle-bar, one day, and studied her eyes as if they would make a nice meal, cocking his black head to one side to see her better, and opening his large, triangular, grey beak, as if to make a beginning on his breakfast, until shooed away. These events and many more Susan absorbed, and they were the beginning of her understanding of the world.

One day, on a new shelf, she came across Bertrand Russell: *The Problems of Philosophy* , and soon a new adventure was in being, as she struggled to understand the arguments about tables which Russell presented.

'What do you make of it?' said John, one evening at tea.

'Not very much,' she conceded, 'but the questions are good.'

'What do you mean?' said Peter.

'He wants to understand how we come to know anything,' she said. 'That's a good question. I me.ean, how do we know that we know? What conditions must be satisfied if we are entitled to say we know something?' Peter said nothing; John smiled.

'What do yo.ou think Peter?' the little high-pitched voice said, as Susan turned her freckled face to him. 'How do you kno.ow mathematics?'

'That's a daft question,' said he, frowning.

'Why is it?' persisted Susan, regarding him levelly through light brown eyes. 'Remember that Bino.omial Theorem you mentioned? How do you kno.ow it's true?'

'Because it is.'

'But that's no good!' said Susan, with shock.

Peter blushed. 'Why not?'

'Because if you know anything yo.ou should be able to prove it. Isn't that what mathematics is about? It's supposed to be certain.'

'It is certain,' said Peter. 'I can prove it. Maths is the only true form of knowledge there is. Truer than physics, truer than history and'—with a not very friendly glance at John—'a whole lot truer than religion.'

'Huh,' said Susan.

'What do you mean, huh?' said Peter.

'Bertra.a.a.nd Ru.s.s.ssell says that mathematics is the subject in which we never know what we are ta.a.a.lking about or whether what we say is true.'

'How would he know?' said Peter, surprised by the power of the words. There was something about them that demanded attention, even if they were slurred.

'He's a mathematician,' said Susan. 'I'm surprised you didn't know that. He wrote a book, with Alfred North Whitehead called *Principia Mathematica*, published in 1910, and it attempted to derive ma.athematics from lo.ogic.'

'But the Binomial Theorem has been proved. I can even prove it myself.'

Susan said, 'Well there's something wrong with the premises. Some of the assumptions behind the theorem have to be wrong.'

John laughed and laughed. Peter flushed bright red at the success of this attack. 'How do you get that? The Binomial Theorem is part of my course. It has to be true.'

Susan said, 'I don't know anything about your course, but I kno.ow that Bertrand Russell tried to put mathematics on a sure foundation by deriving it from logic and failed. So the Bi.i.inomial Theore.em must be wrong, mustn't it? It's just the logical conclusion, isn't it?'

'How do you know all this?' said Peter, with shock, for it was the most profound shock he had ever received; an assault on his most cherished belief—the foundation of his life—for he planned to make a career in mathematical-science.

'I read it in the Encyclopaedia.'

'Well, I don't believe it,' said Peter. 'Show me!' And so, leaving their dinners to get cold, the pair got up from the table, and went to the study and there Susan found the article that told of the controversy in the foundations of mathematics which Russell, everyone agreed, had failed to resolve.

Peter read and read with increasing amazement, and found that the problem was even more intractable. There were other unsolved problems in the foundation of mathematics, which cast doubt on the whole enterprise. A couple of hours later, he got up with a bemused expression on his face, and said to John, who was sitting nursing a glass by the cold fireside, 'Well, that's that. Susan's right. I can hardly believe it! I can hardly believe it!' he repeated, wandering around the room in a circle, as if lost or demented. 'Mathematics isn't certain. That means that nothing is. Where do we go from here? That's what I'd like to know.'

There was a feverish concern to his pacing, and John said, quietly. 'Maybe nothing is certain except that nothing is certain.'

'But how can that be?'

'Well, why not? Why must *anything* be certain when so much in life isn't?'

'But surely there must be something that is fixed, something we can count on being true?'

'There is. God, Jesus, and the ideas connected with them.'

'But you don't believe in a personal God, Dad. What good is an idea?'

'It's all we have, son. And some of us personalise it because it feels better, or it comes more naturally that way. I grew up with the idea of God as a 'him' and I still tend to talk that way, even though I know he's not: that there's no 'him'—at least I think there isn't. The idea of Jesus—all that he involves—is sufficient, and the best we have. Of course, I would like more: certainty about all kinds of things, but I don't expect to get that. It's part of the human condition, this uncertainty we all face. A lot of folk pretend it isn't like that, but it is, and I don't think they do themselves any real good by pretending. It does comfort them, though. But it's not true, and so it's not really desirable.'

Peter almost burst into tears. 'But this is no good! How am I supposed to manage when everything I believe is smashed?'

'It's not a dead duck, for heaven's sake. The fact that mathematics is uncertain is not the end of the world. Who cares about it?'

'I do! It's what my life is about. I wanted to spend my life doing research, discovering things in maths and science, but if it's just a load of baloney why bother? That means I've got to think again, find something else to do.'

'No you don't, you can learn to live with uncertainty, the way the rest of us have to.'

One afternoon, a few days later, when John, as usual, was out, the phone rang and Jean answered it. 'Jim Stewart, here, Mrs Manson. I'm acting for someone who prefers to remain anonymous, someone who is herself acting in the interest of George Buchanan. You know that your husband has changed the system for transporting the old folk to and from church? Well, this is having a damaging effect on George's business. My client has also heard of your daughter Susan's illness, and the need for a large cash sum if she is to get medical treatment. Well, the fact is, she is anxious to help; thinks it would be a Christian act to provide money to help little Susan to be cured. What do you think about that, Mrs Manson?'

'I think it's wonderful!' said Jean. 'It's the answer to all our prayers.'

'That's good. I'm very glad to hear you say so. Now the point is, Mrs Manson, my client has tied the two matters together, so to speak. In return for putting up the money for Susan's treatment, she expects George to have his business restored to him.'

'I see. Well, I can't think there would be any difficulty.'

'That's just it, Mrs Manson. Your husband's being difficult about it.'

'You mean you've spoken to him? He never said so.'

'Yes, well he says he's not prepared to do anything to help George and this has angered my client. She thinks it's ungrateful.'

'What is you would like John to do?'

'He doesn't have to do anything. My client feels that if he will just let the matter drop, it will resolve itself.'

'I don't understand this. It's such a little thing.'

'I was hoping you'd see it that way. Perhaps you could speak to John and get him to change his mind? It's not as if she was asking much.'

'And your client will pay for the whole of Susan's treatment?'

'Yes, without a doubt. All she needs is a little cooperation with this other matter. Perhaps I could phone you in a few days to see how things have worked out?'

The journey to Madeline's could not be put off, but, as John approached the house on foot along the street, there was a strange silence, a sense that he was being watched. A few more people were visible behind the net curtains than usual, it seemed to him.

As before, Madeline was radiant, this time in a short scarlet dress, flowing fair-flecked tresses and made up as if her life depended on it. As soon as he was in the hall, she gave him a kiss full on the lips.

He said, 'I wish you wouldn't do that. It's not right.'

'I can't help myself. I'm head over heels in love with you.' And as he led her into the sitting-room, she added, 'I've been dying for you to come. I can't tell you how often I walked past the Manse hoping for a sight of you.'

'It won't do, Madeline. It's got to stop. In fact, this will be my last visit to you.'

Madeline burst into tears. 'Oh no! You don't mean it. Please come again. I need you so much. I dream about you all the time.'

She sat on the chair opposite, a few feet away and opened her legs revealing all that lay beneath and John blushed and made to get up, but she stopped him, grasping his hands and keeping him in place.

'Don't be like that. I love you, so what does it matter? I want you to see me. I like you to look.'

'Please close your legs.'

She laughed. 'Does it make you excited?'

'Yes, it does. It's more than flesh and blood can stand.'

'Well, then, why not go the whole hog? It's such a little thing and it means so much. You're here and I'm here and I want you. Oh, I really want you.'

'At this very moment people are watching this house to see what is going on. Someone saw us last time.'

Madeline frowned. 'Who? How?'

'I don't know who, but someone saw us and reported it. It's a wonder no one has said anything to you. They have to me.'

'But nothing happened. What was there to say?'

'They saw us, depend upon it. I don't know what they saw but they saw enough.'

'But we didn't do anything.'

'You were undressed from the waist down and I was not far off it.'

'But how could anybody see?'

'Easily. There are windows.'

'But why would anybody do that?'

'They do it all the time, spy on each other. Especially if they think there might be something to see. But, come to think of it, I have a funny feeling I'm being followed. I must pay more attention.'

She laughed. 'Who would follow you? And why?'

'I don't know but I have this sense of doom. As if something is brewing and I don't like it.'

On an impulse, John went to the window and looked out. Across the street behind a net curtain, he could just make out a pair of binoculars. Then, further up the street, he saw a woman standing looking straight at him. 'There are people watching this house,' he said, turned, strode to the kitchen and opened the back door. Behind it he found Sniffy Johnstone, in pilot's jerkin and boiler suit. 'What are you doing here?' John said.

The man seemed at a loss. He sniffed and said, 'Ah wis jist comin' tae see Mrs Grant.'

Madeline, who had come behind John, said, 'Yes?'

Shifting from one foot to the other, nervously, like a schoolboy, Sniffy replied, 'Ah wis wonderin' if mibbe there wis anythin' Ah could dae fur ye?'

'What do you mean?'

'Wull, yer man beein' deed an' aw that, Ah thocht Ah micht be able tae help ye, ye know.'

'I don't need anything from the likes of you,' said Madeline.

'How long have you been there?' said John. 'And why didn't you go to the front door and ring the bell?'

'Uch, Ah didnae wahnt tae be a bother. Ah thocht the back door wid dae as guid as any ither.'

'I don't believe you,' said Madeline. 'You..You've been skulking there for a while haven't you...you...you dirty little bastard, you!'

'Ye don't huv tae talk like tha'. That's no fair. Ah wis jist pluckin' up ma courage tae chap yer door.'

'Well, what have you got a camera hanging round your neck for, then?'

Sniffy blushed. 'Ah niver go withoot it. Ye niver know whit ye might see.'

'You're a bare-faced liar, Johnstone!' said Madeline. 'The world knows you're a sleekit wee spy. That's what you are! Away out of here before I call the police.'

'Let me see that camera,' said John, angrily.

'Naw, Ah'll no'. It's mine.' And John, in his anger, took hold of the strap, by which it hung around Sniffy's neck, and pulled. As Sniffy grasped the camera itself, the strap broke and it fell on the paving under his feet. 'Ye've broke ma camera!' he said, stooping to pick up the pieces.

'A good thing too. Serves you right for spying on people and taking photographs of them when they're not looking.'

That evening over tea, knowing that was the place to achieve maximum effect, Jean taxed John with the matter of the financial offer of medical treatment. Every head lifted, and every item of cutlery was laid down, when the position was made clear.

'It's just a bribe, Jean. George Buchanan's business is suffering because of the loss of the taxis he used to provide. That's why I'm being offered a bribe. To get his business back to what it was.'

Peter said, 'But that's crazy! What's a few taxis, for heaven's sake? Do you mean to say you're turning down five thousand quid for this?' The sense of shock seemed to stand in the very air between them and was shared by everyone present.

'It's not that simple. If you must know, George Buchanan uses the taxi-system to keep in with the old folk. He often arranges for their wills to be signed, provides witnesses and so forth—often the taxi-driver and himself, for the old are usually alone as well. And when they die, he often gets to do the funerals—from which he makes a fat profit—but, worst of all, he often gets left things, bequests of money and goods, by the old people themselves. In other words, he uses the taxi-service to ingratiate himself, and makes a lot of money out of it. Why do you think I'm being offered five thousand pounds? It's not charity but business! He thinks it will be well worth the expenditure. He will make far more than five thousand pounds this year, and every other year, if he can get back to running things the way he's used to.'

Angrily, Jean said, 'But the lawyer said it was a woman that he was acting for.'

'It's not a woman. That's just a ruse to conceal the fact that it's George himself who's behind it.'

'I don't believe this!' said Jean. 'Mr Stewart was very kind and friendly about it. It can't be a bribe! It doesn't sound like a bribe.'

'Do yo.o.ou mean I could go to America and get cur.ur.ed, if we go.o.o.' that money?' said Susan.

'Yes, you could go to America,' said John. 'A cure is not guaranteed. There is no cure. All the consultant would say was that it might help.'

Peter said: 'But if it would help, shouldn't it be tried? At any cost?'

'I would have to tell a lie at the Kirk Session to get that money. Maybe a lot of lies, how do I know? It's not something I do, but I suppose once you tell one you have to go on doing it just to keep that one secret.'

'Why would you have to tell a lie, John,' said Jean, calmly, determined to break down his resistance by self-control. 'All you have to do is keep quiet. Say nothing, and the new system will be dropped all by itself. That's what Mr Stewart said.'

'If I say nothing, I will be asked for my opinion, and if I say nothing then, the Kirk Session will see very plainly that I have been bribed. Don't you see? The fact is, I cannot say nothing. I will have to say something at some point, and what I would have to say is that I think the matter can be dropped. This, I will not do, because it would be a lie.'

'But Daddy, be reasonable,' said Jessica. 'You might not have to say anything. You don't know that.'

'I know it, Jessica, believe me. I just wish it were as easy as Jim Stewart says. You think I wouldn't like to send Susan to America? Of course I would! You all know that. But to do it, I would have to allow George Buchanan to go on milking the old people of their money. It's quite immoral what he's doing. I can't do that. And I can't go about telling lies so that he can go back to doing it again. It's just not in me to behave like that.'

'But think of what you might achieve, Dad!' said Peter. 'I don't believe this! The world's gone mad! You mean you can get five thousand quid for Susan just by keeping your big mouth shut and you won't do it? Isn't your conscience a small thing beside Susan's life?'

For the first time in *his* life, John had nothing to say. For the first time in that family, the head of it seemed to be in a false position.

Finally, John said, 'I see how it must appear to you. It is a matter of calculation, moral calculation; but I think I understand the premises, conclusions and consequences better than any of you, and you'll just have to trust me about it. I am right in this. I'll talk about it again and try to explain it better. Maybe you'll understand it then. But the upshot is that I am being offered a bribe and I can't take it. It's just not in me.'

'Well,' said Peter, 'I don't see how you can hold up your head if you don't!'

'It wouldn't be worth holding up, Peter, if I did. It cannot ever be right to commit a grave wrong in order to help one person, no matter how much you love them. And it would be no different if we knew for a fact that Susan *would* be cured. Self-sacrifice is a fine thing, but taking a bribe, and telling a lot of lies, is not an acceptable sacrifice. No one should have to undergo moral destruction to save life. But it's not just that, don't you see? I have to put a stop to what George Buchanan's doing. It is my duty!'

At Branden Grammar School, Roddy sat with others in the room at the corner on the second floor. It was a class in religious instruction given by Charlie Braddock at the last period on a Friday and the children were restless, eager to be off to their homes for a week-end, free from the rigours of school. Charlie drew a letter out of his pocket and said, "I have a letter to read to you. It says, 'Enjoyed the game on Saturday, even though we lost. The other side played well. They have a young winger who is very fast and a powerful scrum who made the most of difficult conditions. I trust life in Branden continues along its Christian path.' There's more, but it's not about rugby. Yours ever, Graham."

Charlie stopped reading and looked at the class. 'Who do you think that is from and what game is he referring to?'

The class was silent. No one could think of anything to say. Charlie was affronted and abused them. 'Don't you know anything? What do you read? Don't you watch the television news or hear what's going on in the world? What event took place on Saturday?'

Out of the silence, Roddy said, 'Please sir, Scotland played France at rugby.'

'That's right, Roddy. Good boy. So who is the letter from?'

'I don't know, sir.'

'Try, Roddy! Try.' Then getting no response, 'Does nobody know who Graham is?'

Astonishingly, nobody did. Charlie was even more irritated. 'What do you do with your lives? It's time you took an interest in the affairs of your country. You're a patriot, aren't you Roddy? You support Scotland, don't you?'

'Yes, sir.'

'Well, why is it you don't know who was playing for Scotland on Saturday?'

'I don't know, sir. I never saw the match. I was in Greenock playing for the thirds.'

'You should all be ashamed of yourselves. This letter is from Graham McGregor, Scotland's stand-off. Doesn't it make you think?'

Apparently the power of thought was all but dead in Branden that day.

Suddenly excited, Roddy said, 'Did Graham McGregor score?'

'Yes, Roddy. Two tries. Imagine it, scoring two tries for Scotland against France and all he can say for himself when writing to a friend is 'I enjoyed the game.' A hush fell over the class as at something miraculous. 'What does it mean, this letter?' said Charlie.

But no one could say anything for a while, until at last someone suggested, 'Graham McGregor must be very modest, sir.'

'Right, Jimmy. Graham was the man of the match, but he doesn't boast about it. He doesn't advance himself and he even finds time to praise the opposition. What a fine man he is.'

When the bell rang, Charlie asked Roddy to stay behind, and, after the rest had gone, he went over to the door and turned the key.

At four o'clock, after two periods of rugby at Otterhall, Peter was in the gym changing, so he was late if he wanted to catch Charlie Braddock before he left for home. Leaving the others dressing, or in the shower, he threw on his clothes, grabbed up the bag of kit, swept out of the dressing-room and ran along the corridor.

The ferment was still in him. How could mathematics be uncertain? How could all that wonderful, rigorous Euclidean Geometry not be true? Of course it was true! It cried out to be true! It felt right! And yet the Encyclopaedia said it was flawed. To Peter, it was like a confrontation on the Damascus Road—except it was the devil, not God, that had spoken.

Once outside the building, the journey down the hill across the grass to the senior school was made in a mad rush, leaping over fences in a way that even prefects of his seniority were not permitted. On the way, he glanced up and saw that the lights of Charlie's room were still on. With luck, he would still be there. Would still be able to save his, Peter's soul, for that was the thing at stake. The towering spires of mathematics, thousands of years in the making were tottering, the building on the point of collapse. And if it fell? What then? What was he to do? How could he believe in anything again?

The door to the gothic building was flung open unceremoniously and the stairs to the second floor taken at the run. At the door to Room 18, Peter stopped to catch his breath, put one hand on the door-knob, turned it, and knocked with the other. The door did not budge. Disbelief made Peter try to open it again. No result.

It was locked. Amazingly, it was locked. But it was hardly ever locked! Peter looked at his watch and saw that it was ten past four. Maybe Charlie was already away and had left the lights on. Maybe he had gone off somewhere and would be back.

Behind the door, there was silence but tension too. Peter was puzzled. What could Charlie be up to? Was he there?

Peter knocked the door again and called out. 'Can I see you for a minute, sir? I've got a problem I need your help with.'

Silence.

Desperate, Peter hammered on the door and shouted, 'For God's sake, are you there? Is anybody there? I need help!'

Silence.

Peter bent his tall body, put his eye to the keyhole and looked. He could see nothing. The key was in the lock! The door was locked from the inside! Charlie must be there.

'Oh, sir!' Peter shouted with disappointment. 'I know you're in there. Why won't you come?'

But, inside, Charlie had temporarily lost all desire to do that.

Sensing that something was amiss, Peter ran down the stairs and left by the swing door, banging it behind him as he did so. Then, up the hill he went, seeking a place from which to see into Charlie's room, for the windows were on the second floor. Looking around him, Peter saw that the best position from which to look into Charlie's room was from the top of the gatepost of the Primary school on the road above.

The hundred yards uphill were covered fast and then Peter clambered up the gatepost and began to try to balance on the top which was a concrete pyramid. Then down, down into the senior school he looked and could see nothing. The lights were out!

Peter did not so much jump down off the gatepost as fall down in amazement. What could Charlie be up to? Why had he not answered? Why had he opened the door and left so soon after he, Peter, had gone away for a better look inside? It was a mystery; and behind it all, was the thought that

Charlie did not want to see him. Knew of his trouble and did not want to help. It was too much! Charlie was the one teacher in the school Peter admired unreservedly.

Maybe Charlie could yet be caught! Peter began running back the way he had come, down the grassy slope to the senior school. Which exit would he use? Where would he go?

Working it out like a mathematical problem, Peter saw that the route most probable for a successful interdiction, was a circle around the front of the school, from where half the routes available to the town could easily be seen. Running like a four-hundred-yard athlete, he soon encompassed half the school buildings, seeing nobody around, at that hour. Then, on the road below the senior building, he saw a figure wrapped in a raincoat, wearing a felt hat and holding it on with one hand, against the wind, which threatened to tear off the hat. In a trice, Peter was onto him, running fast now to catch up. Down the drive, out the main gate and along the road in pursuit. A hundred yards along the road, by now out of sight of the school-buildings, Peter came up with the man. 'Mr Braddock! Mr Braddock!' he called, but the man did not hear or could not, for the wind, which was against him.

Just behind, Peter shouted, 'Mr Braddock! It's me, Peter.'

And the man turned. It was not Charlie Braddock but Harry Leach, the science teacher. 'Hello, Peter,' he said, stopping, and turning to him, still clamping his hat down on his head. 'What can I do for you?'

Peter stood shaking, panting and disappointed. He shook his head.

'Are you all right, Peter? You don't look well.'

Peter looked back at the school and then his head went down, as if he had been defeated.

'Is there anything I can do to help?'

Peter said nothing for a moment and then, with a sigh of resignation, 'No. No, thank you, Mr Leach. I don't think you can. It's Mr Braddock I need to see.'

'I think he went home, Peter. See him tomorrow. There's a good lad. Well, I'll be off now.'

Peter turned and walked back slowly towards the main gate of the school and, reaching it, stopped and surveyed it. Then, crest-fallen, he carried on along the street heading for the Manse.

That evening at tea, Peter was subdued, still struggling with the problem of the security of mathematics, and the almost equal one of why Charlie Braddock had ignored his appeal for help. It was unimaginable and yet it had happened. What did it all mean? Did Charlie not like him any more? Was that it? The sense of rejection sat like a stone on his head.

Jean said, 'How was school today, Roddy? You were late home. Did you do something wrong and get kept in?'

Roddy blushed at what he had done there, and then, desperate, devised a diversion, an activity at which he was becoming adept. 'It was O.K. Charlie read out a letter from Graham McGregor, the Scottish stand-off. It was really good.'

'What did it say?' said John.

'Just that he enjoyed the game on Saturday. But he didn't say anything about scoring two tries. Imagine not saying!'

'Yes, not many people have scored two tries in an international. So what did he say exactly?'

And Roddy had to tell them and, for a moment it allowed him to forget his own trouble, by immersing himself in this wonder of good behaviour who scored two tries in an international and talked about everybody else but himself.

The meal over, the other children having left, Jean, having asked him to stay behind, said, 'Roddy, are you all right?'

'Yes, Mum.'

'Are you sure? You don't look as healthy as usual.'

'I'm OK, Mum,' said Roddy, blushing, 'I feel fine. Honest.'

John said, 'Don't pester the boy, Jean. He looks all right to me.'

But after Roddy had gone, Jean said, 'There's some funny staining in his underpants.'

John laughed. 'It's natural enough. He's past the age of puberty. It's just the sap rising. It has to do that, you know. It just doesn't wait until he's twenty one and ready for marriage.'

'I know. No, it's not that. It's at the other end. That's where the staining comes from. I'm a little worried. What if he's got something wrong with his bowel?'

'There's no blood, is there?'

'Oh, no. Nothing like that. It's just clear staining, if you see what I mean. Not urine. No. I don't know what it can be. I think we should send him to the doctor.'

Next day, with a pair of underpants he had jettisoned the previous evening on getting home, Jean took Roddy to see Dr Telford, who took a swab and said, 'It's probably nothing, but I'll send it off for testing anyway, just to be on the safe side.'

'He's started changing his pants twice a day, Doctor, haven't you Roddy?'

'It's not every day!' the boy exploded.

'You didn't used to do that. It's just recent. That's not normal, is it, Doctor?'

Telford put down his glasses, and looked at the blushing boy before him and said, 'How often do you change twice a day, Roddy?'

The boy blushed more, if that were possible, and said nothing.

'Come on Roddy!' said Jean, but Roddy would say nothing. Plainly it was all too embarrassing for him. 'It's about three times a week, Doctor,' said Jean, thoughtfully.

'Is that right, Roddy?'

'I don't know,' said the boy.

'You mean it's only three times a week you do this?' said Telford. 'Why don't you do it every day?'

Again, Roddy appeared to have lost the power of speech so that Jean lost her temper. 'Come on, Roddy! Don't waste the doctor's time. Speak up!'

Sounding aggressive, yet frightened, as if he were being assaulted by them, he said, 'I just feel like it sometimes, that's all.'

'Does that mean you don't have staining every day, then? It's just a few times a week?'

'I don't know.'

'Uch, Roddy, why can't you be consistent!' said Jean. 'You must know! You change when you've had staining, don't you?'

Roddy, red-faced at being caught in a lie, said nothing.

'It must be uncomfortable,' said Dr Telford, finally. 'Well, leave it for it now. Come and see me in a couple of weeks. The results will be in by then.'

That night, Jessica could not sleep. There was a sense of deep unease in the family, as if it were members of a rugby scrum drifting away to the far corners of the pitch. Long after midnight, she got up, sat down at the desk and switched on the table light. Slowly and deliberately, she took a sheet of paper from a pile, picked up the cherished fountain pen, and, with a lost expression on her face, looked out of the window into the dark, and then bent her head to write.

> Moonlight, moonlight warm and clear
> Fills the night air far and near.
> Darkness, darkness, that's near too,
> Split spirits roam abroad anew.
> Minds divided, hearts on fire,
> Family strength drained entire.
> Father, mother and children dear

Opposed by doom-laden far flung fear
Bind them, bind them, bind them here.

At nine o'clock next day, Peter met Charlie in the corridor at school. 'Sir, I need to talk to you. Can you spare me a minute?'

'Of course, Peter. I'll tell this class to get on with something and we'll talk.' Charlie went off, leaving Peter standing, went into room 18 and soon came out again, closing the door. 'Now what seems to be the trouble?'

'I've been reading about the Philosophy of Mathematics in the Encyclopaedia. It says that Euclidean Geometry is flawed because of the Parallel Postulate and that Russell's attempt to derive Mathematics from Logic failed. Some of the axioms he had to put in to make it work were unacceptable. Then there's this problem with Set Theory Paul Cohen discovered. Apparently there are two contradictory versions of Set Theory and both are equally valid.' Peter suddenly broke down, bent over, and wept. 'It means that Mathematics is no good, sir, doesn't it?'

'Calm yourself, Peter,' said Charlie. 'It's not that bad! The fact that no one has proved Mathematics to be true doesn't mean that no one will. I think it can be done. It's too wonderful a subject not to be true. I mean'— Charlie's face lit up as if with sunlight, shining from within, and one or two others who were passing stopped to observe and listen—'I mean, Mathematics works so very well! If it didn't work we would have abandoned it long ago, wouldn't we? And it is beautiful, isn't it? We agree on that, I know. So how could it not be true? How can something that beautiful and wonderful and useful not be true? Think of how important Mathematics has been in helping man to create better technology to save life, to prolong life and make it more comfortable for everybody. There are people going into hospitals today who would have died years ago, if it hadn't been for advances in Medical Science and these would be impossible without Mathematics. Life expectancy used to be about thirty; now it's seventy. Think of the millions of extra years that people can enjoy to be alive and well. Isn't that wonderful?'

Peter had stopped weeping, straightened himself, and said, 'So you think it's all right, sir? Oh, thank god!'

'Maybe that should be your research topic. To establish beyond a shadow of a doubt that Mathematics is valid.'

Peter's eyes shone suddenly. 'Do you think that's possible, sir? Do you really think I could do it?'

'I'm quite sure you can try but it will be very difficult. If Bertrand Russell couldn't manage it, it will take a bit of doing, but maybe the world wasn't ready then. Maybe it is now. Maybe out there, in some book written since 1910, is an article or a mathematical device which you will find, and be able to use to to make it work. Who knows? Maybe you'll invent one yourself.'

Peter seemed relieved, delighted and almost convinced. Then he had another objection. 'But what about Gödel's Incompleteness theorems?'

Charlie laughed delightedly. 'So you know about them?'

'What is there to laugh about? It's a disaster! I don't see how anyone can possibly manage to prove that Mathematics is valid.'

'What did Kurt Gödel prove?'

'Gödel showed that any system of knowledge simple enough to include elementary Arithmetic was either inconsistent or incomplete.'

'What's wrong with that?'

'I don't believe it! How can it be true? I mean, if you have a few axioms like one plus one equals two, you should be able to derive all the theorems. It *should* be complete.'

'But Gödel showed that it isn't. It's like the liar paradox. What it means is that all knowledge systems like Mathematics must remain incomplete or there will be a loss of consistency. That isn't a disaster. It just means that the world is a good deal more complex than everybody thought. It also means that to prove a system you will have to do it from outside itself.'

Suddenly Peter saw. His eyes lit up. 'So it's not lost after all! Thank God, that's all I can say.'

Soon after, Charlie said he would have to attend to his class, and Peter, gratefully relieved, went off to find his own. In the tension and excitement he neglected to ask Charlie what had been going on behind the locked door of room 18 the previous night.

That evening, on his way to the Kirk Session, John saw a figure lolling on a park bench in the promenade gardens and decided to investigate. The lights lit up the bare flower-beds and, as he approached, John saw that the man was drinking from a bottle. He was of medium size and build, maybe overweight, and the brown raincoat gave him a crumpled, defeated look. By his side was a case and a couple of paper bags. Then John noticed the tie. There was a gap of an inch between the knot and the collar.

'Hello,' said John. 'It's a cold night for sitting out.'

The man said nothing and John decided to sit down beside him. 'You're not from round here, are you?' and when there was no response, he added, 'Just off the boat, are you?'

They sat together for ten minutes and the man said nothing, John trying and utterly failing to get a reply. Every so often, the man would lift the bottle to his lips and take a sip or two, ignoring John, and the temptation to get up and leave was very great. The church meeting would be under way, and this man acted as if he did not want company. But the minister sat on, chatting inconsequentially, hoping to find out his trouble and offer help.

'Have you somewhere to stay for the night?'

Silence.

'Maybe I could take you to a hotel or boarding house and see that you're booked in. How would that do?'

Silence.

'You could freeze to death out here, you know. Maybe I should get the police. They would help you. Give you a cell to sleep in and some hot food. At least they might, if you've no money.'

Silence.

'Did you ever have any trouble with the police?'—trying to provoke a reaction.

Silence.

Deliberately, John began to float ideas in front of the man's mind, hoping he would reach out and make a connexion. 'Ever been to Ottersay before?'

Silence.

'It's a nice place—beautiful on a good day. The finest scenery in the world, I expect. Mind you, I haven't been anywhere much really. On holiday once in Paris. Then there was the war—I was in the desert myself. Then Normandy. I missed out Italy because of a wound. What about you? I was in the Seaforths. Were you ever in the services?'

Silence. Silence all round, as John waited.

'All the Seaforths came from the north. I'm from there myself. Elgin. Where did you say you were from?' John's eye fell upon the case which stood beside the seat between them. There were labels on it but not enough light to see them clearly. Was there a name on the case? A lot of people put their initials on them.

John pretended to change the position of his feet carelessly and, as if by accident, kicked the case, which fell to one side. The man did not move, and, bending to pick it up, John said, 'Sorry, foolish of me.'

In the half-light from the street-lamps, he could just make out the initials F.X.W. and a half-torn sticker that said, 'Espagna'. 'Ah, you've been in Spain, then?'

Silence.

'I was there once, after the war. Just a few days, but I went to a bull-fight. Did you ever do that? I know it's barbaric and cruel, but there was something magnificent in it. The matador all alone in that vast space and the bull ready to tear him with its horn and toss him, and the crowd, the awful people, ready to boo if he doesn't do well. It's all about courage really, isn't it? The matador I saw was only sixteen—his first bout—and the leading men before had failed, so everybody was restive. There was a danger of it degenerating into a farce. And then this boy walked on. You could see he was scared—terrified. The sweat ran down his face in rivulets. And as the bull charged, he actually shook in front of our eyes, but you knew he wouldn't flinch. Whatever happened he wasn't going to let us down.

'Well, the bull came on like a Sherman tank, only quicker, and, just at the last moment, the boy took a half-step to one side, and the monster went roaring past, missing him by a whisker. And the crowd gasped with amazement. And then it charged again, and again the boy moved out of the way just in the nick of time, and, gradually, very gradually, that boy gained control, and eventually the bull was running at him in short bursts, and every time it just about connected, the boy would disappear in a swirl of cape and the bull would have to turn again.

'Finally, the bull tired, and its head went down, and the boy made a sudden lunge and stabbed it between the shoulders, so that the sword went right in. It sank to the ground and expired.'

In the silence, the man turned and looked at him for the first time, waiting for more. John said, 'There was something beautiful about it, in spite of the smell of blood and death. It was a triumph of the human spirit. The boy reminded everyone present what it was to be a man. What courage is and skill too, and patience and stamina and strength of mind. It was a celebration of man's victory over the environment and the animals that might have killed him; that he had conquered a larger and more powerful and dangerous beast and survived; for the game was about life itself.'

Even in the darkness, John could make out the softness and hurt in the man's eyes. Then, with a sudden flash of insight, it dawned on him that maybe this man had come to Ottersay to die. There was a look of death about him. Was he quite well?

John waited, and presently the man said, 'I was never in Spain. I stole this case. I was never even in the war. I was too feart. I managed to get a reserved occupation; a job that needed somebody. So I was a fire-man in Glesga.'

'That must have been difficult.'

'For some folks. No' for me. Ah always looked after number one. Last in, first out. Ah even left a woman dyin' and didnae help her. Would you credit that? She was lying under a pile o' rubble and I could hear her moans. Not very plain but just. And Ah could see all the blood and guts and Ah couldnae face it, so Ah came away. And when one of the men says, 'Is it clear ower there?' Ah says, 'Aye, it's clear.' And we buggered aff. The woman must have died because a me. Am Ah no' jist a rat? A rotten bugger? And you know? The funny bit is, Ah spent my hale life takin' care tae stay outa trouble and see what happens? Ah get this pain in ma guts and the quack says it's cancer. See me? Ah'm fur the high jump. That's why Ah'm drinkin'.' The man raised the bottle to his lips and took a swig.

'Why did you come here?'

'Tae get away from where Ah wis. Ah thought Ah might just feenish aff here.'

'What about a place to stay?'

'Ah havenay got wan.'

'Have you any money?'

'No' much. No' enough.'

'Maybe I could find you lodgings somewhere?'

'Who would take me in? Ah'm jist a broken-doon wreck. Ah'm no' worth the trouble. You know, when you were telling me about you in the war? Ah goat the idea you were a war-hero. You were, weren't ye?'

'No, I was just an ordinary soldier,' said John, knowing that the truth would only create an undesirable distance between them. Anyway, he never spoke of it, if it was avoidable. No thinking man could take pride in any activity of war; there was always too much suffering. Enough that he had survived. Sometimes, even that seemed an unwanted miracle.

'Well, Ah'm surprised. Ah thought you were. Then this boy. He was a hero, wasn't he?'

'Yes, but we can't all be heroes. The world is run by all the ordinary folk. We're all weaklings really. Some are just lucky that's all.'

'But look at me! What a failure! Ah've never done anythin' at all except run, keep out the way. And now it's gone. In a few months Ah'll be ....out of it.'

As the beginnings of a tear formed in the man's eyes, John said, 'Will you come with me and I'll find you somewhere to stay?'

'Ah havenay any money. All Ah've goat's a few bob. No' enough to stay anywhere. Ah spent my last few quid on drink.'

'Well, you better come home with me, then. But first we'll go to a meeting I have to attend.'

The man seemed so downhearted that John offered to carry the case, and there was no objection. As they walked together through the lighted streets of the town, John pointed out the shops and the sights, as if he were a tour guide. Outside the church, he said, 'Come in,' and the man entered, and then John, leaving him just outside the vestry, opened the door on a scene of violent argument. He stood, looking at them, with the down-at-heel man behind, and there was a hush.

'Sorry I'm late. I met a man who needs help. I'm glad to find you all still here. You might have some suggestions about where he might stay.'

Silence descended upon the room like a wet blanket.

Sensing trouble, John turned to the man and took him next door, where he lit the gas fire and asked him to wait. Once outside the room, the hubbub restarted and then, as he returned to it, silence fell again.

Tom Henderson cleared his throat. 'I'm afraid, minister, there has been a proposal that you be asked to resign.'

'I think you'd better explain,' said John.

Tom seemed embarrassed and looked round as if seeking help. When no one said anything, he said, 'There's talk about you and Madeline Grant.'

John waited and when nothing further came, he said, 'Well, speak up. What kind of talk?'

'You were seen in a compromising position with her. She was half-naked and you were ...You were just about to have relations with her.'

'And who is supposed to have seen this?'

'Jack Johnstone.'

'You mean the man they call Sniffy?'

'Yes. He says you broke his camera. He threatened to charge you with assault. I had to put him off, but he thinks you should resign. If not, he intends to press charges.'

'Is that all? A man—a known peeping Tom—goes about carrying a camera—isn't that suspicious? What kind of folk go around looking in windows with cameras? Does it not occur to you to wonder what his game was?'

'He said he was employed as a detective and his client's name is confidential.'

'A likely tale for a peeping Tom.'

'That's not all,' said George. 'You've lost five thousand pounds to the church funds. Mrs Arbuthnott-Snell offered it to you, and when you turned her down, she left St Margaret's and joined St Bruoc's.'

'And why did she do this?'

'Because you were rude to her. She wanted to buy something for the church and you wanted her gift to pay for salaries like your own.'

'That is a lie. She never offered five thousand. It was fifty, and she was the one who was rude. She wanted me to jump to her bidding and kept me waiting. In spite of it, I was nothing but polite to her. She wanted to buy a flashy thing for the church which she could point to and say: this is mine, my benefice. The kinds of things she was prepared to pay for were more suited to a Catholic church.'

George said, 'What about your heresy? You told the Philosophical Society you didn't believe in a personal God. A lot of folk are saying you're an atheist.'

'I am a believer and follower of Jesus. He and God are one and the same. The difference is semantic, has arisen in another time and place and culture which saw things very differently.'

'What about the Holy Trinity? God, Jesus and the Holy Ghost?'

'They are all the same thing because there can only be one God.'

'But that's not what the church teaches.'

'Some ministers try to make out that Jesus is a kind of second rate God, I grant you that. I can't be held responsible for other ministers' confusions.'

'Do you believe in the virgin birth?' said Calum Smith.

'I believe that Mary was impregnated by a man like every woman who's pregnant.'

There was a sharp intake of breath from Calum.

'Oh, you don't agree, Calum? Would you mind telling me how she managed to conceive, then?'

Calum said nothing.

'You don't know, do you? Does it not make more sense to believe in things that are credible? That they happen in *The Bible* the same way as they happen here and now? Anyway, what does it matter how Jesus came into the world? The fact is he did. I believe that. And we are Christians because we follow his teachings.'

George said, 'But *The Bible* says it was a divine act! That a man was not involved.'

'It was a divine act; it produced a divine man. But it was done by a man. How could it have happened otherwise?'

'But *The Bible* says it did!'

'*The Bible* was written by men. That is the trouble precisely. And, in an age of miracles, they wanted it to seem miraculous. Don't you see, it would sell far better if it was wrapped up in a miracle or two?'

'Are you calling them liars?'

'No. I expect they really thought it was a miracle. The point is, that they had to think it was a miracle. Otherwise, in that society, it was nothing, worthless.'

'But Jesus spoke about God as his father, as a person,' said Bob Forsyth. 'How can you say he's not?'

'In those days they believed in living spirits. It was natural to think of God as a person. Nowadays we don't believe in ghosts and all that stuff. And we see God as a kind of influence for good.'

Bob said, 'But isn't God the creator of all things like The *Bible* says?'

'You mean you believe that God pressed a button one day, and caused an explosion and the bits flew everywhere, and one of them landed here; and he flicked his fingers, and suddenly folk like you and me were walking about? And just to keep us company, he gave us animals and fish as well—except some of them ate us—and he planted trees and crops, so we could become vegetarians?'

There was a silence.

'There's too much evidence against that sort of thing. We can't ignore Astronomy and Darwin's Theory. Genesis just isn't true. So why should anyone believe it?'

Henderson said: 'But it says in Genesis, that the world was made in seven days.'

'That's all a metaphor, Tom. You must see that. How can it be anything else?'

'You think the folk that wrote it made it up then?'

'No. I think they wrote it that way, because that was how they thought. It was written at least six centuries before Christ. They couldn't think the way we do now, with all the advantages of knowledge, in between.'

John looked round at them and saw only shock.

Terry Macleod, white-headed and kilted, said in his Skye sing-song, 'But Mr Manson, we need a creator! God's the creator. You canna do without him! How did it all get here?' There was a genuine distress in Terry, that made John feel and sound compassionate.

'God *is* the creator—in a sense. He is the influence for good that makes every good thing possible, that makes progress.'

'But who made us? The earth? An influence for good couldna manage it just.'

'I don't think anybody made it, if you mean the nuts and bolts of it. I think the universe has always existed, and our wee bit has come together under gravity, and thermonuclear reactions have been set up by the heat generated, when bodies come together fast. The heat's caused by kinetic energy.'

Ellen MacFadyean said, 'But how can you read Genesis from the pulpit, and give sermons on it and things like the Virgin Birth, when you don't believe in them?'

'I don't often use Genesis. I try not to offend people, because I know some of them do believe in things that are unbelievable—things they shouldn't believe! I try to make them see things more clearly. You see, there's no point in letting folk go on believing in things that are not true. If we pretend that they are, we lose all the young folk and, if we do that, the church will just die, because there will be nobody left. We have a duty to keep up to date. It's the only way we can bring in the young and the only way to keep the church in good health.'

Terry said, 'But Christianity canna be brought up to date! *The Bible* says how its meant to be!'

'No, Terry. *The Bible* is man-made, written thousands of years ago, by ignorant men, in a different world, who saw everything differently. We have the discoveries of science. They change everything. So many things are explained now. We don't need these unbelievable ideas in *The Bible*.'

'Are you saying *The Bible* is wrong, then?' said George.

'No, I am saying it's not literally true. But it is metaphorically true.'

'But the resurrection?' said Bob Forsyth, 'Do you believe Christ rose from the dead?'

'It doesn't matter whether Jesus rose from the dead! Can't you see that? We don't need it, so why have it? It makes no difference to what Jesus taught us, whether he rose from the dead or not.'

'But it's the foundation of the Christian faith!' said George. 'Everything depends on it.'

'Not so! The Christian faith depends on the personality of Jesus. Nothing else. In signing up as Christians, we agree to follow his teaching. If the folk who spent years and thousands of pounds trying to prove that Jesus rose from the dead had any sense, they would have ignored the issue, and spent all that energy doing good in the real world. That's what Jesus himself would have done! Don't you see that? Do you think he would have wanted anyone to waste time trying to prove he was divine, when there was so much more good they could do right here and now? Of course not! Jesus is the ideal man with the right priorities. All that mumbo-jumbo adds nothing to his teaching.'

Bob said, 'But Jesus believed in God as a different person, and heaven as a place he was going to.'

'The men that wrote the gospels said this, right enough. That doesn't make it true. It's what they would think he said, given their beliefs in spirits and magic. But even if it is, if he said that, it just goes to show that Jesus was not perfect, that he made mistakes. So what? There is no contradiction in thinking of him as divine and of him misunderstanding the nature of himself.'

'This is blasphemy! Jesus is perfect,' said George.

"Not so! On the cross, Jesus said, 'Eli, Eli, lema sabachthani! My God, my God, why have thou forsaken me?' Do you know what that means? That Jesus didn't understand what he was there for at all! He wasn't forsaken! If the God of The Old Testament existed, if all the literal stuff is true after all, then Jesus didn't know what he was about! For, to bring about good in the world, it was essential that he should die in that way. If Jesus understood, he should have been the last person on earth to say those words.'

'But you believe Jesus went to heaven, surely?' said Ellen, almost in tears.

'After he died, Jesus is supposed to have met two men on the Emmaus Road. Do you know what's wrong with that? None of the gospels will tell you what they spoke about, or where he went afterwards. Don't you think they would have known? Those men would have told everyone, and it would have been remembered. Doesn't that strike you as odd? The same with the Ascension. The accounts in the Gospels differ and they are very hazy about an event that most of the disciples saw. There is something very far wrong with that. It just doesn't add up.'

'But what does it mean? What are you saying?' said Ellen, tearfully.

"That years after the event, a few men wrote it up, and tried to make it cohere by 'remembering' things that never occurred. Not deliberately. At least, not all the time. No, the Gospels are fabrication. There can be no doubt of it. But the point is, it doesn't matter! What does matter is the personality of Jesus, and the insights he gave, in the Sermon on the Mount, like 'Love thy neighbour.' That's why Jesus is worth following."

'What about an afterlife?' said Dr Telford.

'I don't know about that. I know Jesus promised us there is one, but I'm beginning to think that, too, was metaphor.'

'So what are you doing when you perform a burial?'

'Giving comfort to the bereaved. That's my job. I give them hope and try to ease their pain.'

'But you don't believe there is an afterlife?' said the doctor.

'I don't think you go anywhere, if that's what you mean. There's no heaven up there in the sky. We know that now, after discoveries in Astronomy.'

'So what hope is there?'

'The fact that Jesus gave us hope. That's all there is. But it is useful, a comfort, whether there is any real hope or not.'

'Do you mean when we die, that's it?' said Dick Souter.

'Maybe the soul goes somewhere.'

'But you don't think so?' said Souter.

'No, I think the soul stays right here among the survivors. It's part of their memory and it does still influence them. That's immortality of a kind.'

Henderson said, 'Well, minister I think you should leave us, while we deliberate further.'

'Before I go, I would like help with this man I have here with me. I found him on a park bench. I don't think he's any money, and he says he's dying of cancer. Can anyone suggest where he might go?'

There was a silence.

'I'll do it myself, then.' As he reached the door, John turned and added, 'You see, that's what Christianity is really about. The here and now, not the before or the hereafter. It's about doing good in this world, not bothering about the next.' Then John laughed. 'We can't do anything about the next world. It'll come soon enough. All we can do, is do our best in this one. I just wish you'd remember that.'

After John left, George said, 'Well, that's pretty conclusive. He's an atheist, and a fornicator and he's rude to the gentry. What more do we need? He should go.'

'I don't agree,' said Telford. 'He's a very good man.'

'Good, is it?' said George. 'He was late for this meeting. It's not the first time either. He was nearly an hour late! He doesn't give a damn for us, or this church either.'

Nobody said anything, the man dying of cancer being forgotten, in the surge of controversy about John Manson.

'I don't think we should have an atheist for a minister,' said Ellen MacFadyean, wiping her eyes with a handkerchief. 'It doesn't make sense. I thought he believed.....believed what we all believe, what we're supposed to believe.'

'Do you believe in the Virgin Birth, Ellen?' said Telford.

'Yes.'

'Why? It's very improbable, isn't it? Impossible even. Maybe John's right. Maybe it doesn't matter.'

'Of course it matters!' said George angrily. 'You can't join the church unless you believe these things. He doesn't. How did he ever get in the door? How did he get ordained with beliefs like that? He's been acting a lie all these years, and it should be stopped.'

'Maybe he's just changed,' said Telford, calmly. 'Maybe he has come to a new understanding. We should ask him. It all sounds pretty reasonable to me, even if it is heretical.'

At the Manse, John took the man's coat and hung it, with his own, on the hallstand, and then led him, in frayed green Harris-tweed jacket and dirty grey flannels, into the sitting-room, and introduced him to Jean, who was at the fire-side, mending socks. 'Make yourself comfortable, while I put a glass in your hand.'

'John didn't give your name, foolish man that he is,' said Jean, when he had gone out to the study.

'I'm Jock Black,' said the man easing himself into the chair, leaving the suitcase at his side.

When John returned, Jean excused herself, and went upstairs to see to the problem of accommodation. 'Peter,' she said, knocking the door and opening it, 'You'll have to share with Roddy. I'll send him in.'

'Aw, mother! Not again! Don't tell me Dad's found another stray.'

'Enough of that. It's a poor man who's not well, by the looks of him. There's no choice. You know we have to take him in. Would you leave him to walk the streets at night?'

A few minutes later, Roddy, already in pyjamas and half-asleep, crept into Peter's room and occupied the camp-bed Jean had just set up.

'There's nothing to worry about, Mrs Manson,' said Dr Telford, in the surgery, the next day. 'The boy's quite clear.'

Jean was sitting on a chair in front of Telford's old desk with Roddy standing beside her.

'Oh, that's a relief, Doctor. What was the staining?'

Roddy blushed, and Telford looked at the boy over the top of the half-moon specs and said, 'Why don't you read a magazine in the waiting room, Roddy, while your mum and I have a wee chat?'

When Roddy had gone, Telford said, 'They're so embarrassed at his age. You forget how it was. Well, Mrs Manson, it's just normal. That's the age they're at, you know. Semen it was, that's all.'

Jean sat listening in silence, digesting this, for a moment, as Telford tried to explain. 'All boys do it. It's a preparation for intercourse later.'

'But the staining wasn't at the front, Doctor, it was at the behind. You saw it yourself.'

Telford thought for a moment and said, 'Yes, so it was. I hadn't thought of that.' Then, after more reflection, he concluded, 'Maybe he wipes himself there for some reason. How can we tell? And he'll never be able to talk about it.'

Jean was not happy. 'Peter was never like this. At the front, sometimes, but never at the bottom. I don't know what to make of it. I just feel something's wrong. I wish I could put my finger on it.'

'It's quite natural, I assure you, Mrs Manson. Some boys have far more emissions than this.'

At the edge of consciousness, someone was talking. In the dream, Charlie Braddock, in his university-degree-robes, the hood of green silk with a white ermine border, that swept back over the black-gowned shoulders— Charlie was smiling, radiant, addressing an audience of some kind, of which he, Peter, was a member in the front row. And Miss Morrison stepped up on to the stage, dressed in nothing but a suspender belt and stockings. The image of the pert breasts which jiggled as she moved, and the black bush at the crotch, made Peter moan and clutch the hardness, as if it were altogether too much of a burden to bear.

There was talking, a babble of talk. Suddenly, Peter was awake.

The room was in darkness, but, through the curtain, a pale glimmer of light allowed him to see faintly. A noise made him look at Roddy's bed, and he saw the boy sitting bolt upright, staring straight ahead. The eyes were round and prominent, and from the mouth came a babble of meaningless sounds, like words but not words. Presently, the boy fell back as if pole-axed by the effort, and a moment later he was fast asleep, as if he had never been anything else.

At the breakfast table in the morning, between munchings of toast and eggs, Peter said with a smile, 'Oh, little brother was behaving strangely last night.'

There was a silence and Roddy blushed.

Peter laughed and turned to him. 'You sat up straight and started talking nonsense. First example of somebody speaking in tongues I ever saw.'

Everyone laughed, except Jessica, Roddy and Jock, who laughed at nothing.

John said, 'Was there a hint of the languages?'

Peter laughed. 'No. Just gibberish.'

'Do you feel all right, Roddy?' said Jean, connecting it with her other worries.

'I'm all right, Mum.'

At the interval, Jessica visited the school office and, from the timetable displayed outside, learned where Roddy's class would be, last period in the day. Then, after her own class had been registered for the last time, just before the four o'clock bell, she excused herself early and went to stand in the assembly hall within sight of room 10. Soon, the children marched out in straight lines, overseen by the commanding figure of Miss Tate.

Last of all, as if he had no wish to leave the sanctuary of the geography room, came Roddy. Without seeing Jessica, he headed along the west corridor, and trudged up the stairs, Jessica following. Having established from the sound of feet and the slammed door, that he entered number 18, the maths room occupied by Charlie, Jessica retraced her steps and made for the music room on the ground floor of the east wing.

Half an hour she played, half an hour of engrossed concentration, while she surrendered her soul to the genius of Bach, and at the end, before

Miss Carmichael said anything, Jessica said, 'I wonder if I might go off early? There's something I'd like to do.'

'Of course. You deserve a rest. You've been working like a navvy. The piece is faultless. I think you've made tremendous progress in the time. But the competition is only a fortnight away, remember, so you'll have to keep at it. That's the ticket. Do your scales with great care every day, and play your pieces as if they were your one outlet for emotional expression.'

In the hall, at the foot of the stairs, was Billy Buchanan. 'You're early,' he said.

'I know. There's something I want to do. So I came out early. Would you mind not seeing me home today?'

'No, of course not. So long as it's not because of me. I'm not in your bad books am I?'

'No, nothing like that.'

Jessica hung around, and as she made no move, neither did Billy. 'Could I not stay and help? If you're going to wait, I mean.'

'Well, I'd rather you just went today. I need to wait for somebody.'

Billy was crest-fallen. 'I see. Another bloke, eh?'

'No, nothing like that. It's my wee brother. I think something's the matter.'

'Maybe I could keep you company then. How about it?'

'If you must, you must.'

'Where is he?'

'In Charlie's room. I'm going to stand at the end of the corridor and keep an eye on Roddy.'

As they moved across the assembly hall to watch the corridor, Billy said, 'What's it about?'

'I don't know. I just have a feeling that something's bothering him.'

Billy suddenly blushed and blurted out: 'You don't think Charlie's a homo, do you?'

'No, why should I?'

'There's been talk, that's all.'

'What kind of talk?'

'Just that Charlie was taking a shower with one of the boys.'

'You mean in the gym? After a rugby match?'

'Yes, something like that.'

'Well, so what? Charlie must get muddy and sweaty too, when he's refereeing. Who was the boy?'

'I don't know. I didn't pay attention. But I think it was a first year. All I know is that Charlie and the boy were still in the shower, after everybody else left.'

When Roddy appeared, he blushed as soon as he saw them.

'Doing extra maths?' said Jessica, moving off alongside him.

'Yes,' said Roddy, dragging his briefcase as if it were a dead weight.

'I suppose you're gonny be a mathematical genius like Peter, eh?' said Billy, enviously.

'I don't think so.'

'Why do you go, then?' said Jessica. 'Are you backward? No you can't be. You were always good at maths. Good at everything aren't you?'

'I don't know,' said Roddy, dolefully.

As they walked down the steps beside the boy's playground past the rhododendrons, Billy cast a sideways glance. 'When I was in first year I got flung into these. Nearly broke my neck. I never saw you get treated like that. I wonder why it is some folk get all the trouble.'

'Who did it to you?' said Jessica.

'The second and third years,' said Billy. 'It was an initiation ceremony, so they said. But they were just taking it out on us because it happened to them. They seemed to enjoy it, that was the awful bit.'

'Did none of your lot get it?' said Jessica to Roddy.

'Most did. They hadn't cut the branches then, so it wasn't so bad.'

Jessica said, 'Did you hear about Charlie in the shower, with one of the first years?'

Roddy said nothing. But Jessica knew from the red face that it was him.

At the Manse, Roddy immediately ran upstairs, and Jessica heard him close the bedroom door.

Once Billy had been sent home on the pretext that Jessica could 'do some music practice', she went into the kitchen where Jean was preparing the tea.

'Roddy has been doing extra maths. That's why he's late every day.'

Jean turned from the sink to look at her. 'Oh? He never said. It's not like him.'

Jessica waited, but when there was no development, she said, 'There's also a story going about, that Charlie took a shower with one of the first years, after the rugby.'

'I suppose there's not enough showers,' said Jean, cutting the potatoes into thick slices.

'Roddy was the one in the shower and he's very unhappy. I've never seen him so down.'

'Well, how would you like stories circulating about you?' Jean suddenly put down the knife and turned to face Jessica. 'You mean?...'

Jean dried her hands. 'Go and bring Roddy to the study,' she said, marching off to the sitting-room, where John and Jock were playing chess. 'Can I have a word?'

In the study, John sat down at the desk and Jean on the edge of an armchair. 'I think I know what the staining is. It's Charlie Braddock's...' and she told her suspicions.

When he appeared, the boy was like one ready for execution. The head was held low, so that the dark hair fell over the brow. Behind him, Jessica closed the door and stood with her back to it.

Calmly and affably, John said: 'Were you playing rugby yesterday afternoon?'

The boy nodded.

'Did you take a shower afterwards?'

Again there was a barely perceptible nod.

'Did Charlie Braddock take a shower?' said John.

The boy seemed to shrink. Then he nodded.

'He took a shower with you, didn't he?' shouted Jean.

John got up and took her by the shoulders. 'Enough of that. You go and make the tea. I'll bet it's burning.' Jean made no move to leave. Jessica went out to the kitchen to check on the cooking, and soon returned, John having resumed his seat.

'Did Charlie do anything to you in the shower?'

'No,' said the boy, blushing.

'Are you quite sure?' said Jean, taking him by the arm and turning him to face her.

'Of course.'

'So Charlie Braddock shared your shower,' said John, 'but he didn't do anything?'

'Yes.'

John sighed with relief.

Jean said, 'What did Charlie do in the shower?'

'Just washed the mud off his legs. Otterhall was mucky. It had been raining.'

'Well, there's no harm in that, is there?' said John. 'A man's got to wash himself, for heaven's sake.'

'Are you sure, Roddy? Are you sure he didn't do anything to you?'

'Yes, Mum. I'd know wouldn't I?'

In the silence, the tension eased until Jessica said, 'I don't believe it.'

Every eye turned on her. 'What do you mean?' said John, 'Roddy's just told you. Isn't that enough?'

Jessica stood looking at Roddy levelly, and he burst into tears. He said, 'I've told you! Nothing happened in the shower! Why won't you believe me?'

'Because something's troubling you, Roddy,' said Jessica. 'Something's wrong. So wrong.'

'You're the one that's wrong! You always think you're so right! I told you. Nothing happened in the shower.'

'Then it happened somewhere else, didn't it?' said Jessica. 'Was it in his room, Roddy? Is that where it happens?'

The boy fell down on his knees, sobbing as if his last day had come.

John said, 'Did he do something to you in his room, Roddy?'

When there was no answer, John lifted him up and made him look him in the eye, but the boy shut his eyes in a very red face. Jean sat down and the tears came flowing down her cheeks.

'Look, son. I need to know,' said John. 'Did Charlie Braddock do something to you or not?'

'No, Dad. Honest. Nothing happened.'

'Well, thank God for that!' said John. 'Now we can go back to being normal.' Again the tension eased, until John said, 'Why did you take so long to tell us?'

Jessica said, 'Because he didn't like to tell a lie. That's it, isn't it, Roddy? Charlie Braddock's been putting himself inside you, hasn't he?'

The boy burst into renewed sobbing, and Jessica went over to him, grasped him by the shoulders, and comforted him. 'It's better to tell, Roddy. It really is. It's not your fault. It's not. Even if you think it is. It's all Charlie's fault. He shouldn't have taken advantage of you.'

'Is this true, Roddy?' said John. 'Tell me! I need to know.'

But the boy could say nothing for tears and sobs which burst out of him like uncontrollable waves. Then Jean got up and sat him down and dried his eyes. 'Now I want to know. Once and for all. Is it true? Did Charlie do something to you?'

'Yes!' said the boy, between sobs.

'You're quite sure?' said John.

'Yes.'

'How often does it happen?' said Jessica. 'Is it every time you go?'

'Nearly every time.'

'And he does it to you. That's why there's staining?'

'Yes.'

Dressed in jeans and sweater, Peter, who was late for dinner, immediately noticed the silence and general air of catastrophe, as soon as he sat down. 'What's up? Anyone would think there had been a death in the house.' Then he laughed, as he picked up knife and fork and set to.

For a couple of minutes, nothing was said, as everyone pretended to be engrossed. Then Jessica said, 'He'll have to be told, Daddy.'

'I know. Peter, I have some bad news for you. Roddy's been taken advantage of at school.'

'Huh? What do you mean?'

John put his hand on Roddy's, comfortingly. 'I need to tell him, son. Do you understand?'

Face ashen, Roddy nodded.

'Charlie Braddock's been doing things he shouldn't to Roddy.'

Peter let knife and fork drop onto the plate. 'What do you mean?'

'Just what I say. It's been happening after school when he goes for extra maths.'

'I don't believe it! Are you trying to tell me that....' As his voice tailed away, it was as if things unclear before, suddenly made sense. 'So it was you! I tried Charlie's door one day after school and it was locked. I went up the hill and tried to look in the window, but by then the lights were out.'

'When was this?' said John.

'The day I was worried about the foundations of mathematics.'

Peter stood up. 'I don't want any more to eat.' Then he strode out of the room.

'Come back Peter,' said Jean.

'I need to think. This is a disaster. What am I going to do? He's my teacher, for God's sake. I can't manage without him. What am I going to do?'

Three hours later, just as tea was being poured in the sitting-room with the television news blaring out, the sound of a taxi could be heard at the front gate. 'I wonder who that can be?' said John, getting up to go to the front door, which he opened, to discover two figures staggering up the path, in the dark. One, the taller, was Peter.

'What have you been up to?' said John.

'Pi equals three point one four one five nine two six five three five eight nine seven....'

'Drunk. Drunk as a lord!'

'Oh no,' said Jean, at his back, 'on an empty stomach too!'

'Who's this underneath? Oh, it's you Buce!'

'Aye, John, it's me. For once, Ah'm the wan that's sober.'

'Where did he get the money for drink?'

'Ah'm afraid it's ma fault. Ah stood him a few rounds. He seemed tae need it. Telt me all aboot it. Ah willnay tell a soul. Honest. Ah'm the only wan that knows. Ah hope you don't mind?'

'No, you were very good, Buce. I'm glad to see you looking so well. You'd better come in.'

'No, Ah won't, if ye don't mind. Ah've got a taxi waiting. Ah'll away and see the wife. She'll be amazed to see me sober at this time o' night.'

Next morning, John was up early, awakened by the sound of the letter-box flapping. Among the usual bills, was a pink envelope addressed to himself. The handwriting, in blue ink, sloped backwards. He sniffed it warily. Perfumed too. In the study, with the door closed, he opened it and read:

My Darling John,

I've been thinking about you and longing for you every day since we last met. I feel that fate has brought us together and we can do nothing about it. I know you feel that way too. Who can resist the power of love? So don't waste your strength trying to do the impossible. Come to me again, my darling. I'm waiting for you, keeping it warm for you.

Just in case you're worried about being seen I'll leave the front door unlocked at night and expect you any time. Just walk in, my love, and you'll find me ready and waiting.

I love you ! Oh, I love you desperately, darling.

Please come soon.

Your adoring,

Madeline.

John put down the letter, and the images of Madeline came flooding back into his mind. Madeline naked from the waist down. The dark hair at the crotch with a hint of the space between and the lissom legs of youth, and hips that had never borne children and the flat belly. And the urge was upon him, uncontrollable, like a monster. He groaned under the weight of it and, passing the study, Jean heard. 'Is anything wrong?' she said, putting her head round the door.

'No, no. I'm just thinking about the boy. I'll have to go up to school this morning of course.'

'Right. I'll give you a full breakfast. Are you taking him with you?'

'Yes, it's better that way. He'll only fret if left to himself. He should carry on as usual. What's the point of him missing classes?'

'Just so long as there's no extra maths.'

John dropped the letter on the desk, drew the roll-top over and locked it, as usual, with a key. At quarter past nine, he was sitting in the headmaster's office.

'So what brings you here so early, Minister?' said Phil.

'Bad tidings, I'm afraid. It's about young Roddy. The fact is Charlie Braddock's being taking advantage of him.'

'You're not serious?'

Mulholland thought for a moment. 'It's not this story going about, is it? That Charlie took a shower with the boys? Children are always making up stories about their teachers. And the more unlikely the better.'

'No, it's not that. No, we thought at first it was that, but it was far worse. It's been happening after school in the maths room. Been going on for a while. Jean noticed staining on the boys pants, even took him to the doctor, thinking there was something wrong internally...' John's voice dragged away from the awful image, leaving the Head to see it himself.

'I'll have to talk to Charlie, of course. I'll send for him immediately.' After a short phone call to the janitor, Mulholland sat with hands splayed out on the desk, thinking. Then he said, 'Who else knows about this?'

'The family, that's all. Oh, and two others.'

'Will it get spread about, do you think? It could do a lot of damage to the school.'

'I don't think so. I don't want to harm the school's good name—or Roddy's.'

When Charlie arrived in the room, Mulholland said, 'I think I should see Mr Braddock alone, Minister. Would you mind waiting outside.'

The door closed, Charlie was invited to sit down. 'John Manson says you have been committing homosexual acts with his son, Roddy.'

Charlie was aghast. 'It's not true,' he spluttered. 'How could he say such a thing?'

'He says it's been happening after school in your room, under the pretext of extra maths.'

'Well, I absolutely deny it! It's an outrage!'

'I think you should resign. In fact, I'd like your letter of resignation on my table tomorrow morning. You can take the rest of the day off.'

'But I didn't do anything. What have I got to resign for? I won't resign and I won't take the day off. I've got too many important things to do that won't wait.'

'Are you saying this boy's a liar? That his father's a liar?'

'Yes! Yes! What else can it be? Would I do such a thing? Of course not! I'm the Scoutmaster for heaven's sake. I'm the Head of the Scripture Union as well as Head of Mathematics. I'm a lay preacher, for heaven's sake! How can you imagine that I could.. could take advantage of my position?'

'Calm down, Charlie. You're saying the boy's lying, then?'

'Yes.'

'Do you want to confront the boy here?'

'Yes, I'm sure he'll admit the story is a lie.'

The boy was sent for and, when he and his father were present, Phil Mulholland said, 'Well Roddy, this is a most serious charge you're making against Mr Braddock. You do realise it, don't you? He's one of the most experienced teachers we have here, and one of the best. We're very lucky to have him. If you're telling a lie, it would be most unfair. It could be the end of Mr Braddock's career, you know. That's a very serious thing. He has a wife and a small child. What do you think will happen to them if he loses his job?'

Tears rolled down the boy's ashen face, as he stood holding his father by the hand. He said nothing.

'I don't think this is the right way to go about this,' said John. 'The boy's had enough trouble already without this inquisition.'

'But it wouldn't be fair to Mr Braddock to let the matter go without investigation, would it?'

And John had to concede as much.

Charlie bent down and took Roddy's hands in his and looked into his eyes with an expression of tenderness. 'Tell them it isn't true. Please. Just for me. I'm a good man and you know it. I don't deserve to be treated this way.'

The boy looked away, tears flowing down his face, first to his father and then to the Headmaster.

'I need to know, Roddy,' said Mulholland. 'You need to tell me now.' But Roddy said nothing. The sobs kept coming.

John said, 'Have you been going to Mr Braddock's room after school, Roddy?' And when he said nothing, John added, 'Speak up, now. It's important!'

'Yes.'

'Did Mr Braddock make you take your trousers down?'

'Yes.'

'I did nothing of the kind!' said Charlie.

'Did he put himself inside your body?' said Mulholland.

Silence. John said, 'Come on Roddy, speak up! We need to know! Did he do it to you?'

'Yes.'

Charlie turned away in disgust. 'No! No! This is all lies, all lies!'

'So Mr Braddock had sex with you, Roddy? Is that it?' said Mulholland.

'Yes.'

'How often? Once, twice or what?'

'Often.'

'How many times?'

'I don't know. I didn't count. It was nearly every day.'

'How long has this been going on?'

'Since I came to the Secondary.'

'What have you got to say, Charlie?' said Mulholland.

'It's all lies. All lies! I wouldn't do that to Roddy.'

'I think you can go back to your class, Roddy, for now.'

When they were outside, Roddy said to his father, 'I won't need to go to extra maths any more, now, will I, Dad?'

Inside, Charlie, still standing in front of the headmaster's desk, said, 'It's just his word against mine. It's not true and I won't resign.'

'What if I sack you?'

'I'll sue the school for defamation and unjust dismissal. And I'll win too. It's just his word against mine.'

'The matter will have to go to the Director of Education. I suggest you take the rest of the day off.'

'But I've got lessons prepared, classes to teach.' And Charlie refused. Outside the office, he decided to ignore the suggestion and get on with his job. It was what he lived for, wasn't it? So why not just get on with it?

But the very next class was Peter's. They were waiting for him, and as soon as he saw Peter's downcast expression, he knew the difficulty it would cause. Did the others know? Had there been talk? And immediately Charlie realised that Peter would have said nothing, for it would have reflected badly upon himself, if he had.

Ignoring the class, Charlie began his lesson, transmitting to the blackboard: equation after equation as if they weren't there, as if it was a subject he was teaching and not students. It was analysis again: differential equations, one of Charlie's favourite topics.

At first, it was slow going, as Charlie played himself into the structure of the theory. Gradually the power of the ideas gripped him, he started to speak with enthusiasm, and his face became suffused with radiance, and he heard the gasp when the derivation of the indicial equation was made clear and knew that he was safe. Then, ignoring the narrow confines of the syllabus, he wrote down equations of third and fourth order, each time following with the solution, immediately produced like a magician. And then he checked it quickly by differentiation, so they could see it was so. Finally, he wrote down an nth order differential equation with variable coefficients and asked for its solution. It was the first question he had asked, and he waited without looking at the class. There was a silence and then, with a voice choked with emotion, Peter recited what it would have to be, and, for the first time, Charlie turned and smiled at him, and, to Peter, it was as if God had smiled.

As he left the classroom, Peter was in tears, tears of confusion and tears of admiration, that anyone could teach like that, think like that, with such awesome intelligence. Overjoyed and almost unmanned, that such extraordinary power to solve these sophisticated equations—limitless regiments of them—was now, thanks to Charlie, within his grasp. And yet Charlie was a bugger. Literally and inescapably a bugger. There was no room for doubt. Roddy hadn't wanted to admit it, but he, Peter, knew how it was, for he had seen the locked door, knew he had shouted for help, knew that Charlie had heard him, and even, at that very moment he, Charlie, had been stuffing himself into his little brother's back passage. What did he do it for? Why? When he had a wife and a new baby? It was mystifying. And one half of Peter wanted to go and smash his fist into Charlie's face for defiling his little brother, and the other half wanted to kiss his feet for his intellect, for the riches he had given up that day.

When they had left, Charlie closed the door and sat down at the desk, looking forlornly at the pile of exercise books. At least this period was free. He took out a handkerchief and wiped his perspiring face. And then it hit him. The awfulness of it, the humiliation. What would he say to Rhiannon? His throat became suddenly dry and he swallowed. But Rhiannon would stand by him. He knew it in his soul. She had married him because she had no one else, a plain good-hearted lady from a Welsh valley; and she would never give him up, whatever he did. Somehow, that became clear even before the wedding, for he had not concealed it, it would have been dishonourable; and he was not that. Not that, he told himself aloud. He had told her of his....his infatuation; and his struggles to overcome it; and the Greeks, the noble Greeks. His beloved Euclid, Eudoxus, Apollonius... They would have understood. And she had told him it didn't matter; she would help him.

But there was the lie! He had had to lie again! His head went down, and he covered the bald dome with his hands, and tears came. And he knew he had to lie. There was no escape from it. If he ever told the truth, he was finished. His head came up and he looked around the room at the cases full of books, and his face was gradually infused with joy—joy at the treasures there, and a greater joy still at what he was able to do to promote them properly; for that was a gift, a rare gift, and he possessed it, uniquely. His eye alighted on the certificate on the wall, which announced that Charles Braddock M.A., had won the Smithson Medal for the most outstanding teacher of the year. And then he looked down, and he saw before him the jotter of Roderick Manson, 1A, and he opened it and began to flick through the exercises, and suddenly, like a man newly awake, he noticed for the first time how poor the marks had become. In a frenzied burst of activity, he pulled open a drawer and grabbed a mark book; and then, slowly, deliberately, as if in pursuit of his own crime, he turned to the marks of 1A, and ran his finger along the row at Roddy's name, and then stopped, and gave out a gasp. The unthinkable had happened. It was undeniable, the conclusion as self-evident as Q.E.D after a theorem of Euclid: Roddy, Roddy of the dark hair and lissome limbs had declined under his, Charlie's, teaching! It was shattering.

He had been so taken up with his own love, that he had failed to recognise the effect of it on the boy.

What was it about him? The particular thing. The bodily form? Yes, partly; but not all. It was the innocence, the all-round skill; and then there was the courage. He loved the boy's bravery, for Roddy Manson would tackle anyone, of any size, and devil take the consequences. And Charlie thought back to that match between the quail, a class of 30, and the first year—the whole of the first year, he reminded himself, with astonishment, the biggest and the best of 200 of them. The quali had led for three-quarters of the match by a penalty goal scored by Roddy, after he had been illegally neck-tackled, inches from the first year's line. Oh, a glorious, perfectly-timed, heaven-sent strike, that sent the ball soaring high, high between the posts. And for ages, the younger lads had defended their lead, against every driving assault of a team so much bigger, Roddy himself, constantly in the thick of the battle, a prey to kicking feet and punching fists, too difficult to identify in the mud and press of bodies, squirming and shoving and heaving. And then there had been that last attack, when Roddy was alone, inside his own twenty-five, against two big forwards, who jeered at him as they approached; for the ball carrier only had to draw him and pass. But they were close, too close, and Roddy Manson had driven into the pair of them with an arm round both waists and dragged them down into the muck on top of him. But the ball-carrier, with superior strength, had got to his feet and crawled over the line under the posts. So they had lost after all, but Charlie was jubilant, for it was still a triumph.

And now what had he done? The boy was very able. With help he would be a star. And Charlie had fluffed it, ruined it. Turned the boy from a bright prospect, a potential supernova, into a dead planet without life or enthusiasm, and without that, as Charlie knew better than anyone, there was no hope. As he studied the mistakes being made, really looked at them carefully for the first time, it dawned on him that the spark had disappeared. The writing had become slovenly, the accuracy evaporated in a scrawl, impossible to decipher what figures were which. So how *could* one be accurate? It was a scandal, and he himself was to blame. Had he not been so devoted a lover, he would have seen it, and taken preventive action. How could he have done such a thing? It was unthinkable! He had favoured him too much, and turned a blind eye too often. As his great bald dome came up off the perusal of the books, with a flash of intuitive mathematical insight, he realised that it was too late. Too late for him; but also too late for Roddy. But if he had known the full extent of his own accuracy of perception, he would have acted differently thereafter.

Outside, a cloud moved off, revealing the sun, and rays of light shone into the room, striking the glass of a book case, making of it, for an instant, a mirror in which Charlie beheld the reflection of a tear-stained face under a domed bald pate, surrounded by a dark tonsure. Maybe that was where he should be: a monastery, far from the attractions of young boys.

At five o'clock, Jessica came home with Billy. On the kitchen table was a note from Jean saying she had just gone into town to get some milk, and asking Jessica to put on the potatoes when she came in. As Jessica set about this, Billy excused himself and went off to use the toilet. A little while later, he returned. 'Jessica, there's something wrong. You know that picture in the hall? It's gone.'

Jessica went to look, and found that the picture of the bullfighter had indeed disappeared. 'I wonder where it went?' she said, uncomprehending. 'Maybe it's been stolen. Let's look and see if anything else is missing.'

The door to the study lay ajar, and they went in. The roll-top desk had been forced and the top lay open with its lock broken. Papers were strewn about. 'Somebody has broken this!' said Jessica, who knew that nothing of value would be kept there.

'What about the sitting-room? Or the dining-room? We should look there,' said Billy.

Jessica rushed out and searched every inch, looking for things that might be missing. And there was: the decorated plate her mother was fond of, which hung on the wall of the dining room. And a cupboard door lay open, revealing that some of the glasses had disappeared. She rushed upstairs and opened the door to Peter's room. Nothing. Jock's belongings had gone as if he had never been.

'Isn't that awful!' she said at the foot of the stairs. 'Imagine being taken into a home because you've nowhere to stay, because you've no money, and then, when you feel like it, leaving with every little thing that might be of value.'

John and Jean arrived together, with Roddy, whom John had gone specially to meet at the school-gate, before going off to see another parishioner. When he was told, John immediately strode to the study, and gave it a close inspection.

'Did he get anything?' said Jean.

'He's taken the last of the whisky,' said John, holding up an empty bottle. 'A pity,' he smiled wryly. 'I could have done with a shot right now.'

Jessica laughed. 'You mean, you're not angry?'

'It's not as if there's anything of value in this house.'

'But there's the picture of the bull-fighter,' said Jessica. 'That's gone. And that plate with the Athenian on it that Mum likes. And the glasses.'

'Well, maybe he's trying to tell me something. That I should give up drink.'

'Wha.at about bo.ooks?' said Susan, who had just arrived.

'No need to worry. He's not a reading man.' As John spoke, his eye fell on the roll-top desk. He remembered the war-medals, and soon saw that they were not in the secret compartment. Well, he was better rid of them. He might forget the war more easily. Then he looked at the papers scattered on the desk-top. The pink envelope had disappeared.

His expression changed, and Jessica saw it. 'What's the matter, Dad? Is something important missing?'

'A letter. A letter I got this morning. Now, why would he take that?'

'Who was it from?' said Jean.

'A parishioner.'

Billy declined the offer of tea, saying he had to be home by six, and the manner of it, the red-faced stammering nature of it, convinced John that the letter had been appropriated by him, after the fact. But what could he do? Ask the boy for it? And yet it was important. In the wrong hands, it would do a lot of damage.

As Billy walked down the path and opened the gate, John stood watching him, with a wistful expression on his face. All he had to do was run after the boy, take him by the ear and ask for his letter. But John could not bring himself to do it.

When he read the letter, in the sitting room at Silvertrees, George was ecstatic. 'You've done it, boy! Well done! This is all we need.' He read it aloud joyously, ending with the words: '*I know you feel that way too.*' George chuckled and then got out of the chair and did a little, rather unco-ordinated, dance by himself, waving the letter like a flag, and then read it again and laughed with delight. Then he took Betty, who was standing admiring Billy, and danced around the room with her, beaming and smiling, as she had never seen him.

For the first time in his life, Billy, too, was really happy. His father approved of him, loved him at last! And his mother, too, was proud.

'You think... you think I really did well, Daddy?'

'Oh ho! Yes, you did well, son. Manson's for it now. We'll have him out of here in no time! You wait and see what we'll do to him with this.'

'Do you mean they'll have to leave the island? All of them?'

'Of course, son! Then we can go back to where we were. The business will thrive again.' And marvellous vistas crossed the interior of George's mind. Of five funerals a week. No, ten! There had once been ten! What a profit there was that week! And wills, every week another will, to attend the reading of. And taxis humming back and forth, and the till so full it could hardly contain the money.

'But what about Jessica, Dad? What will become of her?'

George turned away from his internal calculations to look at his son. 'She'll have to go with her father, of course. They'll all be leaving.'

'But Dad! I love Jessica. I want her to stay. I couldn't bear it if she left. Please make sure she stays.'

George stopped dancing and looked at Billy without comprehension. 'I can't.'

'But Dad you could fix it, you know you could.'

'Don't be daft, son. I can't. Once this letter goes the rounds, that's it. Manson's for the chop. And the whole bunch of them will be leaving on the first boat. That's what we've been trying to achieve all along.'

'I haven't been trying to do that,' said Billy, tearfully. 'I thought I was just helping you get a small advantage. I never knew you were going to throw Mr Manson out of the town. I wouldn't have done it if I'd known.'

'There, there, Billy. It's all right,' said Betty, going to comfort him. 'You'll get over it. You'll soon forget the Mansons.'

'No I won't! I won't! They're the best people I know. Far better than any others.'

'Not better than your own parents, Billy? You don't mean that,' said Betty.

'I do! I do! They're worth two of any folk. They're really kind and all they get in return is rottenness. They took in a vagrant who said he was dying, and he stole their things and all they did was laugh.'

'What's good about that, for heaven's sake?' said George, sitting down in a chair by the fire. 'They must be daft.'

'They don't have anything of value. The man stole nothing that would fetch any money.'

George laughed. 'But that's daft! Imagine having nothing worth stealing. What's the good of that? What a useless life of failure, to work for forty years and have nothing to show for it. Well, you're OK my boy. Look at the wealth that surrounds you. We can buy and sell the Mansons ten times over. A hundred times! Yes, and still have money left. That's what success is, Billy. It's having things, having the power to get them.'

Billy sobbed and put his hands over his eyes.

'Come on, Billy, enough of that,' said George, 'these people are worth nothing. Forget them.'

'You're wrong, Daddy. It's the exact opposite. I love that family. I think they're all wonderful. Peter's a great rugby player and a mathematical genius. Did you know he got 100% in his last exam? And Susan. She's the cleverest of them all—even if she has got that awful disease. And Jessica! Oh Daddy! There was never anyone like Jessica. I dream about her all the time. She's.. she's terrific. I'm so lucky knowing her, Daddy. What'll I do without her? What'll I do?'

The boy's misery was so evident that George became serious, and ordered Billy to sit down. 'I don't like the way this conversation's going, Billy. I'm really surprised. Surprised and disappointed. I thought I could depend on you for loyalty. You're my own son, for heaven's sake! The business comes first, Billy. You know that. You've always known that.'

Billy considered this for a moment and then sat up straight and said, 'Dad. I want you to give me back that letter. I should never have taken it. It was unthinkable. I don't know what came over me! It was theft. I'm no better than that tramp that stole the pictures and glasses. Oh Dad! Please let me take it back! Please!'

'I will not, son! Now just you listen to me. Put that out of your mind. All you were doing was a bit of work for your father. You've nothing to reproach yourself with. Nothing. How could you not do what I told you? You have to stick with us. We're your flesh and blood.'

'Give me the letter, Dad. Please.' And Billy held out his hand.

George smacked it with the flat of his right hand, keeping the letter in his left. 'Nothing doing, son. If you go on like this, I'll think you're a traitor. These people are worth nothing, and they're nothing to you, besides your own flesh and blood.'

Billy burst out crying again, but seemed to take hold of himself. Through the tears, he said, 'It's not true! They're everything to me. The finest folk I know. They've all been really kind to me. Even Peter, who thinks I'm not good enough for his sister. Do you know what he did? He came to me at Otterhall and showed me how to do a screw kick to touch. Then he taught me to pass the ball right. And I can do it, Dad. Well, I can do the spin-pass. Maybe I'll learn the screw kick. But they're all good, Dad.

Honest! They really are. How can you want to send them away from here? It's crazy!'

'They have to go, ya nut, because the business will suffer if they don't! Do you know how much money I've lost this month because of Manson? Eh? It's thousands! They have to go, son. And by Christ they will! I'll see to it myself.' And to prove it George waved the pink letter, smiling again.

'But Dad!'

'**But** nothing, Billy. You're a rare wee spy! That was a great piece of secret work. Just like James Bond. You should be proud of yourself. A chip off the old block. What do you say, Betty?'

'If you say so, George.' Betty, worried and uncertain, was still standing in the centre of the room. Billy burst into a renewed bout of sobbing, and his mother went to him and stooped over the arm of the chair to comfort him. 'There, there, Billy. You've done well. There's no need to take it so badly.'

'I'm a Judas, that's what I am. That's what Mr Manson was talking about on Sunday. I'm a Judas.'

'You're nothing of the kind, son,' said Betty.

'I betrayed my friends, the best friends I ever had. What else would you call it?'

'You did it to help the family, Billy. Your father needed it. The business needs it.'

At tea, the table was laden with chocolate cake and apple pie, Billy's favourites, and the main dish was fillet-steak and chips, another favourite, but after a few mouthfuls, Billy put down his cutlery and said, 'I'm not hungry. In fact, I feel sick,' and he got up and went off to the downstairs toilet where, a few minutes later, his parents could hear him retching.

Betty rose immediately and went to his aid, returning in a little while to say that he had gone to bed.

'I'm disappointed in that boy,' George told her. 'What he did was marvellous, but if he thinks he betrayed his friends, he's no good to me. How did he get like this, Betty? I don't understand it.'

'Don't worry, it'll all come right in the end, dear. He'll get over it in time.'

'I suppose you're right, ' he said, patting her hand. 'It's a pity we hadn't some more kids. Just in case.'

A tear came to Betty's eye. 'I know. I tried, you know I tried, but it just didn't work out. But Billy's a good boy. You'll see. He'll make good. He won't let us down.'

At nine o'clock, Billy left the house, and began walking down the hill and along the sea front promenade into town, drawn by the Mansons who lived at the other end of it. How had he come to lift the letter? What made him do it? All his father had said was to keep an eye open for a letter. It would be on pink paper. Scented, pink paper. The kinds of letters women wrote. The envelope would be addressed to John Manson. How had his father known this in advance? And after the robbery, when the desk was lying open, he had seen such a letter. Exactly as described. A pink envelope with John Manson's name on it and a letter inside on pink notepaper. His father must be really clever to know that kind of thing.

But why had he done it? He wasn't a thief. He didn't need to steal anything. He already had everything he wanted. 'I just did what my Daddy told me,' he muttered to himself, as he stopped to look across the treacle-black water of the harbour, at the fishing boats moored against the inside of the pier. 'I've always done what he told me.'

The air was balmy, and he turned to look along the promenade, past the gardens and the theatre in the middle, and right at the end up the hill, he could see the looming presence of St Margaret's Manse. And a sob came out of him as the image of Jessica presented itself to him, tall, strong, clever Jessica, with a distinctive quality he dimly recognised as goodness. And he knew he had to go and see her, try to explain, and his steps became more determined and he walked as he had never walked before, with purpose, with ambition, motivated by a need as tremendous as he had ever felt in his life.

What would Jessica want me to do? he said to himself. What would she do in my position? But he knew, as soon as he thought it, that Jessica would never, could never, be in a false position. She was as pure as anybody could be.

At the house, as he waited, after ringing the bell, he was lost and knew it. What would he say? The door was opened by Jessica herself, who said, 'Billy? You look ghastly! What's the matter?' And when he said nothing, just stood gazing at her, with a look of longing and desolation, she added, 'You'd better come in.' That was when he broke down and wept. How could they invite him in, when he had stolen from them, and done them in? It was so like them.

He was led into the sitting-room, where the family were assembled, except for Susan who was already in bed.

John looked at him with interest, and asked him to sit down, and Billy sat, hunched up, like a scared rabbit, white-faced, with large red-rimmed eyes. John said, 'I've never seen you like this before, Billy. Is there anything I can do?'

As sure as anything, John knew what was troubling the boy, but he needed to make the moves himself. There was only so much you can do for someone in need of absolution. First he must ask for it.

Peter, who understood none of it, said, 'What's up, Billy? Have you had bad news?' Grappling with his own, made him more compassionate to others in trouble.

Billy looked at them all, and finally his eyes fastened on Jessica, and the sight of her gave him strength. He knew what he had to do. Suddenly, with the greatest difficulty, he stood up, almost over-balancing in the process. 'I..I..I've..I've g.g.got something to say.'

Conversation ceased and Jean got up, turned off the television, and sat down again. Every eye was upon Billy, expectantly, for here was something new. Billy, who had never in his life taken the initiative, was doing so now, and the sight was interesting. In trembling tones, he said, 'I took the letter. The letter from the desk. I'm so sorry, really very sorry. I didn't know what I was doing. It's just...' The tears began again and he wiped his eyes. 'It's just that I always do what my Daddy tells me. I always have. You would have to know my Daddy to understand. He expects me to, and I do. So when he told me to look for a letter on pink paper to Mr Manson and lift it, I just did it automatically. I'm really sorry. I really am.'

'What's an old letter anyway?' said Roddy. 'What's it matter?'

'How did your father know it would be pink, Billy?' said John.

'I don't know, Mr Manson. I've just no idea. But he knew. He knew.'

Jean said: 'Does it matter, John?'

'Yes, I'm afraid so. It's a letter from Madeline Grant and it puts me in a compromising position.' John sighed. 'There's nothing in it of course. I'm not guilty of anything. But people, nasty people, will think that there is. It's one of the dangers of being a minister. You get your share of crank mail. Well, I've got mine now.'

'I don't see how a letter that's not true can get you into trouble, Dad,' said Peter.

John leaned back in the chair and licked his lips. 'I wish I had a drink, but Jock took it,' and everyone knew then, just how bad it was.

'I..I asked my father for it back, Mr Manson, but he wouldnae give it.'

'That's all right, Billy. I'm proud of you, you know. That was a brave thing you did coming here like this, and owning up. There's not many lads your age could do that.'

Billy's eyes shone through the tears, and he said, with amazement, 'I can stay then? I can stay a wee bit longer?'

'Yes, of course, Billy. Why not? But not too long. It'll soon be bed-time.'

Billy heaved a sigh of relief, and sat down and looked across at Jessica. who smiled at him, and came across to sit on the arm of his chair.

'What will happen to the letter?' said Jean.

'George will show it around the Kirk Session. There's a move to get rid of me. George is behind it, of course. He wants me out of the way, so that he can go back to fleecing the old folk in the congregation. He can't do that with me here. That's why he was so eager to strike a deal. So he could get my support and save all this unpleasantness.'

'Is this true, Billy?' said Jean.

'I don't really know. My Daddy doesn't talk to me about business. All I know is that he's lost thousands, and the letter will get you all kicked out. That's what he said.'

'And what did you say?' said Jessica.

'I tried to get the letter back, but he slapped me and told me not to be disloyal. I told him I felt like Judas for betraying my friends. My best friends. And he got mad, because he said I should take more notice of my own family. But I told him my friends were worth a lot more than my family.' Billy paused and then concluded, 'I wish I didn't have to go back there; but I know I do. I would much rather be here among good folk.'

Billy was given tea and cake and then he and Jessica went out with the dog. As they walked towards the town, Billy said, 'Did you know I'd taken the letter?'

'Not until you were leaving. I knew then.'

'How did you know? How do you know these things?'

'I just knew from your reaction, the way you spoke to my father.'

'Why didn't you say? I mean you could have stopped me. I would have handed it back, and you wouldn't all be in this mess.'

'It was something you had to do yourself. My father knew too and he thought the same.'

'But why? Why? I don't understand you folk at all.'

'It's the way he is. He thought it was the right thing to do, that's all.'

'But it wasn't right! He's in a fine mess now, because of it!'

'No, he was right just the same. If he had challenged you about it, you would have been finished—not because of us. No, because of yourself. He would know that. That's why he said nothing. People have to be allowed to make up their own minds to do good. They should always be given the chance.'

'Even when a disaster happens?'

'Especially then. Who's to know it will be a disaster? Maybe something good will come of it. That's what God wants us to do. Have faith, do the right thing regardless, and everything will come out right in the end.'

As he walked through the town, having left Jessica to make her own way back, Billy wondered where that put him, and had a bright idea, an idea of such dazzling brilliance he was blinded by it. He stopped in the middle of Main Street, empty at that time of night, and looked upwards at the stars and his eyes glistened. Doing good is catching. And having good ideas is a blessed experience, all the more so when they are connected to one's own previous bad behaviour, and solutions to the problem of repentance.

Billy laughed and set off again, skipping with delight, changing course for the High Street, where, outside the police office, he stopped, took out a comb, and drew it through his hair and then tightened the knot in his tie, adjusted the pin, drew his shoulders back, and entered.

For five minutes he stood at the desk and waited. Then he noticed the buzzer and pressed it. A tall man in a sergeant's uniform came from an inner room. 'Billy Buchanan, isn't it?' he said, in an accent from some Hebridean island, 'What can I be doing for you at this time of night?'

'I've come to report a theft.'

Sergeant Macdonald drew a form from below the desk, and took a biro pen from his top pocket. Once Billy's name and address were inscribed with painful slowness by the enormous hands, so plainly unsuited to writing with fragile instruments, he said, 'So what is it that's been stolen?'

'A letter, a letter on pink scented paper addressed to John Manson.'

'You mean the Minister? Where was it stolen from?'

'St Margaret's Manse.'

The Sergeant yawned and then wrote something. 'Have you any idea when?'

'Yes, at ten to five tonight.'

The Sergeant wrote it down and said, 'How do you know?'

'Because I stole it.'

'You stole it? And where is it now?'

'My Dad has it. I want you to get it back and give it to Mr Manson.'

'I will have to confirm this with Mr Manson, first.'

'Go ahead. Phone him now, will you. He's knows all about it.'

'Hold on. Do you know you can be charged with theft? You could even go to the jyle?'

'I don't care. I don't mind being charged or going to jail. I did wrong, but I did it because my Daddy made me do it.'

Macdonald lifted the receiver and dialled. Getting John Manson, he explained the situation.

'I see,' said John. 'It's quite true. I did receive a letter and it has been stolen.'

'Will you be making a complaint, Minister?'

'I don't know. I hadn't thought of it. Do I have to?'

'No, you don't. But it would help if you want the letter back.'

'I see. What would happen to Billy, if I did?'

'I am not able to say, at this stage. It depends on what the Fiscal thinks. It's not very serious. So maybe it'll be dropped. I really don't know.'

'I don't want the boy to be in any trouble. He's been brave enough just owning up to it.'

'I see,' said Sergeant Macdonald. 'Do you want me to get onto his father and ask for the letter, as the boy says?'

'I hadn't thought of that. It might be best. It can do no harm.'

When he had put down the phone, Macdonald said, 'Well, there's been an offence, right enough. I suppose I should phone your father. If he'll give it back, though, maybe the whole thing can be dropped. Mr Manson wouldn't mind, I'm sure. He doesn't want to prosecute.'

As Sergeant Macdonald began to dial, Billy's resolution wavered, for he could sense the impending catastrophe when his father learned of his defection, his betrayal of family loyalty. Had he not been present often enough when George had been informed of acts of disloyalty from other people? The explosion of wrath was terrifying, and the subsequent pursuit of the miscreant, to ensure his utmost discomfort and, if possible, utter destruction, was terrible to see.

'I...I...th.th.think I should go home now,' said Billy, and the Sergeant nodded.

'Aye, I think you maybe should. Your faither's bound to want to see you.'

'I..I.. won't need to go into the cells, will I?'

The bobby laughed. 'No, Billy, no. You won't be arrested, if that's what you mean. Your faither would never forgive us.'

If only Billy had known that was his best line of action: to fear nothing; to demand that he be arrested. For then George would have been worried about how the scandal would affect the family, and in particular himself. But Billy did not have that much perception. Faced with the certainty of George's anger, he wanted only to avoid it.

As he walked home along the sea front, the coming show-down began to affect his newly acquired courage, and it ebbed away like the tide. Up the hill to Silvertrees, he went. At the entrance to the garden, Billy stopped. Could he get into the house unseen? Not easily, he decided. His father would hear him come in; would be waiting for his arrival, ready to club him into submission, with a tirade of curses and maybe more.

It was cold under the stars, and Billy shivered. Unable to face the confrontation, he moved off along the street and dawdled uncertainly on the road overlooking the sea, and, in the distance, the mainland.

For half an hour he sauntered about, and then, realising that George would soon come looking for him, he returned to the house and quietly went around the back, where, locating the key under its appointed stone, he opened the door of the shed in the back garden. There, he made a bed of sorts under some sacks, and lay shivering for a while, until the noise of the car starting up, made him realise that George was leaving the house.

Soon after, Billy entered by the back door, crept up the back stairs to his room, and, after locking the door, an event unprecedented, he went to bed and fell asleep.

At two o'clock in the morning, he was awakened by the sound of George trying to open the door. 'For Christ's sake! A locked door in my own house! I won't have it! Get that bloody door open this minute!'

Billy, made no move; lay cowering between the sheets; and the tears began again.

'Christ!' said George, and put his shoulder to the door and pushed, without effect. Then he took three paces to the other side of the hall and ran at the door side-on, hitting it with all his might, and there was a bang. Then he did it again. And then a third time, and the door jamb gave, in a splintering crack. One final forceful run at the door completed the task, and George burst through it, to land, full-length, on the carpet of the bedroom.

Above him, on the bed, Billy cowered, large-eyed and whimpering with fright.

George picked himself up off the floor and advanced upon the boy. 'Ya wee bastard! To think you're my own son and you go and clipe to the police! What made you do it? Eh?' Without waiting for a reply, George cuffed him on the ear with the flat of the taloned hand and then did it again, harder, for the satisfaction it gave him.

Billy wept and hooted like a stuck pig and George shouted, 'Stop that, ya wee cissy! Can you no' take your punishment like a man?' And the slaps rained upon Billy and they soon made it seem as if he was a man indeed, for he quickly became numb to the pain, surprised by it, into a near-coma of indifference.

Betty appeared at the door, and stood weeping. 'No, George! No, George. Please! No more! He's had enough!' but George was absorbed in the release of emotions he hardly understood himself, and did not let up until, finally, tiredness made him drop his thick-fingered hands.

'I can't get over it! I can hardly believe it! The wee bastard told the cops he stole the letter from Manson.' The statement was uttered with a sense of amazement that such a thing could be possible. How could anyone do such a thing? How could his own flesh and blood do it?

For once Betty was not thinking of herself. Drying her eyes, she said, 'But he did steal it, George. You told him to.'

George was dumbfounded, and for an instant Betty thought he would attack her, but instead, blinking his eyes as if just aroused from sleep, all he said was, 'So I did. So I did.'

Downstairs, at the kitchen table, over a cup of tea, George said, 'He told the police that I made him do it. Can you credit that? I can hardly believe it. I never thought my own son would ever sell me out like that.'

It was on the tip of Betty's tongue to say, 'Since it was true, what else could he say?' but her instinct for self-preservation reasserted itself and she remained silent, leaving George none the wiser about himself.

In the morning, George was up early to complete the work he had begun the night before, of going around the Kirk Session showing the pink letter. Four of them he had seen that night, leaving the last at nearly two o'clock, and only being prevented from continuing, by the absence of lights in any of the other houses he visited. Even George's zeal to make use of the letter, before handing it back to its rightful owner, could not overcome the reluctance to raise the occupants, and with them the entire street of other sleepers. In the circumstances, there was a chance of being taken up for breach of the peace—something to be avoided at all costs. But this morning, that was a different matter. When Sergeant Macdonald had insisted the letter be handed back, George had pleaded illness, saying he would do so the following day by lunchtime. The Sergeant did not accept this. It would have to be first thing. After some negotiating, this was agreed at ten o'clock. The letter to be handed in at the police office.

By then, George intended to get round the entire Kirk Session to show them the original letter, and let them see what sort of man they had for a minister. A fornicator and an adulterer. Unsure before what Manson was, convinced even that he was guilty of nothing much, George was now, thanks to his being in warlike opposition to him, quite certain of his secret sex-life with members of the congregation. As he put it to Dick Souter, 'This is only the tip of the iceberg. Who else is he having on the side? This man is in and outa folks houses all the time. If he can have it off with one, why not with others?' Then, as an afterthought, 'You should keep an eye on your wife.'

As he walked down the stairs of the close afterwards, George smiled, and thought what an inspired salvo that had been. That would do a bit of damage, right enough, for was not Dick Souter, that wee bachle of a man, married to a taller, younger woman with a taste for younger men?

That afternoon, when the letter had been handed into the Manse by a constable, John decided to visit Madeline. The news would be out by now, and it was best to face it boldly, he decided.

The walk through the town on a rare sunny day was pleasant enough; people were out and, for the most part, greeted him as usual. Up the High Street, he went, past the medieval castle with its four round towers, and the great keep with the drawbridge, standing on high grassy lawns, which sloped down to the dark moat, where yard-long pike swirled silently, hunting ducks.

People he met, smiled. The story was not out then. But the walk up the hill to Madeline's house was different. Curtains rustled, and one or two folk found reasons for doing some early gardening, on a day that was still too cold for it.

She let him in immediately and made as if to kiss him, even before the door was shut, but he would have none of it. Turning, he closed the door himself, strode into the living room and sat down.

'You're not pleased with me, then, John?'

As she sat opposite, he noticed that she looked at her very best, like a rose in full bloom. A white blouse with ruffles and a richly-designed black and red patterned skirt and skin-coloured stockings. Her hair, her lovely shiny flecked hair, was swept upwards and held there with combs, in some far more sophisticated creation than he had ever seen in Ottersay, and her face was professionally made up, so that she gave off a kind of honey-coloured glow, with just a blush at the cheeks.

'I got your letter, and it was stolen from me. George Buchanan got hold of it and he intends to use it, to get me the sack.'

'Oh, no!' said Madeline, putting a hand to her mouth. 'But, you've never done anything yet. So how can he get at you?'

'It's the way it's written. It suggests that I have. Anyway, it doesn't matter really. People believe what they want. It's very damaging.'

Madeline shifted her knees nervously and John's eyes could not tear themselves away. There was something irresistible about stockinged legs like these and the gaps above served only to inflame the imagination about what lay beyond. And yet he knew what lay there. He already had an image to gloat over. That was the difficulty precisely: it was so delectably desirable.

Swallowing noisily, as if to keep down the monstrous fires of need that swirled below, in his innards, John said: 'You mustn't write any more letters, Madeline. Will you promise me?'

'But John,' she said, 'why not? I love you. Why shouldn't I write to you since you won't come here?'

'After this, I can't come here. And we'd better not meet at all. You must put me out of your mind, Madeline. It's for the best.'

'I can't John! I can't do without you. You're the only thing keeping me alive! Without you I'm nothing.'

'No. You're a very attractive woman. All you have to do is make yourself available, and some fine young man your own age will come courting. That would be best.'

'But I want you, John, only you!'

'That's just the way it looks, Madeline. It's just post-bereavement depression. You'll get over it.'

'I won't John. I'll..I'll kill myself if you leave me. I will,' and there came into her eyes a fierce passionate look, at once unstable and vulnerable, so that her considerable beauty was enhanced.

John said, 'I won't be blackmailed by talk of suicide. That's all it is. Talk. I've got a wife and family to think of. And I love them, especially my wife. It's her I love, not you. But, even if it's not talk, Madeline, it will make no difference to me. I can't stop you doing away with yourself, if that's what you want to do. Nobody can.'

'But you want me, John! I know you do! I saw your erection.'

'Lust, Madeline, just lust. I'm only flesh and blood. It would be strange if I didn't lust after you. You're a beautiful woman. You've got everything going for you—everything!'

Madeline moved her legs, revealing herself, and John flushed and said, 'I wish you wouldn't do that. I don't want you to.'

'You do so. You know you do. Look at yourself! You're getting big. I can see it.'

'I have to go, now. I can't do this any more. Oh, there's just one question: How did George Buchanan know that you were sending a pink letter to me? I can't fathom it.'

'I don't know!'

'Did he speak to you?'

'No, I don't even know him. Only to see from photos in the paper.'

'Well, somehow he knew that you were writing to me and that the letter was pink. Could he have looked through your window, do you think, while you were writing?'

'No. I wrote it upstairs in bed at night, when I was dreaming about you coming.'

John stood up and made as if to go, and Madeline frantically grabbed at him below the waist, as if to convince herself that what was there, was so for her. 'See, John! Look! I've got it,' she said triumphantly in spite of his efforts to fend her off. 'You do want me. There's the sign. And I need it John. Oh, I need it badly, awful badly. Please, John, Please. Just do it once, just once!'

John detached himself from her, found the door-lock with a trembling hand, opened it and, in a moment, was striding down the path with a very red face and a breathless look about him.

The terraces of Murrayfield were swept with wind and driving rain and the spectators, a few thousand children from Edinburgh private schools, were huddled together in the front of the one and only grand-stand. For the first time, Peter was in a blue jersey and the pride of it was immense, a fierce pride in his country, shared by every one of the others drawn from Scotland's schools. From Nairn and Glasgow, they had come. Several from border towns like Melrose and Hawick, where rugby was not so much a game as a religion, and the rest from the private schools in and around Edinburgh. Three Fettesians were playing that day, and, from the talk the night before, it was plain to Peter that they inhabited a different world, one where the utmost effort was expected on all occasions. The intensity of their lives was in their eyes and expectations and stream-lined muscles. Where else were boys so highly trained? These boys in their houses were at war with each other, twenty-four hours a day. No wonder there were three of them playing for Scotland. The wonder was that it was only three, he observed to another boy, wryly.

The first line-out was a scrappy, rough-and-tumble, with both sides pulling at the ball, and a loose-scrum developed, in which Peter was ballast, mainly. But the next Peter won with a clear jump and two-handed catch, and he released the ball to the Fettesian scrum-half who belted a Garryowen a hundred feet into the air and ran like a hound of hell after it. It descended into the hands of the full-back, stationed on his twenty-five, and the Fettesian and Peter hit him together, so that he fell with the ball bouncing free, and the Scottish stand off, a lad from Watson's, came bursting through to pick up on the full, and streak away to the wing in an arc of blistering pace where, at the last moment, a hairsbreadth from the English line, he was torpedoed into touch at the corner flag, by the opposite wing, who, covering across the field like a lightning bolt, threw his body at full stretch parallel to the grass, and knocked him off the pitch.

From the resulting line-out, inches from the try-line, Peter dexterously palmed the throw to the scrum-half. In a moment, the ball was whistling along the blue line and the outside-centre made a dart through the space in front, but was held by a pair of powerful white arms, and went to ground. Bodies, blue and white, surged into the ruck and heaved and struggled for the ball, which was soon buried deep, never to re-emerge in a finite time; and so the whistle blew and a new scrum was formed.

Back and forth the fighting went, from one line and then to the next, as both sides forgot the majesty of the occasion and played like lion-cubs. At half-time, the score was nothing each, and the Scots had won a moral advantage by having enjoyed more of the ball but, somehow, a try had eluded them, for the English tackled like guided missiles. Peter had jumped well and won good ball and was a decisive factor in the game.

Ten minutes into the second half, his boot split again, along the secondary stitching, and he was forced to cut back on his running. Worse, he was unable to jump quite as high, because he could not get sufficient purchase, for the foot was not contained by the boot. Inexperienced as he was, it never occurred to him to go off, temporarily, to effect a repair. The poverty of your equipment is not something you advertise.

And so he played on with less effect than before, and the English began to win more and more ball. Their stand-off, a blonde six-foot bombshell, began to show his flair. A dazzling side-step took him past his opposite number and, coming up with the Scottish full-back, he threw a dummy that left him standing, scythed past him and coasted to the line, where he touched down between the posts, to roars of amazement and disbelief from the assembled Scottish crowd. Five nothing to England, after the easiest of conversions.

Twenty minutes from time, the Scots were awarded a penalty thirty yards out, half way to the touchline. The Fettesian forward who was the captain, called for Peter who was too embarrassed to reveal that his right boot was no longer functioning as it should. In a daze of confused emotions—wanting, with every fibre of his being, to put the ball over the bar, desperate to be the one who did it, to play an outstanding part, and aware, deeply, powerfully aware, that in that team there just had to be goal kickers with decent boots, who were better able than him to do the job. Why could he not speak up? Why? The occasion, the desperate need, the pride, the unwillingness to seem, even for a moment, unequal to the task.

And so he ran up and let fly, and saw the ball slice towards the right-hand post and, most humiliating, fail even to go the distance. But worse, the boot itself came off and flew several yards. Deeply embarrassed by the sniggers, Peter fetched it and tied it on, thinking as he did so, what a fool he must look to the rest of the teams and the spectators; as if his efforts to conceal the lack of respectable footwear, had somehow revealed itself even more dramatically.

Ten minutes later, another penalty was awarded to the Scots, ten yards further out, and right on the touchline. A Fettesian was called up to take this kick and, amid whoops of joy, sent it flying over the bar between the posts. Five points to three, the English led.

There were no more scores. And Peter knew that if only he had put his kick over, it would have been six-five to Scotland.

Disconsolate, like all his team, Peter soon set off for the train to the west, and Ottersay. The selectors never did find out why he had slowed up about the field, and jumped less well in the second half. The flying boot was assumed to be the result of laces too-loosely tied.

Arrived in Ottersay, he was striding away from the pier, heading for the promenade, when Hector Lamb grinned and accosted him. 'I hear you lost. Tough luck anyway.' But there was a knowing look about Hector, one of Peter's rivals in the sixth year, which made him pause. 'There's a story going around about your old man,' said Hector. 'Apparently he's been stuffing one of his congregation.'

Peter's face became ashen. 'Rubbish. I know all about it. Every minister gets this kind of tripe talked about him.'

Hector smiled, seemingly amused. 'How do you know? Were you there? Were you in it too?'

'I know because I know my father. If you knew him, you'd say the same.'

Determined to have his fun, Hector laughed. 'I bet they all say that. Must be satisfying, helping out all these grieving widows. Maybe I should train for the ministry myself.'

Peter left him then, but the rumour rankled, cut deep into an already troubled psyche, and, as time passed, he began to wonder whether, after all, there was something in Hector's tale. Deeply disturbed by his own sexual fantasies, it seemed to follow that every other male must have the same sort of problem. But would his father do it? What would he, Peter, do if an available woman presented herself? Take full advantage, that was the long and short of it. He dreamed of it all the time.

And so, when Peter met his father that evening and the match was described and commiserations offered, there was a new distance between them. And both John and Jessica sensed it immediately.

Later, Jessica went to Peter's room and knocked. Told to enter, she found him at his desk, deep in the science of mechanics. Sitting on the bed, she said, 'There's a story going around about Dad. Everyone's talking about it.'

'I heard it already,' he replied, looking up from the book.

'You mustn't let it change you. It's not true, you know. We have to stick together and support Dad; weather the storm together. That's how to see it through.'

'Has it occurred to you that it just might be true?'

'No, it has not! How could it be true?'

'Maybe Mrs Grant threw herself at him. How could he resist her? She's really beautiful.'

'You mean you couldn't resist her, is that it?'

Peter blushed. 'No, I don't suppose I could.'

'Dad's different. He's not a boy that's just bursting to do it to someone.'

'How do you know? Maybe all men are the same. I think they are.'

'So if Madeline Grant were to flaunt her charms in front of you, you'd oblige her, is that it?'

'I wouldn't be able to control myself.'

'Well, Dad did control himself. I know as sure as I'm sitting here.'

'How can you know that? You're always so damned sure of yourself.'

'I know Dad, that's how. If he had done anything he shouldn't, he would have been so affected it would show. But it hasn't. He's the same as he's always been.'

'What about the whisky he gets through? It's getting to be half a bottle a night and we can't afford it.'

'Maybe we have to afford it. Maybe he needs it more than anything we need.'

'Well, I think there's something in it. No smoke without fire.'

'You're so wrong, Peter! And you need to be behind him like the rest of us. He needs our trust and all our support. I saw the way he looked at you tonight. He thinks you think he did it. And it made a difference. I wish you could stand fast. This ship could sink if you don't. That's what I came to tell you.'

But Peter lacked the confidence of his sister and, the next day, at school, when the ribbing began, he was deeply affected by it. He, who had gone about the school like a conquering hero—the first boy at Ottersay Grammar to be capped for Scotland—was reduced to a figure of fun, whose father was having a bit on the side. The fact that John was a minister, only made the situation more ridiculous. It affected Peter's concentration at lessons, and after a while, he began to believe it was true. Every detail, embellished in the telling, was made known to him. How John had been seen in a state of arousal, just about to do it, how Madeline had stripped off in her kitchen and poor John Manson had had no defence. How he had actually been seen doing it by another prefect who lived in that same street. Many of the boys admitted that they would like a temptation of that sort themselves. Some even planned to pay a call on the lady, in the hope of some action. After a couple of days of it, a sensitive nature like Peter's had had enough and he began to lash out at anyone who referred to it. Finally, a fight broke out in the prefects room, and some damage was done, as Peter and the enemy crashed about between the bookcases.

When Philip Mulholland appeared, it stopped. Peter's one friend in all this was Dick Breslin, son of a local hotelier, but Dick's attitude was different. 'It's not your fault, Peter. Ok so your father's been stuffing some crumpet. What does it matter, for God's sake? It's not you. Why should it make a difference to *you*?'

'Because I can't look him in the eye. It's as if he's let the side down. And after all we've been through! All the bloody poverty and misery trying to make ends meet. Do you know how little he gets paid? It's peanuts! And now he's turned out to be an adulterer. It's too much! After all that stuff he spouts out of *The Bible*, I can't stand it any more.' And as he said it for the first time, admitted it, there was a feeling of self-revulsion, for in his heart he knew it was not true; it had just become too difficult to stand against the rumour any more. It was much easier to believe it. That way, at least he was not against everybody else, the object of their sniggering.

'Well, if it gets to be beyond you, you can come and stay with me,' said Dick. 'There's plenty of room. Are we not blood-brothers anyway? What are friends for? It would be a privilege to have the first Scottish international in Branden, staying at our hotel.'

'Thanks a lot, Dick, but it's not practical. I couldn't just take your hospitality for nothing.'

'Oh, you needn't worry, old son. Dad's got a job earmarked for you. He wants the pair of us as commis-waiters this summer holiday. You would need to live in, to do the breakfasts. What do you say? You could move in early?'

And so, in the middle of the summer term, having received the reluctant permission of his astonished parents, Peter moved out of the Manse and went to live in The Clyde Hotel, ostensibly to learn to wait at table, while tourists were still few and far between, and attend school as usual, after serving breakfast, and serve dinner from seven in the evening. This still left him a few hours for mathematics, and, as the exams were over, there was no pressing necessity, until he went off to Glasgow University at the end of the summer. Meanwhile, for the first time in his life, he would have money in his pocket.

His defection was everything Jessica feared. It cast a cloud around the house and John Manson was visibly shaken by it, but he would not stand in the boy's way, and he understood his need to distance himself from the Manse.

By special arrangement, the Kirk session met without the minister, to consider what ought to be done.

'I haven't seen the letter,' said Dr Telford, who had been away at the time of George's visits to them. They were sitting, as usual, around the table in the vestry. George handed over a copy of it.

'Where's the original?' said Telford.

'Manson has it,' said George.

'Do you mean he lent it to you so that you could show it to everyone?'

'No, but when he heard it was in my possession he asked for it back.'

'Well, I don't think it means anything,' said Telford reading it through his half-moon specs. 'It's just a woman that's lost her husband imprinting onto the only man who bothers to show her kindness. That's all it is.'

'What do you mean, *imprinting*?' said George.

'It's a term used by Konrad Lorentz about animals, and how they form attachments to their parents. It's the same for humans.'

'Well, I think he's been using her, taking advantage,' said George. 'A lot of us think that.'

'Nothing of the kind!' said Telford. 'And this letter doesn't show this. Is that all you've got against this man? You should be ashamed of yourselves.'

'No, it's not all. There are these other letters.' And, out of a brown envelope, George brought forth a pile of other letters, and passed some of them around.

Telford opened one, written on pink paper and read it aloud, '"My Darling John, I wish you were here beside me. I miss you terribly and can't wait for you to come again.' Is that all? This proves nothing, Nothing! Just that Madeline Grant is a poor depressed soul, starved of sex."

'But what about this?' said George, '"What you suggested I use is nothing to you yourself. Please come again, please. I need you desperately. It is you I must have.'"

'What are you complaining about?' said Telford.

'What is it he suggested she use? And why is it nothing to what he has himself?'

'What's the problem? The woman's lost her husband. She needs to do something. John has simply suggested some suitable surrogate.'

'Well, I think it's disgusting,' said George. 'Imagine a Christian minister making suggestions of that kind, to a woman in his congregation! I'll bet he's been up there himself. I can smell it!'

'Nonsense! He's given her advice. I bet he's given her the go-ahead to do things she feels guilty about. That's his way and he's right. A lot of ministers wouldn't give her the time of day. They would walk past on the other side and leave her to burn. Not John! He gave her comfort. It's what he's best at. And he's not afraid. You think I don't know him? I'm the one person who does, because I attend the same old folk he does, and I see the good he does, and it is uncommon. Out of the ordinary! John Manson's the best medicine some of them get, better than I can give. All I can do is help their bodies; he heals their minds; makes it easier for them to accept their situation. I've seen it many a time. He's a magician, a faith healer, and nobody realises it. And it's all done with goodness. That's all. A commodity in short supply around here this evening.'

In his piping voice, little Dick Souter said, 'But there's this story about her stripping off and him being, well, excited and... and..'

Telford stopped him. 'If Madeline Grant stripped off—and she might, because she is sex-starved—would you not get excited? I know I would! So if John Manson became aroused it's no wonder. But I know this, he did nothing wrong.'

'How do you know?' said Tom Henderson, nervously stroking his dark hair, as he imagined what he would do.

'Because I know him; and because it would kill him if he did. He knows it and I know it.'

George said, 'Are you saying he's got some medical condition that would make it impossible?'

'Yes!' said Telford. 'He suffers from compulsive moral goodness.'

There was an amazed silence.

Looking at the letter again, Telford noticed the creases which had been flattened. Suddenly, he seized another letter out of his neighbour's hand and studied it, seeing again the folds that had been ironed out there too.

'Where did these letters come from, George?'

'I'm not at liberty to say.'

'I think these have been stolen. I bet they were never sent, most of them. Most haven't been finished off. I bet they've been thrown away. That's why they have creases which someone has been careful to iron out. Am I right?'

'It doesn't matter whether they were sent or not,' said George. 'Only that they were written.'

'Where did you get these, George? In Madeline Grant's dustbin? Because if you have, that's theft and if not, it's reset, for someone else must have got them there for you.'

There was a hush for a while. Eventually, Telford said, 'I think we can happily consign all these letters and any others to the waste-bin, don't you.' And so saying, Telford took out a lighter and lit the letter, which he watched burning for a moment, and then got up to put it in the waste-bin where it burned out. 'Give me the others and I'll deal with them,' and, moving quickly, he seized them.

Puce with rage, George shot out of his seat, protesting: 'They're mine! I paid good money for these. Give them here!'

But it was too late, even as George's large talon came within reach, to grab them, they caught fire. George stood back, horrified. Soon they were ashes.

'And we can forget about that other letter which I never saw, because it means nothing anyway,' added the little doctor. George grabbed his small hand in his great fist, and crushed it as if it were a handshake he felt determined to make; and then released the small hand and smiled, as Telford bent double over the waste-bin, shaking the hand in agony, wondering if he would ever be able to operate again.

And George was not finished. Scarlet with humiliation and fuming with frustration, he turned to the others, 'We can't have a minister who attracts such an amount of unfavourable comment. None of the women will admit him to their houses now.'

'How do you know?' croaked Telford, taking a seat at the table again.

'Never you mind. But it's only natural, isn't it, the way he took advantage of Madeline?'

'He didn't take advantage of her! He tried to help her—did what no one else would do. Gave her comfort.'

'What about his heresy?' said George.

'Balderdash! Every Christian's entitled to his own interpretation of *The Bible*. John Manson's beliefs are his own. But I tell you this, if his beliefs are what you say, I'm all for them. They sound pretty sensible to me.'

'But he doesn't believe in the important things,' said Ellen. 'The Virgin Birth, the Resurrection and the Ascension. I'm not even convinced he believes in God! His idea of God sounds a total abstraction to me.'

'Yes, that's right!' said George. 'And there's this matter of the money he lost us by being rude to Mrs Arbuthnott-Snell. We can't afford to have a minister who's rude to the well-to-do. It just costs us money. Think of how that five thousand quid could have been used here.'

Telford said, 'John was right! Do you know what they're doing with that money at St Bruoc's? Spending the whole damn lot on stain-glass windows!'

'What's wrong with that?' said Tom.

'It's a monument to Mrs Arbuthnott-Snell, that's what it is. It's all she wanted. A monument to herself.'

'But she's paying to beautify the church,' said George. 'Where's the harm in it?'

'Paying to glorify herself, more like,' said Telford. 'That money could have been spent on the poor, to alleviate suffering in the third world. It could have saved lives! All it does is cover the congregation in a rosy glow. It's such a waste! Churches are not meant to be palaces. They should be stripped bare, so that all the available funds can be spent on things that matter.'

The meeting broke up then, the issue undecided. Dr Telford had won the day, for the time being. But George was not the only one who was dissatisfied. Several of the others, as people do, had not taken the point, and were merely irritated by the force of Telford's case. For days, they had been thinking that John Manson was sexually involved with Madeline Grant, and, despite Telford's argument, they still thought so. Why? Because they knew that, placed in similar circumstances, most would have made no effort to resist. So how could John Manson? It was unbelievable. The more so, in some cases, because of a tinge of jealousy. Why should he have all the luck?

The capacity of ordinary folk to appreciate and act sensibly on compelling, reasoned argument, is far less than is commonly imagined. An idea once acquired, especially if it has lascivious or unworthy overtones, is difficult to eradicate. Giving someone the benefit of the doubt, is the last thing that many people, left to themselves, will do. It is so much easier and more interesting to believe the worst, and the action is reinforced by the knowledge that if they themselves had been the accused, they would assuredly have been guilty. Thus, a kind of categorical imperative operates among human kind of the form: *I would have done it myself, so he must have.* For some, there is even a corollary which says: *He is such a do-gooder, that I would like it to be true that he failed in this.*

As Jessica's competition was at the end of the week, she didn't see Billy for a few days, was even glad of the extra time for practice, and was largely ignorant of the events at the police station. But when he failed to appear after her concert at school, given before the entire assembly, she feared he must be ill.

That evening, she walked out to Crichton and up the hill to Silvertrees, where she rang the bell. When Betty came to the door, Jessica introduced herself, and asked about Billy. Knowing instinctively what George's attitude would be, Betty did not invite her inside, but kept her standing in the porch, with the door ajar. 'He's been kept in bed for a few days,' she replied.

'What's the matter with him? Is he ill?'

'Just growing pains. Nothing to worry about.'

'Could I see him for a few moments? It might cheer him up?'

'No, I don't think so. His father's given specific instructions.'

'Well, maybe I could come tomorrow and see if he's better, then.'

'I don't think you should bother,' said Betty, stern-faced.

'When do you expect him back at school?'

'Oh, he's not going back. His father says it's time to enter the real world and join the business.'

'Does he want to leave school? He was getting on so well recently. We were all proud of how he was developing. I'm very surprised.'

'Well, his father's not too pleased, that's all I can say.'

It was not unusual for children to leave school at sixteen, but not just before taking their O levels. Jessica knew that something was wrong, and that night, after all the work was done, she wrote Billy a letter. It was intercepted, of course, at George's instructions.

Earlier that evening, John received a phone call from Phil Mulholland. 'The Director has decided that nothing can be done about Charlie Braddock. If he's sacked, he will sue the Education Committee and we don't have a leg to stand on. It's just Roddy's word against his.'

'But there must be other boys. Have you enquired into it?'

'The Director thinks it's impractical. If there were other cases, they would come to light of their own accord.'

'Surely you can do something?'

'I can't go round the school asking for boys who have been taken advantage of. What would I say? *Anyone who has been stuffed by Mr Braddock should report to the office.* It would be ridiculous and undermine the authority of the place.'

'So what do you intend to do?'

'There's nothing we can do—unless other cases come forward by themselves. But I have a feeling Charlie will steer clear of that kind of thing in future.'

'You're not serious?'

'Well, it's a bit dangerous for him, isn't it? Would you do that again in his place?'

'So he gets off Scot free, then?'

'With any luck he'll move off to some other school soon, and the problem will sort itself out.'

'You mean he'll be promoted to another place, where he'll get away with it more easily?'

'There's no need to take it personally.'

'I haven't. But the public needs to be protected against people like him.'

'Look, the Director's anxious to help in any way he can, and it occurred to him that a grant could be awarded to Jessica, to cover her travel and accommodation, during the scholarship competition. How does that grab you?'

'It's good news. I don't how we would manage otherwise.'

'Well, then, I'll say goodnight. By the way, this is the best thing all round, you know. Your son Peter has the best maths teacher he could have. What would he do without Charlie?'

The truth was that John, alone of everybody, understood just how it was with Charlie. He had seen into the heart of the problem when dealing with Joe, and from what Roddy had let slip about Charlie's approach, knew that, for Charlie, it was a kind of philosophy that he genuinely believed in. Where was the harm in an adult having a relationship with a boy, when the adult had so much to offer by way of protection and guidance? The ancient Greeks had not done too badly under the system. There was good reason to think that civilisation only regressed for the two thousand years after the Peloponnesian War.

The correct attitude to adopt became the subject of conversation in the study one evening, when John, sitting with his glass, saw Peter, paying an unexpected visit, on his way upstairs to collect some books; and asked him to come and talk.

'How are your maths lessons, these days?'

Peter sat down in the chair opposite and said, 'It's not the same, of course. I've lost all respect for the man—as a man. But he's a great teacher. The more advanced it gets the better he becomes. He makes it so interesting and it's so clear a child could follow it. It's the structure, really. Everything is sorted out into ideas which lead naturally from one to another, just by following the logic. Questions—the kind you should naturally ask—govern everything. It's beautiful the way he does it. The theory he generates is like poetry—or maybe a story with tension which draws you on from one thing to another. And there's always a surprise—several often—sometimes really miraculous things. The others don't teach like that. There's no structure from them. No natural progression of ideas. All they do is show you how to solve problems in exam papers. I sometimes wonder if the rest of them know what an idea is! Charlie only deals in ideas, and once you've got them that's it! You know you can do anything. The main thing is the enthusiasm. It really is fascinating in itself; but he brings this out, because he can really see how it is. That's the other thing, of course. Charlie can apply it all so efficiently. His mind's like a razor-blade and it doesn't matter how difficult the problem, he slices it to bits in no time, without hesitation. It's a gift.'

Peter sat wondering, marvelling at the man's teaching and then said, quietly, 'He's a genius, I think. I don't think there could be a better maths teacher than Charlie. The best of it is, that he sets it in its historical context. He tells you what Newton was faced with, before he started thinking about it—in the calculus, say. And then he shows you, just as if you were watching Newton, how he got round the obstacle. But it's the power of it, really. He never just does the wee bit in the course for the exam. He goes the whole hog, takes you all the way. Or rather, he tells you you're going and asks some of the questions and you go yourself. He gets us to ask the right questions and we do. That's the magic of it. It's like being a creative mathematician. It's wonderful. Really exciting.'

John had listened with interest. 'The school's not going to sack him and there's nothing I can do about it.'

Peter was shocked. 'It's immoral, Dad. A man like that shouldn't be allowed near kids.'

'I know. But try and see it clearly. The man had a kind of love for Roddy. That's what it has to be. It's too impossibly difficult for him to be anything else. That's why we should try and understand it. The only harm is to Roddy, who must have been very confused and let down by it all. It will have affected his studies. Of course he will never get Charlie as a teacher now, and that's a genuine loss. If things had been different, it would have been marvellous if all of you could have been taught by Charlie.'

'You surely don't condone it, Dad?'

'No, he took advantage of his position, but teachers do that all the time, don't they? If he genuinely believes in it as a philosophy, he wouldn't think it was taking advantage.'

'I don't agree! He must have known.'

'Oh, he knew how others would view it, no doubt. But he may think that he has so much to offer that, on balance, even then, it was the best thing for the boy. Think of all the favoured attention he was receiving—I mean intellectual, all the ideas Charlie was firing at him all the time.'

'If only that was all!' said Peter, exasperated.

'I know and I agree. It seems such an odd thing to do. At least there are no unwanted kids to complicate the matter. That's why relationships outside marriage are wrong, you know. It's nothing to do with *The Bible* or anything so grandiose as moral rules. No, it's just that sex brings with it responsibilities, and some folk are not equipped to meet them. Like children. If a child is born, it has to be brought up by someone. That's the reason it should be avoided.'

'So, if there are no kids it's Ok, Dad?'

'No, if there can be kids, if they are a possible outcome, it must be wrong outside marriage.'

'But the church doesn't believe that! Honestly, the more I hear you, the more I wonder! How did you ever get into the ministry?'

John laughed and refilled his glass. 'Men change. When they're young, there has to be a formula for everything—like your mathematical formulae. You see, living at the age of twenty is very difficult, and so of course young men naturally look for things they can hang onto. They treat morality as if it were a slide-rule. You set the cursor and the answer's staring you in the face. You can read it off the scale. But when they live in the real world and have to adapt to it—which they must do, or it will destroy them—they learn that there are no formulae for most situations; and that people go wrong, and make no progress, if they try and pretend that blindly applying a formula, is the correct action to take.'

'But Dad, doesn't *The Bible* consist of nothing but formulae?'

'Not the New Testament, no. Not the Sermon on the Mount, anyway. There are principles, yes, like love your neighbour. I sometimes think that's the only thing that really matters in *The Bible*. All the rest is propaganda, as a playwright[1] once said. Some of the formulae are certainly unsound and immoral. Peter—the one in *The Bible*—is a bit of a thug. There's a lot of cruelty in *The Bible*, intolerance of others, just because they're weak or different. I don't think Jesus would have approved of either the New Testament or Saint Paul. What a fanatic that wee fella was!'

Peter laughed. 'There you go again, Dad! Knocking the very thing you're supposed to uphold. Maybe it's the drink.'

'The thing to stick to, is the character of Jesus. That's the touchstone of everything. Ask yourself what he would do. Don't just shut your eyes and apply the old formula.'

'So you're not doing anything, then, about Charlie?'

'How can I? What is there to do? All I can achieve is to keep Charlie away from Roddy. I'm doing that and I recognise the price.'

'Some of us don't think Charlie should get away with it. There are moments when I'm so revolted that I just want to go and smash him.'

'That's natural, but resist it. Charlie doesn't deserve it. Violence is not the answer to anything. Try and understand him. He's different from you and me, that's all.'

'But what about Roddy? The damage that's been done?'

'We can't undo that, we have to live with it. Everybody goes through bad experiences. This is one of Roddy's. Maybe it will teach him things he couldn't learn any other way. Who can tell?'

'So everything is for the best in the best of all possible worlds?'

'No, Voltaire showed what rubbish that is. Bad things happen and sometimes we can do nothing about them, and we're scarred by them—for life, even! But these bad things are part of life. They're what it's really about. It's not meant to be a bed of roses. It would be boring if it were. It's a kind of obstacle race, and each one has to do the best he can with what he's given, and what chance brings him.'

'But Dad, suppose you fail? Suppose you get wounded? Some folk die of it right off. Look at Susan! Where is the justice in that?'

---

[1] Alan Sillitoe, in *Saturday Night and Sunday Morning*, 1958.

'Who said anything about justice? Chance is pretty even-handed. You lose some, you win some. Some folk get dealt a pretty raw deal right from the start. But the thing to do is give it all you've got! Do the best you can. There is really nothing else to be done. And if, in the end, you are beaten, killed by some thug, shot by mistake, or contract some disease that kills you in agony, over months or years, the thing has still to be lived through, and we can do that well or badly. We can go crying to the firing squad or we can march there angrily, sensible of the injustice, with our heads held high. In the end, the very end, there is still our pride in ourselves, our sense of honour and strength of will and wit. Until these are taken from us, we are still men and have a duty to behave like it.'

'But how can God do that sort of thing? How does Susan deserve to have a disease? It's just not fair!'

John refilled the glass from the bottle, which he had taken to leaving on the floor by the side of the chair, and settled himself down again, balancing the tumbler on the arm-rest. 'Have you looked at Susan, recently?' he said quietly. 'Do you not see any positive difference?'

'No! How can there be? She slurs her words. She can hardly hold her knife and fork properly. In the evening, when she gets in, she's so weak she can hardly hold her head up.'

'She's the best student of her age I ever saw. I never knew anyone of that age who read as much or as widely and with as much understanding. It's a miracle. The very fact that her life-span is uncertain, and she is constantly reminded of it, seems to have galvanised her.'

'But what good is it, if she dies before she's twenty? It's such a shame!'

'By the time Susan's twenty, she'll have lived several life-times in books. Already, she knows more than I do about lots of things. I saw her at these differential equations last night. You mentioned it once, the last time you were here, and she was off like a greyhound in pursuit. She's been after them ever since.'

'But what are books to living? She'll never fall in love and marry and have children. She'll never have a job. She'll be totally disabled by then.'

'We don't know that for sure. Nobody can foretell the future. Maybe it won't be so bad for her. Maybe she'll last longer. A cure might even be found. But whatever happens, she'll live a full life and one that is her own choice. She might not want the disease, but she always wanted to know and understand. In an odd way, the disease has been a kind of blessing. It has made it possible for her to devote herself totally to what she wants—a life of the mind.'

'I don't see the good of it.'

'You surprise me then. You of all people! She might make an intellectual contribution to the world. She might discover something one day.'

'These are all mights, Dad. I would like a few certainties. I just don't think God should do that kind of thing. Make a wee girl ill like that.'

'Well, here's one certainty: God didn't do it.'

'But if God is all-powerful, he must have done it!'

'Then maybe God isn't all-powerful.'

Peter was suddenly exasperated again. 'You mean God is limited?'

'To the extent that he does not exercise his power, yes.'

'How can he not, Dad? Why doesn't God act to relieve all the suffering of the world?'

'It would be a pretty boring place if he did. I think he leaves it to us because it gives us something to strive for.'

'That doesn't make sense! God sets us problems to solve and stands back even when we fail most of the time.'

'There is progress. Things get better, and a lot of folk would have nothing to do if they weren't trying to do their bit.'

'Well, I don't think there is a God. He would have to behave differently if he really existed.'

Susan had difficulties at school which were unusual. Practical work was a nightmare. Beakers full of liquid would fall from her grasp, and measurements could not be taken, because her hands were not steady enough. At first, there were tears, but, in time, she grew accustomed to being one of a pair who did the paper work, while the other carried out the delicate matter of experiment or handwork. Driven by a hunger that amounted to starvation, for there was so little time, she devoured books as her peers ate ice-creams or sweeties, and soon developed a passion for science, as for everything else. Again, it was the rigour that attracted her, the idea that things could be clearly demonstrated, even if an absolute proof was impossible, a notion she already had, but which many of her peers would never acquire. And yet, she quickly realised that if nothing could be known absolutely, a lot of things could be absolutely falsified.

A chance remark from Roddy one Friday night, caused her to look into his science book. By the Sunday night, she had swallowed it whole and demanded others, which were taken on as casual reading. So textbooks on chemistry and physics appeared on her desk at home, and then at school, and the teacher was happy enough to let her steam ahead, on her own self-propelling fuel, and in any direction she chose. At least, no extra work was necessary to occupy her. Jotters she used up quickly. Pages full of chemical equations were written down, as she delightedly experimented with the possible reactions of substances through their formulae, as a substitute for carrying them out herself. Hungrily, she absorbed the details of the periodic table, memorising the atomic weight of every element, and other data about the construction of the nucleus, and the electrons which travelled around it. Then there was Latin, which she started teaching herself, out of the first year text-book, having borrowed that too from Roddy. Recognising that Latin was useful in English and Chemistry, was enough reason for her to begin to acquire it immediately. And she was soon captivated by the activities of Gaius Julius Caesar in Gaul and Publius Cornelius Scipio in Africa. Caesar, especially, she admired. De Bello Gallico was read in translation, and then, some time afterwards, in the original language. The man's achievements impressed her as few others. How, time after time, with limited forces, he had conquered armies many times the size of his own. How he had chased the Germans across the Rhine after designing and building a bridge in ten days. But it was the terse style she liked most. It spoke legions about the man. But was it true? This also she considered. Maybe he was gilding his lily.

To Susan, the libraries she had access to were treasure houses, and she plundered them constantly, marvelling at every gem, moved to tears even, at times, by the magnificence of the intellectual structures, created by generation upon generation of human genius, whom she admired as no one else. Reading that Newton was one of the three greatest scientists ever, she immediately demanded a copy of the 'Opticks' published in 1703, and was enthralled by the very first real science written in English; entranced by the very empirical character of it, its rough and ready style, as its extraordinary author set out, in ancient tortured phrases, the result of his explorations into the nature of light, as if he were an adventurer, like Francis Drake, undertaking a circumnavigation of the world, suffering every peril and trouble, en route, into the unknown. The world of ideas was Susan's world, it held her captive, and she was often transported to near ecstasy by what she found there.

Every afternoon, when she arrived back from school, the little feet would tramp upstairs, the door would slam, followed by an awesome silence from her room until tea. Then, tired out, she would totter downstairs, spill food and drink unless helped, and even fall asleep in the chair, as if the effort of holding up her head were too weakening. At times, John would have to carry her upstairs to her bedroom, where she would sleep like one dead; but in a few hours, she would be up again, as if recharged with vital energy, reading at her desk, lying on his study floor absorbed in the Encyclopaedia, or sitting up in bed, gorging herself on some new miracle of the mind from a recondite textbook.

The failure of the letters to unseat John Manson, incensed George; but it had not diminished his determination to defeat him. The impulse to fight even harder was irresistible, and, as he felt it rise in himself, he smiled with gratification. Against his sort of indefatigable initiative, what hope had Manson? George had been along this road before and knew what to do.

One evening, George sat down with a typewriter and let fly, and the result, a few hours later, delighted him. It was a letter to the Branden Mercury, the local newspaper, and in it, he excoriated the minister of St Margaret's for immorality, fornication, lying, heresy and behaving with such arrogance and rudeness to prospective donors of gifts, among the great and the good, that they had been compelled to send them elsewhere. It was, if he said it himself, a masterpiece of invective. But how to publish it? Newspapers do not usually print libels.

A visit to Mrs Arbuthnott-Snell, was a master-stroke, for she soon showed how much she disliked the minister, and was easily prevailed upon to write a short note of condemnation, saying how badly he had treated her, and how she had been forced to change churches and take her benefice away from St Margaret's. Armed with this, and mindful of the information about the letters, of which he had photocopies, together with an affidavit from Sniffy, he was ready for any protests the editor might make.

They had often done business before. The editor was worried by the letter, but the promise of £100 for a handshake agreeing the deal, and an identical bonus once it appeared, was sufficient in the end. As George was at pains to point out, the minister was in no position to mount an effective complaint, as he had no money for the legal fees necessary to support a lawsuit. So George could say what he liked and the paper might print it, without fear of prosecution. Past favours of a similar kind were recalled, as a further means of persuasion, but the money was the principal persuader.

When the paper came out that Saturday, the entire town read it, and as George knew it would, it increased his power by an appreciable degree. For many people said to themselves and each other, 'How can he get away with this?' And when, some time later, it was clear that nothing could be done by any supporters of the minister, a lot of people found it interesting, and a few admirable, that George could get away with such a vicious assault on a good man's character. It was the same syndrome as people exhibit, when then they look up to a gangster or a jewel thief, who is clever enough to outwit the law and get away with millions. Superman gone wrong is almost as much a hero as Clark Kent himself, in his fancy suit.

And so the unfitness of John Manson to remain as minister of St Margaret's was made public, and encouraged to fester in the minds of the townsfolk. Of course, John replied to the attack, but when this was shown to George by the editor, as arranged, and he offered to pay again if it was not printed, the editor himself suggested a cleverer alternative. It could be mangled in the printing and the minister made to look a fool, who could not spell or write in sentences. The Mercury was not known for good editing, one standard practice being to cut off one sentence and begin anywhere else that was suitable, to make the words fit—because of laziness as well as lack of time, when a small space had to be filled by a letter at the last minute. So the readership were accustomed to seeing fantastic omissions, discontinuities and downright gibberish, especially when the deadline was close, and the editor could not be bothered to cut a piece and make sense of the result. There had even been occasions, as all knew, when, determined to reveal the extent of the incompetence of some letter-writers, their epistles had been printed, warts and all.

So George agreed that an 'edited reply' should appear and was happy to hand over a couple of big smackers as a tip. And so the letter over John Manson's name was cut, savaged and mis-spelled and the result was a feeble defence, that made the less intelligent townsfolk laugh at his inability to write effectively; while others, more knowledgeable, just shook their heads and blamed the typical incompetence of the newspaper.

The first day of the music competition, Jessica and her teacher caught the steamer to the mainland and then the train to Glasgow, by way of Greenock, Paisley and a dozen smaller places, smoky and filthy every one, because of the many factories along the line, most of them in pre-war buildings with antiquated machinery.

'Are you in love with this boy?' said Miss Carmichael, as they sat together in the coach, with the cello on the floor between them, after Jessica had expressed concern for him.

'No, of course not. He's just a friend.'

'But you think something's the matter with him?'

'His mother says he's left school and I know he doesn't want to do that.'

'He's been taken out of school by his father. Billy went to the police station to confess to having stolen a letter and it's been returned, but George felt betrayed and he has taken it out on Billy. That's why he's left school—that's the scuttlebutt in the staff-room, anyway.'

'Was he beaten-up for it?'

'I think so. It would be in character. George Buchanan's a rough diamond when he's opposed.'

'Can't anything be done about it?'

'What? Because a boy's disloyal to his family, and gets put to work? Where's the harm in that? Anyway, Billy Buchanan's a useless waster.'

'But he behaved so well! He came and told my Dad he'd taken the letter. It was so fine! We were all struck by how much he had grown up.'

'Well, if you go to the under-taker's office during the day, you'll see a very chastened version now, I can tell you.'

Courtesy of the school's general fund, they took adjoining rooms in a small hotel near the Royal College, where the competition was to be held, and then went off to register and find out the arrangements, and, especially, the times appointed for practice. An hour later, Jessica was playing through her pieces in a small room in a corridor full of other small rooms, every one ringing with sound. Then there was lunch in the College Refectory, where they met some of the other contestants.

In the late afternoon, having sat through the contributions of many other instrumentalists, Jessica herself went onto the stage to play.

Others might have had legs like india-rubbers, which conspired to make their solitary progress across the empty floor an unstable entrance; a few were so over-confident they strode on as if marching to war in a tide of exaltation. Jessica was calm and sedate and unruffled. She went to the chair, she sat down, she composed herself and she tuned the cello again.

Then she closed her eyes to the hundreds of watchers and focused on the music in her mind and began to play, slowly and carefully, at first and then, as she surrendered herself to it, with more energy and passion. And the thousand small noises which had accompanied every contestant until then, were hushed. For here was one who lived music; for whom it was a large and necessary part of life; and who commanded attention. There was accuracy and assurance and strength in her playing, and feeling, great gushing quantities of feeling.

When at last she stopped, there was a silence and then a roar from several quarters, cheering from others and clapping, waves of it.

Three others of the many contestants from the whole of Scotland were seen to be in the same league as Jessica. A violinist called Paul Brewster from Bearsden; a blonde horn player, Tom Symon, from George Heriots'; and a large, blousy girl-pianist from St Andrews named Lorraine McCutcheon. All the rest were still very much at the bottom of a learning curve.

That evening, after more practice, followed by dinner, Jessica, in school uniform, was sitting with Miss Carmichael in a lovat-blue suit, in the hotel lounge, when Billy Buchanan entered. He was in a black jerkin, blue jeans and thick-soled shoes of the kind worn by the worst riff-raff.

'I ran away from home,' said Billy, looking woebegone. 'I couldn't stand it any more.'

'What are you going to do?' said Jessica.

'I don't know. I needed to talk to you. I can't do without you.'

Miss Carmichael said, 'Well, Jessica can do without you. Don't you realise she's in a major competition? She needs all her time to practice just to do her best. I think you should go back home and the sooner the better.'

'I've missed the last ferry. I'll have to stay the night.'

'Have you any money?'

'Yes, I raided my savings account.'

'Well, you must go first thing in the morning. I'll phone your parents and tell them you're safe, and will see them by lunch-time tomorrow.'

'I don't think you should,' said Jessica. 'Not until Billy decides what he's going to do.'

'Come with me, Jessica. I must talk to you in private. Billy? You'd better book a room here.'

In her own room upstairs, Miss Carmichael said, 'Now look here. This is the biggest thing that ever happened to you. Don't throw it away on a waster like him. Tell him to go home and he'll go.'

'I can't. Not without hearing what he has to say.'

'What can he have to say to you? What is he to you, anyway? That sort will just drag you down, Jessica. You could fail here because of him.'

'I could fail anyway. Look, I know you mean well but I must go and see if I can help him.'

'Leave him to me, please. I'll deal with him for you.'

'No, I must help him as much as I can.'

'But why?'

'Because he's my friend and he needs me.'

And so Jessica spent most of that night with Billy, listening for the most part, and irritated with herself at being unable to provide real help. Just before they each went to bed, Billy said, 'Do you want me to leave tomorrow? I'll go away if it's putting you off.'

'No, Billy,' she said. 'If you want to stay, it's all right by me. I just hope you don't get too bored.'

Billy laughed for the first time that evening. 'How could I get bored, so long as I'm with you?'

Day followed day, days of interviews, practice and performing, until by Friday, the numbers had been officially whittled down to four, and each was to be given the opportunity to play a whole piece before the entire audience. Billy had stayed with Jessica throughout, an almost invisible spectator, but one whose presence gradually became expected, and whose unqualified admiration was some help to Jessica. He was the adoring audience at practice, accompanied the pair of them, student and teacher, on walks in the nearest park, as Jessica attempted to relax between bouts of playing, and took meals with them. Mostly he said little. His predicament was that strange limbo between childhood and adulthood, aware of the burgeoning needs of identity and yet held back from assuming it, under the weight of parental influence which, even from afar, sat like a great black rook upon his shoulder.

On Thursday evening, the evening before the final stage of the competition, the three were sitting in the hotel-lounge after dinner, in red leather armchairs, when George Buchanan strode into the room.

Before anyone was aware of it, he stood beside Billy, towering over him in the black suit, white shirt and blue, conservative club tie. 'So this is where you are?' said George. 'Absconded from your place of work! I never heard of such a thing! It's a damned disgrace! The whole town's talking about it.'

Billy cringed and blushed and the two women sat with expressions of frozen horror.

'Who gave you the money to stay here?' said George, bitingly.

'It..it's my savings. The money in my sa..savings account.'

'Your savings? You mean the money I earned. You never did a day's work in your life.' This was not entirely true. Some of it was the residue of presents from other relatives. 'Well, just you go and pack your bags, this minute.'

Scarlet with humiliation, Billy stood up and made as if to leave; then thought better of it, and turned to George. 'I'm not going. I'm staying here.'

George's eyes, normally protuberant, seemed to pop out of their sockets. He raised his large talon, and swept it backhanded across Billy's face, so that Billy fell over onto the arm of Miss Carmichael's chair. As Billy rose, snivelling with fear and hurt, with his hand to his face, Jessica stood up. 'That was uncalled for. You should apologise, Mr Buchanan.'

George threw back the glistening head of black hair and laughed. 'Apologise? To him? To my own rotten, disloyal son?'

'Sit down, Billy,' said Jessica. 'You're not going anywhere.'

'Now you listen to me, you hussy, you, I'll decide what my son does. Not you.' But Billy sat gingerly on the seat under the wrathful eye of his father.

'I'm not a hussy, Mr Buchanan,' said Jessica, throwing her head up, so that the red hair swished and caught the light from the chandelier, gleaming like fire, 'and if you can't control yourself in a public place, I'll call for the manager and have you thrown out.'

'Shut your foul mouth, girl!' said George. 'And,' he said to Billy, 'you get upstairs and get packed. Go on!' And George gave him a violent shove in the shoulder that sent him sprawling, uttering renewed bleats of distress like a mistreated sheep.

'I'm going, honest,' said Billy, cowering under his raised arm, as if to ward off the next impending blow.

Billy ran off out of the room and Jessica followed.

George sat down and tried to calm himself.

'I'm sorry about this,' said Miss Carmichael. 'It's just a pity you didn't get here sooner. It could affect Jessica, all this trouble, you know.'

'I don't give a damn about that girl. What's she to me? The daughter of that adulterer that's ruining my business. She's a bad influence on my boy. He's never been the same since she got her claws into him.'

Miss Carmichael said nothing for a while, but George had suddenly appeared in a new light. She stroked her grey hair, thoughtfully. Finally, she said, 'You know, a moment ago, I was on your side. The side of the parent who knows what's best for his child, but now I'm not so sure. This I do know. Jessica Manson's the best thing that's ever happened to your boy. Anyone can see that. The fact is, he's just not good enough for Jessica. Not many people are,' she added, knowingly.

'Uch away with you woman! What do you know? A bloody schoolteacher! Them that canny do have tae teach.'

'The fact is, Mr Buchanan, if you had been properly taught yourself, you wouldn't be such a disaster as a father.'

But George was no longer listening. He got up, crossed the room and headed for the desk. Ten minutes later, he returned. 'They've gone! Done a bunk! Without paying the bill! See what that girl's done! She's led him right up the garden path.'

'Is that all you care about? The bill? Jessica's bill will be paid by me. Your son's you can take care of yourself. I just wish you'd stayed at home. That girl's in the biggest competition of her life tomorrow—the biggest in my life, for that matter. And I just hope she can handle all this trouble you bring with you. Why don't you go home?'

'Go home, nothing! I'm going to track them down. Jesus bloody Christ, they might even take it into their heads to get married! Think of that.'

Margaret Carmichael laughed. 'You can think again. Jessica's not so stupid.'

'What do you mean? You bloody bitch, you. Are you insinuating that my boy's not good enough?'

Miss Carmichael looked at him sadly and then walked out of the room.

With ten minutes to go, there was no sign of Jessica, and Miss Carmichael, who stood at the front door of the building, in a brown tweed coat, was all a-tremble with anxiety and frustrated expectations. Then a taxi drew up, and out climbed Jessica, slightly flushed, in her green burberry, carrying the cello in its case.

Miss Carmichael said, 'Where have you been? You're so late!'

'Don't worry,' said Jessica, making for the dressing rooms. 'I'm quite ready. It'll be all right, you'll see.'

'Where's my son?' said George, advancing towards them from the auditorium, impeccable in black morning coat with black pin-stripe trousers, white shirt and the same blue tie. But the hours of waiting had not mellowed him. If anything he was harsher and more determined than before. As Jessica swept past, he took hold of her shoulder, 'I asked you a question!'

'Take your hands off me. I'm not one of your hirelings,' said Jessica, looking him full in the eye. And when he did, Jessica continued her progress, followed by the two adults.

'Where is my son? I insist on knowing.'

'I don't know where he is, at the moment,' said Jessica over her shoulder, 'but I wouldn't tell you if I knew.'

At the dressing room, George made as if to enter, but Miss Carmichael barred the way. 'You might think you can go where you like, but you're wrong. This far and no further.'

Several minutes later, showing no sign of stress, Jessica walked onto the platform, to play the last concerto of the competition.

The instrument tuned, she sat still, as if riveted to the spot, composing herself, awaiting the conductor. Across the wide expanse of the stage, she could see George, purple of face, expostulating to a Miss Carmichael almost at the limit of her self-control.

Jessica looked to the conductor, and he led the orchestra into the rising tide of the music. On cue, Jessica joined in, calmly, confidently, yet with growing purpose, and the audience were soon as rapt as she herself, allowing the pent-up emotion of a long night of stressful talk to release, soaring on wings of hope and sadness. And many recognised that the piece had never been played this way before; a few that it was not designed to be played this way. It was as if Jessica were herself the composer, altering the mood by a shade, here, and a nuance, there, to reflect her own feeling. But the effect was momentous, as moving and full of power as anything heard that week. There was beauty too; passages where she extracted every last drop of feeling, and all present felt it, shared it, sensed that they were in the presence of the extraordinary, inspired by what they did not know, but inspired, certainly; as though she were revealing, through the harmonies, the harmony of the universe, the sense of one-ness, of love and of God. It vibrated out of her, her every pore, as she bent over the gleaming red cello, her dark-red hair swept back above a face as lovely as an angel, and as pure, clad in a shapeless white dress of no particular distinction, but for which, anyway, there was no need. What need have angels of designer-clothes? And the voice that sang forth was as rich and sweet and succulent, as the finest mulled wine on a winter's day.

At the end, there was a silence, as if the unthinkable had happened, and the beauty had stopped prematurely. Then applause. Great swelling waves of it, as they dashed against the walls and backdrop. And Jessica seemed to come out of a trance and looked up, surprised to see the strings, every one of them, beating their scores with bows. The conductor came down to her and lifted her up, and shouts reverberated around the place.

Three times she went back, but would go no more. It was over. There was only the wait for the result.

'It was wonderful, but it was marginally too slow,' said one judge. 'I agree,' said another. 'But..but..but, she is the best. The best by miles,' said a third. The argument lasted an hour and was settled when someone said, 'She's only sixteen. She can enter next year.'

'I don't agree,' said one. 'She is the best. The most complete artist of them all. I don't care if she played slower than she should. It was magnificent.' But by then, nobody was prepared to listen any more.

There was universal disbelief when Jessica was placed second, behind the eighteen-year-old blonde from St Andrews. But nothing could be done about it. By the mediocre, youth has always been considered a sufficient excuse for ignoring excellence.

Billy met her in the foyer, as they were leaving. 'Oh Jessica, you were brilliant! I was so proud of you!' For all his troubles, Billy had never been so happy. He stood, radiant with life and health, even in leather jacket and jeans, looking as if he had just been converted.

Flushed and frustrated, angry and disappointed, Miss Carmichael said, 'Well I think it's a disgrace! A damn shame! Jessica was easily the best. I'm so shocked! I can't get over it. How could they make a mistake like that? Did you hear the audience?'

And for once, for the first time in his life, Billy recognised that he was needed; for here was a woman who needed comfort—and her a school teacher. He smiled and took her arm, took both their arms, and walked between them, laid his hands upon their shoulders, and walked them out of the place. 'I don't know why you're so upset. Jessica was terrific! Isn't that all that counts?'

Miss Carmichael stopped, looked at him with astonishment, and laughed and shed tears too at the same time. 'You're right, Billy. You know, you're so right! It was a triumph, no matter what anybody says.'

And for a few moments, for a few precious moments, Billy felt himself a man, and his mood lifted higher than it had ever been, and he smiled at the world, for he had a use in it, he was needed and appreciated by people who were special—outstanding, in one case, as he knew.

They were at the pavement, outside, when a taxi drove up, and George got out—a George, immaculate as ever, but on the edge of himself, puce with rage and irritation. He took hold of Billy's collar and heaved him to one side. 'In you go!' he said roughly, and shoved Billy into the vehicle, so that he sprawled on the floor. 'I don't know why you're greeting,' he snarled at Miss Carmichael. 'She was lucky to get mentioned.' George followed, the door slammed, and the taxi tick-ticked away.

'Don't pay any attention to him,' said Miss Carmichael, wiping her face with a tissue, 'some folk are just pig-ignorant.'

'I know. I just wish I could do something about him. He's ruining Billy's life.'

Jean Manson, when she heard on the telephone, was instantly depressed, as if the kitchen wall had fallen in on her. 'So you didn't get the scholarship, then?'

'No.' There was a heavy silence, and Jessica sensed the disappointment. 'It's not the end of the world, Mum. Everybody can't be first.'

'I know, but it would have been such a lift to us all. It's been s.so...so hard recently. I felt we were due a lift.'

'But life's not like that. You don't get lifts just because you think you need them. Anyway, I did well. I got into the final and came second.'

Jean was silent again, a tearless silence, the worst kind.

'Is everything all right?'

'No, everything's not all right. I don't think it'll ever come right again.'

'Oh Mum, don't say that. Try to look on the bright side.'

'How can I? Peter's moved out and your father's very hurt by it. And Susan's worse, and Roddy's morose and not getting on well. His new maths' teacher's no good. Everyone seems to know about it. I think they call him names. People are so cruel. Then there's all this talk about your father. They don't speak to me much, but I can tell it's bad. The truth is, I don't think we can go on here much longer...' and Jean became incoherent due to the tears that bubbled out of her suddenly. 'It would have been so helpful if you could have won something. It would have made it so much better.'

'I'm sorry I didn't, Mum, but I did my best. I couldn't do any better. It just wasn't good enough.'

That evening, after travelling all day, when Jessica again appeared at the Manse, John, alone, was pleased. 'You don't look disappointed, Jessica,' he said, with a hint of a smile. They were at the dining table, having tea.

'I'm not. Why should I be? I played well and I did well.'

'But it means you can't go to the music school,' said Jean, fighting back the tears.

'Mum, I never wanted to go to the music school. I don't want to spend my life sitting on a stage playing the cello. I wouldn't have known what to do if I had won. In a way I'm glad I didn't.'

'Then why did you enter? Why did you do all that work? You're crazy, Jessica,' said Jean, tearfully, burying her head in her hands.

'I didn't mind the work. It was fun. I did it because so many people wanted me to. I didn't want to let them down.'

'I don't understand you! You know what poverty is. You've grown up with it. You don't need to live like this. You could do better. You would have money and good clothes. Live in the best hotels. Want for nothing.'

Jessica laughed. 'I'm surprised at you. I never thought you envied the rich.'

'When you've had a lifetime of the other, you see things differently.'

'So what is it you want to do, Jessica?' said her father, with a wry smile.

Jessica looked around the table at the assembled family, and grinned happily. 'I'm going to be a psychiatrist.'

'You don't mean it?' said Jean. 'A shrink? Isn't that what they call them? Dealing with folk that are crazy. No, Jessica, you mustn't do that. It would be...it would be bad for you. No, I won't have it. You must stick to your music. That's much better. Speak to her John.'

'I want to devote my life to helping people to be happy. To help heal hurt minds.'

'Come on John, set her straight.'

John laughed. 'No I won't. Jessica knows her own mind. Anyway, I agree. It's a very worthy job. We could be doing with one in here right now, I'm thinking.'

'But John, think of the lunatics and bad folk she'll have to meet! It's not good for her.'

'It's not an easy job, I grant you; but it's a job somebody must do. No, we should be proud of Jessica.'

The tea-dishes washed and stowed, Jean put on her coat and went out into the gathering darkness. She had to get away, away from all this trouble and think things out. It was all so intolerable.

Down to the front she walked, and then up the hill to the castellated Bannockburn Tower with the public garden, and the view of the harbour that she liked best, and there she sat down on a garden-seat and surveyed the lights of the town, the little theatre on the promenade, lit up like a fun-fare, with a thousand coloured lights and, farther off, the lines of boats—puffers, yachts and fishing boats mostly, moored for the night; and the lights of hotels and houses, and inside, nearly every one, the people.

She had always liked people, believed that you could find good in them, if you knew how to go about it. Now she was not so sure. They had become a danger. Or was it just that John was a bad man? An atheist masquerading as a minister? Worse, she reflected—and a tear fell at the idea—a randy man, who lusted after the young women of the congregation, and made love to them when opportunity presented itself.

And she knew he was randy. He had hardly made love to her as he used to. That was a sure sign that his interest lay elsewhere. It was so unjust! 'I give my life to him. I bear his children and bring them up and make a reasonable job of it in dreadful poverty, and when I'm old and grey and getting fat and it's too late to change, he rejects me and goes to other women. And every time I ask him to look out for us, to care for his own family by keeping a tight grip on money, he gives it away to some wastrel who will only spend it in the nearest pub. Or he drinks it himself, on the pretext of taking his ministry into the pubs, because that's where the folk with problems are to be found. What was there to do? The situation was impossible! And now this. Madeline Grant. God knows she was a good-looking young woman. Any man would count his blessings for a night with her. Was it really true?' She felt an overpowering need to know.

Suppose it was true. How did it affect her? Could she up and leave them all? Take the kids with her? How would that help? She needed love. She missed it so badly. How would she find it again?

Her reverie was interrupted by footsteps on the gravel, and she looked up into the face of Tom Henderson.

'It's you Jean,' he said, warmly. 'Mind if I sit down?' Taking no reply for assent, he sat close to her, and looked out over the lights of the town. After a silence, he said, 'I often come here at night. It's so peaceful. I used to come here with my wife when she was alive, but that was a long time ago.'

'You miss her then?'

'Oh yes, but the image fades. Sometimes I can hardly remember what she looks like.'

'Surely you have photographs?'

'Yes, but I put them away a long time ago. It seemed best to look forward and put the past behind me.'

'And you've never wanted to remarry?'

'Oh yes. I miss being married. I really miss it terribly.' And beside her, Jean knew the man was on the point of tears.

'What is it you miss?'

Beside her, he seemed to squirm in his seat, as if unsettled by the question, and for a while there was silence, until, suddenly, like a dam bursting, it poured out of him. 'I feel as if I'm only half a man. As if I'm in need of the other half. It's not just bed—though God knows that's important. You can't imagine how it is for a man without a woman. It's so.. so degrading. I don't know how I can talk to you like this. I've never talked to anyone about it before. I hope you'll forgive me. I shouldn't really be unloading my troubles onto you like this. I suppose it's the dark. It's easier somehow.'

'Don't worry about it. It's good for me. I've been sitting here feeling so useless. So it's a relief to be able to help somebody, if only as an ear.'

They sat in silence for a while, until, behind a cloud, the moon came out, a full, splendid moon, which bathed the garden in silvery light; and then Tom said, 'There is a great feeling of uplift for a man when he gets married. It's.. it's very secure having someone in bed with you every night. But..but when it stops...it's terrible. The guilt. I know it shouldn't be like that but it is. You have to go back to behaving as you did when you were a boy. It's so destructive.'

'Surely it's only natural? I mean what else can you do?'

'Some men take a fancy woman. Others even pay them.'

'Have you?'

'No, I'd be too guilty to do that. No, I'm the type that needs just one woman, one good one.'

Silence descended again upon them like a cloak, as both assimilated the remarkable insights into male sexuality which were new to Jean, though not unexpected. Did she not feel the same sense of loss precisely? Then, suddenly, as if a dam of confidence of her own had broken, she said: 'Do you know if my John has been doing it with Madeline Grant?'

The question, asked out of the blue, took Tom Henderson by surprise. But when he looked at her face, shaded as it was in the moonlight, he saw the tear-streaks and knew the seriousness.

'I don't know, and that's the God's truth. But a lot of folk think he has.'

'I don't know what to do about it. What can I do? I'm supposed to carry on as usual, and say nothing, and hope it will blow over, but it's more than flesh and blood can bear. It's killing me!' And the tears came again, and Tom put an arm round her shoulders consolingly, and she sniffed, and thanked him, and snuggled into the crook of his arm.

'If I can ever be any help to you, just let me know—for anything,' he added with determination. 'I'll not see you let down by anyone.'

'You're kind. I appreciate it, Tom,' she said sniffing. 'Sometimes I just don't know what to do or where to turn. A minister's wife's not supposed to turn anywhere. She's supposed to be self-sufficient, but I'm afraid I've got to the end of my tether.' She rose and turned to go.

'Well, Jean, if you ever need somewhere to stay, just come to me. I would love to have you. And I would ask nothing in return. And you can bring the children too. I would expect that.'

'You are a very good man, Tom Henderson, and I'll not forget it.'

'No, I'm not, Jean Manson. It's pure self-interest, so it is. I've watched you for years, aye, and wanted you too. So if you ever need a man, you can have me any time. On any terms you like.'

As she walked homeward, Jean felt better. She was not after all dependent upon someone who might prove to be undependable. They would not be turned out onto the street—her worst fear. There was a solution, for her and the family, if the worst came to the worst. He was a handsome man, Tom Henderson, with a large house in its own grounds and plenty of money. Yes, she told herself, the woman who married him could do a lot worse; and in the way of women, as the days passed, the idea began to float around, suspended within her unconscious, surfacing every so often to the mind's eye, so that she could savour it and explore it. At times, she would be impatient, and put it from her as unworthy, but occasionally, she indulged it like a day dream, and it was like cooling balm on an overheated and wounded spirit.

That night, John made love to her, more as a duty than any access of desire and she enjoyed it, even though the intimacy of old was lacking. The physical need was at least, for the moment, assuaged.

Susan Manson's progress continued like a torrent, racing along rivers of knowledge, spurting here, there, and everywhere, as this fresh fact or idea drove her in that new direction or to ordinarily impenetrable depth. The intellectual ferment was evident in the red-hot forehead, afire and aflame with unquenchable passion. To the family, she was a delight and horror, as well as an object of sympathy to be indulged because of her ill-luck.

Every morning she was up like a lark, pouring over books, then, after breakfast, when questions would emanate from her like sparks which set everyone else ablaze, because of the impossibility of finding adequate responses, she was off to school, where she shone like the rising star she was, increasingly left to her own devices because her intellectual needs were her own, and no teachers now could satisfy them. By late afternoon, she was winding down, as if the continuous effort of mind had worn her out, and she would slur her speech. Tea-time was a nightmare. By then, she would be unable to hold a knife and fork, food would be dropped, embarrassingly, and the mess it created was often enough to spoil the experience for everyone, herself included. Jessica had taken on the task of feeding her, and Susan had grown used to it, though, at times, she would rebel. Then she might just manage to feed herself for a time, but very soon there would be another disaster, and Jessica would step in to hold the spoon or cup, while Jean cleared up the mess.

Once, Peter appeared out of the blue. A tiff with the head chef who had berated his sensitive nature and caused him to seek sanctuary away from the difficult world of work. After the meal, he sought out John in his study.

'She's worse, Dad. Much worse! What are you going to do?'

'There's nothing I can do, son. I wish there was.'

'But it's so awful. I mean, it's spoiling everyone's life, not just hers.'

'Well, we just have to put up with it.' John took a bigger swig than usual from the whisky glass and wondered about Peter.

'There must be something we can do,' said Peter. 'What's the good of religion if it can solve nothing?'

'Everything works for good, to those who love God.'

'But how, Dad? That's just a formula. You don't even believe in God—as a person anyway.'

'I do believe in God, but I don't know what God is. I don't think he is a person. More of a force for good.'

Peter shook his head, dissatisfied. 'It's no good. Nothing's any good any more. I used to think it was all so simple. I would go to uni and study mathematics and do research, and now I don't know where I am. All I know is there isn't any God. No good will come of this disease of Susan's. I feel it in my bones. How could it? She's just going to die! And all this good work of yours over the years. What's the point of it? Where does it get you? The whole town thinks you're an adulterer. That you have sex with young widows on the congregation.'

So that was it. The anger rose in John like lava in a volcano. All the more violently for the accusation being so nearly true. But, as he was forced to recognise, because he had done nothing, he was able to retain his cool. He laughed suddenly, aware that here at least was living proof of the statement 'All things work for good to those who love God.'

Peter said, 'I don't understand you! How can you sit there and laugh?'

'What do you want me to do, deny it or admit it?'

'Well did you?'

'I'm surprised you need to ask. I thought you were cleverer than that. It seems there are areas of human experience about which you have much to learn.'

And so, because of John's pride, Peter went off again to the hotel, still possessed with the idea that his father had been committing adultery with young widows like Madeline Grant.

By now, the town was pretty-well convinced that there had been something untoward. Sniffy Johnstone had definitely seen something. It just had to be immoral whatever it was. Other folk said they had seen them. And then, how could anyone resist Madeline Grant? Her infatuation for her minister was obvious to anyone who spoke to her. To the bystander who asked after her, she would say she was fine and, if asked if she had received any help, she would reply that the minister had been very helpful, and she would blush slightly, as if the help had been rather more than the divine guidance expected, on occasions of adjusting to widowhood.

A few even asked her outright what she thought of him, and a misty look would spread itself across her eyes, and she would say: 'A wonderful man, a wonderful man!' and with such enthusiasm, that there appeared to be no doubt. To Madeline, all the attention was welcome. She was, for whatever reason, a celebrity, and this she took to be because the minister really was considering a move in her direction. Had everyone not been telling her for weeks she was a great catch? Well then, maybe the minister had been hooked, and it was only a matter of time before he came for her.

'Did the minister ever take advantage of you, Madeline?' said one elder, bolder than all the rest, Tom Henderson—he who had an interest in the issue, beyond any man on the island.

'What do you mean? He would never have to take advantage of me,' she said, which left Tom with the thought: so it was that easy. No wonder he fell for her.

But the mystery deepened. Where did they do it? In spite of every effort to observe the couple, they were never seen together now, except on the steps of the church on Sunday, after the service.

Then, a crowd would gather, expectantly, one far greater than the usual gaggle of souls drifting towards the front gate, as if hoping some disaster would strike, some sign from the divine being, of his ultimate displeasure.

One Sunday, affected by his talk with Peter, John chose to speak on the subject of suffering. He took his text from the book of John. 'In the beginning was the Word, and the Word was with God, and the Word was God.'

'There you have it, the mystery of what God is. Is he an old man with a long white beard who lives up in the sky and watches over us, or is he something deeper and more difficult? "The word was God," says John, the favourite disciple. Does not that say everything that need be said? Listen! Pay heed! It is the word that is God. God is the good news! The principles under which men should live. That is our God. That's who he really is. And John makes this clear by telling us that in the beginning was the word. He doesn't say that first there was God and he gave us the word. No! The word is first and foremost. But it occurs simultaneously with God. There is no distinction between God and the word, that is what Saint John is telling us.

"Later he says, 'We know that all things work for good to those that love God.' What are we to make of this? How can the suffering, the needless suffering of a child, ever work for good? How can the death of an old lady, knocked down in the street, work for good? How can a young girl in a third-world country, starved and tortured and raped. How can that work for good? The answer is in ways we cannot see. But with hindsight, if we knew everything that took place before and after the event, we would find, I believe, that the suffering was worthwhile, in some larger way, perhaps by making everyone of us more aware of what our duty is, and what we owe to each other. Perhaps, by her fortitude, that girl who was tortured, affected one of the guards, who afterwards showed compassion to others who fell into his hands. Perhaps that old lady who was knocked down and killed, was instrumental in the erection of a barrier on the street or making it a one-way street, with a special speed-limit. So that many lives were saved thereafter. Or maybe just before she died, she said something to one of the living who was touched by it and affected by it, ever after. It is hard to say what the effect of suffering might be, but it is certain that every suffering has an effect throughout our society and sometimes throughout the world. Why? Because there is always a sign of it. It is like the ripples from a splash which travel across oceans. That's why it can make sense and why Saint John was right when he said "everything works for good to those who love God." The ocean is the world of time and space, the ripple, the tiny iota of suffering which affects all around it and far, far beyond, in time and space.

'Gravity is a force which affects even the most distant objects in the universe, no matter how small. I think that suffering is like that, in the moral universe.

'Suffering is also inevitable. To be is to suffer. Oh, there are pleasures and triumphs even, but what would they be without suffering? It is the other side of the coin, the quality without which the good things would have no meaning. And since to be human is to die, suffer we must at some time, for there is pain in growing up, in being moulded by the experience of life, some of which is necessarily bitter. And we stumble and fall down and injure ourselves all the time, because we are human. And we get illnesses. The nurse gives an injection, a vaccination against a disease like cholera, and for a few days we are not well, but that small illness protects us against a larger and more dangerous one. Finally, illness kills us, for we are not immortal. We must all die one day.

'But there is, you see, an inevitability too, about the principles of Jesus. As life goes on, as the earth whirls around the universe, men do come to a better understanding of how they should live together. And the reason that they do, is well explained by evolution. They learn because of natural selection. More, they learn from the suffering of others how they should behave. As we have learned from Jesus's suffering. In a way, every man is his own Jesus, has his own cross to bear, and many suffer the agony and the pain of it, just as he did.

'I sometimes think that a full life is one very different from what it is commonly taken to be. A life of ease, of comfort with the big house, the flashy car, foreign travel, and dinner twice a week at the Grand Hotel—that's some folks' idea of a life fulfilled. Because that's what they would like. In truth, it is an empty life, one that never pays its dues, never has to struggle and to fail. That is where the fulfilment comes in: the struggle and the failure. Not in success, or ease, but in the fight, hard fought, which, humans being what they are, is inevitably a failure in some way. For in success, there is failure and in failure, success. Man that is born of woman is born to die. It is only the manner of that death that is of interest. Did he die like a vegetable, without a thought in his head? Or did he die fighting to advance the cause of Jesus? Was that what he was trying to do—even if no one saw it, is that what he was doing?'

There was a silence as the congregation considered this, under his impassioned eye. Was this a confession? Some thought so. A few, a few only, saw it as a struggle of a special kind: after a deeper truth.

'There he goes again,' said George, happily, 'God's just a bunch of words. Not a person at all.'

Betty smiled agreement. Her George knew best.

George whispered not too quietly, 'How could it not be right to be successful? To have money and a big car and a house? Doesn't everybody think this? The man's off his rocker.'

It was on the tip of her tongue to say, 'George, what about the rich man and the eye of the needle?' But Betty was not used to arguing with George, so he, whose animosity against John knew no bounds, had no check on his worst excesses.

At the door, as they went out, John stood in grey cassock, shaking hands, and George could not leave it alone. The anger was in him, the pent up fury of frustrated loss of business and now there was this matter of his son, Billy, who stood behind him, a flushing wreck of a young man.

George said, without shaking hands, 'You've gone too far, this time. The world is built on business. Where would we be without it? Can you not see, man? Where would the jobs be without business to make them? And why would men do business if they couldnae improve their standard of living? What would be the point?'

'I'm not against business, George,' said John. 'But money isn't God. It shouldn't be the be-all and end-all the way it is for some business-men. There are higher things. And some business-men are big enough to see it.'

'Don't be daft. We're all in it for the money. What else is there?'

'Goodness, love. The principles of Jesus.'

'Uch away! Since when was God the same as a few principles? You know what you are? An atheist. You should give it up and go back where you came from.'

George strode off with his family trailing behind, but many had heard the exchange and John took it badly. It was a failure and he knew it. It so affected him that he forgot to speak to Billy, who was dragged off by the arm, as if he would be endangered if allowed to remain. To speak truly from the heart and afterwards be condemned in this way was a failure. And others saw that he took it that way, without any attempt to pass it off as something else, and they too regarded it so. For if he felt he had failed, how could they be expected to think him mistaken? The multitude always behaves thus. Believe something good about a man they might not, but if a man says anything against himself, they will believe that in a rush. And if he shows that he believes it so, that is enough. Better than saying.

Lunch that day was a subdued affair, as if the head of the house had suffered a defeat and knew it. Only Jessica tried to cheer the troops.

'That was one of your best sermons, Daddy. It made immediate sense and was really valuable.'

John looked at her with doleful eyes. 'Good of you to say so, but you're just saying it, Jessica. You believe God is a person. How can you agree with my view of it?'

'I know God as a person. I am aware of him. And yet I also know what you meant, and, to those that are not aware of him as a person, you have given the next best thing. For it's these things that God is all about.'

'You can't believe in both at the same time, Jessica. Not even in charity.'

'Why not? Is there so much difference between the feeling of goodness and the principles of goodness?'

'Maybe not, Jessica, maybe not,' said John doubtfully. 'The one is certainly a concomitant of the other. If the principles of goodness mean anything to a person, they must feel good about them. I suppose that's where we meet.' John smiled bleakly. 'Well, if I got to no one else this morning, at least I got to you, Jessica. And I find I'm closer to you than before. That has to be a kind of success among so much failure.'

'It wasn't a failure, Daddy. A lot of people would have learned new things today. They're not all like George Buchanan.'

'No, but a lot of them are, or they follow him, anyway. There are not too many folk who wouldn't prefer a big house, a fancy car, and a fat wage to any amount of goodness. I suppose that's the difficulty. They want the goodness for themselves, and they think they can't have it unless the other fella has less of it. I sometimes wonder if it's worthwhile. Kicking against the pricks. They all want one God and I offer them another.'

'But Daddy, you don't mean that! Your life has meaning because you're trying to show them the way to live.'

'Yes, but how do I go on trying to convince them? What more can I say? They've heard it all before, and still they go on as if it was all mumbo-jumbo. As if I was a witch-doctor who had to be visited once a week just to keep the spirits pacified. But they don't pay attention. What I say means so little to them.'

'No, Daddy, it's not true! They do pay attention! Think what they would be like if they didn't go to church.'

'Would they be so much worse off? I doubt it, Jessica.'

And Jean, who, formerly, would have been the first to head-off a discussion of this kind, sat silent, watchful, like a broody hen, while her family destroyed itself about her. That was what was happening, she knew. The family had only held together before, because she had kept it there, repelling every attempt to disunite it. But now she had lost faith in it. She could see it herself, as she sat wondering at her own silence. And John looked at her and saw the resignation.

She looked around the room and saw only poverty. The bare walls, the threadbare carpet, the chipped table concealed by a table-cloth, so old and washed out that it was frayed at the ends; and the window sashes that were rotten for a lick of paint and let in draughts. But there was no money to buy paint or anything else. There had to be something better than this. And suddenly, she realised that there was and she knew where it was. It had been offered to her, and all she had to do was accept it. Maybe the bed would be better there too. There was nothing quite like a loving man who wanted and needed you. When was the last time she had known that? So long ago.

'Mother! Mummy!' said Jessica. 'Have you nothing to say?'

All Jean could do was shake her head silently, get up, and begin collecting the dishes like an automaton, while inside her, the dream of a new life elsewhere, spread around her mind. Carefully, she gathered them all on a tray so that she would not need to return, and left without another word.

Susan and Roddy waited a moment, and then scuttled off in silence, leaving Jessica, an alarmed Jessica, seated at the table with her father. 'You must do something, Daddy.'

'How is your school-work coming along these days?' he said, trying to divert her.

'It's all right. It's us I'm worried about.'

'All things work for good to those who love God,' said John and laughed, a sad, dreamy laugh as images of how things had once been around that table, flooded his mind. 'I wonder what good will come out of this? Ah well, no good speculating. It just has to be lived through.'

'Can't you do anything?'

'What is there to do? There are times when the right thing to do is stand off and let folk make their own choices.'

'You don't think Mum would leave us?'

The question jolted John back in the seat. Had it really got that far? It must, he supposed, for Jessica, she of the wondrous insight into the interior of people, to have formulated it. 'Why not?' he found himself saying. 'She might leave me at least. This life she has is not exactly paradise.'

'But where would she go? What would she do?'

'There's no shortage of places for a woman like her. And most of them would be a lot less trouble.'

Remarkable insights into the business affairs of George Buchanan were soon to come to light. On Monday, John paid a visit to Willie Bremner, an ex-fishmonger who had done well at his business. The flat was in an expensive property on Ottersay sea front. The door was ajar and John called through. A woman came.

'It's yourself Mr Manson. I'm Mr Bremner's home-help. Will ye come in?'

The lady soon departed, leaving John alone with the old man who was propped up in bed reading a book printed in large type.

'So you haven't been too well, Willie. I thought I hadn't seen you at church for a few weeks.'

'It's my hert, Mr Manson, that's whit it is. I don't think I'll be oot o' here again.'

'No, no, Willie. You'll be up and about soon. You'll see.'

'No Ah'll no'. It's the feenish this time. Ye see Ah don't really want to go on. I could niver get up that stair if I went doon again. No, this is me till I'm cayrried oot in ma box.'

'But you could get help getting up and down. You could even move to a house on the ground floor. Would you like me to see if there's anything suitable?'

'No, no. I'm feenished, I tell ye. I've had enough. I jist want to die in peace. I jist don't have the puff any more. It's aw too much trouble.'

'But there's so much to enjoy!'

'No' for me. I'm fair spent. I've nae puff left.' John sat eyeing Willie, wondering what to do or say. It was always difficult, a situation like this. What could one say to a person, who had had enough of life, and just wanted to die?

'What was it you used to like to do? Did you not play golf?'

'Aye, but no' fur a while now. Ye need puff for that.'

'Well, what about watching it on the telly?'

'It's no' the same. Watching a wee black box. Niver mind. I'm aw sorted oot. I'm ready and waiting. So dinnae you fash yersel' aboot me.'

The sight of someone ready for death had always seemed to John a contradiction in terms. How could one who was still alive do anything but cling to life?

'I've got my papers aw done and signed. George Buchanan was really helpful. He gave me a form tae save goin' tae a lawyer and payin' oot good money. An' one o' he's drivers signed it for me.'

'And what did you do with it?'

'It's here of course, under the mattress. So when Ah'm deed, it'll get found.'

'But who'll find it? Shouldn't it be lodged in a bank or with a solicitor for safety?'

'That costs ye money. They're aw sharks. I've spent a muckle money wi' these and got naething in return. George said I should jist leave it where it can be found. He told me where to put it safe.'

'So George will find it there, is that what you mean?'

'Aye, I suppose so. Yince the doctor's been and certified me properly deed, the undertakers get called.'

'What about relatives? Won't they get it?'

'I've only a couple o' dochters and one o' them lives in Embro'. The ither wan's harum scarum. Ah widdnae want her tae find it.'

'Why not?'

'In case she does something wi'it.'

'So you want George to deal with it then?'

'Well, aye, Ah suppose so.'

'Can I see this will?'

'Whit fur?'

'Just to make sure that it's all you expect it to be.'

The paper was eventually produced by the old man and John opened it to read. 'George gave me the form fur nothing. He's a good lad, thon. And he even typed it up fur me. Ma writin's no' very clear noo.'

The typewriting was so small it could hardly be read.

'Did you agree to George being the undertaker? It says here that he is to have the job.'

'Aye, Ah did. Ye don't want just anybody haunlin' yer corpse. Ye huv tae be careful.'

'I see you've left George your pocket watch. Did you mean to do that?'

'Aye, it's an antique. Handed down. He often admired it, so Ah'm leavin' it tae him.'

'Well, it looks in order right enough.' The will was signed and witnessed by George, and Jack Robinson, one of his drivers. 'So you read it over before signing?'

'No, George read it out tae me. The print's too wee for ma eyes.'

'So you haven't actually read it at all?'

'No, Ah havenay. But it's aw richt, isn't it?'

'Yes, it is. A pity it's such small type. Did George take it away to have it done in his office?'

'No. He did it himsel' on a portable typewriter. On the kitchen table, as a matter of fact.'

Suspicion flooded John's mind, but where was the clue? Had George gone to all this trouble for an antique watch? What was it worth? A hundred pounds? Or was there something more? Something he was missing? There was a funeral too, he reminded himself.

The bequests were varied. The estate was to be divided equally between the daughters but only after several smaller bequests to charities and individuals.

'I see you're leaving £1000 to Miss Stirling. Did you mean that?'

'Aye, Ah did. She was ma wife's best freend and she was good tae me after the wife deed. And Ah'm leavin' money tae ma ither freends.'

'How much?'

'Ah canny mind. Was it no' a hunner each? Or was it a thoosand?'

'Then there's a thousand to the Salvation Army, two thousand to the British Legion and another to the Church. That's very good of you, Willie. I wasn't expecting that.'

'Ah've always supported the church and it's done right by me, Mr Manson.'

'So it was your idea to leave this money, then?'

'Och aye. But George was helpful, very helpful. He's used tae it, though. He has it aw at he's finger-tips.'

'And you're leaving two thousand to the Cat and Dog home in Glasgow and a thousand to St Michael's Home for the old folk in Branden. All I can say, Willie, is that you've been generous. And will there be much left for the children?'

'Och aye, plenty, Mr Manson.'

'You don't have a pet now, do you? I'm surprised you left money to the Cat and Dog Home.'

'That was George's idea. All these old dugs and cats shouldnay get gassed. They should be kept in comfort.'

Later that day, having tried without success to get the number of the Cat and Dog Home, John set off for Glasgow, grudging the fare, but unable to prevent himself. Two and half hours later, after a boat, train and bus journey, he stopped outside the address given in the will. The building was old and decrepit, and the close smelled as if it had been used as a toilet. On the first floor, John stopped at a plaque which announced the existence of the Cat and Dog Home, and hammered the door, there being no bell, without response. Beside it, to the left of the door were other plaques. One for Simmons Kidney and Liver Research Institute. A larger one yet for The Sir Thomas Morton Heart-Lung Research Unit, a fourth for the Henderson Cancer Foundation and a fifth announcing the address of The Headline Trust. What would that be, wondered John? And then he saw: The Headline Trust would be for diseases of the head and brain. With every major ailment covered, how could it fail? All George had to do was encourage every dying person he met, to will a sum of money to the medical research that most concerned them. And George would even supply the name and address. What could be easier?

And so the lawyer dealing with the will would send off the required sum to the address given, never imagining that the high-sounding title was not what it seemed.

John tried every door on the stair, but got no response. It was deserted. But he was pretty sure by now that the tenant or owner of the flat, with the plaques outside, was none other than George himself. It was so easy! No wonder George was incensed at losing the taxi service for the old folks. He needed that, to make contact and keep in touch regularly. George would be the one person the lonely old folk could depend on; and for every one who had a caring relative, there would be another who had none and whose friends had all died. Yes, George would always be on hand to advise when the question of a will came up. And if he was not, the drivers would be primed to keep him informed. And so he would take his typewriter to the house with a blank will and offer—out of the goodness of his heart—to type it up. And he would drop the suggestion about leaving money to medical research, and he happened to know the names and addresses of some worthy charities. Except that they were names of his own registered companies, and he alone would be able to draw cheques.

It was almost foolproof.

Some old folk would not agree to leave money to his charities. Even then, George would still do well out of the funeral and gifts to himself for his good service. But often, if there was any real money especially, they would be happy to put some of it into a worthy cause. Then, George would do very well out of it. No wonder he drove a Mercedes, lived in a grand house, and dined royally at the Grand Hotel.

How to prove it? That was the problem that engaged John during the journey back to Branden. It was best handed over to the police, he realised. And so to see Inspector Lovell, he went, and found him still in the station, where John related all that he knew and what he suspected.

It was ten o'clock at night before John reached the Manse, where he found Jessica sitting alone in the front room. 'Mum's gone out. I don't know where,' she said accusingly. 'She went out an hour ago for a walk. You might have left a message. We've been worried about you.'

'I'm sorry. I phoned, but there was no one at home. I had to go to Glasgow. Something important. Very important.'

'What could be more important than the trouble here?'

'Surprising as it may seem, there are bigger things than this family.'

'Such as?'

'I can't talk about it. Wouldn't be right to broadcast suspicions until they're verified.'

After a sandwich and a glass of milk, John felt refreshed but still unsettled and he decided to go for a walk. Maybe he would meet Jean and he could talk over his worries.

Along the sea front he went, and then, on impulse, up the Gallowgate and on up the steep back-road to the school where, at the top, he stood, for a while, looking down on the great gothic structure, easily seen against the sky. Inside, in the assembly hall around which the classrooms were constructed, he could see the large board of dux-medal winners, each name emblazoned in gold, for there was a single light above the dais, where the headmaster was wont to address the throng of students and staff, in their lines. Would any of the other Manson children have their names inscribed there, he wondered? How would Peter manage, now that he had lost faith in Charlie Braddock? And Jessica, the all-rounder, blessed with such a powerful inward eye, that saw into the soul of everyone she met.

He laid his hands on the wall overlooking the playground and breathed deeply. All the knowledge there was to be had there and how much it meant. But why? Why have we so much reverence for it? Is it the pleasure it gives? Not wholly, he realised, for a lot of it was competition, one mind struggling to score more marks than another. And working so hard that pleasure seemed to have no place at all. What then? Was it the usefulness of it? A passport to another place of competition and then a good job, maybe? Yes, that was it. The dux board was a symbol of success in the rat-race, nothing more. And yet if there were no excellence, what then?

But it was more than that, he knew. Much more! It was the contact with other intelligences—not of the present so much as the past. Shakespeare and Dickens and Newton and Plato and Beethoven; and a host of other luminaries. What they had provided was so interesting, so enriching, so worthwhile, beyond any material benefit they might confer, like jobs or security.

Not far off, he heard a sound and realised that it was people talking. They were on the seat on the top-most part of the hill, under the old castellated Bannockburn Tower, owned by the local Council. There was a garden around it, where the public could sit and look down on the harbour. Oh well, others went for walks on cold nights. Lovers probably, he thought, smiling. How long ago was it that he had met Jean outside, because there was nowhere else to meet?

It was time to leave and he began to walk to the end of the low wall above the school, so that he could descend to the road below by the path, but, as he did so, something made him pause. What was it? Why, it was a voice. He found himself stopping to listen and wondered at himself; and then he knew. He knew it as well as he knew his own. Better. It was Jean and she was deep in conversation with someone on a seat in the garden. He stood uncertainly for a while and listened, and heard the voices and knew who they were, and their motive for being there.

Suddenly, a strangled gasp came from him, and he made as if to interrupt the seated figures, silhouetted against the sky, clinging to each other, as he could easily see, on the bench. Then he stopped, and turned about, and tottered down the path to the street below, feeling as if an iron band had gripped his chest, so that he could hardly breathe. At the street, he held onto the wall bounding the lower part of the school, and rested, feeling as if his soul were bleeding out of him.

Somehow, he got himself down the brae to his home and into bed, where he lay in a ferment of loss, a prey to every fear. So Jean had left him! The unthinkable had happened. And the reasons for the defection were clear enough. What was he to do? And he knew he would do nothing. Some choices must be left to those who make them. And so, he lay for hours, silently, grieving at the loss, and suffering the irreparable desolation of his spirit.

It was after midnight before she appeared. He lay on the edge of the bed, and pretended sleep because he was afraid to speak. The whole panjandrum of hurt and terror would have come rolling out of him, and demeaned and degraded him, on the barbs of her rejection.

She crept into bed, and soon he heard the change in her breathing, as she fell asleep, a sleep that was well-satisfied, he reflected; and the tears welled-up and he lay, stiff with worry, and fear, at the loneliness ahead, until even he, hours later, dozed off.

Jean was up early, and, from the sounds of her activities, he knew she was happy; and he knew why. Rising late, he shaved and went down to the kitchen and found a full breakfast awaiting him. He sat down without a word, grey-faced, and began to eat. When he had finished, she came across with the tea-pot to refill his cup and he looked up at her, and found her face serene.

'What are you going to tell the children?' he said.

She looked at him blankly. Then she blushed. 'I don't know what you mean.'

'You do. We'll have to discuss it sometime.'

John sat for a while, hoping she would say something, but when she did not, he rose and went to his study, and tried fitfully to work on his sermon.

An hour later she brought a mug of coffee and said, 'Did you have a nice day on the mainland, yesterday?'

'No. I phoned, but you were out. I left on the noon steamer.'

'Madeline Grant was off the island, yesterday.'

John looked at her levelly, 'I didn't know that. She wasn't on my boat. Or if she was I didn't see her.'

'And you didn't see her over there?'

'No.'

'What were you doing, then?'

'Following up a hunch. I'm pretty sure George Buchanan has been making a lot of money out of bequests from our old folk. He gets them to leave money to medical charities, but they are just companies he owns.'

'It's not possible. I don't believe it. What have you done about it?'

'Given it to the police.'

They were silent for a moment, looking at each other, until he said, 'Does it make a difference?'

'What?'

'That I wasn't with Madeline Grant.'

She blushed. 'No, how could it?'

'So it is like that,' he said.

Jean flushed bright scarlet and left the room; and a little while later, he heard her go out. He had been sitting brooding over the sermon, though doing nothing constructive. He was too upset for work. Once, he got up explosively, and paced around the room; but soon sat down again. Anger might be natural; but it was no solution. If Jean did leave him, it would be because she wanted to, and, he conceded, because she had the right. There was a limit to what a spouse had to put up with; and only the spouse could decide what it was.

Church that Sunday was crammed to overflowing and it never occurred to John that the cause might be the quality of the sermon of the week before. To him, they had come to mock; for in a hot-house like the Isle of Branden, how could two people, one of them the minister's wife, carry on an affair without somebody finding out? They had come to enjoy a spectacle, and to gloat over every nuance they could interpret to their own purposes.

And yet it was not so, for none knew of the affair yet. It was too soon begun.

He took as his text, the story of the return of the prodigal, and, after the tale was told, he asked what it meant.

'Was it fair that the son who had held his place and kept his patrimony intact, should suffer at the return of the prodigal? The man who has been a trial to his parents and has spent everything, wasting it on the fleshpots, throwing away, with careless abandon, all that his father earned for him, and gave him freely?' John's voice was strong and carried far into the kirk. But, looking up at him, Jean realised that there was a pallor about him she'd never seen before. She had been staring sightlessly ahead, absorbed in a daydream of a new love and a new life, rich in all the bounties the old life had denied her. But her attention was caught. John was speaking about forgiveness.

'Is any man or woman without blemish? Is there a perfect living being? Of course not. Then why cannot we forgive? But, I hear you say, if a man hurts me, should I not make sure that he will not do so again? Should I not learn from experience and shun him in the future? No, says the Gospel. No matter what the prodigal has done, what sins he has committed, what losses we have sustained because of his folly, we should take him back, welcome him and celebrate his return. That is what we are told to do. No matter what hurts we have suffered, we should take all repentance and greet it with gladness. We should not bear grudges and set people from us because they have offended us or wounded us. They should always be given a second chance and a third and a fourth even. For people are human and can be expected to err and, so long as they repent, we should accept them again with a joyful heart. That is the message of the Gospel. And it is what we all should do.'

Some there took it for a message about himself, and looked at Jean and she, seeing them, took it to mean that they knew about her own folly.

At the door afterwards, as Madeline Grant came towards him, people hung about to look, and whispered together, and John saw it and forgave them. Where another man, aware of the danger, would have turned away and ignored her, he was kindness and sweetness personified.

'And how are you, Madeline? It's good to see you,' he told her, taking both her hands in his. There was to be nothing but warmth; for he was not going to be affected by any stiffness of response.

'I'm fine. I haven't seen you for a while. Maybe you'll call this week and have tea.'

'No, Madeline, not this week,' he said, with a smile. 'You must take yourself out to the dancing and the pictures. Some lucky young fella will soon snap you up and make you happy again.'

John passed on to the next person and Madeline went off with a strained face. Before long, Jean was standing in front of him and John smiled. 'What's up, Jean? Did you forget the Sunday School?' and Jean blushed.

'I don't know what I was thinking of.'

There were titters of laughter round about, as the worst sort of onlookers overheard, but John ignored them, and smiled on her, as he would at any struggling member of the congregation.

Outside the kirk, she stood for a while chatting inconsequentially with some of the older women, until a man's voice said, beside her, 'Hello, Jean.' It was Tom Henderson looking at his handsomest, dark hair swept back in a wave and with a red carnation in the button-hole of his dark suit.

She turned to speak to him, and the radiance of her smile was there for all to see. And John saw it and was instantly desolate.

The police came in the afternoon. John was in his study and they were shown in and sat down at the hearth-side, leaving John in his chair at the desk.

'There are no plaques on the door of 817 Pittenweem Street,' said Sergeant Mills. 'There have been plaques but they've been taken away. Four of them, as you said.'

'But how did he know to go and take them off?' said John.

'We went to see Willie Bremner. It seems he mentioned it to George Buchanan the very next day. George goes there a lot.'

He would, reflected John. He would keep in close touch with anyone on his last legs if there was money at stake. The will might have to be changed at the last minute, and he would want to make sure he arranged it. He would also want good warning of any possible trouble.

'What did Willie say? Was that any use?'

'Not enough to go on. It's just suspicion. The companies are bogus, as you suggested. They're registered in the name of Roy MacPhail of the same address. We traced cheques from lawyers here to a bank in Glasgow where they were cashed, but the description of the man MacPhail doesn't match George Buchanan.'

'So he has an accomplice?'

'Maybe. Maybe he just uses a disguise. It's so easy to do.'

'But how did he get a bank account under a false name?'

'Easily, if you have a few other false documents to identify you. Almost anything can be had for a price. But we don't think he would need to pay much just to get a bank account. Banks are not very particular who uses them. A false passport could have been bought and then resold for the same money. Maybe he just stole someone's driving licence, used the name, changed the address and gave it back, or said he'd found it.'

'So there's nothing on George, then?'

'I'm afraid not, Mr Manson. There just isn't enough to stand up in court.'

'But surely there's the will? Willie Bremner has a will which George typed and it has this fictitious company and address?'

'There is a will, right enough, but Buchanan says he thought that was the right address of the Cat and Dog Home. He can't remember where he saw it. An advert in some newspaper, he says.' As they left, the sergeant said, 'At least you've put a stop to it, for now.'

'Do you mean he might start this up again?'

'When things quiet down, he might. It's a very easy scam to arrange. Anyone can rent an address, and put up a few plaques for important companies to get mail there—some companies behave in exactly this way, to save office-space and staff. The lawyers who send off the cheques should make sure of them before they do, but in the nature of things they don't. They're lazy. So long as they get their own money, a lot of them don't care about anybody else's. No, if a lawyer sees that money has been left to a medical charity, he'll usually pay up without another thought.'

'But surely lawyers check up?' said John, indignantly.

'How? How can you check up on a company? It could take ages. Never mind the cost of the phone calls. No, I can understand lawyers not wanting to spend time on that. Why would they? They don't get paid for that kind of work.'

'But wouldn't the lawyer notice that the same address cropped up, time after time?'

'A lot of different lawyers are involved. Anyway, it'll be a different charity for each will—maybe not even every one George is involved in. And then, the matter of addresses will be left to the office-staff. What lawyer would bother himself?'

The constable said, 'The lawyer might be in on it, you know. There's a lot of money in this. Or there could be.'

With sudden insight, John said, 'He might even have several addresses like Pittenweem Street, which he changes regularly, and other charities. If he used each once only, he would never get spotted. It's foolproof.'

And so the upshot was that the police could do nothing, because George had covered his tracks. They promised to keep the matter under notice, but John realised that proof would be hard to get. It would even be worth George's while to rent a property just once for the sake of the bequest and then change it for another. Glasgow was full of rented property, which could be had for a song. If he were careful, George would never get caught.

That evening before tea, Jean said, 'What are you going to do about George?'

'Nothing. He might even be innocent.'

'But how? You should face him with it.'

'No. I don't know it for a fact. It's just possible that he had nothing to gain himself. Who knows what has happened here? It looks clear enough, but without the evidence it's not a fact. So there is nothing to be done and nothing to say.'

'But shouldn't you try and get evidence?'

'I'm not a detective. I have other things to do than go snooping.'

'But if others won't do it, surely...'

'No. It's not my line. It's degrading and it's not my business.'

'So you won't lift a hand to help all these old folk?'

'I already have. I've done more than most, and more than I should, maybe. But I've put it in other hands now. I have to keep myself clean, don't you see? It's fundamental.'

She looked at him with blank amazement, but said nothing. There was no more lucrative source of money—really big money—than the old and infirm, all of whose assets were up for grabs when they died. And George Buchanan operated a system he had carefully perfected over the years, for reaping a share of it.

George had been busy on his own account. Dining selected members of the Kirk Session, one at a time, in the Grand Hotel, finding out what favours they might need, and arranging them on the spot; even handing dapper little Dick Souter five hundred pounds in cash across the table, in a pretended access of generosity, for that worthy's current expenses—a master stroke, as George, smilingly remembered with pleasure, afterwards. 'You can pay me back some day, Dick,' George had said, with a grin. 'There's no hurry.' Nor was there. As George knew, Dick would never be able to pay it back; and so it would remain an extended loan; but just in case, George had him sign a paper admitting the debt; and knew that he had just acquired a very useful acolyte. For how could Dick ever go against his wishes in future? George had bought him with that loan and smiled at the cheapness of the purchase. And when Dick had flushed and stammered out his thanks, never seeing the real reason behind the transaction, George smiled amiably at the small man with the trim moustache, who looked at him with such admiration and awe, that anyone should carry five hundred pounds, still less, that he should part with it so readily, to help out a friend, for that is what George proclaimed himself to be, and was believed.

Then there was Ellen MacFadyean, whose mother lived in a council house in a bad position on Balaclava Crescent, in the Crimea, among all the worst criminals on the island. It was at a corner, which every drunken inhabitant of the area had to pass on his way home from carousing. At week-ends, the garden was strewn with empty cans and bottles and, most nights, between closing time and midnight, the street rang with curses and occasional brawls, as drunk men made their erratic and disoriented journeys to their homes from the pubs. 'No problem, Ellen, no problem!' said George, when he heard; and, the very next day, a letter was sent out informing Ellen's mother that she was to move out of the Crimea, to a council house in Maple Grove, among the Madeline Grants of this world, where respectability was a byword. All George had to do was discover some old wife living on her own there, who had got behind with her council rent payments and ruthlessly arrange a swap. Difficulty, there was none; but if there had been, if there had been a complaint, George would have found some other quid pro quo to make it stand, like free transport for the unwanted incumbent, and maybe a subsidy—courtesy of himself, if need be—for her rent, 'to give her time to recover her financial standing.' And the old lady would move gratefully enough, being unaware of the problems of the new house until it was too late. He had done it all before. Making room for folk in Maple Grove was one of George's specialities.

Once, a woman had complained, and refused to go to the Crimea, but George killed her protest as if it were a flea. Taking one hard look at the woman, who was over eighty, yellow of face and racked by cancer, he announced, 'You can have free transport and free rent till the end of your days.' And many people, when they heard it, thought him a very Christian gentleman, to help out an old woman in this way, never thinking that there might be something in it for him, and that the woman would soon be dead anyway, costing him nothing much.

Even Bob Forsyth was a walk-over. George had so many dealings with the bank that mistakes by its employees were inevitable, in an industry where an error rate of seven percent is average. All George had to do in that quarter, was turn the screw upon the legendary inefficiency of a tin-pot bank on a small island, and Bob was his for life. But there was no need to go further. As George easily calculated, the hysteria generated among the others, by his carefully cultivated fifth-column, was itself enough to precipitate the desired outcome. Thus, when Dr Telford, meeting her in the street, said to Ellen MacFadyean, 'I just hope the witch-hunt against the minister is over,' she replied, 'It's no witch-hunt. The man's done wrong. Who knows what more he might do if we leave him be.'

And when Telford recoiled with shock, and replied, 'Can't you see that George Buchanan is behind this? He has a vested interest in it.' Ellen even became angry: 'Nothing of the kind! George Buchanan is one of the finest men I know.' And proceeded to tell him her version of how good he had been to her mother. The doctor wondered at the story afterwards, picked over it as if it were refuse and him a scavenging dog, but he could see nothing there. Plainly, there had been a vacancy at Maple Grove, and George had acted sensibly by moving a woman in need.

At George's suggestion, for he knew exactly how the land lay, and that he need not play a more active part, Ellen MacFadyean, as a woman elder, was given the task of interviewing Madeline, as a preliminary—just to sound her out about appearing at an enquiry, as George delicately phrased it; without putting the woman's back up, by making any kind of suggestions. Once Ellen mentioned that Sniffy Johnstone would be giving evidence to the Presbytery, it became immediately clear to Madeline that she must also do so, if only to clear her name. And if she had any reluctance to appear on the side against the minister, it was modified by the need to protect her own reputation. As George had put it to Ellen, the necessity of her appearing must be made clear to her; and it was. The betrayal, though none saw it that way, was made easier by Ellen's assurance that no harm was likely to come to John Manson, when so many folk thought well of him. It was, said Ellen, persuaded thus by George, a routine investigation 'to clear the air'. By such seemingly innocent and gentle manipulations, are the most devious cruelties engineered.

One day, then, a letter was delivered to the Manse. As John opened it in the hall and read it, Jean knew it instinctively for trouble. His face paled and he let it drop by his side in a shaking hand. The shock and surprise in him were plain. Then he turned to her and smiled wanly. 'Well, they've done it, Jean. I never thought they would. That it would come to this. But they have. There's going to be a disciplinary hearing. I'm to be hauled up before the presbytery.'

'What for?' but as soon as she said it she knew. The whole town knew.

'They don't say. They will tell me when they see me. There's just a date and a time and a place.'

Later that morning, Hugh Etherington phoned. As he spoke, John wondered, for the little man had never said more than two words together in the history of their acquaintance. He had a deep voice for such a small man. When John's church was full to overflowing, his was scantily attended.

'I wanted to warn you about the hearing, John. The charges will be "conduct unbecoming." I thought you should know in advance.'

'Is that all? It'll be this talk about Madeline Grant, I suppose.'

'Not quite all. Some of the elders think your beliefs have become too avant garde, if you follow me.' There was a silence while John considered this.

'It's kind of you to get in touch, Hugh.'

'Not at all, not at all. It's the least I could do. I just hope it turns out all right. Good luck, John.'

Some men would have been galvanised into action to make for themselves an effective defence. They would have spent the morning on the telephone, raising supporters. John was not such a man. He already had plans for the day, people to see, people he could not delay seeing, least of all when he himself was under attack. And so, when he went his rounds, he made no mention of his own trouble.

Somehow, the news had preceded him onto the streets, and everywhere he went there were strange looks, a few people crossed to the other side rather than stop and talk, and some pretended not to notice him. The few who greeted him as usual were almost regretful, apologetic at what was happening to him, as if it were a phenomenon that had to be endured and lived through.

On the Wednesday, when he appeared at the hall adjoining St Bride's, for that was Rob McCall's church, and he was moderator of the presbytery, it was to find the sparse interior dominated by a long trestle-table, behind which sat two ministers and four elders of his own: George Buchanan, Tom Henderson, Dr Telford and Ellen MacFadyean.

Rob, brown-haired, in a black suit, said, 'Sit down, John, sit down. I'm sorry about this—we all are. This is a preliminary meeting to investigate complaints against you. One is, that you have been taking advantage of your position as minister, with a young widow on your congregation.' The speaker paused, adjusted his spectacles, and read the name off the sheet in front of him. 'Madeline Grant.'

There was a silence, while John was given time to consider the charge. Gradually, a flush spread its way up his face and all present saw it and took it for guilt. The proof positive. And yet it was only the guilt attending images once seen, and once imagined. For John was guilty about that. He had lusted after her, though he had done nothing. Presently John said, 'I did nothing to be ashamed of with Madeline Grant.'

'It's claimed that you were seen in a compromising position with her. That sexual intercourse can reasonably be inferred to have occurred afterwards between you.'

The shock of the words paralysed John, made him feel disembodied, somehow, as if it were someone else that this catastrophe was happening to. Eventually, choking back the acid that rose up out of his stomach into his throat, he said, 'It's true that I was put in a compromising position by Madeline. She had been suffering from stress after a bereavement. She was having great difficulty adjusting to her changed way of life. I visited her in the normal course of pastoral work, and advised her as best I could. Unfortunately, she formed an attachment to me. Imagined herself in love with me, and that made things difficult for us both.'

'But you didn't take advantage of her?'

'No.'

'How often did you see her?'

'After the funeral? Three or four times.'

'At her home?'

'Yes.'

'Was there anyone else present?'

'No, I don't think so.'

'Did you see her anywhere else?'

'Only at church.'

Rob said, 'Well, evidence will be produced that you did take advantage of her. So you should prepare yourself for that.'

'What evidence? Since there was nothing untoward, there is no evidence.'

George said, 'I'm afraid there is. Madeline Grant has agreed to give her side of it. And you were seen by a third party. So there's plenty of evidence.'

John felt as if the floor under his feet had been pulled away. How could Madeline Grant say anything against him? If he had been unwell before, now he felt as if his very mental stability were in the balance.

Rob said, 'There is another matter, John. It's your beliefs. There is a feeling in the Kirk Session that you no longer believe in things that, as a, minister you should. To be precise, that you don't believe in the Virgin Birth or the Resurrection or the Ascension and the Last Day. Also, that your idea of God has become a bit abstract.'

'Since God is unknowable,' said John, 'he is likely to be a bit abstract for anyone. How could anything be more abstract than something that has no limits and is indefinable?'

'But you don't think he's a person,' said George, aggressively, out of a face the colour of a salmon too long in the river, as if the issue were of utmost importance—which it was, to him.

'Well, he's not a person like you or I, George. God is more like a spirit, a manifestation of goodness and benevolence. To say that God is a person is too simple.'

Rob said, 'Do you object to some people having a personal God?'

'If they think it's their own God, yes. There is only one God and it's every one's. At least there ought to be one God. Unfortunately, some folk worship false Gods.'

'But do you think God is a being?' said George.

'What do you mean by a being? Something alive and tangible that can be touched?'

'Do you think God is a being?' shouted George.

'I think there is an influence for good, observable in the world, which is characterised by all that we hold most virtuous and that we cherish. To the extent that this influence is present among us, perceivable in the behaviour of people towards one another, the influence is a being, for it is just as alive as you and I.'

'It's just as I said,' George thundered, 'your God is just a bunch of principles. It's not a real God at all.'

'What is your real God, then, George? An old man with a white beard striding across the sky?'

'No, dammit.'

'Then what kind of being are you talking about? The one sure thing about God is that he cannot be known, and cannot be spoken of clearly or meaningfully, for he is beyond comprehension.'

George leaned back in his chair, thinking, and then suddenly pounced back. 'Do you think God created the earth and its people?'

'To the extent that an influence for good is at work in creation, yes.'

'So you believe in Genesis, then?'

'No. I don't think the world was made in seven days. Genesis is only a metaphor of what took place, written down thousands of years ago for an ignorant people. Hundreds of years of science have changed our perception of how things came to be. We understand the process better than the men who wrote *The Bible.*'

'But did God do it all?'

'In a way, yes. There is forward motion, eternal change and what directs this is God.'

'What about Christ? Is he the son of God?'

'Metaphorically, yes.'

'You mean not really?'

'No. God isn't the kind of being, if he is a being, who would have a son.'

'So you don't believe in the Virgin Birth and the Resurrection and Ascension?'

'I think Jesus was fathered by a man, probably Joseph, and that he was not fully dead after the crucifixion. There have been other cases since, of people coming to, after they seemed to be dead.'

'But *The Bible* speaks of an immaculate conception and that Jesus rose from the dead!'

'*The Bible* is just a misunderstanding of the possibilities, written by credulous men. That's all. It's no big deal and it doesn't matter. What does matter is what Jesus taught us to do and to try to be. The consequences of divinity, not divinity itself.'

'But John,' said Rob, 'you're supposed to believe in the Resurrection and the Life. It's absolutely fundamental.'

'I do believe in the Resurrection—as a metaphor. Jesus lives—among us in our thoughts and expectations and ideals. He guides me, and it is my mission to help him to guide others.'

'But you don't believe in the literal Resurrection then?'

'I believe that Jesus either wasn't properly dead or his heart started up again after he was put in the cave. What happened to the body of Jesus isn't important. What does matter is that he said certain things and they remain with us. It is through them that he lives still.'

'And the Ascension?'

'The body was buried. A physical corpse does not just evaporate. All the disciples saw it happen, saw him die finally. What was it they saw? *The Bible* doesn't say. Why not? Because it was more convenient to let folk think it was something supernatural, befitting their idea of the Son of God.'

'So they lied, then?'

'No, the authors of *The Bible,* or their transcribers, modified the text to make the success of the young church more likely.'

'They lied then!' said George.

'No, they were just not allowed to tell the whole truth by their reporters. Remember it was all written down sixty years later.'

'You think *they* lied, then?'

'Not necessarily. Maybe they just saw the world differently from us. The supernatural was so much a part of their world, that it was natural to give it a role in the description of any events, including the Biblical ones. Do you think anyone reporting an event today, that happened sixty years ago, would get it right? Of course not!'

'But this is heresy!' said George.

'Is it? Does it not appear to you to be the truth? Isn't that what the church has been working towards all the centuries since? Every year there is a new change of view, slight maybe, but it's there.'

'And what about an afterlife?'

'The soul does not go anywhere; there is nowhere to go; no heaven, no hell that is not here on earth. Why do we need a hell to go to, when we are very good at making our own?'

Dr Telford said, 'What are you doing when you perform a burial?'

'Comforting the bereaved. I offer respect to the dead and try to summarise the good things about them. That's what we should remember. I utter the well-known litanies and I mean them well. I help them get over it as much as I can. I offer real help to the living. I go along with what they believe, as far as possible. It's my duty to help them. If they press me, I don't pretend that I think there is a better world to go to. Death isn't a blessing for any but those in pain. It is the start of non-being. How could that be a good? Did you ever hear the Pope or any other churchman of any denomination pray for death? No! When they come out of hospital after their operations, they are as thankful as anyone still to be alive. They praise God for their deliverance! How could that make sense if there really is a heavenly paradise to go to? And wouldn't they know if there was? They are the most religious folk on earth. If there really is a heaven, then we should all be praying for death and cursing life. None of us do. In our hearts, we know when we die that's it. The rest is propaganda, illusion.

'There is an afterlife but only of a metaphorical kind: we live on in the memories of those who knew us and we can still have an influence on future events that way.'

Rob McCall said, 'I think we should leave it for now, John, while we take the time to consider our response. Meanwhile, as moderator, I must suspend you from duty, pending a decision, but I must say that what you have said already convinces me, that your beliefs are no longer compatible with the requirements of the Kirk.'

Tea, that evening, was a sumptuous affair, as if Jean, sensing disaster, had laid on a feast to dull the pain. John was in such high spirits that Jessica was soon able to ask, 'How did it go?'

'I said what I had to say. I'm glad I did.'

Jessica objected, 'But did you get through?'

'They understood my position.'

'But will you get off?' said Jean.

'Probably not. I told the truth as I see it. That isn't the truth as the church sees it. Though it should be.'

'You mean you admitted you're an atheist?'

'I'm not an atheist.'

But long afterwards, when the children were upstairs in bed, or at their work, he was seated in his chair by the cold fire-side, with the whisky, wondering what the future would bring, when the front-door banged, and a few minutes later, after a murmured conversation in the hall, Peter suddenly appeared and joined him, seating himself in the armchair opposite.

'Mother said you told them! Why did you have to tell them?'

'I told the truth. What else would you have me do?'

Peter got out of his seat and paced the room in a ferment, saying, 'You could have toned it down a bit. You didn't need to admit you were an atheist.'

'I didn't say I was an atheist. I'm not.'

'But you don't believe in a personal God! That's what an atheist is. You talk about God as if he were a person but you know he isn't. To you he's just all the things you think you ought to do. Can't you see what I mean? How can these things be God, a personal God, that created the earth and the things on it? The Presbytery will never understand how you ever became a minister, still less that you should remain one. You're finished, Dad, finished! And what's going to become of the rest of us? Mum and the kids? You, without a job.'

John was surprised and shocked by the attack, and remained silent for a while, considering it. It had to be the independent existence Peter had enjoyed for a few months. It had hardened him. Made him question things more directly, because of the distance between them. John had lost his authority over Peter. And, in a sudden flash, John realised that it was gone forever, like snow melted by the radiant energy of a new-found confidence which would challenge anything—especially anything in the past.

But there was more and that was degrading. It was pitiful to discover that Peter really thought that he, John, ought to have lied. That too, he saw. That one's first born son, the chief hope of one's life, should have somehow conceived a standpoint so base and demeaning, was degrading to John himself, because he took full responsibility for the dereliction.

In the silence which fell upon the room, he heard the click of the front door-latch and knew that Jean had gone out, closing the door silently behind her, in the vain hope he would not overhear.

And then, in the act of raising the glass to his lips, John saw one thing more, most fatal of all. Peter was right. His critics were right. The God of John Manson was not identical to the God of *The Bible*, no matter what latitude of interpretation was permitted; for John Manson's God was a way of life, a manner of being, not a being itself. And there was a discernible distance between the two. 'Like an abyss!' he said aloud, and laughed at the idea, after the words tumbled out, and then choked and broke into a burst of coughing.

If there was no God, no person to worship, no creator, no power beyond man, what else was there? What hope could there be in a pile of principles? He sat with his head in his hands and murmured to no one in particular, 'I've just been pissing into the wind. That's all. Going through the motions. Not really knowing what I was about.'

Peter said, 'You know there isn't any God, don't you? You can see it at last. The only thing at work in this rotten world is chance. It determines everything! And it is absolutely amoral. It strikes the good just as often as the bad. There is no reward for being good. It's all a confidence trick. And the wonder is that you've swallowed it so long. Why can't you see what a waste your life is?'

Worried, but exultant too, as he felt the power of his own anger, Peter watched him from the study doorway, and John rose out of his chair, left the room like a ghost, passing his son without a word, fumbled his way into the old black burberry, and left by the front door, forgetting to close it. It swung crazily in the wind, as Peter stared down the path at the retreating figure. He stood for a while, as the wind blew into the hall, rustling coats on their pegs, as if they were being prepared by an unseen hand for flight from that place. Suddenly it seemed a hateful home, a dreadful town. Peter felt as if, out there in the darkness, every eye was upon him and for the worst of reasons. He who craved approval, blanched in fright at the criticism of the community. What would become of him? Why had his father let him down?

John walked the streets like a man who has lost all sense of direction. Along the front to the town-centre and the Watergate and then back along the main street to the Gallowgate and along the front street again, head bowed against the breeze and mindless of the people who came and went out of pubs and cinemas and chip-shops. At last, he fetched up at Crichton, the posh part of town, and stood on the point where once his hat had rolled, like a spinning-top, into the sea. Hands on the railing, he looked seaward, towards the distant lights of Greenock, discernible through a cleft in the hills; but elsewhere, all was darkness, except for the waves which smashed against the sea-wall below him.

Above, between the scudding clouds were stars, and he watched them for a while and smiled suddenly. For if there were stars, if there was a limitless universe as men said, there had to be a first cause. And it was no counter-argument to cry: infinite regression. All that mattered was the cause of all this, he told himself, spreading his hands and arms wide in the cold air, and encompassing in his mind's eye, the entire production of the universe. The cause of all this was God. It was unknown and unknowable— inconceivable that men should ever be in a position to understand it, any of it! Well then, there was a mystery; and that was much of what men meant by God. Copleston[1] was right. All the contingent beings of the universe could only be explained by a necessary being, independent of everything. That necessary being was God. But what kind of God? The God of the old Testament? A whimsical, all powerful, cantankerous old bugger.—Aye, bugger, he told himself, and laughed ruefully at the expression. How many lives had been buggered up by God, one way and another? What business had God setting tests for folk like Abraham? Imagine telling him to put his son to death! What for? What cruelty! Was that the act of a loving God? And what about all the people, these millions the Israelites slew with the aid of God? All the Egyptians that died in the Dead Sea? And even Goliath the Philistine, killed by a boy with a sling-shot. Was that fair? Was it the action of a loving God? Would not an all powerful, all loving God be above that sort of thing? Nor was it the case that only the bad folk were killed by God, or his chosen people. A lot of them, in the nature of things, just had to be good. God could not be only the God of the Israelites! He was everybody's God! If, he said quietly, aloud, he is a being at all.

That was it precisely! God was not a being, and not all powerful, and not all loving. Peter was right about that. Blind chance does govern our affairs, except for this, he told himself: the spirit of goodness that is abroad. The good in people that makes them help each other, often at great sacrifice to themselves. The only other part of God was the word itself: the good news, the principles by which men should live. So Copleston was wrong after all. And John saw suddenly why. Copleston's argument was just a variant of the ontological one. And that is what killed it. For Kant had shown that existence is not a predicate. A necessary being might be the only explanation Copleston could think of, to explain all the contingent beings of the universe, but that was no ground for the assertion that a necessary being exists. And John smiled wryly, as he recalled the old chestnut which explained it beautifully. I can invent a name like a Muggle-dorpel[2] and even

---

[1] Father Copleston, S.J. who argued with Bertrand Russell on a radio programme circa 1960.

[2] See p 317, para 5

give it any properties I like, such as omnipotence, goodness and a host of others. But once I have finished inventing it, I cannot say that it exists. Not even if it is perfect. Because even perfection cannot be conceptualised into existence.

And yet there are still the principles by which men should live and the spirit of goodness given us by Jesus, which yet manifests itself among us.

John sighed with relief. At least I still have a God—of a kind. He set off again, back into the town, and it flashed into his mind that Peter was wrong about there being no reward for being good. There is a reward! The man who is good, is a better man in himself! The quality of his life is better. And it is not a matter of money or comforts or prestige. These are not the true measure of the quality of life. For the worst sort of rogue, the most abject criminal—even the Eichmanns of this world, murderers of millions—can have these inessential exterior things. No! It is the inner peace of the soul that is the issue, that is the test of a man's quality of life. And a man can have this special sense of self, even in the most extreme suffering; on the point of death, even—the worst kind of death.

What must it have been like for the martyr, the faggots igniting at his feet, who looked steadfastly at his murderers with understanding and compassion, and forgave them? In that moment, he would transcend himself; be more complete, greater by far than the sum of his parts, than he had ever been. Nor is this private thing the only reward for goodness. For what we do affects others; our good is reflected outwards like sunshine, and many may profit from it in diverse ways. Whatever such a man died for, would be marked indelibly on the minds of all who saw it. Beyond that, some would cease to be what they were, if they did not die for their beliefs.

But was it really so? Was Eichmann a tortured soul while the trains drew into Auschwitz with their human cargo? And John could see that he was not. All that time, Eichmann would have been basking in the glory of his own efficiency as an administrator, a task revered among his sort. And after? Once the full calumny of the world had fallen upon him, what then? Would Eichmann then have been remorseful? And John remembered the trial of the old man and knew it was not so. There was no remorse. The man was immune. That was the true horror: he remained ignorant of his guilt. So he, John, was wrong after all. Virtue is not its own reward, at least in serenity. You can have that whatever crimes against humanity you commit. But for John himself it was the reward, because that was how he was.

There was a strange consolation in these reflections, as if, under the extreme pressure upon him, of so many forces combining to destroy him, he was enabled to make fresh insights which renewed and sharpened his faith, by the tempering process of the fire of condemnation.

But the feeling of uplift did not last long. By the time he reached the harbour again, and the familiar streets of the town, reality intervened. Confronted yet again by the ignominy that awaited him behind those closed doors and curtained windows, his agony returned. What could he do about it? That was the difficulty. A minister had no one to apply to for help. No real friend, no superior certainly among the townsfolk.

In a moment of weakness, and he immediately felt it as such, he thought of Buce MacSween, who liked him, admired him even; his one success, however incomplete, of conversion. And on impulse, he headed for MacTavish's Bar by the castle, which stood like some mediaeval sentry, silhouetted against the sky, overlooking the town. The street was quiet, and on his left, below a wall with a railing, lay the deep moat, which glimmered under the moon. For a moment, he stood outside the bar, looking across the road at the great rectangular keep, between the vast round stone towers, with the drawbridge leading into the castle yard, and wondered how many others like himself had suffered down the ages, without adequate justification. Was life inevitably unjust? And he saw that it was. For, as every individual's life is at the mercy of the ignorant and largely uncaring populace around him, some of whom have deep reasons for his destruction, how could it be anything else?

Morosely, with a face fit for a funeral, he entered, to find his short friend standing over a half pint, beside some other men; Gavin Saxby, a tall broad farmer, with a shock of unkempt brown hair, still in dungarees and tackety boots. Then there was Harry McCusker, a fencing contractor, a rough-handed fellow, six and half feet tall; built to match, with a bald head surrounded by tufts of red hair. McCusker, too, was in working clothes: jeans, donkey-jacket and wellingtons, still covered in glaur. And Jock Lyle, a skinny plumber, with fair hair and a face like an underdone bread-roll, in shirt, tie, badminton-club blazer and grey flannels.

Unknown to John, there had just been a discussion about the minister who had been 'shaggin' the young widow'.

'He hasnae been shaggin' anybody,' Buce had said, sorrowfully, staring at the drink in their cheering, multi-coloured bottles, lined up against the wall.

McCusker laughed, scratching his red head. 'How do you ken? Wis it you that did it?' and Saxby guffawed.

'Don't be daft! Ah jist know he widnae dae that,' said Buce.

'How did he get seen, then?' said Saxby. 'Sniffy saw him through a windae. An' hauf the toon kens he's been up at her hoose lookin' fur it.'

To Buce, McCusker, concluded, 'You're jist a stupit wee bastart! Aw body else kens. Christ! It stauns tae reason, the man's shaggin' the wumman. She's a bloody good ride.'

Buce's dander was up, but, as he turned and looked them over, he knew he would get nowhere in a scrap. They would hold him off with their long arms, and tease the life out of him. He would be made a laughing stock. As he said nothing, Saxby smiled, knowing he had beaten him, and McCusker laid a knowing finger against his red-freckled nose and said, 'Ye ken whit gets me? If the fucken minister wisnae shaggin' her, Ah micht get in there masel'.'

'You?' said Saxby, laughing, 'You couldnae get within smellin' range. She widnae have ye at ony price. Yuv been shaggin' ower mony sheep.' To Buce, he added, 'Huv ye seen ony baldy heidit red sheep runnin' aboot?' Everybody laughed then, including McCusker.

So when John walked in and parked himself at the bar, on the other side of Buce, there was an uneasy silence. John asked them what they wanted, and all admitted to having a drink already. 'What about you, Buce?' said John, 'you'll take a half?'

But Buce, without a word of thanks, hunched himself over his half pint and said he would not.

'Aye, richt!' said McCusker, 'It wid knock ye ower!' and the other two laughed. Buce reddened at this self-evident truth, and said nothing, looking straight ahead over the glass.

In the silence that followed, John ordered a whisky for himself and said, 'How are things?' And all Buce would say in reply, was, 'Fine, fine.' No word of interest in John, who felt the coldness, the feeling of being shut out, and he stood uncertainly for a short time, himself making a careful study of the various bottles lined up for inspection, on the other side of the bar. And then, when nothing came, no word of help or enquiry of how he did, the others having turned away, talking to one another in a murmur, he saw how it was; and the pain cut into him like a dirk. The injustice skewered his self-respect. Ashen-faced, he drained his glass in one swallow and turned to go. 'Well, I'll be off, gents,' he told them, and, as the door swung behind him, he heard the laughter as a new joke was cracked, and he knew who was the butt of it.

But he was wrong. Inside, annoyed with his own betrayal, Buce had just ordered a double whisky to assuage the fault. It was that which had caused the laughter. 'Ye coulda had yin fur nuthin'!' said Lyle to him.

'Yer a fucken stupit wee bastart, richt enough,' added McCusker and then, insultingly, 'Aren't ye?' and when Buce said nothing, 'Come on, ya wee bugger, admit it!'

Buce drained the double in one, laid it on the bar deliberately, and fired a right hand shot into McCusker's guts. Then, a vast, rough, red-hairy hand reached out and grabbed Buce by the shirt-front, and slowly raised him off the ground. And the others laughed at the sight of Buce's legs kicking futilely in the air, unable to make contact with the floor. Then the other hand laid the pint on the bar and moved across Buce's face slowly, and took hold of his nose and tweaked it viciously. The laughter around was intense, and so sustained, that other folk appeared from the back room, to watch the entertainment. Buce was smashing lefts and rights into the flanks of the giant and kicking his short legs at McCusker's tree-trunk stanchions, which however, soon closed up, to make further attack impossible; and the spare hand clamped his arms. Then the pair left by the swing doors and men rushed to follow.

McCusker crossed the darkened street carrying his burden as if it were a dead sheep, or one anyway, in the jerking stage of the last rites of passage, and marched onto the drawbridge to the great keep, raised Buce still higher, moving him out across the rail, over the moat, and let go.

When the splash sounded, a splash like a depth charge, twenty feet high, there was a riot of laughter in the street, as ten people, soon joined by others, at the noise of commotion, many of them still clutching glasses half full of alcohol, came to watch.

Then there was silence. Until Lyle, peering down into the dark, said, 'Is he droont?' which provoked more laughter, and Saxby leaned out over the railing of the drawbridge, and said, 'Naw. The wee bugger can swim after aw'.' Then he laughed. 'He's on the bank, shakin' himsel' lik' a dug.' By then, McCusker, soon to be joined by the others, had returned to the bar and ordered up another bevy.

From the bar, John set off energetically, as if action was the cure to his frenzied feelings, but it was an aimless progress, more designed to tire him out than take him anywhere.

After a mile or so, uphill, at a lively pace, which tired him more than usual, he stopped to catch his breath and looked around, and he suddenly wondered what Madeline had agreed to say. Without any decision, his steps led him to the housing scheme and her gate, which he laid his hand upon. The curtains were closed, but there were still lights within. And he stood at the gate and thought of her, conjuring up images, remembering the dark mound between her lissome thighs and the pale pink lips that nestled underneath. Should he go in and knock on her door?

His head lifted—and everything else with it, he complained grimly, and then, wearily, laughed aloud at himself. The weakness of the flesh. Was there no end to it? Must he be forever tortured? The danger was too great. At least he had done no wrong so far. If he went in, even to ask innocent and perfectly proper questions which he was entitled to do, what harm might befall him? Would not the temptation prove too much? Of course, he told himself. I'm only flesh and blood. Along the street behind him, a door opened and someone came out to walk a dog, and John was startled out of his calculation, and set off again with long strides.

On impulse, he walked through the town and up the back road to the school. It was there, at the top of the hill, near the Bannockburn Tower, that he paused for breath, strangely tired yet again. And then, silently, he opened the gate to the park in front and moved into the garden and listened.

There was no sound. Maybe they'd given it up, he told himself in a leap of hope, but as he traversed the grass verge, keeping off the gravel, he began to hear sounds, not talk, but sounds, and the closer he came to the seat that faced the sea and provided such a fine view of the town and the harbour, the clearer it became that two people were on the seat and that they were engrossed in each other.

John stopped behind a large shrub and listened, and then, between two large branches, he made out the figures in the darkness, silhouetted against the night sky. The woman was astride the man, facing him, and he could dimly see that her dress was rucked up around her waist, showing the entire length of her thigh. Presently, John saw the man's hands on her waist moving her up and down on him. And the sounds of moaning and kissing and sucking came across the narrow strip of grass. Then a gap in the clouds bared the moon, and he saw clearly, saw the woman's face with her eyes shut in the grip of ecstasy, and at first he couldn't make out who it was. Then, in unison with her movements on the man, the woman said, 'Oh God...... Oh God..... Oh God! God! God! God!' and he knew who it was.

He stood for a while, rooted to the spot, listening to the murmured love talk, and the tears fell down his cheeks. A surge of hot anger washed over him, and he made as if to move in on them. Images of him tearing Jean away and punching Tom to pulp, shot like star-shell into his consciousness, and his breath came in quick gulps, as the adrenaline surged through him, like the minutes before a commando raid. But he stopped himself, halted the sudden spring into action, that would, he knew with utter certainty, cause the most unmanageable and unchristian chaos. His limbs relaxed, he crouched down again behind the bush. Then, fearing discovery, and suffused with guilt at the realisation of having himself become a peeping Tom, he silently stole back the way he had come, fighting back the sobs that threatened to engulf him and reveal his presence. With hand to mouth to stifle the uncontrollable anguish, he made his way down the path to the road, and as he did so, though he knew he had acted rightly, he felt emasculated, rejected, replaced and defeated.

Buce's state of mind was as bad as it had ever been. Somehow, so confused was he by drink and the assault on his dignity, that he had got out on the wrong bank, the inner one where the castle stood. He would have to re-enter the water to get out of the place. Then he would have to climb up the wall onto the street. It was a disaster. Half an hour later, sodden and dripping, his psyche shattered, he was once again on the street, on the other side of the castle from the bar, near the museum. As he slunk off home, it occurred to him that maybe he had got his just deserts, for behaving so badly to John Manson.

The walk up the High Street was a nightmare, a squelching progress in the chill, made worse by the freezing waters of the stinking moat. Buce lifted his sleeve and sniffed, and said, loudly, 'Jesus!' and then shivered from head to foot, and passed on. And then a door opened and a man came out with a carrier bag and Buce knew instantly what it was. It gave him an idea. The best antidote to a soaking was a drink. Squaring his shoulders manfully and licking his lips first, for a moment, while he stood outside savouring the idea, he entered the off-licence. It was empty and there was no need to beat a hurried retreat. He asked for a quarter bottle, but before it arrived, changed his mind to a half bottle. It wasn't just for the cold, he told himself, it was for his betrayal, for being a rotter. The man eyed him, but did not notice the soaking garments until Buce squeaked out, leaving a trail of damp footsteps and a puddle on the floor at the counter.

Buce had the bottle out immediately and began sipping. By the time he reached the Park, it was half gone and so was he; but he resolved to persist, even though, by this time, his movements were more than a little erratic. As he crossed the road, a car whizzed past with horn sounding and lights flashing, but Buce paid it no heed, contenting himself with an indistinct remark to the fresh air, that whatever it was, 'it had nae bloody business tae be there.' The slope to the council house was negotiated with greatest difficulty in a blur, so that he could hardly see where he was going, and he navigated by some sixth sense. Somehow, the drink probably, his notion of right and left had been seriously diminished and he took a wrong turning. At last he stood, wavering, like a sapling in a high wind, as he studied the dwelling. The number on the door seemed a touch unfamiliar. No matter, this was it, he decided. Knowing that beyond, there might be certain difficulties to be encountered, such as a nagging wife, he lifted the bottle for a final reviver and took in half of what remained, the other half descending via his chin on its way to the ground, by way of the lapel of his jacket and his trouser leg. The bottle fell to the pavement and smashed.

Strangely, the door-handle seemed to elude his grasp, and he said to it, 'Come here, wull ye!' And then he fell against it and made contact and, magically, the effort to turn it was a success, so that the door opened and he fell inside, immediately after. The door slammed shut behind him and a voice said, 'S'that you Wullie?'

Buce set his hands on the wall and levered himself upright. 'Aye, S'me, aw right!' The name did have an unfamiliar ring to it, but Buce was beyond complaining.

'Pit oot the light, then, pal, and come oan through.'

Buce fell against the switch and the light went out. Then, swaying perilously, he moved in the pitch darkness through the bedroom door opposite, like a blindman after an orgy.

'Christ! Yur like a brew'ry! Get yur claes aff.'

Buce turned slightly in the direction of the voice and began to divest himself of jacket, shirt and trousers. Laden with water, this was easier than usual, for they fell off, to the least touch, under the weight.

'Mind yur shoes, tae!' And Buce got these off too. A moment later, he was in the bed and the cover spread over him. A hand felt for him, and withdrew suddenly. 'Christ, yer cauld, Wullie! Ye kin wait till ye've waarmed up.' But that same cold, which until then had kept Buce in the land of the conscious, was now rapidly receding, as the heat of the bed and its other inhabitant spread through him. A few minutes later, he was snoring and his partner, hearing it, turned over and went off to sleep.

Around two o'clock, the front door of the house opened, and Wullie, himself far gone with drink, tottered into the hall, and missing the light switch, soon found himself in the lounge, where he crashed out on the couch.

Not till 8.30 am did Wullie get up. He dressed and shaved and called out, 'Isa, come oan. Get ma breakfast, fur God's sake.' Just to make sure, he popped his head around the bedroom door and blinked with disbelief, for there in bed with his wife lay Buce MacSween. 'So that's it, is it! Get up ya wee bugger! Wait till Ah git a knife. Jist you wait!' And Wullie took off for the kitchen, in search of a weapon.

'Wha's a madder?' said Buce, awakening, to find Isa Gardner sitting up in bed in a negligee with eyes like saucers. Then, as Wullie Gardner appeared through the open door carrying the breadknife, she shouted, 'Thur's a man in ma bed! It's that wee sleekit fulla MacSween. Get oot! Get oot, ya wee bastard!' And Buce got out, like a greyhound out of a trap, and Wullie made a stab at him which missed and, in an instant, Buce was through the door and into the hall, with his hand on the front doorknob, heaving it open, hotly pursued by Wullie, still reeling with the aftermath of drink, screaming, 'Stand and fight like a man, ya wee bugger!' which was hardly realistic, given the difference in weaponry, and the fact that Buce was undressed.

The door open, there was no alternative to flight, naked flight, along a street with people on their way to work, and the postman and the newspaper-boy making their deliveries. All activity stopped, to allow the uninhibited observation of Buce MacSween's journey along the street and across the main road into his own, and up the path to his house. And the laughter of it, the riotous bellowing guffaws wrought in some onlookers, by Buce's microscopic majesty, brought others, even at such an early hour, to their windows, to see the spectacle for themselves.

George was careful not to visit Madeline openly, in case what was being said about John, should, in some way, apply to himself; for people would be watching her house for every strange man who came and went there. So he phoned her one evening, and told her he wanted to see her about Mr Manson. No, he wouldn't discuss it over the phone. Nor would he see her publicly.

Madeline was curious, too curious not to meet. She agreed to walk up to the golf course that evening, leaving home at nine, and meet George on the road.

Some way out of town, among high trees, where the street was not supplied with many lamp standards, the pick-up took place, observed by no one.

'There's been a lot a talk about you,' said George, when she was installed beside him and the car was on its way. 'The whole town's agog with it. They know about you and John Manson. You fancy him, don't you?'

'It's none of your business! Is that what this is about? You can just stop here and let me get off.'

'Hold on, Madeline, hold on,' said George calmingly. 'I know you think Manson's a great guy, but you don't really know him, do you? There, you see, I'm on your side. I don't think you did anything. But the town does. They think you've been having it off, the two of ye.'

'We haven't!'

'Well that's fine, then. We're on the same side. The only thing is....' and George paused to consider what line he should take, given the wicket he'd been given to bat on.

'Well? Come on, out with it.'

'Manson says you flaunted yourself at him. That you tried to get him to take advantage of you.'

'That's not true,' she said, red-faced, for she knew it was, but could not admit it. And George smiled to himself.

'He's saying you stripped off in front of him.'

'I never did! That's a lie... a lie,' and that was true, and George knew it.

'He says you took his whatsit out. Did you?'

'No, I would never do such a thing! That...that's outrageous!' but George guessed that was not true. He waited to see if she would say anything, and when she did not, he knew for sure. She had just confirmed it by her reaction. Any other woman would have been full of questions about who had said such a thing, what their evidence was and more indignation. Madeline had been along that road and knew the answers. Who had seen, and that he had seen truly. She could never admit such a thing, even though it was so. What woman could admit to such an act?

'Well, I just thought you should know what kind a man you're involved with. What he's saying about you behind your back.'

And George knew it was enough and he stopped to let her out and as she left him, silently, with her head down, he knew he'd made a dent in her infatuation big enough to make waves at the holy inquisition, as he thought of it. And that she would be no trouble at a hearing. Pride would make her tell the lies he needed. He would see her again, by and by, bring her a present. Flowers or perfume or chocolates. And in time, he would wear her down, sweeten her opposition, and take every opportunity to undermine her trust in Manson. It was simple really, he reflected, as he enjoyed the stately comfort of the Mercedes. Most people could be got to believe anything. Folk like Madeline Grant were simpletons. All you had to do was cultivate them in the right way, make them feel important and show that you liked them. Give them presents and butter them up, and then, gradually, you could work yourself in. Give them the pitch about doing good for mankind and all that crap. It worked every time. Once you brought them round to thinking you were a friend, they'd never go against you. You could always hold it up over them. Most of them would rather save a friend than do the right thing by the justice system, in which they had only a vague understanding anyway.

Then there was the power thing. Some friends were worth having, worth making allowances for, even worth doing things for; because a powerful friend could do things for you in return. Lend you money, get you things at cost price, and favours at no cost at all. And then, at least in George's case, there were grants of all kinds he could arrange. George was as powerful as anyone on Branden, and the exercise of that power was an important aspect of retaining and extending it.

George was proud of himself that night. Had he not done a power of work that day? The Council elections were soon to take place and he had got himself put up for provost, chief councillor of the town. Against him was Hannah Schneider, a local girl, born Hannah Stevenson, who had done post-graduate work in Germany, before the war. She had done an ordinary thing, one many students do: she had fallen in love. And as her husband's work took him to the United States, she naturally accompanied him. There, she lived for twenty years, while Europe was tearing itself apart. When in 1958, her husband had died suddenly, she returned to her island home with a grown-up son and, well-provided-for by an American pension, she had entered local politics and voluntary work of various kinds.

What George had spent all day doing, in between wheeling and dealing, was spreading the message that Ottersay ought not to have a German as provost. This on top of running a business and overseeing the destruction of John Manson. He had been up with the lark and on his feet since six; and now, consulting his watch, it was after ten. That was industry, for you, he told himself approvingly.

And there had been arguments, people to overwhelm; for some had pointed out that Hannah Schneider might have a German name, but she was as much a native of Ottersay as George himself. To which George had replied that anyone who married a German was unfit for a responsible post in Ottersay, or anywhere else. Had they not just finished fighting a war with the bastards? And had not a few hundred men of Branden been killed in the event? And there was no answer to that, for most people were unaware of the details of Hannah Schneider's husband's life, if only because she had been reluctant to reveal them.

She had never married in the years since his death, and never thought of it, even though she was still a good-looking woman. Talk about her husband was not something she encouraged. Too many memories were unleashed by it. Some loves are too engrossing, ever to get over completely.

But George knew. He had made it his business to find out, employing a detective in Glasgow to do so. Mr Schneider had not been a German but a fourth generation American citizen, with a German name, who had gone there, like Hannah, to study in the best place for his specialist subject. On graduation, he had naturally returned to his homeland to set up in practice— a medical practice. He had chosen to study in Freiburg because that was where the foremost expert in the world on arterio-sclerotic disease was located.

In effect, George was spreading the rumour that Hannah had married a German, when he knew quite well that this was not so; and knew that his lie was unlikely to be uncovered, if only because the lady herself was still half-in love with a dead husband and would not want it discussed.

Sniffy had been employed to dig up anything locally that might be useful, but without success: the lady led a blameless life, occasionally holding quiet dinner parties for a few friends in her large sandstone house on the hill, at Crichton. As a councillor, she had been discreet, tactful and efficient, where George was abrasive, if energetic. Most of the councillors were taken with her quiet honesty and industry, and her aptitude for defusing situations, which might otherwise have brought about an outbreak of fisticuffs, at council meetings. There was a warmth about Hannah, a quiet willingness to keep everyone together, which was an ideal quality in a lord provost presiding over so many diverse personalities, all engaged in different and sometimes competing managerial tasks.

That night, as he drove through the streets of the town, wondering what other measures he could take to see off this challenge to his ambitions, George saw three figures enter a close, not far from the Sheriff Court. One of them looked familiar. The youth reminded him of Billy, but he cast aside the idea, for what would Billy be doing round the back of a pub in Ottersay, after it closed for the night?

But it *was* Billy. Since he had been abducted from the company of Jessica and Miss Carmichael, and beaten up again by George, Billy's life had taken an opposite tack. Removed from school, he now spent every day learning the art of dealing with the bodies of the dead. How to clean the body after death, close off the various orifices with cotton wool, how to make the face look as it once did in life, by the addition of rouge and mascara and other cosmetics; and the difficult matter of maintaining an expression of suitable solemnity whenever the relatives were around, and during the funeral itself, without betraying the joy that the very event signified a good profit for the firm, of which he was the son and heir.

Never very happy at the best of times—which he had enjoyed with Jessica—he was now reduced to an attitude of moroseness; as if the need to seem solemn so often, affected his everyday mood. Jessica, he rarely saw, and then fleetingly, as he drove past in a hearse or one of the taxis, when the usual driver was indisposed and there was a rush on. As George had put it to him, 'See if you ever speak to that girl again? I'll send you to the army, so I will!' And that prospect had seemed so terrible that Billy had wilted. Once, in a brief attempt at recovering his manhood, he had retorted to his father, 'Maybe I wouldn't get into the army.'

But George had killed that stone-dead: 'We'll make it the foreign legion, then. They're not fussy. They take anybody.' And the idea of marching across the Sahara, pursued by thousands of armed tribesmen, had frightened Billy, as George knew it would. Privately, George would do no such thing. He knew that the person who returned would be outside his control, then. The army was just the place to provide Billy with the confidence he needed; but then he would not have been available to George as an acolyte, willing or unwilling.

No, George was determined to keep Billy at heel, so that he would learn all the tricks of the trade in the business. That was the best education he could imagine for a son and heir. But, as with his own education, he knew it was best to leave it until the youth had fully grown up and developed his own appetites. The time to pass on the real secrets would be when either Billy had noticed them or George began to get tired of doing it all himself, which was some considerable way off.

Life as an apprentice undertaker was not a complete disaster. An older youth, Tommy Forbes, one of the employees, had a sense of mischief which Billy soon learned to enjoy. Where Billy was short and plump, Tommy was tall and thin, with dark hair sleeked back, and a short thin moustache which he was cultivating. Tommy was a natty dresser who played on Saturdays for the Ottersay Victoria, a local football team. On Saturday evenings, he went to the dancing, in the hope of 'getting a lumber', which is to say, a lady willing to enjoy his services for the evening. This difficult feat had only been managed twice during the holiday season, when there were available girls, ignorant of his track-record, who were plentiful. But Tommy made it seem as if he was a man of experience and Billy soon fell under his spell.

Deprived of other role models, what could he do but learn to admire those nearest him? Of course, he still hankered after the Manson family, and, to begin with, even went walking in the direction of the Manse of an evening, on the off chance of seeing Jessica, but a new life beckoned and he was soon absorbed by it.

Tommy was a mischievous soul who enjoyed a jest at the expense of the dead. For a while, he was careful not to offend the boss's son until, one day, a teacher named Violet Morrison collapsed and died in class. As both boys had been at the receiving end of Morrison's wit and tawse, they viewed the body with more than ordinary interest. Here, for once, their tormentor lay within their power.

Tommy studied the entrance to the vagina and, after stuffing it with cotton wool, said, 'Christ, Ah wonner how far up it goes?' He took a pencil from his pocket and poked it inside. Then, pushing the little rubber at the end with his thumb, he began to shove the pencil up inside. When it would go no further, Tommy marked the position with his finger, withdrew it and held it up to reveal the length. 'Ah don't think that's big enough fur me.' And he laughed. 'Ah wid huv been too much fur hur. But you could huv a shot, Billy. Huv ye had yer hole yet? Ye could huv a trial run. Shove it up there and see how it feels. Ur ye game?'

At first, subdued by this irreverence, Billy said nothing, but then Tommy was careless in moving the corpse and it slid onto the floor, like a huge slab of beef and the sight of it, arms and legs sticking straight out like a robot, struck Tommy as extremely funny, and he burst out laughing and laughed so much that Billy found himself joining in. It was the start of a friendship, and soon they were going about together in the evenings after work.

At first, George had Billy watched, but as time went on and he was seen more and more in the company of Tommy Forbes, George smiled to himself and heaved a secret sigh of relief that his son was now on the right track, associating with 'the right sort' of local people. What George did not know was that Tommy had just befriended John Ryan.

The son of an Irish labourer who had settled on Branden after the war, Ryan was a rarity, even for an island with a population of eight thousand. Growing up in a large family was difficult when there were so many mouths to feed, but there was the chapel and the Catholic primary school, which had a good effect on many from a similar background. Of course the father took a good drink, and a sizeable fraction of the wages he earned as a council labourer disappeared down his throat. But it wasn't the father's callousness, or the mother's lack of interest in a son who was never in the house, but always out gallivanting outwith her control from an early age. No, it was the boy himself, mainly; the particular combination of genes he had been endowed with. He was strong and aggressive and rather unfeeling. Life taught him early about pain but, somehow, did not deter him from the kind of acts which were punished. Having no aptitude for school-work, he soon found his own gift: he could terrorise everybody else his own age and there were always followers who would support his ventures, because they had no competence of any kind. And so, at school, he had a gang, much feared, and when he left school at the first opportunity, whereat his teachers sighed with relief, he found a succession of temporary jobs, being 'let go' after a few days because of unpunctuality or cheek or fighting or stealing, all of which, in Ryan's world, were everyday activities.

Of more than average height, with a lean, wiry strength, and brown hair, he had strange, rather hooded eyes, fish-like in their lack of expression, and his progress about the small, sea-enclosed world of Branden was shark-like, slow moving and yet relentless, ever on the qui vive for any sign of weakness or carelessness in his brethren, which he would immediately try to exploit, often without adequate regard to the risks and consequences. Ryan was rarely seen to smile, but would snigger at the discomforts of others, especially if he himself were the cause.

At that time, he was sixteen, a year younger than Tommy Forbes. They had teemed up for the obvious reason that both were bored during the winter evenings. When most people their age were either students or members of social clubs like the Boys Brigade or the Scouts or played sports like football, badminton, rugby or golf, these disciplines had never appealed to John Ryan. And so he found himself wandering the streets at night, looking vaguely for action of some kind; for at that difficult age, before the blood has cooled and the arteries start to stiffen, a youth needs something to do. And then there was no money to do it with. His mother claimed the lion's share of anything he earned. So the need for action and money led naturally to the idea of robbery. What was an active lad to do for fags and drink and a bit of excitement at the amusements and the pictures? He had to have money.

It was over a pint in the Seamen's Arms, that Ryan admitted that the drink he'd just bought came from the proceeds of a robbery. Tommy was interested. Here was a form of excitement he'd never before experienced. This might be worth trying. It would be something to do during the week. And there was money in it. He was game to have a go.

Ryan accepted his new recruit readily enough. It was company, someone to talk to while it went on, and then it was useful at times to have another pair of hands to give a heave up over a wall, or help move the stuff, or even just keep watch.

And so, for several months, there had been a spate of robberies, where shops of one kind or another were broken into during the early hours of the morning, or late at night. They got a TV and hi-fi equipment and fenced it off to Gaby McMonigle, the local general trader, for a quarter of its resale value. Then there was a lot of lead off a roof that Gaby told them about. Mostly it was shops, pubs best of all, where occasionally the cash was left overnight to be banked the next day; and there was fun in it, as they sat in the dark, drinking free booze.

One night, Tommy and Billy were together, when they met John Ryan on his way to do another job. Assured that it was just a lark, Billy went along. It was a pub again. While John forced the back door with a jemmy he carried concealed in the deep pockets of an old raincoat, Tommy kept watch in the street. Then, the pair went in, leaving Billy outside. Hearing muffled laughter, he decided to follow and soon he too was partaking of some free refreshment. The till had been cleared, but there was booze in plenty and they helped themselves, filling pockets with bottles of beer and spirits.

In the street afterwards, they looked like a threesome who had enjoyed rather a protracted night's drinking and availed themselves of a good carry out. A few hours later, spent on the seats of the shelters on the sea front, Billy staggered home and remembered to conceal the bottles in the garden shed at the rear of the house, before letting himself in. Of course he was sick almost as soon as his head hit the pillow, but he made it to the sink and cleared up after himself, and nothing was noticed in the morning. So began this new pattern in his life and there was an increased confidence of a kind, that he could have such good fun with his 'mates.'

These days, George was hardly ever at home, and, when he was, it was only to sleep, so he noticed nothing unusual about his son. Every day, he took this or that useful person to lunch at the Grand Hotel, where he always had the best table. There he would ingratiate himself and discover what favours, if any, would serve to move the person to his side; and if there was no movement, because Hannah Schneider was preferred and the man was honourable, George would smile and offer his hand at the end of it and say,

'No hard feelings,' and the target would think him a good fellow, even if he wasn't the best person for provost.

The afternoon when the fateful meeting to decide who would be the provost, duly arrived. Round the table were the retiring provost, Gordon Wright, a local baker, and sundry others including the two contestants. They were asked to say why they thought they should be elected. Hannah spoke in her quiet, calm way, promised to do her best, and, as she had been well-educated and was far-travelled and experienced, she thought she would manage to carry out her duties satisfactorily. There was no bombast and no passion. It was a laid-back presentation of her worth.

George, said, 'I am a businessman here and a good one. Some say, the best, the most successful. This town depends on trade, the kind of thing I know about better than Mrs Schneider, here,' reminding them of her German name. 'I have energy and initiative. I know I would be good at this, good for the town. I can bring in a lot of business to the folk here. We need it, more work. Too many are unemployed. I don't think she can do that so well. She hasn't the experience. Then, we've never had a woman provost and I don't think this is the time to change. There's a reason, you see. There has to be. Our forefathers knew it was better to have a man in charge. Men are more reliable, not liable to break down or have period pains and things that get in the way of work.'

'I object to that,' said Tom Robertson, owner of the tweed-mill. 'There's no reason to talk this way. It's bad manners.'

'It's the plain truth! Do you men want to have a woman set over you? Well I don't.'

And after much wrangling, allied to all the dealing he'd done beforehand, promising this and that, George managed to get elected by a whisker. An immediate consequence was an increase in his stature, as perceived by all connected with the Kirk Session.

At the meeting to decide the fate of John Manson, as Lord Provost of the town and leading citizen, George was allocated a leading role.

After the examination of John's theological position, by Rob McCall, Madeline was invited to join them and give evidence.

'It's been said, Madeline,' said George, 'that you and John have been having an affair. In fact, your relationship with him is the talk of the town. So perhaps you would be good enough to give your side of it.'

As Madeline said nothing—the idea that it was an affair actually appealed to her—if only it were! she thought—George said, 'Mr Manson visited your house after your husband died, didn't he?'

Madeline nodded.

'And did you find his visits helpful?'

Madeline blushed. 'Yes, I did.'

'Was there any affection between you?'

'Oh yes. A kiss or two coming and going.'

'And he took part in this?'

'Yes.'

'Now someone saw you both together in your kitchen. Evidence has been given on this point. This man says you were undressed below the waist and the minister exposed himself to you. Would you like to explain how that happened.'

'It was just one of these things. It happens you know, between people when they get attracted.'

'And were you attracted to the minister?'

'Yes.'

'Was he attracted to you?'

'Yes.'

'How did you know?'

Madeline blushed, deeply. 'Because....because it showed. You can't hide that kind of thing.'

'And did he expose himself to you?'

'Yes.'

'So you saw it, then?'

'Yes.'

'And did he take off your clothes?'

'No, I did that myself.'

George turned to the others, 'I think we have enough now. The minister exposed himself to Madeline. We don't need to know what they did after that.'

Dr Telford said, 'I don't believe that John Manson would expose himself to anyone. How did it happen?'

'How should I know,' said Madeline. 'It just did. Maybe it just kind of popped out, the way they do.' There were smiles and a few laughs. Madeline blushed and added, with a touch of pride, 'Looking at me, made him very excited.'

John was invited to question Madeline but he refused to do so. She had endured too much already, he thought. Anyway, he wouldn't be able to ask her those kinds of questions.

Telford tried to argue that the minister had done nothing, 'because it just popped out,' but the fact that it had done so at all, allowed George to shoot him down with the remark, 'It doesn't matter. We canny have it popping out with other young widows or other folks wives.' That was enough.

John was called in to hear the decision. George said, 'We find that you have behaved improperly with regard to one of your parishioners and that, together with your new views, no longer fit you for the post of minister to this congregation. We would like you therefore to resign. The committee have generously allowed you to take that route rather than be sacked.'

John sat in silence for a while before replying, 'I won't resign. I've done nothing I'm ashamed of.'

After a short consultation among them, the final step was agreed by a majority. George said, 'In that case, Mr Manson, you are dismissed.' And the wonder of it was that after such a quantity of labour for this very result, George could keep a straight face and not reveal the joy that filled him. To a man of power, a man who will spend his money for it, curry favour with every rotten swine in the place, a man who will lick other folks boots and solve their problems when they are none of his concern, and actually degrading to get mixed up in—to such a man, the successful wielding of power is like manna to a starving soul, like a rain-shower of gold pieces of the very kind he now expected to receive once again, from the very citizens clustered about him. It was a terrific piece of work, and he capped it by an expression of regret, of a senior elder doing his duty with reluctance. That was the measure of his success: everyone was taken in.

For a few moments, John sat motionless, looking straight ahead at George and then his gaze swung to Madeline, who seemed transfixed, on the point of tears, for all she had wanted was to clear her name and if the minister had been issued a mild reproof, what matter? She had done nothing wrong. How could it be her fault if she was so beautiful that men were excited by her? She stood up and said, 'This is not right! Not fair! John Manson's the best minister we could have!'

'I agree,' said Dr Telford.

'Have you anything to say?' said George.

'I've done nothing wrong and my theological position is not inconsistent with my being a minister of the church.' He stood up. 'I forgive you,' he said, turned and left the room.

People were still going about as John walked through the town, and he nodded right and left to them, as if nothing had happened, but his face was scarlet with humiliation and, as he looked at each passer-by, he was driven to wonder what they would think of him when they heard. And, in the middle of all the suffering and depth of torment, as he crossed the High Street, observed by several folk as if he were suddenly the bearer of a fatal disease, like leprosy, it dawned on him, that his predicament was like Jesus. His march homeward, like the walk to Calvary. And it cheered him. He had done no wrong. His conscience was clear.

But the mood soon received a devastating jolt. At the corner of the front street, Byron Webster accosted him. 'See you ya bastard? You were gonny fuck ma wife, weren't ye? Yuv been shaggin' the widaw weemen. Haven't ye?' And as John made to pass him on the pavement, Byron, who stank of drink, took a wild swing with his right fist and John ducked under it; but he stepped on the edge of the pavement and tripped and fell into the gutter, which was still filthy and mucky from a recent shower of rain.

As John got to his feet, Byron took another swing at him and nearly connected, and as John sped off along the road, as if his entrails were about to fall out, his coat defiled by wet, black muck, he heard Byron call after him, 'See if you fucken speak tae ma wife, ya bastard, Ah'll fucken do ye. De ye hear me, noo? Ah'll fucken cut yer prick aff and stick it up yer arse.'

Several people heard it; no one objected; all of them reported it; and all with their element of glee. That night, the whole town knew of it; and the majority—the vast, stupid, amoral, majority—enjoyed it.

In the Manse, Jean was waiting.

'They dismissed me. I'm sorry,' John said, as he took off the defiled coat and hung it up. When Jean did not seem upset, he added, 'What will you do?'

'I've made up my mind. I'm going to stay with Tom Henderson. I..I've been seeing a bit of him lately and he's offered to fill the breach.'

John laughed suddenly out of a face shot with hurt and strain. 'Yes, I noticed he'd been doing that.'

'What do you mean?'

'I'm sorry, I shouldn't have said that. It was unkind. I saw you together up on the hill. Forgive me. I didn't know it was you but I saw two figures and I had to be sure.'

Jean blushed. 'Oh, God! How did you know?'

'I heard you once before. I was upset then too, and I had to go and make sure.'

She said, 'I'll take the children so you won't have that bother.'

'I thought you might.' The calm litanies of separation were all the more wounding for their banality.

'I'm sorry,' said Jean, struggling to hold back the tears.

'I know. Don't think about it.'

'What will you do? You'll come and see the children, won't you?'

'Of course—I really don't know. Go on staying here, until they kick me out finally. I suppose they'll give me a deadline.'

When the children were assembled after returning from school, Jean told them that their father had lost his job and they were going to stay with Tom Henderson.

'Well I'm not,' said Jessica. 'I'm staying.'

'But there's no money and we have to move out.'

'I don't care about the money,' said Jessica. 'And the house doesn't matter. It's people that count. '

'Where are you going to live?' said Jean.

'With my dad, wherever he lives. Even folk on the dole live somewhere, don't they? Well, that's where I'm going. With dad.'

'But you could live in a grand house with Tom and me. There'll be plenty money. Think of it! No more scraping and scrimping.'

'I never minded that. I won't leave my dad in his hour of need. Not for you or anyone. I'm shocked at you. It's despicable!'

Jean coloured, as the shot went home, but collected herself. This was no time for hysterics. There were things to arrange, and she would not let any outburst get in the way of the course she planned to take. 'Well maybe it's for the best. At least he'll have somebody to look after him. You'll come and see us, won't you?'

'I'm not sure I'll want to. You can come and see me for a change.'

Jean already had the bags packed. She opened the door and carried them outside, leaving the children to stand in the hall, uncertainly. Susan said, 'What a.abo.out my bo.oks?'

'They're all packed,' said Jean. Then she stood in the doorway, with the two younger children between her and John. 'Say goodbye to your father, then,' she told them. And Susan snuggled into him and lifted her head to kiss him, but deep down there was that old memory, and it came to mind as Susan lifted her chestnut head and looked at him levelly out of the brown eyes and freckled face. No, Susan made no protest. Where Jean went she would naturally follow, as surely as QED after a proof in Euclid.

Roddy just stood, gawkily, dark head inclined downward so that his face was partly covered. Like a lump of stone, he was, bewildered and bemused, stripped of all initiative, as he had been so often before, under different circumstances, by Charlie Braddock. Jessica went to him and gave him a hug; then passed him over to John and said, 'Can't you do anything, Dad?'

'No,' he replied, out of a voice that sounded as if he were dying, 'people have to want to live together. They must be given the space to make the choice.'

'But—'

'What kind of life would it be if they were made to stay? Better they should find out what the grass is like on the other side of the fence, than stay here and dream of what might have been.'

Jean took the two youngest by the hand, hustled them outside and closed the door. Behind it, looking at them through the glass, Jessica and

John, with arms around each other, and tears in their eyes, watched them walk down the path carrying the bags and get into the waiting blue Jaguar.

When the matter of the minister's date of leaving was raised by Dr Telford, George was thoughtful and said finally, that, a decision having been taken, they could afford to be merciful. There was no need to turf him out neck and crop. 'Let's say nothing about it for now. I'll write him a letter confirming the decision but I won't say when he has to leave.' Telford was surprised and pleased by this attitude. It seemed to be a very Christian one in the circumstances.

Ellen said, 'But he'll have to be got out of the Manse to make room for the next man. It might hold up the takeover. The sooner he's out the better—now it's all decided. The poor man! What a shame! I just wish we'd never started this. I feel so bad about it. And you know what? He's the one man in this place I could have gone to about this kind of trouble. But how can I go to him with this? When I've helped to destroy him? I feel like a pariah!'

And George had nothing to say to her, because it was not his aim to offer comfort. Instead, he congratulated himself on the brilliance of his manipulations, for, in spite of everything, they still didn't know the measure of his achievement. As he waved and smiled and drove off in the Mercedes, thinking with pleasure of the rich times ahead, because now he had only fools to deal with, he began to justify to himself his merciful treatment of John Manson. He had been right, he concluded. What good was John Manson to him, if he were forced out of the Manse? The man might even leave the island, which was the likeliest outcome. That would not do at all. For George had not done with him yet. No. When one has a power like George's, it feeds on what it touches, and never lets go until it has extracted every last drop of blood. Everyone has to see that the power is fully applied. That is how to augment it: by its continual exercise, to maximum effect.

Leaving Madeline three days to forget about John Manson, three days when she alternately fretted about him losing his job and imagined that he might come to her after all—for news of Jean's defection had spread through the town; and some thought it just punishment from a wrathful God, for taking advantage of a widow in his flock—George met her again by arrangement.

When she was beside him in the car, he said, 'You know what folk are saying, don't you?'

'About me? How should I?'

'They're saying that Manson's lost his job because of you. If you hadn't flaunted yourself in front of him, he wouldn't have done anything.'

'I didn't flaunt myself and he didn't do anything!' she protested.

George laughed. 'You've got to be kidding. He took his whatsit out. Is that doing nothing? And you took off your clothes. You were half-naked, for God's sake! Naked from the waist down. Are you trying to tell me that's not asking for it?'

'I..I thought he wanted me. I know he did. He did want me and I wanted him. What else was I supposed to do?'

George put a calming arm on her shoulder and said, 'Look, I don't blame you. I blame him for leading you on. But the thing is, the whole town thinks you led him on. That if you hadn't done that he'd still be in a job.'

'But that's not true! It's not my fault! I didn't do anything wrong.'

'Well, a lotta folk think you did. I don't know how you can hold your head up here.'

Madeline wept. 'I don't know what to do. It's such a mess.'

'There's only one way to clear yourself. You'll have to make a complaint to the police. Then people will understand that you weren't to blame.'

'But I couldn't do that! How could I cause him more trouble? It wouldn't be fair. He's suffered enough.'

'Nothing need come of it. All you have to do is make a complaint officially. There won't be enough evidence to go to court with. So it'll be quietly dropped. But at least folk will know where the blame lies.'

'But there is no blame!'

'The town thinks you're to blame. That's what you've got to contend with.'

'But I'm not!'

'Well, they won't believe you unless you act as if you are blameless.'

'But how will it affect him?'

'He'll be leaving the island anyway. He'll get a new job elsewhere. How can it matter what the town thinks of him?'

Madeline would agree to nothing, as George knew she would, but a seed had been planted, and George himself would see that it sprouted. It was just a matter of a few of the right kind of taunts being shouted after her, and George would arrange that easily.

Susan was the most difficult about the move, but once her books had been shifted and she realised that Tom's house possessed a complete set of up-to-date Encyclopaedias, to which she had unlimited access, she settled down fast enough. Roddy and she had never known such splendour. Oakfield House was a detached villa standing in three acres of well-tended gardens, with an imposing drive large enough to accommodate the two cars Tom owned, one of which was at Jean's disposal to take them to and from school. They had a bedroom each, some distance from Tom's and, for the time being, Jean maintained the fiction that they were just staying there until the matter of their father's situation had clarified itself. Thus she kept her things in a separate room of her own. Of course, when the children were in bed, the two lovers were free to do as they liked and they did, with the children none the wiser. Staying with 'Uncle Tom' presented no problems, and seemed like a holiday, in such palatial surroundings, dining off excellent food on fine plate, with no chores expected, because Tom employed both a cook and a maid, to do the cleaning.

Tom himself was solicitous over Susan's tendency to spill food and drink at meal-times, and would quietly help Jean clean up after her. And when she asked some question which flummoxed him, he would wisely admit his ignorance. One evening, trying to close the gap between him and the children, he suggested they watch 'Mastermind', a quiz show, on the wide-screen colour television, so much better than the black and white one in the Manse. After a few minutes, Susan rose and said, 'This is no good. It's just a lot of people trying to remember a lot of facts.'

'But they must be clever to do that,' said Tom.

'No, if that's all they can do with their time, they.ey're no..ot clever. They've had to tra.avel there and wait for it to start and ma.ay be stay the night. And for what? It's a waste of time.'

'But there are prizes,' said Tom, with amazement. 'They become famous. Just imagine if you won, we'd be very proud of you.'

'Well, I wouldn't bo.other. Clever people aren't interested in facts, only in ideas. And wha.at makes them clever is that they can think up their own.'

And so, what John would have understood instinctively, Tom did not, and he lost ground in comparison.

The night they left, the night of the hearing, was as difficult as John could ever remember. He brooded over a whisky for a time, thinking of how things used to be, wondering at the injustice of it all. Perhaps he should have put up more of a defence, overcome his scruples about questioning Madeline, described the situation from his point of view. But he knew he could not have done it. It was all bad enough without being stated in front of all these folk. How did a man—and him a minister—discuss his erection before other men and women? It was unthinkable. But the loss of Jean and the children hurt deeply. It was as if his life had been assaulted in some way, the joy extracted—permanently—with a pair of pliers, by some mysterious and invisible dentist, who had not bothered about anaesthetic.

After an hour of it, Jessica appeared in his study and noticed the untouched glass. 'You should have a drink, Dad, it'll do you good.' And she went to the cupboard, took out a glass and poured a small one for her self.

'In fact, I'll have one too, if you don't mind. Keep you company. What do you say?'

She held the glass up, waiting for his decision, unwilling to go ahead without his agreement.

John looked at her sadly and sighed. 'You're the apple of my eye, Jessica, do you know that?' And tears came to his own. 'It's when the going gets tough that you find out who your friends are.' He reached for her and she put down the glass and knelt and embraced him. And his hands stroked the long dark-red tresses.

'Oh, Dad, it's so unfair! But I'm behind you, whatever you do.'

'I know, and I'm grateful. You'll never know how much. But don't be too hard on them, Jessica. On the evidence they had, it's not a surprising decision. If I didn't know any better, maybe I'd have done the same myself.'

'Where did it all go wrong, Dad? I mean why did it happen?'

'I'm not sure. I did nothing wrong. I'm just flesh and blood. At least, that's what I keep telling myself. But maybe I'm wrong.' He looked at her and set her at arms length. 'I *was* attracted to that woman, you know. She's young and beautiful. How could I not be? I'm only human. But I didn't do anything I shouldn't. Not a thing.'

'I know. And it's natural to be attracted to other people. It happens a lot.'

'How do you know?'

'It's easy. I know people. I see what they're like. Anyway, it wouldn't be natural not to look over the fence at the other man's woman. The point is just to look.'

'Yes, but that's not so easy. The imagination can run riot.'

'I know about that too. But even then, there are loyalties that hold the best people back.'

Jessica rose early the next morning and made breakfast. When John did not appear as usual, she set it on a tray and took it up to him, with the newspaper. 'I have to go to school, but you have a lie in for a change. You could do with a rest.'

John laughed. 'I'm not used to being pampered.'

'Well, it's time you had a shot at it.'

He was still in his blue and white striped pyjamas when the door-bell rang. He turned over and ignored it. Who could it be anyway? But it rang again and again and the noise of it seemed to assault his mind, still woozy with drink, as if it were a chain-saw.

Muttering curses, he got up and went down to see who it was, thinking it must be a parcel delivery.

He opened the door to find Madeline on the door step, Madeline in a white blouse, red suit, hat and matching shoes, looking at her matchless best, as if attending an interview for a job.

'I know there's no one else at home. I have to talk to you.' And when John's surprise produced no response, she added, 'Well, can I come in?'

He opened the door wider, soundlessly, mindless of the fact that he had not even bothered to put on a dressing robe, and she entered and headed for the sitting-room, where she sat down.

'Can I get you something? A cup of tea or coffee?'

'No need. Not yet. I want to know what you're going to do.'

'I don't know,' he said, sitting down opposite. 'I haven't had a chance to think yet. I suppose I'll sign on the dole and look for another job. Though at my time of life, it'll be difficult.'

'I don't mean that. I was thinking more along the lines of what are you going to do about us?'

'I don't understand you. Nothing.'

'But why, John? I know that Jean's left you. I came here as soon as I heard. And I know she's supposed to be staying with Tom Henderson temporarily, but I don't buy that. I hope you don't. You don't do you?'

'No, it's not temporary.'

'So she is sleeping with him, then! I knew it! As soon as I heard, I knew how it must be!' Madeline's eyes lit up triumphantly, and she leaned forward and put her hands on John's knees, just as he had once done to her. It was his own instinctive reaction of compassion exactly. 'Well then, what about it?'

'I don't know what you mean,' said John, though he knew well enough as soon as he said it, and wanted space to get himself in order.

'You need a wife, John, and I need a husband. Anyway I love you, and you at least find me attractive.'

John fell back in the chair as if he had been punched.

'I know you must think it's awful of me to come here like this after what I said at the hearing. But what else could I do? It wouldn't have been honest to have stayed away, would it? And then that.. that man Sniffy had his say. I had to go and defend myself, didn't I?'

'Yes, Madeline, I understand how it is. But I'm just taken aback by this. I need to think.'

Madeline lay back and made sure the short skirt crept up revealing herself, and John's eyes saw the slim legs vanishing into a pair of the flimsiest briefs he'd ever seen. Old images surfaced in his mind. He remembered what lay beneath that tiny veil, and the knowledge choked him at the same time as he felt stirred to the depths by it. He stood up, and Madeline immediately said, 'You see! You are attracted! Look at you!'

'I'll make some tea. Something stronger even. Drink. That's what I need. Even if it isn't midday.'

As he left the room hurriedly, she followed him, saying, 'I'll take a drink too, anything. And I'm coming. I'm not letting you out of my sight. Don't you see that this is a blessing in disguise? Now Jean's left you—shown her true colours—now we can be together. What do you say? Why don't we forget about drink and do it right here? I haven't had it for so long! And I've thought about doing it with you so many times. Please, John, please.' They were in the study by then, and he turned frantically, having failed to find the bottle that should have been on the table. She was right behind him, and she laid her hand on him and muttered huskily, 'God, it's a cannon you've got.' And she put her hand inside and pulled it out and fondled it. Then, still holding him in one hand, she rucked up her skirt and sat on the table. 'I'm not letting you go this time.' And she pulled him to her and reached down and moved her flimsy briefs to one side and inserted him.

The rest was reflex, an action that human flesh was not designed to deny or prevent. The age-old instinct to propagate, impregnate, pour himself into her, took root and ruled him, so that he stood over her, thrusting into the pulsating midst of her, having to bend over because of the strength of the erection, which was like a ramrod, parallel to him. And the moans of her ecstasy, so soon in coming, excited him the more, and he thrust and thrust and then having reached the maximum depth possible, simply moved around in her. And her arms were round his neck, her eyes closed, like his, and they mated as driven lovers mate, as mankind has always mated when moved by forces greater than itself. And the glory of it, the uninhibited pleasure of it, was very heaven!

Outside, watching, through the whole of it, the beginning, and everything up to that moment of utter fulfilment, stood Jessica, riveted by the scene, peeking around the window-frame, and she saw all and blinked and looked again. And then, as silently as she had come, during the school interval, just to check up on her parent and make sure he was all right, and without disturbing him from his first morning as a member of the great army of unemployed—as silently, Jessica stole off round the house, and down the path, where she carefully closed the gate, and ran back to her lessons; confused and, for once, red of face, she who, understanding herself and others, usually had no feelings of guilt. But this was different. This was her father, the living god of her earthly life. And the knowledge that he had sexual feelings, that he could be so aroused and for another woman, was a shock, which needed absorbing, digesting in the inner reaches of her soul. It was, for a while at least, as if her nerves had gone haywire. She sat in the classroom, where a very interesting lesson on history was going on, and heard nothing; and when asked a question, could answer nothing: sat speechless, in a mysterious solemnity, which attracted the attention of the teacher, used to her alertness and spontaneous insight. Presently, Jessica managed to admit that she wasn't feeling very well; and that was enough to divert him.

Sensibly, she tried to reason her way out of it. I know my father has a penis. If he didn't have, we wouldn't be here. It was just the size of it! It was disturbing. All this she told herself. It was so unexpected: that it could be so strong and, admit it, beautiful! A gasp escaped her, one that no one else heard, as the lesson continued. Suddenly, she could sit there no longer. She rose and excused herself, and went to the toilet where she locked the door, sat down and soon brought herself to orgasm, blinded by the image of her father's powerful penis penetrating that...that woman's vagina, and the balls that seemed to jiggle against it. Imagining it as her own, her own, receiving such a blessing; and the thrill of it coursed through her; and she continued through it, tormented by the need, afloat on waves of excitement; and for the rest of the period and half the next, she dreamed and masturbated; and at the end of it, she just sat there, thinking it through, trying to come to terms with it, her father's sexuality, so rampantly available; and her own desire; and his betrayal and her own response, uncontrolled, uncontrollable. And gradually, as if through a fog, came the realisation that her own involuntary sexual need, was little different from her father's.

When it was all over, John made tea and they had that whisky and then John found some biscuits and Madeline wouldn't have any, because Jean had made them, and they sat and marvelled at each other, and before the tea was finished, John drained his glass and stood up, with a hand out.

'Ready for more are you?' said Madeline, licking her lips, and allowed herself to be led upstairs to a bedroom, once occupied by a child, and they did it again, more slowly and with great tenderness and kindness. And at the end, when they lay quietly, Madeline felt the silence descend upon him and said, 'What's wrong?'

And John wept. 'That was lovely, terrific. All the better for having imagined it so many times.'

'So what's the matter then?'

'It's just that it can't go on.'

'Why not? I love you and you like me—a lot! I know, I can tell.'

'But it's not love, Madeline. It'll never be that, don't you see? And I'm too old for you and I've no job. It's hopeless.'

'No, it's not! It's ideal. I've got enough money for the two of us. And you'll have the dole. Maybe you'll get a job, but it doesn't matter anyway, does it?'

'Yes, it does. It matters to me.'

'We could go away and live somewhere else, where you're not known.'

'It isn't that. It just isn't right for us. I'm too old for you. In ten years time I'll be past it, unable to do it at all, and you'll need a younger man. And you'll find one too. You're beautiful, Madeline. Very beautiful. You'll see. I'm right, and you'll thank me for this some day.'

Madeline was hurt, disappointed and angry all at the same time. 'You're wrong. So wrong! What's wrong with a few years? We've just had fantastic sex and we'll go on having it. No fear!'

'That's it, Madeline, it was just sex. What do we have in common? Not much. You don't know what an abyss lies between people of different education and values. Its..its not bridgeable, no basis for marriage. We just wouldn't get on. What if you wanted to go dancing? You'd like that, wouldn't you?'

'Yes, I'd be so proud, with you on my arm.'

'You're only proud of what I was, what I used to be; not what I am now, what I'm becoming. I'm finished, Madeline, don't you see that?' She said nothing and he added. 'I wouldn't go. I don't dance. So you'd have to find someone else to dance with, and I'd get jealous, and it would be a hopeless mess.'

'But dancing's not every thing.'

'What else would we do together?'

'Watch tv? Go to the pictures?'

'Tv, pictures and bed? That's a fine basis for marriage!'

'It's all most folk have. What's wrong with it, for God's sake?'

'Everything. God most of all. I'm...I'm not the kind of ordinary chap that would be contented with that, Madeline. It's not enough for me. It never could be.'

'But you just got your marching orders. Kicked out. Are you saying you still want to do God's work? I thought you didn't believe in it.'

'I do believe in it! There's no finer work than the work I do—did! And I do believe in God, even if it is a bit abstract.'

'So you don't want me, then? This was all just a quick fling?'

'I'm afraid so.'

Madeline said nothing. Angrily, she got out of bed and got dressed. Then, as she made for the door, she turned. 'You'll never get a better offer, John. But I've had enough. Once I'm through that door, I'm not coming back. So make up your mind.'

John lay back in the bed watching her in silence.

'Is that all you've got to say? Nothing.'

'Yes. I'm sorry. But that's how it is. I'm very grateful to you for coming.'

'Don't thank me, for God's sake, John. I thought you really fancied me. I was wrong.'

'No, you were not wrong. I just don't want to marry you, that's all.'

'So you'll fuck me any time you feel like it, but you don't want commitment. Is that it?'

'If you throw yourself at me the way you just did, I won't be able to resist. It's not as if I've got anybody else. I need it just like you. But that's all it would be, Madeline. Sex. And that's not good enough for you. I want something better for you.'

'Huh! Something better for yourself, more like. I'm off.'

George spoke to Tommy Forbes on his own. 'Something I want you to do for me, son. You'll have heard about the minister and Madeline Grant. Well, I don't want that bitch getting off with it. She ruined a good man there, ye know, Tommy. I want you to get a hold of her in passing, just by accident, you know. And say something like this to her. 'Fucked any more ministers, have you?' And give her a grin. 'Can you do that, Tommy?'

'Aye, nae problem, Mr Buchanan, anything you say.'

'Would it cause you any trouble?'

'Naw. Serve the bitch right, so it would.'

'So you'll do it then?'

'Aye, Ah'll see her today. Ah usually pass her goin' for ma lunch. She goes out to do her shoppin' then.' But it occurred to Tommy to wonder why it was. 'What's it for anyway, Mr Buchanan?'

'Just a Christian duty, Tommy, that's all. Trying to bring her to her senses.'

Sure enough, Tommy passed her at lunchtime, and said what he'd been told to say. Madeline was angry, red-faced, with the sheer indignity of it. 'You keep your remarks to yourself, you...you...skinny big lout!'

Tommy laughed. 'Ah'll gie ye a shot masel, if ye've nae mair ministers.'

'Just you keep your rotten mouth shut, you delinquent, you!'

But as Madeline went on her way, the taunt rankled. Was that what people thought of her? A tart who flaunted herself because she needed men? A tear came, and, surreptitiously, she wiped it away, determined to keep up appearances.

When, the very next day, another taunt was hurled at her, by another man she did not know, the message went home like a cannon shot. And it never occurred to her to wonder who that man was or whether he, too, was employed by George Buchanan, as a taxi driver. Enough, that he was a man, another person who thought her tainted.

The idea that her reputation had suffered, because of her association with John Manson, one in which she held herself guiltless—for how could it be her fault if men found her attractive?—preyed on her mind. And if the solution was merely as simple as laying a complaint, a complaint she had every right to make, she believed, for had she not been the woman at home, recently bereaved, sex-starved and vulnerable? Then why not? It stood to reason it was not her fault but his, for getting so attracted to her. And how could she help it, if she were attractive?

One evening, she phoned the Manse. Jessica picked up the phone, and when she found out who it was, she was brusque. 'I'll get him. Wait, please,' she said, through gritted teeth, and Madeline received another intimation of her folly.

'How are you, John?' said Madeline when he came to the phone.

'Fine, Madeline, fine,' said John.

'Have you had any second thoughts?'

'No.'

'So you really don't want me, then?'

'Not in the long term, if that's what you mean.'

'But why, John? Why? I don't understand it. You're attracted, I know you are.'

'It takes more than that, Madeline. Much more. It's a difference in how we view life, that's all. But it matters.'

Madeline was silent, nursing her sadness, for the thought of a night with John had been pleasant. Now the rancour returned, as it does to a woman scorned. 'I've been at the butt end of a lot of bad talk because of you, John. And I don't know what to do.'

'I suppose it's inevitable. All I can advise is to meet it with Christian goodness.'

'What good is that? What good has it done you?'

'It's the only good, Madeline, whatever happens, whatever people say or do.'

'It's been suggested to me that the best way out is to lay a complaint against you. Then the town will know I'm not to blame. I know it wouldn't be very nice for you, John, but nothing would come of it. There's no evidence. So it could hardly hurt you more than you've been hurt already.'

John said nothing, took the hurt into himself and absorbed it. How could people be so unfeeling, so cruel? If he needed confirmation that Madeline was not worthy of his love, he had just received it.

'Would you mind, John?'

In a choked voice, John said, 'Yes.'

'But you would understand, wouldn't you?'

'I understand you, yes. I'll ring off now, if you don't mind, Madeline.'

George started the process of finding a new minister that day. Adverts were taken out in *Life and Work,* the Church of Scotland magazine. But when the issue of setting a deadline for John Manson's removal from the Manse was raised, he was in no hurry. George would drag out the period of finding a newcomer, until it suited him, so that John Manson would remain in Ottersay until he, George, had finished with him. And that would depend upon the date of the trial.

The police were not slow in beating a path to the Manse door, once the complaint was noted in the office, and Madeline's statement taken down. Then there was Sniffy to see, and his statements. After that, it was a matter for the Procurator Fiscal, and George had already made standing arrangements in that quarter. A typist in the office kept him informed of all the cases under consideration, so he became aware of the possibility of prosecution, as soon as it became an issue.

The judiciary is, of course, independent of all arms of government, even the local variety—in principle. In practice, a powerful provost can have an important effect on how things are seen by the Fiscal.

George invited her to lunch at the Grand Hotel, and devoted a couple of hours to buttering her up and softening her, with fine wines and the best cuisine of the island. Ostensibly, it was just a routine effort by the new head of local government to socialise with another leading figure. Only near the end, did the matter of the minister raise itself. George remarked that he had spent part of the morning making adverts for a new one, and admitted, sadly, that John Manson's demise had been unfortunate. Still, he said, you couldn't allow that kind of thing in a town like Ottersay. It just wouldn't do to have a minister exposing himself to young women in the congregation.

As a woman herself, the Fiscal could not agree more.

'Who knows how far it went?' added George. 'Maybe he went the whole hog with her. We'll never know now, will we? It looks like it. Why would Jean Manson have moved out like that? Maybe he's been doing it for some time, with all the young widows. Who can tell? Anyway, we've made sure it won't happen here any more, haven't we? It remains to make sure he doesn't do it anywhere else.'

And that was enough for the Fiscal to see his drift, and she was sufficiently seduced by the splendour of his hospitality, to smile upon his ideas.

The initiation of Billy Buchanan into the criminal underworld of Branden took a further step, one night, when the trio paid a visit to Sandyport, the town in the next bay along the coast from Ottersay. There were several pubs and shops there, on the sea front, and it was felt that one of them would be accessible.

While John Ryan was working with his jemmy on the back window of the chip shop, a police car drove up a side street. Work stopped dead, and the three hid in the shadows. Then, upstairs, a door creaked and a window was thrown open. There was muffled conversation, as if others in the building were watching the police. Ryan set off and the others followed. Running fast, on rubber-soled shoes, he headed for the =darkness, and that was inland, away from the sea, and away from the roads.

They paused for breath at the top of a field, from which the lights of Sandyport could be seen spread out below. As it seemed wise to avoid the streets, in case they were picked up, they set off across country, on a little-used lane, towards Ottersay, and reached the outskirts half an hour later.

They were passing the school, on the road above and behind, when Ryan noticed an open window and, ever the opportunist, made a bee-line for it. Inside, was a science lab. Tommy, who joined him, remembered it. 'This is old Leitch's room. I used tae sit there,' he added, pointing to a place at one of the laboratory benches.

Ryan tried the doors to cupboards, but they were locked. 'No' much here then, eh ?' But Tommy remembered something. He went to a tall cupboard, reached up and lifted down a bottle. 'It's still here.'

'What is it?'

'Sodium.'

'Is that no' salt?'

'Naw. Metallic Sodium. It's like a bomb. Put it in water and it flies all ower the place like a speed boat.'

'Ah thought ye said it was like a bomb?'

'Leitch said it was. If you used a big bit.'

And so outside, they went looking for some water, and found a burn in the ditch beside the road to the Otterhall rugby ground. Under a lamp-standard, they considered the contents of the bottle. Inside, were two large thick sticks of a greyish substance. 'Have you got a knife?' said Tommy.

Of course Ryan had a knife. He might never have been in the Scouts, but he was always prepared. Watched by Billy and John, Tommy removed one of the sticks with a handkerchief wrapped round his fist, and held it on the road, while cutting a slice half an inch thick.

'What's the hanky for?' said Billy.

'To stop it burning your hand.'

Tommy picked up the slice on the blade, lifted it above the burn and shook it, until it dropped into the water. There was an explosion and the water burst up in the air as if a depth-charge had gone off. The boys jumped back, but all three were soaked when the water fell down on them.

'Christ! That was something!' said Ryan. 'We could have some rare fun wi' that stuff doon the harbour. Maybe we could blow up a boat.'

'What for?' said Billy, who had been a silent bystander all this time.

'For fun!' said Tommy, 'whit else?'

The next day was a Sunday, and the trio met, by arrangement, at the harbour, Ryan with the bottle, and inside, the two sticks of sodium in their preserving solution. They were considering which of the many boats to sink, when Billy noticed a ceremony of some kind at the square, close by. 'There's my Dad,' he said. 'That'll be the new fountain being opened.'

The fountain was not exactly in the style of Bernini, but it was large and ornate and cost several thousand pounds of the tax-payers money to commission and erect. A life-size figure of a nude had been sculpted to form a centre-piece, and from her mouth, a stream of water was filling a circular area about twenty feet in diameter, where, it was expected, birds would come to drink. The author of the project, one of the councillors, had wisely suggested that the cost would be recovered, if it were put about that throwing coins into the depths would bring good luck.

George stood at the rim, in the finery of his office: black, three-cornered hat with gold trimming, ermine-edged robes of gold and silver, and wearing his huge gold chain of office. Beside him, were the other worthies of the council and, around these, many of the locals who had come to observe the proceedings. A red tape had been stretched across the growing pond, to the neck of the lady standing in the centre, and beyond to the other rim. George was making a speech, prior to cutting the tape.

'What if,' said Tommy, with calm deliberation, to Ryan 'What if a piece of this stuff was to land in the fountain?'

The two boys looked at each other with wonder. 'On ye go,' said Ryan. And without another word, Tommy put on a glove, took out the largest stick, handed the bottle to Ryan, who stuck it up his jooks, and sauntered over to the fountain where the ceremony was in progress.

So many others were doing the same thing, that no one took particular notice of him. The crowd around George had swollen by the time he reached the back row. Tommy listened for a while and then looked round. No one was behind him, and the coast was clear. He took several steps backwards, turned, launched the stick of sodium into the air, like a hand-grenade, and then began to saunter back to the harbour.

There was a blinding flash as the sodium made contact with the pond, and a terrific explosion of smoke, followed by a great whoosh of water, forty feet into the air, which, when it came down, soaked everyone within ten feet, many of whom had been blown backwards onto the flagstones. A tidal wave of water flowed everywhere around.

By the time Tommy reached the harbour-side, Ryan, overcome with laughter at the chaos wrought among the establishment, had almost fallen into the water off the quay, while Billy stood gawping with amazement, and a tinge of unexpected pleasure, at the alteration to his father's dignity.

When the smoke cleared, and people got up, shook off the water, and began to take stock, the nude figure, the cause of much prior comment, was found to have developed a crack in a most unseemly part of her anatomy, as if the wrath of God had insisted that human representations should resemble them, even in those ways which the more prudish elements were anxious to conceal. Worse, the lady no longer spouted forth water from her curvacious mouth, but from the very part of her torso, from which, in time of difficulty, were she alive, water might actually be expected.

The great dish of the pond was also cracked into several large pieces. Worst of all, from George's point of view, his dignity and the dignity of the moment, had been assaulted. His hat, the wide-brimmed, beloved three-cornered hat, which every Brandonian worth his salt aspired to wear, was missing.

Then, for a while, there was universal confusion, as police cars whizzed around, sirens blaring; the island's two ambulances drove up in a welter of sound; and every fire-engine in the place joined in. Soon, like a community under a Red Indian attack which has been compelled to laager its wagons for the purpose of defence, the square and its people were surrounded by fire engines, police cars and ambulances, and the various dignitaries, whose amour propre had been so violently insulted, began to confront the world again with bemused expressions of wonder. Though a few folk could vaguely recall a splash before 'Tommy's final solution', most could remember nothing, for the shock of the blast had dimmed every other recent memory beyond recall.

And so the police were powerless, and the populace reduced to the wildest forms of speculation in every pub and tea-room in Branden. Some said it was an earthquake of sudden violence which had cracked open the fountain. Have we not seen earthquakes before? they said. And they had, once, during the war. One geriatric, with scattered wits, was sufficiently forgetful, as to suggest that it had been the result of a bomb dropped by a late Heinkel, intended for Greenock. The religious, some at least, thought it was an act of God, occasioned by the unseemly display of the nude, but which, they were compelled to admit, was, after the explosion, a good deal more risqué. Many deemed it a UFO of a particularly violent kind. But the more historically-minded, reflecting that in days gone by, invaders had been killed and probably buried in that very place, considered that it was a supernatural phenomenon, caused by the demons and bad spirits who lurked underneath. Another variation of this theory, promulgated by a sect of religious witnesses, had it that, of course, it was the Devil's work; while the more knowledgeable about current affairs, mindful of the 'close' proximity of the island to another much larger, inferred that it must be the IRA, who had undertaken to extend their theatre of operations to the Scottish islands.

Wisely, now, the three youths standing over by the harbour, controlled their laughter. Indeed, the power of the spectacle was such that they were reduced to stupefied wonder at the scale of their achievement.

As a matter of routine, a constable came across to the three 'Indians' to ask them if they had seen anything, but was deflected when Ryan said, 'Aye, an explosion,' and proceeded to give a blow by blow description of the event, once it had taken place, which was not what was intended. To the question, 'Do you know what caused it?' they each, of course, denied all knowledge. Fortunately, the constable did not see the bulge in Ryan's jooks.

An hour after the event, the celebrated black three-cornered hat, minus the gold braid, was found: on the head of an angel on the war memorial, whence it had alighted having been borne on the wind, after propulsion into the atmosphere.

In the days that followed, a forensic team arrived from Glasgow, who scoured the area, without result. There had been an explosion, which everybody knew, but caused by whom or what, remained a mystery. The bomb, if it had been a bomb, was blown to smithereens so small as to defy discovery. In truth, the sodium had vaporised altogether, but no one thought of that. Even offers of rewards in the media for 'persons having knowledge of..' yielded nothing of interest, as Ryan reluctantly concluded that turning in Tommy Forbes would merely incriminate himself and earn him nothing. Mr Leitch, who was nearing retiring age, and whose memory was not what it was, never did notice the missing bottle of sodium. How could he miss what was not there to be seen? And the next year at that time, when he came to do the same experiment again, he scratched his head, thinking that he ought to have some about the place, but where, he could not say. A search revealed nothing. Oh, well, he concluded, I must have used it all up over the years. He retired soon after; and so the sodium was never missed. Even if he had missed it, he would never have said so. It would have reflected badly on him. However, unforeseen events were soon to make it impossible that he would notice the loss.

Thus, the event was filed alongside the Marie Celeste and the Bermuda Triangle, as a mystery beyond compare, recorded in local anthologies of history and places less important to Brandonians, like the Scottish Office and the British Museum. In old age, when drunk, Ryan would tell how he had set up the whole thing, with the aid of a couple of folk in his gang. But no one believed him. He couldn't even spell the name of the substance used, still less understand why it might have the desired effect. How could a stick of stuff out of a school science-lab cause that amount of trouble? No way! How could someone as stupid as Ryan—made stupider by drink over the years—elude the combined efforts of the Branden constabulary? It was impossible. Only the scientifically literate would have understood, and they never got to hear Ryan's ravings.

The day of the trial arrived. John Manson, in his only dark-grey suit, blue stock and white dog collar, walked across the town and up the hill towards the castle, beside which stood the Sheriff Court House. The sun shone, the grassy lawns gleamed like emerald and light sparkled on the moat. He was passing MacTavish's Bar when, on the other side of the street, he saw the slovenly figure of Saxby and the bald, red-haired giant Harry McCusker emerge from the swing doors, after an all night session of drinking. Saxby reeled, drunkenly, and called across, 'Guid mornin' tae ye, minister!' doffing his bunnet and making an attempt at a low bow, which, however, nearly caused him to overbalance into the gutter. Straightening himself up to his full height, he added, 'Ah hear yer tae get the chop, Mr Manson.' McCusker laughed and fell against the pub door, which swung inwards and deposited him once more inside. 'Yu'll be lookin' fur a joab. Ye should ask, Harry here. The pair o' ye wid get oan fine. He's a rerr wan fur the sheep.'

John, nervous already, was humiliated. He strode on, with a scarlet face, pursued by the sounds of laughter, as Saxby fell about the pavement and McCusker, roaring like a bull, once again appeared on the street and rolled in the gutter.

The progress to the court was a nightmare, through the swing doors, and up the steps to the first floor, the target of every interested eye assembled, particularly, to enjoy the sight of a minister on trial. Finally, he was met by the bailiff and shown to his seat in the dock where he sat between two policemen, one of whom had been involved in following up George Buchanan's scam with the wills.

At the command 'Court. Court Rise,' everyone stood, while Sheriff Jamie Gorse mounted the bench in his red and saffron robes, like some great oriental spider, rubbing his hands together, as if relishing the prospect of an old enemy caught in his web.

Set high above the proletariat, the bench in the Scottish Court is protected by a bulwark strong enough to withstand the impact of a cannonade. From this defended eminence, the Sheriff in grey wig, symbol of accumulated wisdom, and much prejudice, surveys the motley under him, and endeavours to control the accused and their supporters, often half drunk, or euphoric on 'ecstasy' or some other drug. In days gone by, Sheriffs would have sheltered behind their defences, while assailed with missiles such as stones and bottles—emptied first, of course, to make the feat possible— and suffered attack on life and limb, with claymore, cutlass and dirk.

Below the Sheriff's bastion, is a large table, at which sit the lawyers, in their black gowns. On the right, the jury, and the reporters, most important of all, whose duty is to mislead the public into the belief that they are being properly protected. Near the jury, under the terrifying eye of the Sheriff, is the dock, where sits the accused, two police on either side of him; and, facing the Sheriff, the audience; comprising, so often, friends and enemies of the accused; the curious; and the old and the poor and infirm, who only want a free place to sit out of the cold, and often snore through the proceedings.

The Fiscal, Miss Templeton, a slim blue-eyed wisp of a girl, in a black dress and gown, with an angelic face half-hidden under waves of corn, set these in motion, by reading out the charges. To wit, on February 6th 1963, John Manson had committed an act of indecent exposure at the house of one Madeline Grant, of 19 Maple Grove, Ottersay. It had been considered necessary to bring the case, she said, regretfully, notwithstanding the employment of the accused, because of public disquiet.

As her first witness, she called Madeline, and, after some delay, hair freshly permed and in her best suit of dark blue—the Fiscal had told her to avoid loud colours—Madeline appeared, took the stand, was sworn in, and identified.

Miss Templeton said, 'Do you see the Reverend John Manson in the court?'

'Yes,' said Madeline, and was encouraged to point to him, which she did.

'Did John Manson visit you after your husband's death?'
Madeline told how he had paid her several visits.
'Did you think that John Manson was attracted to you?'
'Yes.'
'Could you tell the court why this was?'
Madeline blushed. 'I could see it in his trousers.' A few folk tittered.
'What was it you saw?'
'A kind of lump.'
'You mean an erection?'
'Yes.'
'You're sure it wasn't a hernia?'
'No. It was definitely an erection.'
'Now, on the sixth February 1963, did John Manson visit you?'
'Yes.'

'And did he get an erection then?' The hush was omnipresent, as everyone waited.

'Yes.'

'Was there anyone else in the house?'

'No. Just him and me.'

'And what did you do when you saw his erection?'

'I went off to make some tea.'

'You thought to defuse the situation?'

Madeline thought for a moment and agreed.

'Would you tell the court what happened in the kitchen.'

'I turned round when the kettle boiled to make the tea and when I turned back again, I noticed that his penis was sticking out of his trousers.' There were gasps from various sectors of the court, and the Sheriff called for quiet.

The Fiscal licked her lips, for she had spent hours over this very point beforehand with the witness, and said, 'Do you mean that the erection was so large that his penis had appeared over the top of his waistband, or that he had unfastened his flies?'

'His flies were open.'

'And what did you do?'

'I told him to put it away.'

'And did he?'

'Yes.'

'And what did you do then?'

'I poured out some tea and handed him a cup.'

'And did he go away soon after?'

'Yes.'

John sat with head bowed and face flushed. Is this really happening to me, he asked himself? And his legs felt like disconnected jellies and his jaw dropped when he realised it was so. His breath came in gasps and his face turned purple. How could Madeline say such things? How could she subject another human being to such humiliation? And why to him, of all people?

What John did not know, was that for people of lesser intellect than his own, telling lies was easier, because the untrained memory is a comparatively flexible instrument. Since Madeline herself could not be guilty, someone else had to be, and that someone was John Manson. How was he guilty? What did he do? That was something one worked out. The mind, any mind, easily forgets what is inconvenient, and adds what is. Thus, is justice perverted, time without end.

Sheriffs are aware of this, devise stratagems for the elucidation of the truth, and, miraculously, often succeed in discovering it, amidst the festering swamps of the various enfeebled minds they have to deal with. In an effort to jog a witnesses' memory, one sheriff of large intellect and greater soul, once sang the Sash—a highly inflammatory song—on his bench. Alas, he learnt nothing and the public wrongly inferred he was anti-catholic, as well as deranged by drink, both untrue. In this case, the Fiscal had simply pressed Madeline for an account acceptable to herself, one that would justify her complaint to the police, and—which Madeline, with very considerable assistance, provided—this was enough for a charge to be brought.

The defence lawyer, Dick Langmuir, an elegant, dapper figure in black gown, with grey hair, stood up to cross-examine.

'Were John Manson's visits useful to you?'

'Yes.'

'Why was that?'

'I was feeling lonely and guilty after my husband took his own life. John told me it wasn't my fault and made me feel as if I was a worthy person.'

'Did you ever discuss sex?'

'No, I don't think so.'

'Isn't it true that you told John Manson you were missing the sex you used to have with your husband?'

'I don't remember anything like that.'

'Did you ever behave provocatively in front of John Manson? Did you ever display the top of your thighs to him, while you were sitting together? Or deliberately show off your knickers to him?'

The Fiscal rose. 'My Lord, I object to this line of questioning. This is irrelevant and deeply embarrassing to the witness.'

'Yet I must allow it, Miss Templeton,' said Sheriff Gorse.

Having time to collect herself, it was all the easier for Madeline to reply: 'No.'

'You mean you never at any time flaunted yourself at John Manson?'

'No.'

'You never at any time showed off your underwear?'

'No.'

'So you are saying that you did nothing which might have excited this man?'

'Yes. I mean I never did.'

'Mrs Grant, do you realise what humiliation you are causing this man? He is a man of the cloth. His reputation will be ruined by what you are saying.'

'Yes.'

'Is there some reason why you are making this complaint?'

'No.'

'How can it be 'no', Mrs Grant? You are complaining about something relatively harmless. Yet it is very very damaging to my client.'

'I suppose I think he shouldn't do that kind of thing' —Looking at the Fiscal, for support— 'And I have a duty to see that he doesn't do it again.'

'Is there anything wrong in a man getting an erection?'

'No, I suppose it's natural.'

'So where is the wrong, then?'

'He shouldn't show it off.'

'You mean he shouldn't expose it so that it can be seen?'

'Yes.'

'And you are asking the court to believe that my client, who has never had a conviction in fifty years of life, who has never at any time attracted the slightest criticism of his conduct, took out his penis to show it to you?'

Madeline blushed, and said, 'Yes.'

'Did John Manson make any advance upon you, as if to have sex with you?'

'No.'

'Did he suggest that you might have sex with him?'

'No.'

'Did you suggest that you have sex with him?'

'No.'

'Mrs Grant, I put it to you that you flaunted yourself before John Manson, and when he got an erection as any man would, you unzipped his flies and exposed it.'

'No.'

'And you took off your clothing below the waist, and sat on the kitchen table and begged him to have sex with you. Isn't that what happened?'

'No, I never! I couldn't do that!'

'Did John Manson make a further visit to your house after this occasion?'

'Yes.'

'And did you admit him to the house?'

'Yes.'

'Why was that?'

'Well, I couldn't leave him standing at the door.'

'Even though he had exposed himself to you on the earlier visit?'

'Yes.'

'When was this second visit?'

'About two weeks later.'

'And it didn't bother you? You didn't feel threatened by it?'

'No, I suppose not.'

'Isn't it true, that you wanted to see him again, and you kissed him at the door?'

'Yes.'

'Is that how women usually react to men who have exposed themselves to them?'

'I suppose not.'

'Why did you, then?'

'I liked him. I was lonely and he gave me comfort.'

'But he never at any time made love to you or fondled you?'

'No.'

After the letters were brought up and sundry other matters, Madeline was released. Sniffy Johnstone was called next and, carefully instructed by George to omit all reference to Madeline's active part in the events, gave exactly corroborating evidence. So for Sniffy, all that happened was that John Manson exposed himself and then, asked to do so, put it away. At George's suggestion, Sniffy was in a red and brown check suit—the kind associated with the quicker elements of the racing fraternity, whom he admired above all—a black shirt, of the sort favoured by the Mafia, and a tie—what a tie! Lemon yellow with a dusky nude dancing all over it. George might have defined the clothes, but he couldn't be expected to imagine what colours or designs would be chosen. His manipulations were not perfect, after all.

'Where were you when you saw this?' said Langmuir.

'Jist ootside the kitchen. I looked in the windae tae see if anybody was at hame.'

'And why had you come there? For what purpose?'

'Tae see if Mrs Grant needed ony help. I knew she was a widow wumman and she was in a state. Jist daein' the Christian thing, ye ken,' he added, trying to look saintly.

'Isn't it true that you were employed to snoop on John Manson?'

'No.'

'What is your profession?'

'Ah'm unemployed.'

'Are you on the dole, then?'

'Yes,' he sniffed, lowering his head, as if in an act of contrition and apology.

'Do you ever do work on the side?'

'No' me.'

'So you have never ever made any money on the side, during the years of your unemployment?'

The witness sniffed and replied, 'No.'

'Have you ever had a job?'

'I was a private dick once in Glesca.'

'When was that?'

'Five year ago.'

'And you haven't worked since?'

'No.'

'Why did you stop being a private eye?'

'I was laid aff.'

'You mean you were no good at the job?'

'Naw. There wis nae work. Divorce got easier. So folk didnae need witnesses for citing as correspondents.'

'I put it to you that ever since you came here, you have worked irregularly on the side as a private eye or snoop.'

'No, that's no' true. I widnae cheat the government.'

Laughter echoed around the courtroom at this admission of idealism; and Sniffy looked about him with amazement that anyone might disbelieve his sworn oath.

John Manson told the truth, the whole truth and nothing but the truth. Of course, he had never volunteered information about Madeline's visit to the Manse, so he was never asked any questions about it, by Langmuir, and the Fiscal did not consider cross examination necessary. From her standpoint, the case was open and shut. Most of those present, including the jury, agreed with her. Two separate witnesses, no matter that one was a rogue, had corroborated each other effectively. Why would anyone believe a minister, so recently unfrocked?

'Have you anything more, Mr Langmuir?' said the Sheriff, wearily, looking almost sorrowfully at the minister in the dock.

'Yes, my Lord. I call Jessica Manson.'

John Manson's head swivelled, as he heard the name, and again at the footsteps that soon followed. Apparently, he was not expecting this turn of events, and there was a sudden buzz of comment in the packed court, which caused Sheriff Gorse to bang his gavel and growl at them for silence.

Jessica was sworn in and identified.

Langmuir said, 'Would you tell the court what happened, the day after your father lost his job.'

Jessica stood in her white dress, with her red hair cascading down onto her shoulders, for all the world like an avenging angel. Her cheeks were flushed and her eyes fiery.

'I got up early to make my father breakfast in bed.'

'That wasn't usual, was it? Why was that?'

'He had just been sacked and my mother had left him. So he was very upset and down-hearted. I wanted to look after him.'

'You were the only one left in the Manse, besides your father?'

'Yes. My mother took the children with her. Except for Peter, who was staying in a hotel because he had a job there.'

'Why did you stay?'

'Because I love my father and I think he's a very good man. The best. And I think it's despicable the way he's been treated.'

'Now, after you gave your father his breakfast in bed, did you then go to school?'

'Yes.'

'You didn't think you should remain to look after him?'

'He wouldn't have let me.'

'Did you return from school to see how he was?'

'Yes. At the morning interval. I ran home. It's not far.'

'What did you see?'

'I didn't have much time and I didn't want to intrude too much. So I didn't go into the house.'

'Why was this?'

'I thought he might be drinking. He wouldn't have wanted me to see that.'

'So you were content to spy on him from outside?'

'Yes. I suppose that's what it was.'

'And what was your object?'

'Just to assure myself that he was all right.'

'So you looked in at a back window?'

'Yes, the study window.'

'And what did you see?'

'I saw Madeline Grant and him. Dad was still in pyjamas. Madeline took out his penis in one hand and she rucked up her dress with the other.'

'And did your father resist?'

'Not much. He was too excited to do anything.'

'So what happened next?'

'Madeline pushed her knickers aside and inserted my father's penis into her.'

'Where into her?'

'Into her vagina.'

'You are sure of this?'

'Absolutely! I saw it all.'

'And then?'

'My father and she began to make love.'

'Did your father move in and out of Madeline Grant?'

'No. She inserted him and pulled him onto her. Then they just moved together.'

'What did you do then?'

'I left.'

'You didn't think to interrupt them?'

'No. It was a private matter. Nothing to do with me.'

'Did you feel it was wrong?'

'At first. I felt angry. As if he'd let the side down for the very first time. Somehow, I knew it was the first time. I also felt jealous. But later, when I had a chance to think it out, I realised that it was all for the best. My father was in a state. Very depressed at being sacked and my mother leaving him. It was the best thing for him. Anyway, he hadn't done anything. No man could have resisted Madeline, the way she carried on.'

'Has your father spoken to you about this?'

'No.'

'Has he seen Madeline Grant since then?'

'No.'

'How do you know?'

'Because he hasn't been out of the house since. And I've been on holiday. So I've been at home all the time.'

'Has there been any contact between them since?'

'Madeline phoned him. I overheard the conversation. She wanted him to marry her. He refused. He said they lived in different worlds. She was upset and then annoyed by his rejection.'

The Fiscal rose to cross-examine, resplendent in black dress and gown, with her coiffeured golden hair and peach complexion, a perfect contrast to Jessica in white, with red hair tumbling to her shoulders.

'Isn't it true that you couldn't possibly see your father's penis being inserted into Mrs Grant's vagina, because her thighs were in the way?'

'No. She was sitting at an angle to me with her legs spread wide. I could see right into her vagina. She was gasping for it.'

'Why didn't she see you?'

'Because her eyes were shut most of the time. She was really excited. When they were open, she was looking at my father as if she could eat him. She was in no state to notice anything else.'

'I put it to you that this is a total fabrication trumped up because you know your father is guilty, and you are a loving daughter anxious to protect him?'

'Not so! I couldn't tell lies to save my father. He would never let me.'

'But look Jessica,' said the Fiscal cajollingly, 'it just isn't possible for people to make love when the woman still has her underwear on. Is it?'

'Yes it is! I saw it happen. Mrs Grant was wearing knickers like tissue paper. You could see right through them and they were easily brushed aside out of the way, as if they never existed.'

'You admitted that you were jealous when you saw the couple making love. Isn't it true that you were so jealous that your father loved Mrs Grant, and not you, that you made this up this whole story?'

'No. If you think I would make up a story like this and tell it in public, you are a complete fool. This kind of thing, nobody invents.'

A wave of sympathy rolled across the court and in that moment, the Fiscal knew she had lost the case.

She made one final last effort to break down Jessica. 'If your father made love to Mrs Grant, as you say, don't you think he betrayed his vows of marriage and ordination?'

'No! His wife, my mother, had just walked out. She's been fornicating with Tom Henderson ever since. Any fool can see that. My father was absolved from those marriage vows when my mother walked out on him. She couldn't have chosen a worse moment—the very day he was sacked. Unjustifiably! As to his vows as a minister. These don't prohibit him behaving as a man. He's just flesh and blood, for heaven's sake! Anyway, he didn't misbehave. He didn't take advantage of Mrs Grant. He was deliberately seduced by her. Nobody, no man, could have done anything else.'

Scornfully, the Fiscal shouted, 'So you have no regrets for your father's behaviour?'

'Yes. I regret that he lives here. He's too good a man for the people of this town. They don't deserve him. That's all I regret. I'm glad he got a little pleasure out of Madeline Grant, even though it wasn't his idea, and he didn't initiate it. But I know he'll never go to her. She's just not good enough!'

'Your loyalty is commendable,' said the Fiscal, reddening under the onslaught, 'but you can't avoid the fact that he has just been unfrocked. Sacked for conduct unbecoming.'

'He should never have been sacked! They'll never get a better minister than my dad. All he did was go into a situation to help somebody when other ministers would have been too scared.'

'But he is an atheist! Isn't that a good reason in itself, for his dismissal?'

'It's not true. He may not believe in an old man up in the sky, but that doesn't mean he doesn't believe in a God, and do everything he can to support that belief.'

Sneeringly, irritated at having backed a loser, the Fiscal said, 'And what kind of God is that, may one ask?'

'One identical to goodness. The principles of goodness. If you want another name for it, call it love. My father believes with all his soul in the power of love. And the duty of every man, himself especially, to further that cause, at any cost to himself.'

There was a silence at first; and then a hum of approval, that became first a buzz and then a wave of delight, as some people began to clap and a few others to cheer. A drunk man stood up waving a half-filled bottle and cried enthusiastically, 'Here's tae ye, lassie! Yer a chip aff the auld block!'

The case was over. John's acquittal inevitable. The trial had lasted half the day and the decision was not reached until 7 pm. Afterwards, there was a discussion among some of the Kirk Session, about the outcome. Bob Forsyth and Dick Souter, agreed that there had been so much trouble already that—even though the minister was innocent, very good at his job, and even sufficiently in tune with the doctrine—he should not be reinstated. Efforts by Dr Telford and others to change their minds were unavailing. Some folk are always too stupid to see that the amount of trouble produced is no criterion for deciding what ought to be done. Indeed, the trouble had even been caused to the minister, not by him; but they easily forgot that, and no amount of argument would persuade them. And so a deputation of the others went to George, as head of the Kirk Session, to see about the minister's reinstatement, but George, with an air of sorrow, not altogether assumed for the occasion, informed them that he had already written, offering the post to another minister. There was now no vacancy, at St Margaret's or anywhere else on the island. He had also written to John Manson, telling him to vacate the Manse by the end of the week. Later that night, George sat down and wrote his letters.

At lunchtime, that day, the three embryo gangsters met by arrangement at a shelter on the sea front, where they consumed fish suppers and cans of beer. It was while they were reliving the spectacle at the fountain, that Tommy wondered what they could do with the remaining stick of sodium. Greatly daring, Billy suggested blowing up the public baths.

'What fur?' said Ryan.

'For fun? Isn't that why we blew up the fountain?'

But common sense prevailed. They would not get off with that kind of thing a second time. It would be a pity to get caught. No, a public spectacle was definitely out, they agreed. Then Ryan, who was always hard-up, suggested fishing. They could row out in a boat in one of the lochs and throw the stick in. That would kill a lot of fish, which could be sold.

'That's daft,' said Billy. 'Who needs money? I've got plenty.'

'Let's see it, then,' said Ryan, with disbelief. 'You can share out wi' yer pals.'

And it was then Tommy had his idea, one of blinding simplicity, the immediate answer to all their dreams of an independent life, free from the need to work, enabling them to buy fancy clothes, fast cars and pick up birds by the dozen.

'Why don't we rob a bank?' said Tommy.

There was a silence, while they each considered the implications. To Billy, it was horrendous, conjuring up images of Dartmoor prison; himself in clothing covered with arrowheads. But the others thought it brilliant. 'God, even if we got caught, we would be heroes!' said Tommy, exultantly. 'And when we got back from the nick, we'd get all the burds chasin' us.'

Though he had been caught before, often, it never occurred to Ryan that he would get caught, whatever happened to the others. All he could think about was all the money a bank would contain. It was, to him, a tremendous idea. The big time! For if Ryan dreamed of anything, it was himself in a cashmere suit with a flower in the buttonhole, smoking a big cigar like Al Capone, on his way down the stairs of his hotel, surrounded by henchmen.

'That one stick isn't enough to blow a safe,' said Billy, hoping to divert them. But Tommy was so motivated, that his inventive genius was working to full capacity.

'We could go and look for mair. There's other science labs. And a science-store. We'll gather all we can and then figure out a way tae break in and set it off.'

So at 4.30, that evening, after work, they set off for the school, which they knew at that hour on a Friday, would be quite deserted, locked-up for the week-end.

Because that was the day of the trial, Tom Henderson determined to divert Jean as much as possible, for she might be expected to have qualms about her situation then, as never before. Masterfully, he told her he was taking her out to dinner that evening, and beforehand, he intended to buy her some new clothes, among them, a new dress, to be chosen by both, in consultation. Stopping work early, he collected her at the house and drove off in the blue Jaguar to the harbour, directly onto the ferry.

'Where are we going?' said Jean. 'How can we get back in time for the last boat and what about the children? They have to be picked up from school.'

"Don't worry, I've arranged everything. Maggie's collecting them. And the biggest surprise of all is that Maggie's staying over the week-end.'

'What for?'

'To baby-sit. We'll make a week-end of it in Glasgow. Stay in a hotel, go to the shows. But first, we'll visit the shops this afternoon.'

Jean was a little dubious at first, but allowed herself to be persuaded. Here was the opportunity of a lifetime. New clothes—plural! What woman would not be seduced by that alone? Then there was the hotel. The Central, she was soon informed. Grandest of the grand, unimaginably posh, at which Jean had often cast a yearning glance on her way through the station, lugging far too much baggage, to or from a bus, at Buchanan Street. Now, at last, she was going to stay. Really belong there, as a right! It was bliss. And not for a night of bed and breakfast, but a whole weekend! Full board! And then there were the shows. Jean had always wanted to go to the theatre. The bright lights had exercised a half-guilty attraction, but there had never been money for that kind of thing. Now it was all happening to her, and the excitement was like a flame, which grew and grew.

And as Tom saw it, he smiled to himself at his success in diverting her attention from the home-front, John's disgrace, and her own betrayal, though he thought it more a case of going to a better provider.

Later that day, at three o'clock, Roddy Manson was taking a note from his teacher to the school office, when, in the centre of the huge assembly hall, to which all corridors converged, he met Charlie Braddock carrying bags of books and files. 'Oh, Roddy,' he said, 'This is my last day here, you know. I'm going off to a new job in England.'

Roddy blushed and stood uncertainly. Then, manfully, he thrust out a hand and said, 'Well, I hope you get on well, there, sir.'

Charlie was moved. 'I wonder if you would do me a last favour, Roddy?'

'If I can, sir.'

'Well, come along to my room after four. I've got a present for you. Just to show there's no hard feelings. What do you say?'

Roddy agreed, but as he made his way to the office, doubts began to assail him. What if Charlie wanted to have a go at him again? One for the road. Wasn't that the expression?

By four o'clock, Roddy had worked himself into a state. Should he go or shouldn't he? It was the Christian thing to let bygones be bygones; go and accept the present. That's what he should do. But then, maybe there was more to it. Maybe he was going to have his back passage stuffed again. What should he do?

As soon as the bell rang, he left the school and ran down the road to the Manse. He would ask his father. He would know what to do. Maybe come with him, just in case.

But the Manse was empty, locked up. Disconsolately, Roddy climbed up the hill to the school expecting Jessica any minute, on her way home; for Jessica had not said anything about going to the trial. In fact, Roddy had been left in blissful ignorance that there was to be a trial.

Back in the playground, Roddy hung about in a confused state of mind, unwilling to enter the school, to entrust himself to Charlie Braddock, when there was no one else around; yet unwilling to leave, because he had been asked to go and see Charlie, and he had promised to do so. And a promise was a promise. Unhappily, then, Roddy waited outside the school building, hoping and expecting that Charlie would eventually appear, and the present could be handed over outside, where safety lay. As the front of the building looked empty, closed-up, he decided to walk around it and see if Charlie's lights were still on.

Charlie was leaving because of him, that much was clear; and Roddy, as he dolefully wandered around the outside, felt sorry about it; the more so, since Charlie was such a great teacher, as everyone knew. It seemed only right that he should say goodbye properly, as Charlie wanted. And yet, Roddy had never wanted Charlie's affection, certainly not that way. It must be himself, there had to be something wrong with him to cause that kind of behaviour. It wasn't right. It didn't feel right. In fact, as he blushed again, thinking about it, it was downright queer. For an instant, Roddy found himself wondering what it must feel like to do that to someone. But the idea of doing it to Charlie, made him shudder. The man had haunches like sides of beef. And the guilt of it, the inexplicable awfulness of it, struck him. Decidedly, there were places you had no business to put yourself. Revulsion, of himself for his part in it, seeped down inside him and seemed to split his personality, so that he felt lost, adrift, disoriented; slightly mad, even, as if out of control, a deeply disturbing sensation.

By this time, Maggie had driven up in Tom's second car, and collected Susan from the Primary school, at the top of the hill. For a quarter of an hour, she waited for Roddy on the road above the secondary, in the usual place. Finally, when he did not appear, Susan suggested that he might have gone to the Manse to see his father. 'That'll be it,' said Maggie. 'He'll just have to walk out to Oakfield or get the bus.' She decided to leave him, and was soon driving along the sea front towards Crichton, thinking of how she would spend that night; for, in the late evening, once the kids were in bed, she had arranged to admit her boyfriend, Gordon, to the house. They would have the run of the place. Mr Henderson had even agreed that she could have a friend to keep her company, though nothing had been said about it being a boy. Tom had been too excited by his own devious arrangements, to consider the possibility that Maggie might have fleshly desires of her own.

Before tea, Susan was quickly immersed in books again, for an hour; and after a hurried meal, helped by Maggie, she got back into them. At seven o'clock, feeling very tired, she said to Maggie, 'Ma.aybe yo.ou should phone and see if Ro.oddy's at the Ma.anse. Just to ma.ake sure. I'm go.oing to bed.' Yawning with fatigue, after a week of unremitting labour, with a host of subjects far in advance of her peers, she was soon in bed and fast asleep.

Maggie phoned, but as Jessica and John were still at the court, finishing off the trial, there was no reply. Oh, well, Maggie thought, maybe he's out with his father or sister. He'll show up sometime.

By quarter to five, the embryo gangsters were sauntering round the school, 'casing the joint'; trying door handles and looking for a way in. There were no lights on except the single bulb in the assembly hall, which cast a gloomy glow over that vast empty chamber and the dux board on the wall. On his lonely look-out for Mr Braddock, Roddy spotted them and hid in an alcove; but he was too late.

'What huv we got here?' said Ryan, pouncing suddenly, and emerging, after a scuffle, from a dark corner of the playground with the figure of Roddy, whom he had by the scruff of the neck. 'What are you up tae? Plannin' tae rob the school, eh?'

'No. I'm waiting for Mr Braddock to come out.'

Tommy laughed. 'What fur? So he can shove it up yer arse?'

Roddy, back against the wall, blushed and stammered, 'N.n.no. I..I..I'm sup..p.posed to collect a g.g.g.going-away present.'

Tommy laughed louder and Ryan joined in. 'Why did ye no' go tae his room then?' said Ryan.

'I.I..I didn't like to.'

There was more laughter, and Billy found himself joining in. Tommy said, 'So he was gonny stuff yer chocolate box! That's it, isn't it? Yur scared he's gonny do it again.'

Tommy was exultant at his insight. What a joke too! To stay out here all that time waiting. 'Ah know what kind a present he had in mind fur you! A big fucken cock, that's what!' While Ryan was still considering the possibilities presented by this new development, Tommy added 'What are we gonny do wi' him? We canny leave him tae clipe on us.'

'Take him wi' us,' said Ryan. 'That makes him an accessory. He'll no' tell, then.' In truth, Ryan's education might be limited, but in his short life he had already experienced enough of the law, to have picked up some important words and concepts his peers had yet to learn.

At the back of the building, Ryan climbed up and knocked a hole in a window, with the jemmy, stuck his hand in, and released the catch. Then, the window was pushed up and he climbed in. 'Shove that wee bugger in next,' said Ryan, and there were sniggers outside at the joke Ryan never intended; for to him, anyone was a bugger, if he was not actually on his team.

Inside, Roddy firmly held in an iron clasp by Ryan, they went in search of the science labs, making their way along the silent corridors. Doors were forced opened with the jemmy and cupboards searched. Four labs on the ground floor of the west wing were rifled in this way without success.

In the science-store, adjoining, they were confronted by cupboards full of chemicals, beakers, pipettes, bottles, jars and packs of every commodity a science lab should have; and shelves of exam papers, old and new, marked and unmarked, and exercise jotters and hard-backed science notebooks and flimsy, one sheet, test papers, heaped in neat piles.

'What is it you're looking for?' said Roddy, innocently.

To conceal the fact that he had forgotten the name of it, Ryan said, 'Never you mind.' Then, tiring of the appendage, the burden of looking after their hostage, and his eyes falling upon a coil of rope-like stuff, he announced, 'Wull tie this bugger up. Save haudin' ontae him.'

In a few minutes, Roddy was tied firmly, hand and foot, to one of the gas taps on the preparation-bench.

It was then that Billy reached up to a shelf and brought down a bottle, the same size as the one they already possessed. 'This looks like it.' Boldly, determined to play his part, he wrenched off the glass stopper and grabbing the top sheet from a pile of test papers, to protect his hand, reached inside and hauled out a thick stick of about the same size as the sodium. He held it up to the light cast from the window. 'I think this is it,' he announced triumphantly. 'Two sticks.'

'That's no' enough,' concluded Tommy. 'See if we can find any mair. We need as many as we can get. A bank safe's a tough proposition.' Tommy adopted a swagger, at that phrase, for surely that sounded like real gangsters?

Billy laid the stick, still wrapped in paper, down upon the bench, and proceeded to extend his investigations, along with the others.

A few minutes later, Ryan sniffed. 'Is there somethin' burnin'?' Looking around, he saw, on the bench, just behind the trussed body of Roddy Manson, the cylinder of stuff, still wrapped in paper. 'Christ, look at thon!' And, as they turned to look, the paper suddenly caught fire. The cylinder of stuff was glowing.

Tommy rummaged in a cupboard for a pair of tongs, seized the incendiary stick and raised it aloft. 'That's phosphorus, you dopes!' shouted

Roddy, unable to see, but sensing what it must be from the problem and the stink it made. 'Don't you know anything? It catches fire in air! Get rid of it.'

Tommy tried to carry it, holding it at arms-length to the sink, where he thought it would be best placed, but Roddy yelled again. 'Not there, fool. Put it back in the bottle!'

Indecision made Tommy drop the glowing cylinder, which rolled along the floor towards the cupboard full of papers, still with burning paper wrapped around it, stopped only by the wooden cupboard itself.

'What'll Ah do? What'll Ah do?' cried Tommy, still holding the tongs.

'Pick it up! Put it back in the bottle!' called Roddy, calmer now, realising the need for self-control, twisting himself round to watch.

Tommy stooped and tried to pick up the fiery cylinder, which was whooshing flames and sparks in every direction, without success. Every time he tried, something untoward happened. It would roll away. Then a piece broke off. Then another. Finally, while the others stood transfixed by the increasing blaze, as it continued to ignite in the still air, Tommy succeeded in picking up a chunk of it and took it to the bottle. With difficulty, he managed to shove it into the formalin and stood back, coughing from the sudden effusion of smoke that issued forth.

'The other bits ! The other bits!' called Roddy.

But by the time Tommy reached the biggest with the tongs, it was well alight, really hot, burning with a white fierceness right in the centre, and, underneath, the wooden floor was on fire. 'Christ get a bucket of water, some'day!' cried Tommy, grabbing at the fiery cylinder. Then, holding it up at arms-length, he began to turn, when something, a change in its mass maybe, as it was burnt up in the air, caused it to slip out of the tongs, and it fell among the test papers, piled one on top of another, sheet on sheet, easiest of all to catch fire.

For a moment, Tommy and the others stood mesmerised by the speed of the flames, as they spread around the cupboard, until, in seconds, it was an inferno.

'Christ! Let's get outa here, boys,' said Tommy, and he made for the door. Ryan and he were soon in the corridor running as fast as they could. At the door, standing screaming and crying, stood Billy, looking after them. 'What about Roddy? What about Roddy?'

Ryan stopped and turned: 'Leave the wee bugger. He'll just tell on us!'

'But he's tied up, for God's sake!'

'Never mind! Leave him! Save yersel'!' Ryan took one last look at Billy standing formlessly, like a jelly-baby, and Tommy called. 'Ah'm outa here!' And the pair fled, as smoke billowed after them. Hearing this, Roddy screamed, a plaintive animal cry of distress.

To his credit, Billy returned into the blazing room, where Roddy was struggling frantically to free himself. By now, the flames had engulfed the cupboard full of papers, and had begun to attack bottles of chemicals, some of which had started to explode and react with others nearby. The floor was well alight and the smoke and heat were intense.

'Get the fire-extinguisher!' cried Roddy, through the tears, and broke out coughing because of the smoke entering his lungs.

But Billy couldn't see it for the smoke and the dark, even with the flames all around. 'Where is it?'

'I don't know,' called Roddy, in a queer strangled voice, as he fought to breathe the last unused air around him, spluttering with the noxious fumes, as he inhaled them along with it. Then, suddenly, he keeled over, and lay slumped, his body still anchored to the gas tap.

Billy moved backwards to the doorway, driven there by heat and flame and the impossibility of taking a breath. The entire cupboard area was ablaze with bright banners of yellow and red and blue and green—from the burning chemicals—swirling and curling along under the ceiling, as if caressing it, with a hot passion; and, even as he watched, horrorstruck, the wooden floor had become an inferno of flame which surged in every direction, engulfing the preparation-bench and even the figure slumped behind it.

Then there was a sudden, ear-splitting bang, as the gas-pipe on the wall exploded; and something, a wet thing, hit Billy full in the face. He felt himself simultaneously propelled with an implacable, powerful, mysterious force against the opposite wall of the corridor, against which he slammed, and then slid downwards, until he was seated on the wooden floor, with his back to it. Inside the room, all was confusion and smoke and flame and the stink of roasting flesh and utter destruction.

Billy knew, then, that there was no need to remain. Wearily, he got to his feet and wiped off the thing which had struck him and fallen in his lap, yet seemed to stick there on his clothing. As he did so, a shout of utter terror rose in his mouth, closely followed by a violent retching, as he brought up his stomach contents. The thing that had hit him was an ear, Roddy's ear, severed clean off by a fragment of bursting glass, dripping blood, but partly roasted, which was why it had a tendency to stick to him.

Like a man aged suddenly, made half-blind and weary, by travails too terrible to absorb, he made his way along the corridor to the open window and climbed out.

There was no sign of the others.

Across the playground, he tottered, and down the path to the road, and then down the avenue to the Manse, where he stopped and looked in over the gate. The storm door was closed and there were no lights on. So there was nothing to be done. Down the street he staggered, gaining composure, as the night air chilled him, happily meeting no one, until he reached the sea front. By then, he was anxious to get away, but once, he stopped, and looked in a shop-window, and saw the reflection of a youth with a black face and once-white shirt, with marks that looked like blood on it. The shirt was flapping open at the neck, which meant that somehow he had lost his tie.

Billy crossed over to the gardens which, for hundreds of yards, separate the town from the promenade and the sea. Gathering up fistfuls of grass, he wiped his face and shirt, before going on along the road to Crichton.

Entering by the back door, and using the back stair, he was able to strip off, wash and change without being seen. The shirt, he rinsed, and left to dry on the radiator in his room. Then he lay on his bed, in a stupor. And it felt as if a burden of immense weight had just descended upon his shoulders; and he sensed he would have to bear it all his life; and also, as if the bindings of his personality had become loosened and the small taut strength he had found in the company of the Mansons, had begun to dissolve and slide away out of him, leaving behind fragments of being, where before there had been a tenuous whole.

By the time the two Mansons, walking hand in hand, reached the road up to the Manse, they were aware that a catastrophe had occurred. The sky above the great gothic school was glowing from the burning building beneath. Windows could he heard shattering in the heat generated by the incineration of so much wood, and flames could be seen being fanned into great yellow banners, as the breeze entered and fed them.

As they reached the front gate, they were passed by fire-engines which soon were setting up hoses and spraying futile quantities of foam and water. Without a word spoken, they carried on up the hill and joined a group of townsfolk already gathered, as if at a wake, to observe the bonfire of Branden's best building.

Phil Mulholland was there, with his wife, and Miss Carmichael and Mr Leach, and soon the town council and people from all over, who had seen the conflagration from afar. The police, too, were in evidence, and a broken window at the rear of the building was soon discovered by a searching torchlight, to have been the means of entry. The catch was still undone and the window itself wide open. Phil and the janitor confirmed that there had been no broken windows, nor had this window been open when the school was closed for the week-end. 'Well, that's how they got in,' said Sergeant Strong, 'the question is, who was it, and what were they after?'

The school burned for three days, with a heat that was unusual, due to the amount of wood in its construction. The central roof fell in upon the assembly hall, but above the science wing, the roof held, because the wind had come from that direction, blowing the flames towards the centre of the building, away from the fire's source.

After such a day of humiliation and trial, the strain was telling on John Manson, and Jessica urged him home, made him some hot cocoa, and packed him off to bed, like a sick child. Not until late the next morning, did the phone ring and the questions begin, about the whereabouts of Roddy.

Jessica's face was full of alarm when she told her father. The police were informed and Sergeant Strong and a wpc were soon at the door.

Strong said, 'Could he have been involved in the fire last night, do you think? Had he any sort of grudge against the school?'

Jessica and John looked at each other and John said, 'He wouldn't have been at the school after hours if it was avoidable.' And the sergeant wanted to know why, and the whole story of the problem with Charlie Braddock had to be told. Wpc McCready said, 'Mr Braddock left the school yesterday for a new job. Do you think there is any connexion?' But no one could think of one. Then the sergeant said, 'You were on trial at the court yesterday, weren't you? Could Roddy have wanted to take revenge for that?'

John said, 'You mean by starting a fire in the school? No. He had too much respect for learning.'

But the Police did not agree. Roddy had been angry at the school for Mr Braddock's conduct and that, coupled with the humiliation his father was having to suffer, had made him flip, become an arsonist. Two and two, not for the first time, were put together, to make five.

The question was: where was Roddy? On Tuesday, forensic scientists from Glasgow were poking about the remains and, in the science-store, they came across a familiar black mark on the earth and some charred fragments, besides, the remains of the preparation-bench. On it, they found one thing more, a few black, thread-like fibres, dangling from a gas tap which was twisted and buckled with heat. What were these? Whatever they were, the conclusion was clear: someone had died at the spot. The skull was carefully examined and observed to be from a child or young adult, and was taken away for dental investigation.

Within a few hours more, Sergeant Strong and wpc McCready were able to confirm to the Mansons that it was indeed the remains of Roddy. When the police left, they sat together, in a state of mutual shock and astonishment. Jessica poured whisky for them both and, after he'd taken a slug, John said, quietly, 'I had the feeling, a few months ago, that everything was going to be winter from hereon. And it has. I wonder if spring will ever come again.'

When the death of Roddy came to light, the news soon spread through the town, and once again the Mansons were on the receiving end, dark looks following them wherever they went. But the Inspector assigned to investigate the case for the Fiscal was not satisfied. Why had the boy not escaped? He could so easily have walked along the corridor back to the open window, where he came from, and got clear. Why would he remain in the room to burn to death in such an excruciating fashion? Overcome suddenly by fumes? God knows, the science-store would have contained a rich variety of gases once the chemicals went up. But there were the thin black strands at the gas tap. Experiments suggested these might be rope of a type the science-store had in stock. Well then, was Roddy Manson burned to death because he was *unable* to escape? Had someone tied him up? Who else might have been in the school at that time? And why would they have tied up Roddy Manson in the store?

Charlie Braddock was tracked down on the mainland and interviewed. Yes, he had arranged to see Roddy after school, but Roddy had never arrived. And after waiting till 4.20pm, Charlie had then caught the steamer for the mainland at 4.45. The idea that Charlie might have started the fire himself and left Roddy tied up in it, as some kind of revenge for having to leave the place, was interesting, but unlikely. The fire had not started before 6pm at the earliest, and, by then, Charlie was in a train, half-way to Glasgow.

Every child in the school was interviewed, and every teacher and auxiliary, without success. Then, it was the turn of every criminal and every young person in the town.

Ryan, who was by now, an important suspect, gave his usual bravura performance. 'Whit de ye mean, where was ah? How the hell should ah know where ah wis a hale week ago.'

'But you've thought about it, and you do know, don't you?' said Sergeant Strong.

'Aye, right. Ah wis wi' ma pals. We were doon the front wi' a cairry oot.'

'Can you not speak English!'

'Why should ah? Ah'm no' English.'

'The sea front? Where at the sea front?'

'The shelters doon by the puttin' green. The wans near the pier.'

And as Tommy gave corroborating evidence, there was no fulcrum for changing the statement.

Billy was a different proposition. Dressed in his best silver-grey suit—with white shirt and conservative-club tie, a nice touch suggested by George, with a matching handkerchief in the top pocket—at first sight, Billy looked as if he'd sprung from the upper echelons of society. But underneath the rich exterior, his legs were like loose elastic and his stomach like a butter churn. The Ryans and Forbes's of this world might be able to face down the combined might of the local police force, because they had seen it done in too many crime films, not to have learned, but Billy would never have enough self-confidence for that. Every time he looked like taking a small step in that direction, George had successfully stolen it from him.

'So you were drinking in the shelters at the sea front, with Ryan and Forbes?'

'Yes,' said Billy, thinking he had done well to manage that much, for that was what had been agreed between them. And when a chap needs an alibi, he is never so happy as when he finds one is available. But what an alibi!

Sergeant Strong looked at him suspiciously. 'What is someone like you drinking in a public place on a Friday night, with the likes of John Ryan?'

The question seemed to float around the smoke-filled air, for a while, and Billy contemplated it and reddened, as the enormity of the blunder came home to him. 'Tommy Forbes works with me, and Ryan's Tommy's pal. So, of course, we're all pals together.'

'So you are all pals together?'

'Yes.'

'Does your father know about this?'

'I don't know. He knows I go about with Tommy.'

'But not about Ryan, I bet.'

Billy shrugged his shoulders.

'Did you know Roddy Manson?'

'Yes.'

'What did you think of him?'

'I liked him. He was good at rugby and he was my girl-friend's brother.' And the story of how he had to give up seeing Jessica had to come out.

'What did you think of Roddy being used by Mr Braddock?'

'I thought it was a shame. Awful.'

'So you had nothing against Roddy, then?'

'No.'

And so Billy Buchanan was released, to return to his every-workaday life, and thought himself successful, but, as he walked the corridor in the police station, he caught the eye of Inspector Mirrilees, a thin, dark-haired, slight man, for a policeman, but possessed of a sixth sense, well-developed by two decades of detective work. The very relief on Billy's sweating face, was enough to warrant a second glance; and then the unco-ordinated nature of the movements, told of extraordinary stress.

On impulse, he went into the room, where Sergeant Strong was filing the papers. 'What did you get on that one?'

'Nothing. Son of the Provost. Big cheese. It couldn't be him.'

'Maybe, but he knows something.' And Mirrilees began to ask about the family, what was known about George, the father—provost or no provost. And then, as so often in a police investigation, skeletons, or their constituents, started falling out of cupboards everywhere. An hour later, a full scale meeting of the entire local force was called and Mirrilees said, 'The boy Buchanan knows something. We need to find out what it is. I think he might fold if we took him in overnight, but I don't want to do that yet. It seems his father was close to being charged for misappropriation of old folks' money. And that's recent. The Minister, Manson, discovered it, but it couldn't be made to stick. Maybe there's a connexion between George Buchanan and the death of Roddy Manson. Could it be that Roddy knew something and Buchanan knocked him off, or had him knocked him off?'

Sergeant Strong laughed. 'Oh, sir, give's a break! George Buchanan's the biggest fish in the pond. Why would he have to go about setting fire to kids?'

'I don't know, Colin, that's for you to find out. But there seems to have been some kind of vendetta between Buchanan and the Minister. Is that accidental? Did the Minister get the heave because of what he knew about George? How is the Minister's son involved? It needs looking at.'

There was a silence while they imbibed these odd possibilities. Then, as he always did at such meetings, Mirrilees, said, 'What I want to know right now is, are there any other funny connexions between Buchanan and anybody else I should know about? Something queer. Anything. Think about it. Any unexplained happening that doesn't quite add up. Only you locals would know. Come on now!'

After a silence, wpc McCready mentioned that Buchanan had employed a private detective from time to time. Strong and others laughed. 'Sniffy Johnstone? A private dick? That'll be the day.'

'Ignore nothing, folks!' said Mirrilees. 'I want to know everything this man knows about Buchanan. All the jobs he's done for him. And the son. Everything he's got on either. And anything else he might know. Don't forget that. Frighten it out of him, if need be.'

It was then that Constable Menzies said, 'What about Jim Grant's death? I've never been happy about that.' Every eye turned to survey this normally quiet man who seemed so slow and dull. Pressed further, he added, for the benefit of the off-the-island police, 'He cropped himself in the car, out at Rhueilan. Connected up a hose-pipe and gassed himself.'

'Well what about it, then?' said Strong.

'I drove his car back to town after the body went in the ambulance. I had to adjust the seat.'

'So what?' said Mirrilees.

'Well, I'm six foot three and Jim was six four. Why should I have to adjust the seat?'

'Maybe you've got short legs or he has,' suggested Strong.

'No. We had very similar builds. I remember, because I borrowed his cricket flannels one time.'

'What adjustment did you make?'

'I had to get more room. It was as if a guy with much shorter legs had been driving.'

'Maybe he had to move the seat back to fix the hosepipe,' said Strong.

'What for?' said Menzies. 'I've always wondered about it.'

'So what you're saying is that maybe Buchanan knocked off Jim Grant?'

Menzies said, 'No, I don't. But I've never understood why he did it like that. He was a cheery big fella, right up to the end. And this thing about the seat having to be moved has always worried me.'

Mirrilees, to whom nothing was impossible, walked about thinking for a while, and then said, finally, 'Well, it just might be that Manson was not the first to learn about the scam George Buchanan was working. Maybe somehow, Jim Grant got the scent of it. And just maybe Buchanan cropped him.'

Strong shook his head in disbelief. 'You've got to be kidding, sir. Honest. How could Buchanan do it here in this place, without being seen?'

'Maybe he was seen, and no one realises it yet. It wouldn't be the first time that a man was cropped right in front of folk, who saw nothing and, as far as they were concerned, it was just a natural death.'

Derisively, Strong said, 'So somebody drove the car there, attached the hosepipe and then hitched a lift back?'

'Or walked, in the dark, at night. He wouldn't be seen then. Or just maybe he was seen. Find out. Ask everybody that lives out there if they ever saw George Buchanan walking that road at night.'

'But how would he get Jim out there? Jim wouldn't go. He was no fool.'

'Maybe he had no choice.'

'You don't seriously mean he was taken there at the point of a gun?'

'No, that wouldn't do at all. Grant would have to be unconscious before the gassing. That would have left a mark or two.' Mirrilees thought for a moment, before adding, 'What about the post mortem?'

'Death by carbon monoxide poisoning,' said McCready.

'What was in his stomach? Get the file.'

Menzies said, 'Jim Grant was on holiday when he cropped himself.'

'So what?' said Strong.

'Well, he never went anywhere, and he usually went off every holiday he had. I got the idea he was working on something, on his own, like.' There was a silence, until Menzies added, 'Whatever it was, it was definitely big stuff. Hush-hush.'

Strong laughed. 'What could be hush-hush in this place? De ye mean he was playin' at James Bond, or what?' Other men laughed.

The file was pulled and handed to Mirrilees, who opened and read.

'Sleeping pills and rum and coke,' he announced, and looked skywards, thinking. 'Maybe that's it then,' said Mirrilees. 'You meet a man in a bar for a private drink—something an eminent councillor could easily do—especially since they knew each other. I see they were both on the Kirk Session. The meeting could be for any number of reasons. Maybe this man Manson was one of them. Why wouldn't two members of a Kirk Session meet for a private chat about their minister? And where better than a pub? In a back room maybe, out of earshot. Once they're having a drink, George goes out to the bar to buy a round. On the way back, he slips in some sleeping pills and makes sure they dissolve. And there's no problem because Grant drinks coke with his rum. Maybe the pills are water soluble instantly, who knows? Later, once Grant is feeling the effects, George asks for a lift somewhere; and during the journey, Grant feels unwell. So the other man takes over the wheel, and, while Grant lies back to sleep, he drives the car to some lonely spot and attaches the hose-pipe.'

'Jim Grant always drank Baccardi and Coke,' said Menzies.

'But what if he came to?' said Sergeant Strong, with evident disbelief. 'He would have the goods on whoever did it!'

'Buchanan would stay until it was all over, just in case someone came along and found it, or Grant woke up. And if either of these happened, Buchanan would say he was parked there, taking a leak while his friend slept it off.'

'Grant would never swallow that, if he woke up.'

'No. He would be suspicious. Maybe that's why so many sleeping pills were used. To make sure he would stay asleep. It doesn't take that many, and if they were washed down with several drinks, it was easy as pie.'

There was a silence for a while, and then Mirrilees, who had been walking up and down thoughtfully, turned and added. 'You know, if Grant fell asleep at all, it was easy. All Buchanan had to do was attach the hosepipe to the exhaust and then hold the end of it at Grant's nose. He would have been inhaling gas right from the start. So how could he possibly wake up? He would be a goner immediately. The hosepipe would then be stuck in the window to make it look like he did it himself.'

Mirrilees said to Menzies, 'Where was the hosepipe introduced?

'Through a quarter light on the driver's side.'

'Did he do anything to stop the gas escaping?' said Mirrilees, handing the file to Strong.

'The door seals were taped and a travelling rug was stuffed in the gap between the open window and the hose.'

Scornfully, Strong said, 'How could the murderer tape the car from the inside?'

'Easy', said Mirrilees. 'He gives Grant a good dose of gas. Maybe crops him completely holding the hose at his face. And then, having killed him, he tapes the car inside and finishes it off by taping the driver's door through the window.'

'Why would he bother to tape it, if he'd killed him already?'

'To divert us from the fact that the pipe was held at his nose.'

'But what about the travelling rug around the hose?' said Strong.

'How wide was the tape?' said Mirrilees.

'Two inches. Parcel tape,' said Strong, reading from the file.

'Big enough to tape the gap for the hose between the window and the frame?'

'Yes,' said Menzies, with surprise.

'That's why he used the travelling rug. He couldn't tape that from outside. But he could shove a travelling rug half way in, and by turning the quarter light and pulling it, make it close the gap.' But Mirrilees, threw up his hands in disgust at a new idea: 'So long as some of the rug is inside, who is to say it wasn't all done from there?'

Mirrilees was dissatisfied, his idea fallen at the last. But he stood deep in thought for a moment and then announced, 'That's it! Don't you see that's it! Grant didn't do it! Any policeman knows that tape isn't necessary! Only an amateur would think it was. If Grant did it himself, he wouldn't have bothered with tape!'

A few days later, in the building which held the Sheriff Court and the Council Chambers, the Mansons attended a meeting at the Procurator Fiscal's office. Miss Templeton was gracious to John Manson, shook hands, and offered her sympathy, which was heartfelt, in spite of their recent meeting in the court upstairs. Presently, Jean arrived, with Tom Henderson, as escort, and the three were seated in front of the Fiscal's desk. She introduced Inspector Mirrilees, thin and dark-haired, in a charcoal-grey suit, sitting on her right; a bald, fair, forensic dentist, Archie McCallum, in a green-checked sports jacket, on her left and, beyond him, a young, brown-haired police scientist with a pock-marked face, in a grey suit, called Jim Pendreigh.

'It's not mandatory to hold a meeting like this, Mr and Mrs Manson, but, in the circumstances, it seemed only fair. I've asked the people assembled here to determine what they can about the fire, and I must now decide what action to take. I think it is best that you should be fully informed about the matter.'

Mirrilees described the events of the fire and told how the remains of a human had been found in the science-store of the school; and that a careful search had produced no other signs of deaths elsewhere. Referring to notes, Jim Pendreigh, told how the remains had been discovered near a partly-melted gas tap. The only physical evidence was the full skeleton, much charred, of a young male, on which there were no suspicious abrasions. Archie McCallum confirmed that the teeth identified Roddy Manson; and everything else confirmed that view. In his opinion, it was definitely Roddy.

Jean let out a sob and lowered her head on her hands.

'What was the cause of death?' said the Fiscal, frowning under the blonde hair.

Pendreigh said, 'It's hard to say, as there is no corpse to examine. However, in a case like this, he probably died of asphyxiation.'

'Why is there no corpse?' said John.

'The building had wood-panelling and wooden floors and cupboards. Then it happened in the science-store, where there were large quantities of chemicals, of all kinds. Some of these are highly inflammable.'

Pendreigh seemed disinclined to continue, and Miss Templeton had to say, 'Please, go on.'

'The heat of the blaze was so intense that the fat on the boy caught fire. It would have been like a chip-pan going up. Except it wasn't a chip-pan, but a young boy. There was a stain on the earth under where the floor-boards had been. That was all that remained of the boy's flesh and internal organs. Just a big grease-stain. The bones were burnt black.'

The Fiscal looked down at her notes and said, 'Can you explain why the boy did not escape?'

Pendreigh referred to his notes and said, 'Beside the grease stain, a few lengths of burnt fibre were wrapped round a gas tap. This had been on a preparation-bench in the middle of the room. The bench, being wooden, was badly burned. Experiments have identified the fibre as coming from a coil of rope in the store. But the ashes of it were still wound round the tap.'

'Are you saying the boy was unable to escape because he was tied up?' said the Fiscal.

'Yes.'

'So the boy's fat caught fire and cremated his corpse? Why didn't the rope burn completely?' she added.

'Because it contained strands of asbestos, which is non-inflammable. The rope was, to a certain extent, heat and fire-proof. It was used for sealing vessels which were being heated near flames.'

Miss Templeton said, 'Well, I think that's clear enough. The boy was killed by persons unknown. So I am ordering a murder enquiry.'

Jean sobbed. 'But you don't think anyone deliberately killed Roddy, do you?'

'No, Mrs Manson, it doesn't look like it. But it's at least culpable homicide.'

'What happens, now?' said John.

'Police will be brought from the mainland to assist Mr Mirrilees,' said the Fiscal.

The funeral was a cold wind-swept occasion in the cemetery beside St Bride's, at the top of the High Street. The town council were present, George prominent among them, in full regalia—the black hat having been restored with new braid—which he liked to wear; the police, firemen, a few pupils from the school, and many of the staff, including Phil Mulholland, who looked ashen, after so many disasters to his empire. Even Charlie Braddock had come, and that, thought John, had taken courage. For who on Branden now, did not know the full story of his leaving?

John had asked Hugh Etherington to do the service, and he stood bareheaded in the rain, in his old black burberry, with Jessica beside him. Peter was nowhere to be seen for a while, until he was found to have been lingering at the back, out of sight, having arrived late. Jean, was there, with Tom, standing beside her, and little Susan on the other side.

Once, as they listened to the eulogy about a life cut so pitifully short, John looked across at Jean, sorrowfully, and without rancour, though he was acquainted, by now, like everyone, at her doings just before the boy's death. In a town like Ottersay, every coming and going on the ferry is noticed and reported. And Maggie, a very distraught Maggie, had told her side of it, as soon as Tom gave her notice to quit her job.

As the crowd broke up, and men and women began to say a word to Tom Henderson before leaving, for there was to be no refreshment afterwards in a hotel or at the Manse—John's stipend did not run to such extravagance—Susan said to Jean, at his side. 'Mummy, I want to go and see Daddy.' And without waiting for permission, she walked to where John was, and put her little hand in his pocket, while he was speaking to George, who, for the gloss it would add to his image, was busy making a point of offering condolences. While he did so, Susan looked across at her mother and Tom Henderson, and the conviction grew in her that memories were nothing beside the loyalty of flesh and blood; and there was no doubt where loyalty was due.

And so, three of the remaining Mansons walked wearily back together, to the car-park, where a taxi waited. They climbed in, and, without a word said, the driver drove off. No one enquired whether Susan was to stay or not; and Jean was too far behind to do anything about it.

That night, Jessica took up her pen and wrote:

What is the meaning
 Of a young life's death?
What is the good
Of so short a breath?
Where is the sense
Of his frantic fright?
In a smoke-filled room
On an endless night?

And yet I know
That good there is
In that untimely
Death of his.
We'll never know
What plan he served
For a fiery fate
So undeserved.

Perhaps the grief enriches us,
Deepens and develops
The dark reaches of the soul
Untouched by joy
 Yet, the ultimate goal.

And so Jessica had begun to find out how to write a poem. The essence of it was not to search for rhyme. Instead, to find a first line, one that sounded right, and say what she felt, truly, seeking for meaning above all, and her inner voice, the musical one, would naturally speak in cadences of the kind necessary, for the fulfilment she sought. Only afterwards, did she realise that some of it did rhyme; and that was where the structure and the power came from.

As it turned out, a council house would not easily be forthcoming to an incomer to Glasgow—or anywhere else. Only in Ottersay, was a house likely to be allocated immediately. A week later, then, the Mansons removed to number 29 Sevastopol Street, situated in the area known locally as The Crimea, not merely because so many of its streets were named after events in that war. It was the worst housing scheme on the island and Sevastopol the worst street. Its one useful feature to the Mansons, at that time, was the presence of an empty house.

Here it was, but two doors along, where lived the Ryans, of inglorious name, and, at the far end, the Clancys, noted performers in the pubs of Ottersay, where they had a knack of fighting with glasses—broken first to make the outcome more interesting—or bottles or chairs—anything that came easily to hand. One street down, in front, were the McKittericks, a tribe of short, broad-shouldered, tinker folk, whose aptitude for surreptitious theft was legendary. Once, caught on the ferry with a brass cannon in a battered lorry they had borrowed, Pop McKitterick had replied to the policeman's question where he had got it. 'Haw sur, ah bocht it oota Merryhull Barracks.' And was promptly arrested, for had not Maryhill Barracks closed down many years before? And had not the British Army made advances to their ordnance since the invention of cannon? Such were the new neighbours of the Mansons.

The house was the top flat on one side of a four flat villa, reached by an inside stair. There were only three bedrooms, but, as John half-laughingly put it, with a tear in one eye, there were only three of them now, so there was still a room each. Then there was a kitchen big enough to eat in, and a sitting-room and a bathroom. Central heating there was none, but they couldn't afford that anyway.

Of course the decor was a lot worse, but that couldn't be helped. A dog had scratched the doors, children had made blackboards of the walls, and a cat had used a bedroom as a toilet, but it was a home, and they had a right to be there. Outside, an overgrown hedge obscured the flat below and the grass around was littered with paper and in need of cutting. 'It will have to do,' said John, finally. 'At least it's not quite a stable.'

And the tears came, and the girls sat down beside him, not for the last time, in front of an unlit fire, and comforted him.

'And what about you, Susan?' he said, after drying his eyes. 'Can you stand slumming with your old broken-down dad?'

Susan snuggled into his side, 'Yes. I ca.an.' Then she yawned. 'I'm so.o ti.ired. And its o.only two o'clock.'

Susan's medical problem had worsened, if anything. Now she spilled anything that was not held for her, and tiredness seemed to affect her earlier in the day. After a few hours of ordinary life, her head would fall to one side, as if she lacked the strength in the neck muscles to keep it upright. So she took to supporting it on the side of a high-backed wing chair, which suited her purpose.

And yet, when energy allowed, and that was every waking hour of the day, Susan's mind continued to flourish at an astonishing rate. One day, she came across a book called *Calculus Made Easy*, by Silvanus P. Thomson, and began to read, for she had heard of this magical mathematical subject, and was attracted to it for the extension to her power it would afford. Thus began the greatest adventure of her life, as she would tell it later, and her worst surprise.

The book was elementary and provided facility, without the labour of full technical understanding. Susan was soon differentiating and integrating functions that Peter himself could only just manage. Here was a sense of pure mastery over symbols which were complicated and beautiful, formulas which sat up and begged to be savoured like the finest pictures, and marvelled at for their limitless power. And Susan could derive them for herself! But what did it mean? And that question took her to Newton and Leibniz and the idea of the limit. For one evening, like a thunder-flash, it hit her that the entire book by Thomson was wrong! Nearly everything in it had been got by dividing by zero, and it was a fundamental axiom that such a process produced an infinite result! Catastrophe! Thomson had oversimplified the issue to make it accessible. But what was the truth? A desperate frantic search was made of every book in the adult library, until the idea of the limit was found and grasped and absorbed, and Susan was off again into the secure and rigorous world of epsilons and deltas, where a proof really was a proof!

Curious about the name Silvanus Thomson, Susan learned that he was the grandson of the great Sir William Thomson, later, Lord Kelvin, and, reading about him, she came across his definition of a mathematician, as someone to whom it was obvious that

$$\int_{-inf}^{inf} e^{-X^2}\, dx = \sqrt{\pi}$$

And Susan was off again. What did this equation mean? Why was it true? And after that, how did one make it obvious to oneself? That is, confronted by such a challenge, Susan, she of the vaulting mind and no time, decided to try to make herself a mathematician in Kelvin's eyes. And so, by the end of the summer term, just before the final exam in her last year of primary school, Susan had found the gamma functions in a book—ordered specially from the central library, because Ottersay had never needed such a book before—learned to deal with them, revelled in the simple rules of combination, and understood how to prove Kelvin's result. And, if it was not quite as obvious to her as Kelvin intended, it was, nonetheless, a tremendous achievement for a child of twelve, working unaided, driven by needs and ambitions which were, admittedly, extraordinary.

The ecstasy she experienced on reaching the summit of her dreams is impossible to convey. It was like the view from Everest, that first time; the pure, clear light of truth shining upon structures of immense and unmatchable beauty. Far off, she sensed, lay legions of other summits, now, within a few years march. All the days of her life, it brought tears to her eyes, whenever she thought of that moment of truth, that time of intellectual awakening. Calculus, she realised, was a power without compare, which could conquer the world.

With fear and irritation, Miss Mather, her teacher, observed the books and jotters covered with equations and derivations which beggared belief. She could so easily be killed by an innocent question, for they lay far beyond her experience, long multiplication and division being the summit of her mathematical competence. Miss Mather disliked Susan. Her talent and intellectual energy were unattractive because Miss Mather could play no part in their development, or take any credit for them.

After the final exam for the outgoing primary class was held, then, Miss Mather was delighted to announce that Kathy Crawford, who was very efficient at long multiplication and division, was first in the class, and Susan Manson second. A stunned silence greeted this announcement, for the world knew about Susan. But Miss Mather explained that Susan had lost a few marks, here and there, for untidiness, and had even made an arithmetical slip in one of the long multiplications. And so the genius of Branden, who could with profit have attended Glasgow University instead of proceeding down the hill to Branden Grammar, was placed second, because her teacher was incapable of measuring, still less comprehending, the extent of her knowledge and skill. If what Susan could do were laid alongside Kathy's accomplishments, there was no room for argument. The criteria by which the winner had been judged, were simply, utterly, inadequate. It was like condemning Einstein because he could not be bothered to be careful about arithmetic, which mathematics is not really about.

Of course there may have been extraneous factors, such as the 'well known' fact—despite the trial—that John Manson had been fornicating with young women on his congregation, taking advantage of their vulnerability;

but it was mainly stupidity. And was he not Susan's father? And how could it be right to give the dux medal to the daughter of a man like that? It stood to reason that she must have bad blood. Those who know primary schools from the inside, will understand this mentality very well.

None of the staff in the primary school understood the true nature of the school's failure. Of all those in the school, only Susan did. She alone knew—was the only one who could know—just how far ahead she was; and that she was already in front of Peter. It was the first time that anyone ever really saw her cry. Since her illness, she had borne every obstacle presented to her by life, with stoical determination and unquenchable spirit. Now she was confronted with an injustice, the full extent of which she alone could appreciate. Since Charlie Braddock had left the island, there was not another mind on Branden who had ever heard of gamma functions. Thus was it, that she wept in class, she wept outside, and she wept all the way home up the road to the Crimea.

'It's not fair, Daddy!' she said, tearfully, at her new home, in a state that was pitiful to see. 'Kathy doesn't know anything worth knowing!'

'Do you like the things you know, Susan?' said John, with a sympathetic but rueful smile.

'Oh, yes! They're wo.onderful! 'Specially the gam.ma functions!'

'Well, does it matter that Kathy gets the school prize? Look at what you've got?'

And Susan saw that it was so; was almost bowled over by the shock of it. There were no riches to compare with the ideas in her mind; no prizes were ever going to be more important, or more productive of joy, than these mental worlds she was so fortunately empowered to make her own.

For a week or two, John did not go out much, except to buy some cheap paint and wall-paper to brighten the place up. Then there was the back garden, long overgrown, and his responsibility. He set to with a will, but onlookers wondered at him, for he seemed out of breath too easily. Not used to hard to work, said some, failing to understand his; but the smiling girls, at least, were considered an important addition to the sorority at the Crimea. Definitely upper crust, but acceptable, because there were no airs and graces. They said 'hello' to everyone, no matter who, or what the reply.

The exams, conducted in church halls, in lieu of a school-building, were soon over and Jessica was named dux medallist of the senior school. That night, John supplied an iced fruitcake with lemonade as a special treat, this being about the limit of his pocket and imagination in such matters; but it was well received. Susan, it was, stuck a candle in it and cajoled the medallist to blow it out, as if it were her birthday. So Jessica's name was to be inscribed in gold on the dux board beneath Peter's, except that now there was no board. It had been destroyed in the fire. Still, it was a great feat and John's spirits rose for a while.

He said: 'One day, there'll be another board, Susan, when the new school's built and maybe your name will appear there with the others.'

'Ma.aybe it will just be as bad there; and I'll lose marks for bad writing or carelessness.'

'That's always a possibility,' said John. 'You'll have to learn to write very neatly, be very tidy and do your counting accurately. But you know what really matters, don't you? That's the main thing. What would you like to be when you grow up?'

'A professor who discovers things and writes important books and papers.'

'Well, I think you might succeed, even allowing for the Miss Mathers of this world.'

'It's ju.ust a pity,' said Susan, 'that Ro.oddy can't have his na.ame on the dux board.'

A few days before, Susan had been leaving school to walk up the road to the Crimea, when she was met by Jean, in a designer-suit of deep emerald, tailored to perfection. The gleaming blue Jaguar, driven by Tom Henderson, had stopped just ahead.

'I was wondering when you're going to come back and stay with me,' said Jean, taking her hand.

Susan allowed herself to be led towards the car, but stopped. 'I ha.ave my own room in a new house no.ow. It's not very posh, but my Da.addy's there. I couldn't leave him again.' She looked up at Jean openly, innocently, and Jean's heart was melted by it.

'Well, won't you just come for tea or something?'

'No,' said Susan decisively, 'I ha.ave to get back to Da.addy and make sure he's all right. We have to stick together and look a.after each other no.ow.' And so she left, leaving a very distraught mother beside a very fancy car.

Susan's early memory of her father would never be eradicated, but, because of the power of her mind, she had met, in books, too many excellent examples of humanity at its finest, not to be affected by it, uplifted as much by the nobility of Caesar, as by his energy, intellect and power of command. And so, for Susan, loyalty to the cause she deemed right, was the overwhelming principle.

In the few weeks limbo after school finally broke up for the summer holiday, Jessica had time to reflect upon the events of the past year; and, as she went over them in her mind, on a solitary walk over the hills to the other side of the island, she remembered that she hadn't seen Billy at the funeral.

One street up from the Crimea, farm-land began; a few fields away was Otterhall, dry at last in summer, and empty, for cricket was played elsewhere at the Park, downhill, near the loch. There was a walk through woods, where pheasants would soon build nests full of golden eggs, and then across another farm to the centre of the island, where, from the height of a hill on the moor, all the other islands of the Firth could be seen basking in the silver sea, which sparkled in the sunshine. And she lay for a while on a grassy hummock, looking into the west, at the stark mountains of Orrin and all the way beyond, to Kintyre.

Above, high in the blue, a lark sang to himself, at the joy of such a day, and Jessica was conscious of a fellow feeling with him, as if her own aspirations were as high and as promising. And the rays of the bright sun shone through the trees not far off, and lit her, so that she was bathed in heavenly light; and she lay still, in the silence now, for the lark had moved off, aware, deeply and powerfully aware, of God. And a feeling of extreme goodness and benevolence washed through her; and she let it be, and savoured it and moved not at all, for a very long time.

When she got up to go, the sun had disappeared, and she shivered. And again, as she wended her way homeward, tentatively, as if fragile, following an experience of an unusual kind, she thought of Billy and wondered what it meant. Was God trying to tell her something?

He had not been at the funeral. Yet he had known Roddy and liked him, she thought. His dad had been there and everyone else who knew him. And then, knowing Billy, she wondered at the omission. What had become of him? Now that he was working, he was hardly ever about during the day; and at night, Jessica had been too involved with school-work and all the recent trouble, to get out much.

One evening, on a sunny summer Saturday, she had been visiting Joe Gorman, in Bridgeton Street, as usual, for the weekly game of chess. She would arrive around four o'clock and hoover the house, make the bed, put the washing in the machine and hang it up to dry on the pulley, just before leaving. Then there was dusting and tidying and making sure that everything was as it should be. All the while, she would tell Joe the news and try to cheer him up. Then, around 5.30, or so, she would make his tea, often bringing a cake she had baked, specially, for desert. Afterwards, they would play a game of chess and Joe would get soundly beaten.

Once, when Jessica seemed to be making more mistakes than usual, Joe said, 'Whit's wrong wi'ye? Are ye no feelin' well?'

And when Jessica smiled and replied, 'No. I feel fine,' he replied: 'So that's it! Tryin' tae give me a chance, is it? There'll be nae mair o' that, young lady. Ye've tae play yer best and dinnae mind an auld fool, like me.'

'Why shouldn't I let you win sometimes? What's wrong with it?'

'Everythin'! Ah wid ken ye wur daein' it, fur wan. And fur another, it's no fair tae you. Yer a grand player; and ye should aye play yer best. Itherwise, ye might get intae the habit o' losin', like. And that'll jist no dae at aw.'

Gradually, there was less and less to do, as if Joe had felt under so much of an obligation, that he should try to do more for himself.

It was all working out quite well, thought Jessica, as she walked home that evening, in the late sunshine. But Joe was still afraid to go out during the day, and she knew that if she were ever to stop her visits, the loss would affect him badly. Yet, there was satisfaction in the work. On impulse, the night being young, she turned right and not left, crossed the road at the Gallowgate and began to stroll along the wide promenade towards the harbour, where holiday-makers were ambling, and many folk playing putting, on the two excellent eighteen-hole courses that were laid out on the vast lawns, on both sides of the Little Theatre.

It was on the promenade that she met Billy. He was dressed in a smart suit, as if heading for the dancing at the Palais, and he seemed altogether more mature, taller, heavier, as if the tide of battle had washed over him a few times, and left its mark. But when he saw Jessica, his demeanour altered. He was glad to see her, but there was more. A fearfulness too, which caused Jessica to say, 'I suppose your father put a veto on seeing me.'

'Yes, I'm to get sent to the army if I don't do what I'm told.'

'And do you?'

'Most of the time,' he said, with a cheeky, shallow grin.

'But you enjoy your work? And being retired from school?' she joked.

Billy sighed. 'It's ok, I suppose.'

'Well that's fine then, I mustn't interrupt you. I'll be going.'

But as Jessica made to go, Billy suddenly looked so piteous, that she stopped and stared at him. And he broke down, bubbling noisy tears, saying, 'No, it's not the same! Not the same at all. I've done so many wrong things. So many! And I can't do anything about it! Not a thing. It's beyond that.'

'Here, Billy, come and sit down,' said Jessica, leading him to a bench seat. 'Tell me about it. It can't be that bad. Nothing's ever that bad.'

'It is! It is! I wish it wasn't, but it is!'

And for a short while, Billy sat down on the seat, with Jessica beside him, looking compassionate and concerned. And it seemed as if he would bare his soul, for she was the one person he could talk to, but time passed and he said nothing. The consequences of confession were appalling, unthinkable. She would loathe and detest him; he would be reviled by the entire town; worst of all, his father would kill him. Finally, almost gasping for breath, he stood up, looking as if praying that the earth would swallow him. He said, 'I've got to go. I can't talk about it. It's just not possible,' and he ran off along the promenade, leaving Jessica more than ever convinced that God had been trying to tell her something. Later, much later, she would often think of that moment; for, though she took no dramatic action on this occasion, because it would have involved pursuit and intrusion, it taught her thereafter, to listen even more intently to her inner voice, and do whatever good it seemed to suggest, even at the cost of rebuff.

Another person was suffering the angst of adjusting to the consequences of her actions. Guilt lay like a lump of granite on Jean's breast. She was cossetted, coddled, well-fed and dressed, but when Tom went off to work every morning, she was left with nothing to do but brood about her dereliction. And Susan's defection only made it worse. Tom had offered to abduct the child outside the school, but Jean would not stoop to that. Susan was not well, and to cause her further anxiety was unthinkable. Twice more, Jean met Susan on the road after school came out, and there were tearful scenes, but Susan was adamant. She would not go with her mother in the car, even for a cup of tea somewhere. And with great sensitivity, Susan had never mentioned the matter to either her father or Jessica.

To Susan, it would have been indecent even to have gone that far. There had been betrayals enough.

One day, John said to her, 'Have you seen your mother?' to which Susan replied, 'Yes, Daddy. I spoke to her a few times,' and John did not enquire further.

Peter, embarrassed by the changed fortunes of the family, never appeared. For such as he, it would have been unthinkable to have been seen walking in the Crimea. How would he have faced his friends? But then he had no real friends, none who could overlook the disasters in his family, because he himself was of most worth. Ironically, the only person who would have known about a visit to the Crimea, was Peter himself, for none of his friends would be seen dead there either.

One day in mid-summer, a day of breathless hush, as the whole world seemed to be growing, surging upward, Jean, a queenly version, in pink designer-suit, with matching hat and shoes, descended from the bus, and knocked at the door of number 29 Sevastopol Street. Susan, who answered it, a tired Susan, for it was late afternoon, was instantly reinvigorated, and exclaimed, 'Oh, Mummy! How nice to see you!' gave her a hug, and led her upstairs along the narrow corridor, on a strip of threadbare carpet Jean recognised from times past.

John got up out of his chair and smiled, and Jessica, who was in the kitchen baking scones, dressed in jeans, white T shirt and pinafore, came to look, grinned, and said, 'Hello Mum.' And Jean, taking off the hat to reveal the kind of permanent wave of lacquered hair she was fast becoming used to, burst into tears; and for a moment, stood as if frozen like a snowman exposed to the sun, as they swam down her cheeks, removing the cosmetics so lovingly applied and at such trouble. John took her by the arm and led her to the best chair, his own, and said, 'There, there now! No need for that. No need at all!' and sat her down and then took a stiff-backed dining chair from the table, and settled on it nearby.

'I'll make some tea, will I, folks?' said Jessica, chirpily, adding, 'Come on Susan, you come and help, for a change.'

But Jean said, 'No. Just stay where you are, girls. My fine girls! You don't know how much I've missed you!' And she got up and embraced one and then the other, and stood for a moment between the two of them, head raised skyward as if praying. Then, wiping the tears away, she said, 'I've been such a fool! I'm so sorry! Could you ever forgive me? Could you?'

'Of course, Mummy,' said Susan. 'Can't we Daddy?' And all John could do was blink back a tear and nod. And though nothing more was said and nothing had been decided, the Manson family knew it was on the mend.

Tea was soon served, and the girls were telling their news and John spoke quietly of his new life—how he had been having a rest, doing gardening and going for walks and, ruefully, how he had taken up interior decoration for the first time. And Jean made admiring comments about the choice of wall-paper, and overlooked the wrinkles here and there. Jessica's scones were soon ready, eaten hot off the griddle, with fresh butter and strawberry jam she had made from strawberries given by the man next door who worked in a nursery. And, after the tea and scones had disappeared and there seemed nothing left to say, John broke the silence of the group with, 'Let's have a wee prayer, shall we?'

'Yes,' said Jessica, 'why not? You haven't said a word of that since we came here—except for grace at meal times.'

'Dear God, thank you for bringing us together again. It has brought comfort here when we needed it. Amen.'

And it was all that needed saying, even if it was said to an abstract God.

Then Jessica took Susan out for a walk, leaving the two adults to themselves. And they sat for a while, like children, until John said, 'How have you been?'

'Awful! Just awful! It was a punishment wasn't it? Roddy going like that. All because I went off to Glasgow enjoying myself and left him. If I hadn't done that, it would never have happened.'

'Now, now,' said John, 'It's no punishment. God doesn't work that way. How could anyone, man or God, wish for the death of a wee boy, like that? It's just not so. It's chance, that's all it is. Being in the wrong place at the wrong time. God had nothing to do with it; and it's no punishment. There was a baby-sitter, wasn't there? Everything had been done as it should? Well, there's no blame. It's just a pity that Charlie Braddock asked Roddy to his room, and Roddy was too scared to go. He must have hung about.'

'But what happened then?'

'Somebody came along and tied him up. And then a fire started; and Roddy couldn't get out. That's all there is. It's not your fault.'

'But why did they leave Roddy like that to get burnt?'

'Maybe they tried to save him and couldn't. That's probably what happened.'

'John, John, can you ever forgive me?'

'For going off with Tom Henderson, you mean?' and John turned away for a moment and thought about it. 'I was hurt when you left, of course; but it's understandable. You thought I'd been with Madeline Grant. Then there was all the flak I was having to take. It couldn't have been easy for you, Jean. And then, there was a marvellous alternative. Big house, posh car, and all the trimmings, everything you'd been deprived of because you married a minister. No, Jean, I don't blame you, not in my heart, anyway.'

'I was worried about having a place to stay, you know. Making ends meet, when we got thrown out.' Jean looked around her at the home they had made for themselves. It was not much, but it was home; and it was their own doing and their own place. That gave it an aura, a special light and quality, her own current establishment could never have. Oakfield was wonderful, of course: all mod cons, served and waited upon, hand and foot, wanting for nothing—even having a very loving man for company, who admired her and thought her of most worth—no matter her betrayal of others. But she realised that all that comfort was not worth a jot besides the loss of her children—for they had made their choice, as she had—not worth the loss of such a man as John Manson, who could look down the barrels of adversity and take what was coming, without flinching and without losing his soul. And she saw that what she had given up was infinitely better than what she had acquired. And for a time she sat there, weeping soundlessly, and would not be comforted.

Sooner than expected, the girls returned, for Susan was tiring fast and had to be held up some of the way. And by the time she reached home, all she wanted to do was go to bed directly and sleep.

Jessica made the evening meal and the three others sat down together quietly and companionably, remembering so many times past, when they had all of them dined at the Manse. 'Have you seen Peter?' said John, presently.

'Once or twice. He's very busy in the hotel, now that summer's here and the tourists are hopping. But he seems happy enough.'

Jean insisted on doing the washing up, just as in the old days, borrowing a pinafore to keep the new suit clean. And then they sat together in the old worn chairs by the unlit fire-side, and it was time for Jean to go, and everyone knew and waited to see what she would say.

At ten, as darkness began to fall, a towelled mop of chestnut hair rounded the door and said, 'Is Mummy still here?' and seeing she was, bounded into the room in nothing but pyjamas. 'Look, I'm not tired now,' and sat down on the floor between her mother's knees.

Finally, Jean rose and said, 'Well,' and they all stood up, and Jean embraced Susan and then Jessica, and looked at John, but was too embarrassed to do it to him. Then she moved to the door and they followed, and she walked along the corridor, turning her head from time to time, making remarks to them, about how nice they had got the place, when everyone knew it was untrue, and not worth anything, beside her new residence. And, as she began to descend the stair, they could see the tears begin and she moved down and Susan was behind her, touching her back, as if guiding her but reluctant to let go, and Jessica and John, arm in arm, followed and watched from the small landing at the bend in the stair. At the bottom, Jean put her fingers on the door-handle, and slowly, very slowly, opened the door wide, and then she turned to look at them, and the tears streamed down her face. 'I don't want to go,' she said. And nobody said anything for a moment; until John said, very deliberately, 'You don't have to go. Why don't you stay. That's what we'd all like very much.'

'Do you mean it?' said Jean. 'I can stay the night?'

'Of course. But why don't you just stay for good?' said John.

'But..but what about my things.....'

'What are a few things? Forget them. Who needs them. We need you, and maybe you need us. That's what counts.'

And so, to smiles of relief, and sighs of contentment at this turn of events, from the girls, Jean closed the door, and came upstairs again.

John offered to sleep on the sofa and give up his room to Jean, but Jessica solved the problem. 'Susan can move in with me—on the bed we keep in case Peter comes; and Mum can go into Susan's room.'

A little later, as everyone was about to fall asleep, there was more silent rejoicing among them than at any time for months.

Next morning early, Jean was up preparing breakfast; and, as there was nothing but a loaf of bread and a few eggs in the cupboard, she went off to the wee shop round the corner, where, with Tom Henderson's money, she bought bacon and black pudding and sausage and corn flakes and bread rolls and butter and marmalade and fresh orange juice. Half an hour later, attracted by the sounds and smells of sizzling, everyone was trying to set the table and getting in each other's way, until laughter broke out. The meal was a triumph, even if it was held courtesy of Tom Henderson.

But further, Jean would not go. 'Are there any of my old dresses here?' she enquired. Mercifully, there were, so she changed into the least dowdy and stored the new pink suit in Susan's wardrobe, wondering, as she did so, whether it would ever be right to wear it again.

A flurry of house-cleaning and washing and gardening went on by the Mansons for a while; and then John arrived for a cup of tea and, with studied carefulness, suggested a walk to the Park; for it would not entail a parade through the streets, making of Jean a talking point to every passer-by.

Ottersay Park is one of the marvels of the place, under-rated by the natives only because they take so much other beauty for granted. It lies to the south of the Crimea, across half a dozen fields, in a valley, before the great Loch, with the causeway across, dividing it into two massive areas of water, one reedy and muddy, the other, surrounded by tall conifers, dark and brooding, where fish feed in plenty. Privately, John considered the walk through the Park and around the loch, one of God's gifts to the folk of Branden.

And so, with the dog on the lead, the four Mansons, the mother dressed more appropriately now, left the house and the grubby poverty of Sevastopol Street, and entered fields of ripening corn, on the way down the hill towards the Park. And the few people who saw them go, wondered at their joy; some astounded that Jean could have gone back like that; while others would not believe the move permanent. For who would give up Oakfield for the Crimea? Even in that cesspot of villainy, however, there was some goodness. In the wee shop, Mary Ryan was heard to say to a neighbour, 'Ah'm richt gled efter aw their troubles.'

The stroll downhill, across fields aglow with bursting growth and birdsong, made John Manson himself feel like singing. And he began to sing, in a rich high tenor, and with great emotion, almost quavering at times:

> 'Jesus calls us! O'er the tumult
> Of our life's wild restless sea,
> Day by day his voice is sounding,
> Saying, 'Christian, follow me.'

And the children smiled, and joined in, and soon Jean, too, was singing, at the joy of such a walk on such a day, under a cloudless sky, among all the sights and sounds of summer, after so many long nights in places she should not have been.

Crossing the road from Ottersay, which bisected the island, with Susan's hand in his pocket, John Manson soon stood overlooking the Park, which spread from one side of the town to the other, around the north side of the great loch. Tennis courts there were, and a vast grassy area used for shinty and cricket, and for many things besides: picnics and rounders, for the space was truly phenomenal. Beyond the kiosk, where games equipment was hired and ices sold, was a children's area with swings and roundabouts and a paddling pool, and farther off, across the Mill Lade, the great expanse where football was played, ending finally at the cottage hospital. At the south edge of the Park, on a mound that kept the loch in its rightful place, lay a tree-lined track, known as the lover's walk, where generations of Brandonians had courted, and below which, on the slope to the playing areas, concealed by a few thousand rhododendrons, glorious in spring, they were even known to have made love.

Down the hill to the kiosk, went the Mansons, past the tennis courts and the cricket square to the curling pond, dry now, until the sluice was opened from the stream. And John wondered at it. For years, there had been no curling on Branden, there being no sustained frost to make it possible. Perhaps the world was getting warmer. What other changes would time bring? And he thought of the churches and the dwindling congregations in some. They were giving up their God, under the impact of a higher standard of living and too many interesting ways of spending their leisure. Where would it end? Immorality was rife—not the kind that he or Jean had been guilty of, men and women had always made mistakes. No, it was the idea that there were things one ought to do, that was being lost. The temporary happiness of the individual was all that seemed to count now, fleeting though it might be.

As they went along, meeting the road around the loch, and following it through the trees and right across the bridge, there was little talk among them; it was a time of silent communion, as each soul sought out the others and felt their presence, and there was an inner peace in the family it had not seen for many a day.

Surveillance of George Buchanan had been going on continually and a most exhaustive search made of the benificiaries of deceased persons for a few years back, in every lawyer's office on the island. A substantial sum of money had been steadily flowing into a number of medical and other charities, like the Heart, Lung Foundation and the Cat and Dog home, all of them located at addresses in Glasgow, such as that discovered by John Manson, but every time they called at the door, it was to discover that the office had moved.

The question the police were anxious to answer was where had the charities moved to? No wills recently lodged with the lawyers made any reference to these, which meant that either the scam had been given up, or put on ice, or the wills had been retained by their authors.

One morning, George was observed to catch the ferry and was shadowed by two detectives. Arrived at the mainland, he took the train to Glasgow, and headed for the gents toilets in Central Station. It was there that he lost them. The two men waited outside for half an hour and did not see him come out. When one entered the place himself, there was no sign of George.

All afternoon, they waited and watched the concourse, and four hours later, in plenty of time for the last train, they observed him again, dressed as before, in black suit and trench coat, carrying the same large hold-all of the morning. Evidently, George had changed clothes in the toilet; disguising himself so effectively, that he had escaped notice on the way out.

Unfortunately, a ferry is a confined space, and policemen are usually tall, so it did not take George long to observe them, and remember their presence on the outgoing journey.

Mirrilees was annoyed. The next time George caught the ferry at the pier, he was picked up at Wemyss Bay and followed discreetly by a man and woman. He left the Central Station without entering the toilet or adopting a disguise, taking a taxi to a building in Mayflower Street, where he visited the office of a well-known firm of architects with a senior partner called Mackinnon-Smythe. The police saw him enter, but were unable to follow and, a little later, when he emerged, they were no wiser.

Inside, George had just received ten thousand pounds in cash, as a downpayment for services rendered. The block of buildings between Bridgeton Street and Mill-Lade Street, in Ottersay, was to be demolished, by order of the council—which is to say, George, who had retained control of planning—and the new development attracting grants totalling one million pounds was to be orchestrated by the Mayflower Street firm. They were tied in with a cartel of contractors, which would make the matter of profit elementary: three of them would tender, but all would share in the outcome, which was prearranged, by sub-contracting out some of the work from the leading tender to the others. The costing was done by the architects and their associates. All George had to do was get it approved. Some of the ten thousand pounds would be devoted to sweetening enough of his fellow councillors to make it a fait accompli; even then, there would still be a healthy sum for George; and an equal bonus at the completion. The architects and associates would earn about 15 % of the total contract, so they were happy—happier still, because of the inflation of the price to double its real value. The cost had been inflated to twice its real cost for an elementary reason: the maximum possible grant was 50%. So the real cost of the project was one million pounds and the public was paying all of it! The firm behind it, also associated with the architects, surveyors etc, would get several new buildings, many of them shops, for nothing, which they would rent out until they were sold off.

As George sat in the first class carriage on the way to Wemyss Bay, he smiled to himself, for he doubted that it would be necessary to spend more than the cost of a few dinners at the Grand Hotel. That would be enough to convince the few councillors necessary. But he might have to grease a few palms in the Burgh Surveyor's office. Still, he was used to that and so were they. Why would anyone object?

Investigating the fire, Police interviews of townsfolk had not borne fruit; nor had the window through which the arsonists entered been much use: finger prints were plentiful, but, as there had been several comings and goings, through the same small aperture, they had intermingled, smudging each other and rendering the sharp impression necessary, beyond recognition. George himself was the only lead and he would keep his head down, now, knowing it, suspending all activity until the police left and the coast was clear for the resurrection of the phoenix.

Sniffy Johnstone had known nothing, or nothing at least that was incriminating to George; and Billy, when in desperation, he was called in again for questioning, managed, through sheer paralysed fright, to repel all efforts to incriminate him.

'We know you knew the boy Roddy well,' they had said, over and over 'and we think you know what happened to him. So why don't you tell us? We're not saying you had a hand in it. We just want to know, that's all.' But Billy had remained like a dumb animal; and it was eventually concluded that he could not know anything. For how could he sit there, hour after hour, otherwise? When, in truth, he was too terrified of his father to admit to wrong-doing of any kind. Being the provost's son was a further complication, as the time-limit for holding him for questioning could not be breached.

The problem of how George Buchanan would have got a hose-pipe to attach to the exhaust of Jim Grant's car was fully investigated. The pipe itself had been bought at an ironmonger on the main street but no one could remember by whom. They had sold plenty of that kind of hose-pipe all over the island during the year. Whether Jim Grant or George Buchanan had ever bought some was unknown. Yet, the length of it was too bulky to be carried in the voluminous pockets of a trench-coat. So if George had anything to do with it, he must have carried it in a bag. And why not? Why should not a councillor be carrying a bag when he goes to meet someone in a pub? People often carry bags on such occasions, especially if they have just come from business or work of some kind. So there was nothing to go on.

Inspector Mirrilees was at his wits end to think of something useful to do, and he decided to stand down the investigation. Officers were needed for other cases elsewhere.

For the last time, he drove up the hill to the school, taking a look at the scene of the conflagration, before leaving the island. Miraculously, the outer stone walls still stood but the interior was a shambles of charred beams and ashes. Some of the roof had survived, the part above the source of the fire, because of the explosion and the direction of the wind, which had spread the fire away from that area.

As Mirrilees sat in the car, wondering whether there was not something else he could have done, he saw a movement in the building, and decided to investigate. Inside, carefully avoiding the ashes and debris as far as possible, he found John Manson, in the old grey suit, white dog-collar and blue stock, who turned to him, at his approach. 'I was just remembering where Roddy died,' he said, wearily. 'The demolition crew moves in tomorrow. So there'll soon be nothing left.' Then John pointed to the centre of the room, 'This is where it happened, isn't it?'

'Yes,' said Mirrilees. 'That was the preparation-bench. There's the gas tap, and there was a bunsen for heating chemicals. He was tied to the tap, we think.' And after a silence, as they contemplated the spot where the boy had died, each imagining the frenzied attempt to escape, and the failure of breath, and the chip-pan fire he had become, Mirrilees, added, 'I am very sorry, you know. And sorrier still that we couldn't find out who did it.'

'It doesn't matter,' said John. 'I'm sure it wasn't deliberate. It was just an accident. Maybe a prank of some kind. These things happen.'

'You don't feel anger, then?'

'What good is anger? I miss the boy,' he said, choking back a tear, 'he was my flesh and blood, mine to raise and guide and help mature, and I was proud of him. He was a good boy in so many ways. He had promise; and now he's gone. What might he have become if he had lived?' And the tears came then, and John made no effort to conceal them. He sobbed, 'I don't understand it. Why him, of all people? I try to tell myself it was just bad luck, but it's hard to accept. There's so much about life we'll never understand.'

Rays of sunshine streamed through the windows, from which the glass had mostly blown out long ago.

In a voice of infinite sadness, John said, 'It's as if we can't help but kill each other. An innocent—my boy—is going about the world doing his lawful business and, by chance—blind chance—he bumps into folk who tie him up and, because a fire starts, he gets killed. It's just awful; and it happens all the time, everywhere in the world. Hell isn't somewhere else, it's right here and now. Why would we need to go there because we're bad, when we're so good at making it so for ourselves and other folk?' He shook his head and added, 'It doesn't matter who did it. It's enough that he's dead.'

Mirrilees said, 'I'm afraid it does matter, though. It's not just the death and the damage. It's what they might go on to do. That's why I'm sorry we're giving it up. But there are just no leads, you see.'

As Mirrilees turned to leave, something sparkled, something under a charred timber, in what would have been the corridor, just outside the doorway to the science-store. Curious, he went over to it and moved the debris with his foot, and when he felt something there, some small object, he stooped and fished it out of the muck and rubble. Holding it up to the light, he said, 'Now there's a thing.' And he blew on it and brushed it.

'What is it?' said John, without much interest.

'A tie-pin.'

'Well, I suppose all sorts of odds and ends lie buried here.'

'But this is unusual. See! That's a diamond, if I'm not mistaken. This is a very expensive article. Not the kind of thing you find in schools.' Weighing it carefully in his hand, he added, 'This is just near the door. I wonder if it was left here by one of the culprits?'

'What would they be doing with expensive jewellery?'

'Just what I was thinking. It is most odd.'

John Manson refused the lift home which Mirrilees offered, electing to ascend the hill to the Crimea, on foot.

Across the front of the gaunt, ravaged, building he went, to the path which rose steeply to the Bannockburn Tower with its castellated eaves, and, by the time he reached the gate on the road above the rear of the school, he was panting for breath. Then, standing with his hand on the gate, he looked along at the seat which stood on the gravel with such a splendid view of the town. And the images of Jean astride Tom Henderson flooded his mind. And the pain began; at first a small pain, but as he looked over at the shrub from behind which he had observed the lovers, it gradually grew worse, and he clasped his hand to his chest and stood uncertainly. What should he do? What does one do, with a pain like that, when there is so far to go, and nearly all of it uphill, a hill as steep as any in Branden?

Sensibly, John tottered across to the seat and sat down with a thump; and there he sat for half an hour, resting. But he didn't like sitting there, for the image of Jean's new-found joy continued to appear before him and cut at his vitals. The place to be, was home, he decided, and he got up and began to walk unsteadily to the gate, manoeuvred himself outside, and then started to struggle up the hill to Sevastopol Street. The incline was severe, with grass on one side, so that not too many windows overlooked his progress. Twice, he stopped, and rested, panting with the effort, steadying himself with a hand on the fence of a garden on his left. Then the trudge continued. At the very steepest part, the pain suddenly became alarming, and he was forced to sit down on the pavement, feet splayed out, with his back to the fence. There he sat for half an hour, feeling, if anything, no better, and unable to face the effort necessary to get up and struggle onward.

A lady with a pram went past, a woman with all the vigour of youth about her, who said, 'Are you all right, Mr Manson?' And John, who hated to be a burden, replied, 'Yes, oh yes. I'm just having a wee rest. It's this steep hill, you know. Think nothing of it.'

So the woman, who had urgent things to do, went off thankfully, glad that she did not have to step out of her world to help another, and mindless of his evident distress, so obvious in one sitting down on the pavement.

John struggled to his feet and tried to go on, but a yard or two further up the hill, he was forced to sit down again. It was comical really, he reflected, to be unable to stand up properly and walk to his home. If it weren't for the pain, the worsening pain in his chest and limbs, which felt gradually weaker, it would be laughable. A grown man who couldn't walk. Ridiculous.

And so he rested until another woman came along and a similar conversation took place. Again he got up and struggled onwards as best he could; but this time, the woman waited below him, and observed his progress. Seeing his difficulty, she returned and said, 'You're not well, are you, Minister? Just you wait there and I'll phone for the ambulance.' And off she went to the phone-box at the top of the hill, enviably, with steps as light as a gazelle. But John was embarrassed at causing so much trouble and called after her, 'There's no need. Don't bother,' and he lifted himself up once more and then, in the midst of the effort of that first upward step, his world collapsed and him with it. Down he fell, like a tree-trunk, newly axed, by the cumulative ravages of time. Too much worry, too much disappointment, too much humiliation and too many betrayals. Why is it that we kill each other? was his last thought.

The rest of it was a blur, an occasional sense of movement and the noises of people talking, seemingly far off, and in between, periods of unconsciousness.

By the greatest good luck, the tie-pin was remembered at Shand's Gift shop, on the front street, the place where anyone who was anyone, bought expensive presents. 'Yes,' said the shop assistant, 'I would know this anywhere. George Buchanan bought this less than a year ago.'

'How can you be so sure?' said Mirrilees, making an effort to hide his excitement.

'Just look at it! That's no ordinary diamond. That cost a fortune. You don't forget that kind of thing.'

'So you haven't sold any others like it?'

'No. We've never *had* another like it.'

But when the tie-pin was taken by the police to Silvertrees, and shown to George, he denied owning it. Then, looking more carefully, he said, with surprise, 'This is Billy's. Betty, didn't I buy this for Billy's birthday?' And Betty confirmed it. Then, backtracking quickly, George said, 'Maybe it's just like the one I bought Billy. What's it about anyway?'

Mirrilees said, 'It was found at the scene of the fire. The girl in the gift shop is positive it's the one they sold to you. If you gave it to Billy, it follows that he was in the school at the time of the fire.'

'Uch away with you!' said George. 'Billy's left school. He left months before the fire.'

'That's what I mean,' said Mirrilees, 'What was he doing there when he had left the place?'

George's head went up, as if he'd been jabbed in the jaw. 'Well, he must have lost it. Left it there. And the fire burnt everything and brought it to light.'

'Did he report losing it?'

'I don't know. Not to me.'

'An expensive present like that?'

'He wouldn't want to admit losing it, maybe,' said Betty.

Mirrilees said, 'I don't think he did lose it. If he'd lost it in a school corridor, it would have been found.'

'Maybe it fell behind something, out of sight, like I said,' chipped in George, far from confidently.

'I doubt it,' said Mirrilees. 'School corridors are left deliberately empty, so that people can easily get to where they want to go. Getting them from one class-room to the next, is a major problem. It uses up time, you see; and can cause indiscipline, if not supervised.'

That was enough for now, and Mirrilees knew it. Leave them to stew over it and harass the boy for a while. But if Mirrilees had known what harassment would mean in this case, he would have reconsidered. Returned to the police-station, he called a halt to the evacuation of the force, and rebooked a room for himself in the town.

It was in the Greenock hospital, where he had been taken, that the vindication of all John's troubles was provided, though only he viewed it as such.

He was lying in bed surrounded by the family, some of it at least, telling them how well he was and how well-treated; and how he expected to be out in a week or two, when Susan yawned, and John suggested she go to the hospital café to buy some sweets. For during his stay, he had often thought about Susan's tiredness. Maybe sugar was the answer. More energy to drive her wee frame.

'A.all right, Da.addy,' said Susan, reluctantly. 'But I don't wa.ant sweets. A cup of tea might be the thi.ing.'

'Just make sure it has plenty of sugar, then,' said John. 'You go with her Jessica.'

'I do.on't ne.ed help, Da.addy,' said Susan, but Jessica went anyway, knowing the problem of managing crockery.

At the cafeteria, Susan had all the expected difficulty with the tea cup, which, before Jessica could intervene, slipped and fell on the floor where it smashed. Susan was upset and cried impotently, at such a public display of weakness. It was then that a passing doctor, in a white coat, who had observed the entire proceedings, approached.

'Excuse my asking,' he said, to Susan, in a caring, curious way, 'but would you mind coming with me?'

'What for?' said Jessica.

'She's not well,' said the Doctor.

'We know,' said Jessica, 'She has Motor Neurone Disease.'

'I see,' said the Doctor, looking dubious. 'My name's Webster,' he said, holding out his hand. Jessica took it, and then Susan. 'I.I'm Su.usa.an,' she said, slurring as usual.

Alert with excitement and deeply interested, Webster said, 'Do you get tired progressively throughout the day?'

'Ye.es, I have to go and sleep in the afternoo.oon.'

'Well, I'd like you to come with me, while I carry out some tests.'

'Bu.ut my Dad.dy's in here. He.e's the one we've co.ome to see.'

But Webster insisted, telling them that Susan's condition had been a special research interest of his, and that conceivably they might be able to help him. Reluctantly, but thinking to do *him* a good turn, the girls followed him into the bowels of the great hospital. Five minutes later they were in his consulting room where tests were carried out and Susan's symptoms carefully described. How she got more and more tired during the day and, though she wanted to be active, how she utterly lacked the energy necessary. And yet, how a little sleep was invigorating. Finally, he said, 'Well, I have good news for you. I don't think you have Motor Neurone Disease. What you have is Myasthenia Gravis.'

'Does that make a difference?' said Jessica.

'Oh, yes! If I'm right, I can treat this and Susan will be completely free of it.'

'Wo.ould there be a.an o.operation?' said Susan, worriedly.

'Maybe. Maybe not. It depends. Sometimes we cut out a bit of the thymus gland; but often all it takes is steroids.'

'How do we make sure?' said Jessica.

'I am fairly sure already. The best thing to do is try the steroid cocktail and see what happens. If that doesn't work, then the thymus may have to come out. What we have to do is suppress the attack of your own body on the acetylcholine receptor.'

When the rest of the family heard, there was amazement, disbelief, at first, and then they were overjoyed; and Dr Webster came to the ward to explain it: how a number of people had been incorrectly diagnosed as having Motor Neurone Disease, because the symptoms described by the patient had not been attended to sufficiently. The standard test just couldn't be relied upon, he told them. How Myasthenia Gravis, a disorder of the junction between nerve and muscle, results in weakness or, more precisely, fatigability of different muscle groups. Commonest in women in their twenties, it can occur in any age-group and affects about 4,000 people in Britain. Classically, people wake feeling spry but, as the day progresses, they begin to tire, start seeing double or find it difficult to carry on a prolonged conversation, as their speech becomes slurred. Meals become an ordeal: sufferers spill their food, as they find it difficult to move the fork from plate to mouth; develop pain around the shoulder, from the strain of trying to keep their head upright. By the early afternoon, they often feel exhausted and retire to bed, after which they feel their batteries have been recharged, albeit temporarily. Mysathenics have a spectrum of symptoms, and it is at the two extremes of the very mild and the severe that patients may be told they are either neurotic or have a rapidly progressive fatal muscle disease.

The vital symptom is that tiredness becomes gradually worse throughout the day. This is often missed, and hence Motor Neurone Disease is often mistakenly diagnosed.

Dr Webster explained it clearly, and when the family had heard him out they all knew that a cure was at hand. The rejoicing made Dr Webster's day. How often does a doctor pick up a misdiagnosis like that and change a young life? Rarely! But when it happens is it is like a miracle.

Since the fire, Billy had changed. Friendly, even subservient to Tommy Forbes before, he now did everything possible to avoid his company, and Tommy noticed. Once, when they were working alone together on a corpse, Tommy raised the matter.

'Ye've jist got tae keep yer mooth shut, Billy. That's aw.' But, when Billy made no reply and continued as morosely as ever, Tommy added, 'See if you talk? See if you split on yer mates? You'll get done, so you will. And it'll no' be jist an ordinary doin'. Ye'll git the hale lot. Ye know what Ryan's like. If you split on him, ye'll feenish up like this fella here,' pointing to the corpse.

'Don't be daft,' said Billy.

'Daft, is it?' said Tommy. 'Ah'm no' daft. Neither's Ryan. If we get fun oot we'll get the jyle. Years and years. Too mony bloody years! Do ye think we fancy that? Bein' locked up half wur lives? Nae chance!' Tommy looked around, and seeing the coast still clear, put his head close to Billy's and murmured, 'See if you gie them as much as a cheep, we'll get ye. We'll come back here out the jyle and stuff you like wan o' they cadavers. Yer faither'll huv tae gie ye a special, tae cover up the mess.' After work, Billy had taken to drinking by himself in the Branden Arms, sitting mournfully over pints for a few hours, until the pangs of hunger became intolerable. By the time he arrived home, dinner would be over, and scraps would have to be got out of the fridge. Betty, ever indulgent, and taking this new behaviour as a sign of maturity, would often make him a reheat.

When Mirrilees arrived, George had been about to sit down to dinner. By the time he left, George had lost his appetite. Like a black rhino, working itself up into a temper because of the approach of an undesirable, he had paced the floor and snorted and fumed so much, that Betty had stayed out of the way in the kitchen.

'Sit down there,' said George, pointing to an armchair by the fire, when at last Billy entered. Hearing the commotion, Betty appeared at the door of the sitting-room, nervously drying her hands in her apron. When Billy was seated, cowering in the chair, George said, 'Where is your tie-pin? The one with the big diamond I bought for your birthday?' This from a menacing, purple-faced George, seemingly capable of uttering fire and smoke, so pent-up was his anger.

'I don't know,' said Billy, involuntarily curling himself into as much of a hedgehog-like ball as he was able, in the confined space of the chair.

'Have you lost it?'

'Yes... I don't know. I just don't know where it is.'

'Well I know where it is. The police have it. They found it in the school near where that boy was killed.'

The silence stood between them like smoke. Billy didn't know where to look or what to do. Involuntarily, he made preliminary moves to escape, to run, anywhere...anywhere out of that place, away...away from his father. George stopped him rising with one broad hand which pushed him down again.

'Well, what have you got to say?'

'Nothing. I don't know how it got there.'

'Uch away! You must have lost it there! You must have been there! The cops think you did it. Don't you see?'

'I didn't do anything.'

'But you were there, weren't you?'

'No...No. It wasnae me! Honest!' And Billy drew into himself, like the hedgehog into its protective covering, psychically, as well as physically. But George was not in the same position as the police. They might not be able to beat the truth out of him, but George had no such compunction. 'Don't you understand what you've done? The business is under threat! The cops are looking into everything! And now this! You go and tie up a boy and set fire to the school. What did you do it for? '

'I never did anything,' said Billy, wearily, trembling, in a voice that sounded detached, distant.

George slapped him viciously on the face. One way and then the other.

'Admit it, ya wee bastard! You did it! I know you did it!'

'No Ah didnae,' sobbed Billy, casting a fearful look of pity at his mum. But there was no help from that quarter, and he knew it.

'Yer a bloody wee liar!' said George, and punched him full on the face, a clubbing blow that bounced his head off the chair-back. Then George rained punches at him for a little, and then pulled him out of the chair and sat him on the floor, kneeling above him with his hands on his throat. 'Now, ya bastard! Are ye gonny talk? Let's hear what ye did.'

But, surprisingly, blood showing on his face in three places, Billy said nothing.

Trying a different tactic, and yet partly sorry for what he had already done, George put an arm around his shoulders and said, 'Look, for God's sake, Billy, we need tae tae know what ye did. Then we can take precautions. I'll advise you what to do. Now come on, talk, for Christ's sake!'

As Billy sat, silently, one eye closing, like a punch-drunk boxer, Betty cried and said, 'Oh please, Billy, please! Tell your father what happened. He'll put it right, you'll see.'

So Billy relented and told them, in a flat deathless voice, just as it happened. How they had gone to the school and broken in, to see if they could find anything useful in the science-store.

'Useful? Like what?'

'Explosives, I don't know. Some stuff like dynamite.'

'Dynamite? What for?'

'To blow up a bank.'

'Christ save us! Who got you into this? Who else was there?'

When Billy told him, he begged that George would not split on them.

'Split on them? Damn right I will! They're the ones got you into trouble. Aren't they?'

'It was just an accident,' said Billy. 'I tried to free Roddy but it was too hot, too smoky. I couldnay breathe. Then there was this explosion, and I got blown across the room and out the door.'

'So you didn't tie him up?'

'No' me. I didn't want any of it.'

George got up and paced the floor, thinking, and said, finally. 'You're an accessory after the fact. You'll get done for manslaughter and arson. You could get ten years.'

Betty sobbed. 'What are we going to do, George?' she cried, piteously, 'What are we going to do?'

George stopped pacing and turned to him. 'You mustn't admit you did this! Deny everything, it's the only way!'

'What about the tie-pin, George?'

'You'll have to say you lost it. Then there's nothing they can do to you. Say you didn't report it, because you were afraid of what we would say. It's an expensive piece, after all. That should do it. But you'll have to stand out against them. Can you do it, son? Can you do it?' As he said it, George clamped a large talon on Billy's shoulder, but knew, just as soon as he asked, that Billy couldn't do it. Had he not just proved that he could be broken down? George made a noise of irritation and turned away to pace the floor again and think.

Betty said, 'But surely he didn't do anything wrong? He tried to save the boy, didn't he?'

Impatiently, George said, 'He was there. He broke into the school. He climbed in with the others. He stood by, while they tied up the boy. That's all they need.' Turning to Billy, he said, 'How did the fire start?'

'I don't know. Some stuff in a jar. When you take it out it just lights up. Roddy said it was phosphorus or something.'

'Did you try and put it back in the jar?'

'No, it was Tommy. He tried, but a bit broke off and fell in the papers. Then all hell let loose. It all went up so suddenly. Like a bonfire.'

'And what did you do?'

'Me? Nothing. I just stood and watched.'

'Ya bloody zombie!'

Staring into the fire, George could see it all, as the images came to mind. Then he shook his head, ruefully. 'It won't do!' he shouted, like an animal in pain. 'There's nothing we can do!'

'But surely these other boys....' said Betty tearfully. 'It's really their fault.'

'That doesnae matter. Our son's involved. Our Billy. He'll go down along with them. Oh Christ!' and George exploded a curving right hook in the direction of Billy, which grazed his head and made him shrink against the chair. 'Yer a bloody disgrace! I wonder where you came from! Christ, how did I ever deserve you?' He turned away sighing, and then turned back to the stupefied boy who lay on the floor, his back against the armchair with legs spread, and screamed, 'Ye know, it would be better if you hadnay been born!' Then dismissively, 'Away to your room, away wi' ye!' And, as Billy slunk off silently, like a shot skunk, George called after him. 'Do you realise that if it hadnay been for you—you being so spineless—this would never have happened? And that boy would never have got burnt to death? He would be alive and kicking! Do you know what it'll cost to rebuild that school? Do ye? It's a fortune, that's what it is!' And he began to pace the floor again, 'Christ we'll never live this down. The wee bastard will talk! I guarantee it!' Almost in tears, he swung on Betty and said, 'Are you sure he's my son? Or did you let some other man put the leg over ye? Eh? Ah canny believe this! I jist canny believe it!' And then in a sudden torrent of self-pity, he shouted, almost sobbing, 'The wee bastard's done us in! He's done us in! And me the provost too. All that bloody work! All that scheming and skill, for Christ's sake! All wasted. The bugger's done us in!' And not for a moment did it occur to George that perhaps he might himself bear some responsibility for his son's lack of backbone.

That same evening, for lack of money to pay everyone's fare, Jessica went to Greenock alone. And later was glad of it, for many children never have the opportunity to talk to their parents, and first realise it only when it is no longer possible. John was sitting up in bed, but Jessica was still uneasy at the cast of his face, which seemed aged. He soon brightened at the prospect of mental things, the touching of minds.

He asked if she still intended to be a psychiatrist, and when she confirmed it, he said, 'What was it that gave you the idea?'

'It was Charlie Braddock. He didn't just teach us mathematics, you know. There were other things, like psychology.' And when pressed to explain, Jessica said, 'Well, you'll have to pay close attention,' and when John agreed, she told him how Charlie had drawn eighteen sets of four lines on the blackboard. Each set was a single yellow line with three white ones beside it. One of the white lines was the same length or nearly, as the yellow line; the other two white lines were of very different lengths.

'Charlie told us we were going to play a trick on an unsuspecting student, brought in specially for the purpose. He would say that he was holding an intelligence test and that students had been drawn at random from their classes to take part. But during the test, by arrangement beforehand, we would answer some of the questions incorrectly to see what effect it had on the unsuspecting student.' Jessica explained how Charlie had told them to give the correct answers to the first six questions and tell the same lie for the next twelve. 'So when the student joined us, Charlie told all of us, as if for the first time, that we were all having a wee test, and then he pointed to the first set of lines and said, "Which white line is nearest in length to the yellow one?" Of course, the answer was blindingly obvious. It was meant to be. And we all put our hands up for white line number three, say. And so, six sets of lines were dealt with. And by the end of them, the unsuspecting student, would begin to think this test was easy. But then, on the seventh set, everyone in the group, except the unsuspecting student, would give the same wrong answer. And Charlie had arranged things so that the unsuspecting student could see everyone else's response.

'Well, the unsuspecting student might answer correctly the first time and the second, but soon, because of the group pressure—the effect of all these hands going up, even when the answer was wildly wrong—he would start putting up his hand when ever the group did. In other words, the effect of the group, was to make that one unsuspecting student make responses which were blindingly false! And all because of group pressure.'

'And this made you want to be a psychiatrist?'

'Not just this. But do you see how important it was? People are easily got to say things that are completely wrong. In other words, people in groups are dangerous. That made it such a good lesson. We were all stunned by how easily even strong characters could be forced to fit it in with things which were quite wrong, that defied the evidence of their own senses.'

Doubtfully, John said, 'It must have been humiliating for the unsuspecting student.'

'It was, of course, and Charlie always explained it, and told how most people were affected this way. The point was to be aware of the danger. I thought it was a good lesson. And it was worth the trauma. The unsuspecting student learned as much as any of us. And could take care in the future. We all stood up and applauded when the school captain, a powerful character, stood out against us all. You could see the stress; he was sweating and really worried by it; but he did it.'

John said, 'The problem is that it only takes one man, one bad egg, to get the group around to his way of thinking, and then any outsider who joins gets pressured into doing things he ordinarily wouldn't.'

'Do you think that happened here, with you?' said Jessica. 'I've wondered what brought this about. It was all so orchestrated, so pre-determined, as if someone had pulled strings and we were puppets bouncing about, bumping into each other.'

'You mean George Buchanan? I think it goes deeper than that, with him.' But John wouldn't speak ill of a man not able to defend himself, to Jessica at least, at that moment. Anyway, he had put the matter—what he knew of it—into the hands of the police. It was not his business to rake over men's lives. Mischievously, he said, 'And do you believe all this stuff in Freud, about the importance of childhood and sex and all that?'

'Some of it, yes. Whether I believe it or not, hardly matters. It's a question of learning ways to help people get over their troubles and lead healthy lives. So many folk don't do that. They're unhappy most of the time.'

'Yes, hell is other people. If it weren't for them, most of us would be happy. But we would be nothing without them. It's learning to live together that is the problem. That's where Jesus comes in; but a lot of folk never understand that, or they forget it.'

Later that night, returned to Branden, Jessica sat in her room and wondered about her father. Whether he would survive and what his death would mean. Taking the fountain pen and a scrap of paper, she began to write:

> Not in the sunlight of our souls
> Are we known,
> But in desperate gloom
> Our courage shown.
> In our faith in what is right
> And our just progress
> To the tomb,
> Near or far,
> Which beckons, relentless,
> To a still eternity.

Another visitor was Joe Gorman. John was delighted to see him and conscious of the honour. It had meant Joe having to dress himself up, and take himself out into the forbidding streets of Ottersay, in the full light of day; and pay the fare for the ferry and the bus to Greenock—a tremendous undertaking for a lonely soul, afraid to go out, and with little money. His scant hair was brushed back and looked clean, like the rest of him, and he wore a new grey suit and black, shiny shoes.

'No, no!' said Joe, refusing to be thanked, after handing over a large box of chocolates and a paperback thriller, 'Ah jist had tae come and see ye, when Ah heard. You were good tae me, the best. Ah never knew anyone as good as you. And what Ah came to say is how sorry Ah am that Ah didnae come and see you before—when it really mattered. When you were having your trial and all that terrible fuss. God knows Ah knew it wis aw wrong, aw jist bloody rubbish! How could Ah no' come an' speak up fur ye?' And Joe broke down and wept and covered his head in his hands.

'Listen, Joe, listen!' said John. 'There's a lot of folk who're not afraid to go out, folk with a lot of clout in Branden—yes, and some of them used to speaking up. And none of them did. So don't blame yourself, man. The very fact that you've come to see me today gladdens my heart. So dry your eye and hold your head up. You are a good friend, Joe. And I'm proud to know you.'

Joe shook his head and looked up, 'Ah canny tell ye how much that means tae me, Minister. Ah'm fair knocked over by ye.'

'Maybe I'll call the nurse and order you a bed, then, Joe. And you can stay and keep me company.' And Joe enjoyed the joke and even managed a laugh.

'Ah'll jist sit doon here,' said Joe. 'This'll dae fine.' But when he had done so, he would not let it go; it mattered too much to him; as if the same phenomenon had been applied to his own case, so very long ago, when he had felt the cruelty around him, the humiliating ostracism, which had confined him like a prisoner to his hovel. And for Joe's own good, John had to try and answer him. 'It just seems to be the way we are, Joe. When the group takes against one poor soul, never mind the reason, nobody has the courage to stand up and speak up.'

'But why? That's what Ah want tae know. Are we aw' jist cowards?'

'We're like sheep, Joe, just sheep; and we follow the herd. The trouble really starts when a rogue ram takes charge and leads them out of the field and up the garden path. Then they destroy everything. It just takes one black sheep.'

'But why does nobody tell him to go tae hell?'

'Because they're afraid. He has the kind of power that can really hurt them. And he gets the power over them, first of all, because he devotes himself to serving them in small things so that he can manipulate them in large ones.'

'You mean fixing them up wi' favours and such?'

'Yes, but it goes beyond that, Joe. They owe him and he calls in his marker when he needs it. And they string along, even if it's a bit dubious, because he's become too powerful and too important to ignore. They never realise at the time just how dubious it is, of course. After that first time, it becomes habit-forming. They even begin to see the world the way he does, from his point of view. That's why the garden path can come to seem very attractive; though, left to themselves, the grass in the field is what they'd prefer.'

'Is it just that, then?'

'It's very easy to get people to do wrong. Most of them will do anything for a powerful friend, especially if it doesn't seem much wrong. Most folk don't have much moral sense. They're very vague about right and wrong, and easily put their own interest before anything. Millions of folk routinely steal small things, cheat the customs duty or pay less tax than they should, by failing to declare their true income. So getting folk like that to do wrong, a little wrong, that combines with others to make a great one, is easy. It's the times too, looking out for number one, has become the new categorical imperative.

'Sometimes it's deeper, so deep we can hardly see what's happening. Some men, Joe, will pay for information and even pay ordinary folk—in favours or money—who have not the least idea what they're being used for, to do things which bring pressure to bear on a weak link, knowing that there is a chance, often just a chance, but a good one, that the link will crack and do things it usually wouldn't. And all because there's a deep game being played. It's all politics, Joe. And most of the population are never aware they're being stung.'

On another occasion, it was Jean's turn to visit John, taking the ferry and the bus to Greenock in the late afternoon, in time for a half hour visit before returning to catch the last ferry.

John said, 'I'm glad you came alone, for once, Jean. Gives us a chance to talk.'

Jean looked, once more, like the manse-lady, in ill-fitting, low-cost, nondescript clothing, in this case the grey dress under the dark-blue trench coat, which had seen better days; and there was no money now for expensive hair-dressing. She sat down and handed over a poke containing an apple tart she'd baked, and John was pleased by it. She said, 'I wanted to say how sorry I am. Say it properly, I mean. I've never been able to before. I was wrong. So wrong! I was so disloyal! I don't know what came over me. I just got frightened. About being on the street and having no money. And all that talk. It was just too much for me. I just couldn't stand it any more. Can you forgive me?'

'Yes, of course, Jean. You were only human, like everybody else. You did really well to put up with me for so long. I appreciate it. I do.'

They sat for a while, in companionable silence, until Jean said, 'Will it ever be the same again between us, do you think?'

And John said, 'No, I don't suppose it will. Life isn't like that, and there's no good pretending it is. People change. They get changed by each other. Sometimes we rub each other the right way, but just as often it's the wrong way. I sometimes think we kill each other a little every day. And yet, there's so much joy in people too. Sometimes we help each other to grow.'

'So, there's no chance for us, then?' she said, with tears on the way. 'Is that what you're saying?'

'No, if I got out of here, we would have some kind of life again. But I won't be coming home, Jean. Don't ask me how I know, but I do.'

'Oh, don't say that John, don't!' and the tears began to come. 'What would we do without you?'

'You would all get along a lot better. Now here's what I want to say to you. I want you to listen and pay attention and remember it, for I might not get another chance. If I don't make it out of here, I want you to go back to Tom Henderson.' As Jean gasped and made to interrupt, John held up his hand to prevent her. 'I mean what I say. Tom must think a lot of you and I know you think a lot of him. That's a good thing, not something to worry about or feel guilty about. It gives you another chance, you see, when I'm gone.'

'But John, how can you? After all that's happened.'

'It's maybe all for the best. Everything works for good to those who love God, remember?' he laughed sadly, as if it were a joke. 'If I hadn't come in here with a heart attack, Susan would never have been cured and you would have had to go soldiering on as a Manse-wife, with no money and no spare time and nothing to do but be a skivvy. No, Jean, don't you see? It's all for the best!'

'But it's not, it's not, John! You talk as if you were leaving us. Oh, you're not, you're not! And it's all my fault!' And the tears fell down.

'No, Jean. I'm done anyway. Used up. The old ticker's about ticked its last tock. Just don't you feel guilty about anything. Anything! Remember that. You're only human and you're better than most. But you must expect to fail some of the time, and when you do, you must forgive yourself. As I do. As everyone should. As God does, if there is one up there somewhere.' Then he laughed. 'I'll find out soon enough. You know, between you and me, I'm a little curious about dying. But I don't think there's anything in it at all. One minute you're there and the next you're not. The point is, it's no big deal.'

In this way, they took their farewells and, later, John went to sleep. At four o'clock the next morning, he found himself awake. A dim light penetrated the curtain at the window, and the room was silent except for the sound of snoring from other sleepers around him. He tried to move his head, which was uncomfortable, and could not, for there was a sense of weakness he had never felt before. He tried to move his left foot, with the same result; and then his right hand. Nothing. Nothing would move. Round the body, he went, in his mind, trying to budge something, some little thing; just to persuade himself he was still alive; but there was nothing doing. Not a part of himself could he move. And yet he felt the interior weakness, as if it were creeping up on him from all sides. Finally, he gave up and a tear rolled down his cheek.

The sense of isolation was as terrible as anything he had ever known. He tried to mutter a prayer, to call out—anything to confirm his existence; and heard nothing, for no movement of the lips took place; and he lay, motionless, for a time, staring upwards at the ceiling, listening to the sounds of lives around him. And he envied them their slow breaths and occasional rustlings under blankets, as a limb changed position. And in his mind, he prayed to God, as if it were a person and not a bunch of principles or an unanswerable question, and then, tiring still further, from the effort, and the additional weakness induced by the realisation that there was no one there listening, no bright angel beckoning, he lay in deepest sorrow, in the blackest pit of gloom he had ever known. We come into the world alone and we leave it alone, he thought, and, in between, we fight the battle of life as well as we are able. And maybe, he conceded, to himself, just possibly, our efforts and sufferings make it a little easier for the next generation. And yet, he thought, finally—his last ever thought—there is joy amidst the suffering and, while we live, we can ease the sufferings of our fellows.

At eight-thirty the next morning, Sergeant Strong and Constable Menzies arrived at Silvertrees, expecting to find the family at breakfast, before going to work. Betty—a very exhausted Betty, after dosing with sleeping-pills at George's suggestion—showed them into the dining room where they told George, still at his bacon and eggs, that they wanted Billy for questioning. 'Well, he's not down yet,' said George, wearily, as if his soul were a lump of lead. 'Away and rouse him, Betty.'

And so they waited and presently Betty, still reeling with tiredness, returned to the dining room. 'He's not there,' she said, surprised. 'I've looked everywhere and he's not in the house.'

'Where can he be?" said George, unimpressed. 'Is his bed slept in?'

'He's been lying on it, I think. I can't imagine where he'd go to.'

George did not bother to get up, continued his close examination of the newspaper. The police soon checked the house. 'Is there anywhere else he might be?' said Strong, eventually.

But as no one could think of anywhere, the police went into the garden. In the shed, they found Billy, hanging by the neck. A rope had been thrown over a rafter and he had stood on a tool box before kicking it away. His face was blue-grey when they cut him down.

Thus, three days later, there were two funerals, in Ottersay Cemetery, at the head of the High Street, where the sun streamed down out of a pale-blue sky and the air was windless, soundless, as if even the birds had paused to respect the last rites of passage of two citizens of Branden.

Somehow, the circumstances of Billy's death had circulated, and his part in the fire, and the death of Roddy Manson surmised, and made known. And it had to be him alone who bore the blame, for George could not reveal the names of the real culprits: that would have condemned Billy for sure.

Even the suspicion that he alone was responsible, was preferable to the certainty that he was an accessory. Then there was George himself, a man subdued, a man in anguish even, at the loss of an only child, without hope of another, so late in life. And Mirrilees wondered, as he watched him play his part in the ceremony. What a pity he had left Billy to his father's mercies! How unfortunate that Strong had jumped in and tried to save a life already lost, for all he did, really, was spoil the spoor, the tracks that might have told exactly what did happen that night. Had the boy done it himself? Had he been pushed that far by what George had said? Billy must have known he was not guilty of anything much. Apart from being a bystander. All this Mirrilees guessed for himself. No, the culprits were the other two. And nothing could be done about them, because Billy would not be saying. And George could not speak up—if he had got it out of Billy, which seemed inevitable, given his death. Had George been so pushed himself, that he took the boy and hanged him? Undoubtedly, that was the best solution from his point of view. If Billy had been charged and found guilty, it would have ruined George. And maybe his business too. Strong and others had pooh-poohed the idea. But it was a strange coincidence that Sergeant Grant and Billy should have died when it looked so helpful to George. Ah well, Mirrilees said to himself, maybe we'll never know the truth.

Seeing nothing of interest, he walked up the path to the Manson funeral, where he saw Jessica, tall, slim and graceful, in the old green rain-coat, but looking like a Celtic queen, so poised and firm and full of warmth and intelligence, red hair blowing free in the light breeze, like the peoples' flag, and the eye clear and full of purpose. Some way from the grave, near Mirrilees himself, stood Jean, distraught, weaker and knowing it, and Susan, the child who had, after so many troubled months, found a cure, as if it were a miracle. Behind Jessica, at the grave, stood Peter, solemn and sorrowful, but he came forward soon enough to take a cord, and lay the coffin to its resting place.

In a lull in the proceedings, a man, a man with mousy brown hair, in an old brown trench-coat, stained and dirty, a tramp, probably, Mirrilees decided, detached himself from the crowd, went up to Jean Manson and handed over something to her, which glinted in the sunshine, and Mirrilees, curious, went closer to overhear. It was a medal, said the man. A Military Cross. There had been another one, he told her, a D.S.O., but he had sold that one. Mirrilees heard the man say how sorry he was, and then he moved off and disappeared among the crowd.

As a last act, Jessica stepped forward and addressed them all in a voice, vibrant with emotion and regret, but pleasure too. And just as she began to speak, Billy having already been laid down, George heard, and decided to put in an appearance for form's sake, as a good provost should.

Wearily, therefore, under the combined weight of the provost's gown and the gold chain of office, he began to climb the hill to where the great crowd stood around John Manson.

Jessica spoke out strongly, so that all could hear. 'I have listened to what has been said about my father and I feel impelled to add my piece. For I knew him as none of you; in triumph, when he moved us to tears in the pulpit—myself among them—and in the darkest hour of failure, when you had all deserted him. For that is what you did. And that is the true measure of the man. How was he at the darkest hour? How did he bear himself when he was alone, defenceless and half-dead already with the weight of your ignominy? And I tell you, I am proud of him! No man could have stood that so well. You killed him by it; and he forgave you. You destroyed his living and his life and he understood your failings. You thought the worst of him, when he was only good, a man withal, but a good one through and through. I think, I hope, my father has not died in vain. He taught us things by his sacrifice. To love one another; to defend each other, to stand up and speak up when evil men pull their strings for their own advancement and their own profit.' And Jessica's head turned to look down the hill at George, struggling up the path under the weight of his finery, which he liked to wear on every opportunity, and every head turned to look, and saw the object of her interest.

'What we have seen here is just an everyday crucifixion. So long as men remain blind to the antics of the evil among us; so long as they remain deaf to the truth and hear only the lies, skilfully spread by those who would supplant the good; so long as they remain silent and do not lend their aid to good men in need; so long will crucifixion be an everyday affair.

'My father believed in love and he was willing to die for it. And he loved you, all of you—even the worst among you, the thief and the murderer. He was not a perfect man but he tried to be. I know, as well as any one here, just how hard he tried. And if he failed a little, who does not? Who among us is perfect? I forgave my father his faults easily. I relish his goodness and I ask you to learn from his sacrifice. Evil flourishes when good men do nothing. So let all good men combine, and lift each other up and protect the right. Be vigilant! Use the brains God gave you. And be courageous. Above all, be a good neighbour, and believe in the power of love. For that power comes from you and you alone. My father thought, you see, that the power of God is in us. It is the goodness we all are capable of. I ask you never to lose sight of these things.'

And, as the crowd began to disperse and make their way, in ones and twos and threes, down the path, passing George, not one of them said a word to him, though he nodded to right and left. And as he stood alone now, watching them retreat from the cemetery, he viewed them without regret for their snubs. He knew they would forget this day soon enough. Many would come creeping back to eat again from his hand, when memories dimmed; and others would fudge his failures in their own woolly heads and find him not guilty. For that is how people are.

THE   END

EPILOGUE: Appendix 1

Since some may doubt that the kind of mathematical precocity described in the case of one of the young characters herein is possible, it is worth explaining further. It has been decided to try to reveal some of the mathematical elements of this, despite the objections of some non mathematical people. Why have a mathematical appendix in a novel? Because the maths is beautiful and yet simple, though it may appear complex. It is also very powerful: lends itself to many important applications. There is another side to this inclusion. Every writer should write to the limit of his ability, not the ability of the least able reader. Nor should this put anyone off, for it comes after the novel, the story, has been told.

So there is no good reason to object to some mathematics at this stage. It is here for the sake of the few, perhaps the very few, from this island and far more elsewhere, who will be interested and willing to spend the time and effort understanding these things.

The principle of working to the highest level and not the lowest was one I applied when I was enjoying my most successful years of teaching. Very few were switched off by this. Even without full understanding, they got the flavour of it. And that was exciting. This was obviously real maths which had great power, not simple boring stuff done for exams. On the contrary, that school soon became the most successful in the country and that department, of which I was head, the most successful in terms of national awards achieved over a period of several years and even after its charges left for university where a succession of scholarships and awards was won by them. But it was very different from every other. The drive, the emphasis, was not on passing exams —though these results were outstanding—but towards the experience and appreciation of mathematical ideas, often far beyond any narrow syllabus. Students were solving differential equations while still in their early teens. A few could prove the Einstein-Lorentz equations at 12 and do it publicly, without notes, in front of the maths club. Always, the answer to the question: do you really understand this apparently complex matter? was decided by whether they could produce the goods in this way under this kind of pressure. And they were questioned closely about it. The kinds of things that were done after the E-L equations were Maxwell's equations which most able children would do in the fourth year [aged 15 to16] after they had absorbed the principles of Calculus. Then followed the irrationality and transcendence of e and π. A book like *Famous Problems of Elementary Geometry*[3] by Felix Klein was a useful source here. Some went on to grapple with Einstein's Gravitational Equation, having first absorbed the ideas of Tensor Calculus. One pupil returned after 4 university terms to announce that he had just caught up with school work. ie he was then just beginning to encounter things he had not seen before. He [and another soon after] won a John Welsh Mathematical Bursary at Edinburgh at the end of his 2nd or 3rd year there. So their skill was independent of the school, autonomous, self motivating and self sufficient. The advantages to the student of this kind of preparation were considerable. My pupils were afraid of nothing and wanted nothing so much as to be presented every day with a fresh diet of intellectual wonders. Better still, deprived of any stimulus, they would find it for themselves and teach themselves. As some parents reported, in the evenings, in each others houses they would play at maths.

They were encouraged to come along after school with any sort of problem: usually having failed to understand some difficult line in an advanced proof or stuck with some brainteaser and I would endeavour to resolve the puzzle, trying very hard to think my way around it with nothing else to help but the textbook itself. A few times I failed but even in trying to do this, off the cuff, something useful was invariably learned. The matter was clearer if not completely clear. This was a kind of upper limit on this procedure.

---

[3] An expansion of lectures given at Gottingen University in 1894

I remember attending a Gifford Lecture at Edinburgh in 1972 when John Lucas first informed me[4] of Godel's Theorem: that any system of knowledge dependent only on elementary arithmetic was either incomplete or inconsistent. This was extraordinary. I did not believe it. At a maths conference, I came across a book in the university bookshop with the proof: 'Godel's Proof'[5]. I immediately gave up the conference and read the book. Ecstasy! Returned to my workplace, every able mind in the place was made aware of the result and, over a period of several weeks, the proof was explained on the board in the maths club after school. That theorem and its corollaries were staggering, for they seemed to cast into doubt the very certainty of mathematics. A simple arithmetical system should be capable of completion: deriving all the possible theorems in it. Not so! The Liar Paradox makes that impossible.

Another side to this is that there have been mathematically precocious children like Ruth Lawrence who entered Oxford aged about ten directly from primary school. Her tutor there was Professor Sir Michael Atiyah of St Catherine's College. I met Michael, as he then was, a few times at maths and science conferences. Since the possibility of really young children absorbing advanced mathematics was nothing new to me, the subject did not crop up very much in conversation. His interest, I expect, was that his niece was a probationer in my department at that time and he wanted to know what I thought of her prospects as a teacher (she may have given him the gist of my original and unusually successful doings). We attended a few lectures in company together and I attended one or two of his. Michael eventually won a Fields Medal [equivalent to the Nobel prize] for maths and was successively President both of the Royal Society and the Royal Society of Edinburgh.

Serving as I did on the Scottish Mathematical Council, attending so many conferences, giving lectures in universities and colleges and writing in so many journals as I did, I was well placed to see what was going on in other maths departments. I believe nothing like what I was doing was going on anywhere else in the country and do not think it had been done before (or since). Some schools were very good at preparing for exams but that is all they deemed worthwhile. Investigating the upper reaches of the subject for the sake of interest and excitement was very different from becoming skilled at scholarship-type problems. Since 1985 (when I left to go abroad) the mathematical content of school maths has been in sharp decline. Before that time, in my department, the ablest would do A level maths London University a month or two after higher, get an A, and in the sixth year would do all five papers usually to a very high standard (A's again), each of them worth an A level, which I later taught in two colleges abroad: A level Pure and Applied and Further maths, Cambridge Board. So I am well placed to make the comparison. On leaving that comprehensive school, they would be able to solve many second order differential equations, would be good at probability theory, be able to solve a fine range of problems in mechanics and be competent computer programmers as well as group theorists. Above all, they had exceptional enthusiasm and experience beyond their years of advanced ideas.

The idea of presenting young students, a dozen or so years of age, with the statement of Lord Kelvin that a mathematician is one to whom it is obvious that $\int e^{-x} dx = \sqrt{\pi}$ (with infinite limits) and setting them the challenge of understanding it, even if it never became obvious, was my own, I used it all the time as a stimulus and I do not know of anyone else who did this. Undoubtedly, it was very effective in creating an interest in the subject and in

---

[4] That year, exceptionally, there were 4 Gifford lecturers, all dealing with the concept of mind: CH Waddington, Geneticist, Anthony Kenny, Philosopher, Christopher Longuet-Higgins, Artificial Intelligence expert, and John Lucas, Theologian. Each took turns in the main lecture before comments by the others.

[5] by Nagel and Newman pub Routledge, Kegan & Paul, 1959 repr 1976

motivating children to learn. It gave them an obvious cachet to be embarked on this quest—
a kind of holy grail— assured of admission to an elite group, if successful. The question was
not, will I understand this? But when? Can I do it by the time I am 16, as some could. The
fact that many of my students were winning renown was known and this was an incentive.
There was an expectation that others could do the same. Of course it was my creed that no
one should have limits imposed upon him. Every student was made aware of his or her
immense potential.

It should therefore be seen as a feather in the cap of this little island that one of its sons
should have mixed in the high company of mathematicians like Sir Michael, Sir Herman
Bondi[6] who (along with Professor Patterson, then Chairman of the Scottish Mathematical
Council) sponsored my fellowship in maths and offered an introduction to a book I wrote
and even, when it failed to find a publisher, to co author one, and John Conway[7], discoverer
of the Surreal numbers, then a reader in Cambridge at Sydney Sussex College and latterly of
Princeton Institute for Advanced Study, eventual home of Einstein who lived there for many
years in a detached, clapboard house at 112 Mercer Street. I also encountered, briefly at a
conference at Oxford, Sir Roger Penrose who gave the best lecture I ever heard. At Durham,
c1981, he told us about efforts to tile the infinite plain with kites and darts. The mathematics
that came out of it was wonderful. He had just flown in from Harvard where he had been
telling the American mathematical community. [The cynic might call this name-dropping.
Nothing of the kind! These experiences inspired my own teaching.] Roger's tome: *The Road
to Reality*, [the bible on physics] is a terrific piece of work and would have been set as a
challenge to my secondary pupils had I still been at the chalk face.

---

[6] When I had to do with Hermann he was Master of Churchill College, Cambridge, and
Head of the Natural Environment Research Council, having been before that, the
Government's Chief Scientist at the Dept of Energy. His greatest achievement perhaps, is as
co author of the Steady State Theory along with Samuel Gold and Sir Fred Hoyle. When
Hermann was on the platform presenting prizes to some of my students at St Andrews
College, Glasgow, it was a particular pleasure to tell those that sat beside me in the audience
all about the meetings in a Lyons Coffee House when this discovery was made—at least
according to the accounts then current in the mathematical community. Later, Lady
Christine Bondi informed me that the earliest and most productive conversations were in the
Bondi's flat in Trinity Street, Cambridge. Hermann gave a very successful 13 hour series on
TV explaining Einstein's Relativity Theory. That day, when I learned that Hermann would
like to talk to our first prizewinner, Jim McColm, I ran across the college hunting him, for I
knew Hermann would not stay long. It took nearly half an hour to find Jim but I got him to
Hermann's side and left him there to have a one-to-one with one of the great scientists of the
age.

[7] Conway was a colleague of John Wiles at Princeton, who managed to prove Fermat's Last
Theorem [which had remained unproved, even believed unprovable by many, for centuries],
having deliberately stayed away from the College in case anyone like Conway got involved
and took some of his credit. I spent a few days in Conway's company at a maths conference
in Liverpool at which he was giving a lecture. We attended other lectures together and
talked mathematics until 4 in the morning. As I was returning along the corridor with coffee
to keep me awake, John would continue his argument when I was still yards from the door
of my room. His energy was inexhaustible. He was a talker and not a writer. Writing he
found difficult. His discoveries of Surreal numbers and their properties, for example, were
written up by Donald Knuth. John Brent, Professor of Maths at Cape Town, a contemporary
at Cambridge, told me that Conway nearly failed his Phd because he had difficulty writing
things down. See later.

This has become a very mathematical epilogue. I set out to account for the presence of mathematical precocity: to show that it exists and that the character invented is not impossible—far from it in her unusual circumstances. Since I have dealt with the maths projects' success of my pupils to a limited extent, it will, I see, be worthwhile, to reveal some more of this. Some good will come from it, I hope. This will seem less of an unconditional triumph. The downside is always worthwhile.

In an eight year period, 29 prizes for maths projects were won by my pupils out of about 60 awarded to Scotland as a whole. One student, Michael Crawford, won first prize in every year but sixth year. So he won 5 of them, all first prizes. He also won other national prizes for problem solving. Why did he not win in the sixth year? Because he did not compete! He would not do a project in his final year at school because the school failed to recognise his excellence. And with the mathematical knowledge at his command he could, I believe, have achieved something very remarkable, maybe even an utterly fresh discovery. He could have worked on one of the great theorems still to be proved by anyone. This is what I would probably have suggested: in number theory, say. One of Hilbert's problems, anyway.

How did the school fail him?[8] There is a common belief that a school glories in its successes. Not so! The capacity for jealousy and resentment is proportional to the success achieved. If these students win so many prizes for maths, was the question, why do they not win prizes for chemistry? Or physics? Or some other subject? The fact that there were not—then at least—many opportunities to compete for other subjects is forgotten. Someone, perhaps Professor Patterson of Aberdeen, or a predecessor in the Scottish Mathematical Council, had set up the prizes for Scotland in maths, with funding, and the rest of the academic community was lagging in this important innovative means of stimulating development. [At George Watson's College, when these prizes first became available around 1968, I was strongly encouraged to use projects and the prizes which could be competed for, as a means of encouraging interest in the subject; and in that school, any kind of success was wanted and lauded, without reservation. I remember a student of mine winning one of the first prizes awarded: for a programme to play chess. I encouraged him to seek help from the local university computer dept which he did.] But only later, as head of maths in a comprehensive was this early experience developed further by me.

And so, every fresh success in one department causes increased gloom for the others who have none to report. And so, to resolve this, efforts are made to diminish the success or tarnish it. Only within a staff of unusual decency will this not occur.

In this case, the point of attack was elementary: the prizes for maths were mainly for mathematics projects whose most obvious characteristic was that the subject chosen was in advance of the expected mathematical level of that age of student. It was easy then to claim that the project was created by the teacher and not the student. Only the teacher and the student could know each other's contribution. Some would also claim that the parent and had done it for the student—a clear impossibility in many cases, given the relative ignorance of the parents.

The test—the test I laid down as standard practice in my school—was to close-question the student and one or two were found not to understand what they had produced; and failed accordingly; project not presented to any competition, marked down in course work. [At this time (1976-84), projects were not officially part of the educational curriculum; that came after I left the country, around 1985. But they were a part of my department's curriculum, at

---

[8] David Hilbert, a Professor at Gottingen, in 1914, I think, stated about 34 problems at a maths conference in which he, in effect, challenged everyone to solve. In the years since many have been solved: The Four Colour problem, Fermat's Last Theorem and the Prime Number Problem, among others.

my insistence]. The best test was to have the student give a public presentation, always the case in a matter of some difficulty— but always a matter of great beauty and power as well: nothing was ever done because it was merely difficult.

What was my contribution? As a stimulator of intellectual excitement, that mainly; but it had to be shown, the matter had to be explained, step by step, at least at the start. You had to reveal not only the excitement but that the ideas, whatever they were, lay within their power to grasp. I remember making great efforts to try to explain the various steps in the derivations of the results I wanted to show. Since Michael Crawford won five first prizes out of the 29 awarded to our students in my eight years there, I will relate his story, mainly.

At the maths club, I began to talk about The Theory of Relativity, mentioning its remarkable consequences. At great speed, time passes more slowly; you would age more slowly if travelling at near the speed of light relative to someone who was stationary; the speed of light cannot be exceeded. These were the hooks: the stimuli used to develop interest. I explained the Einstein-Lorentz equations, some of them, to the dozen or so students present, Michael aged 12 among them. The method was simple. The hardest part was the idea that dividing a finite number by zero produced infinity, an idea sharpened a few years later by the idea of the limit.

Divide 1 by 0.1 and what do you get? 10. Divide 1 by 0.01 and what do you get? 100. Divide 1 by 0.001 and what do you get? 1,000. Divide 1 by 0.0000001 and what do you get? 1,000,000. So when the number in the denominator gets smaller and smaller, the quotient (the answer) becomes larger and larger. This is why the mass of an object travelling very fast becomes larger and larger, for it is affected by a factor[9] in the denominator which gradually tends to zero [everything relative to an observer, of course]. I explained about the national competition, the prize of £40 [I never earned more from the Times Educational Supplement for a full page article, then, so this was a large sum in 1976] and that this would make a good topic. Michael was interested and I told him he would have to explain the whole thing and above all, understand it totally. He took this on, I gave him an elementary textbook, he asked very few questions and eventually derived all four equations in public before an audience of about twenty, without difficulty and without notes. He answered questions successfully. The project was submitted and eventually, after submission, was awarded first prize for that age group in Scotland.

I took about a dozen pupils to the prizegiving (in Jordanhill College, I think) so that the others would be stimulated by his success. What was next? Kelvin's definition of a mathematician[10]. But you need to understand Calculus for that, I said. I explained how important this was. I then gave him 'Calculus Made Easy,' by Sylvanus P. Thomson, Lord Kelvin[11]'s grandson. Michael read this by himself and asked few questions. I soon cleared up some of the work in it, with limits, explaining these, [Sylvanus left this out, rightly, in a first textbook]. Before long, I was setting Michael special exams in maths for him alone, apart from the usual ones, to test his understanding and knowledge: his ability to integrate and differentiate and solve problems using these. He was still only fifteen. Whether

---

[9] The Fitzgerald factor.

[10] Kelvin's definition is not a sine qua non. It is just a sign that the person described is a mathematician; one used to dealing with advanced notation. A short-hand way of defining the creature.

[11] Sir William Thomson became Lord Kelvin. He was second wrangler at Cambridge, beaten by Parkinson, a man who focused on exams. Kelvin was the greater scientist, Parkinson, never heard of again. The Tripos then was full of out-dated 200 year old Newtonian Lemmas which had to be memorized and unrealistic problem solving like jumping through hoops: creativity was not measured; speed was.

Kelvin's result ever became obvious to Michael, while still at school, is hard to say. But he soon understood that the result was true and what power of application it produced. Since he could write down the equation very easily, I think it fair to say that it was for him obvious. Of course he knew what it meant: the area under the exponential curve.

Once he had Calculus the whole world of mathematical analysis opened up to him. Soon he could integrate and differentiate many things and knew about Maclaurin[12] Series and the others that follow. I soon tested this by setting him exams on calculus under full exam conditions, in which he excelled.

The next challenge was the Maxwell Equations. There are four of these and usually they are nowadays expressed in vector calculus notation.[13] It was not long before the proof of the equations fell to Michael's understanding. I think I helped him over the first hurdles of vector notation[14] but he learned a lot himself. I think another student got the prize for a project on these equations, Michael having moved on to the irrationality of e and pi.

In the fifth year, Michael chose [at my suggestion and for reasons I gave] to attempt a project on Quantum Mechanics. I gave him some books. That is, I looked for and found books simple enough for him to manage. I think even these included Tensor Calculus. Late in the year he came with a few questions, two or three. The first pair I managed to figure out answers which seemed to satisfy him. The third question I could not answer. At that time in the session I knew I did not have the time to investigate this deep matter. 'I don't understand it then,' he said. 'Then you must leave it out,' was my response. The project was submitted but including only work that he understood. In due time, Michael was awarded first prize for that category. I was quite satisfied that he understood all that he had submitted. Prof Mackie [15]of Edinburgh who wrote the report said: the project was remarkable but he did not see how it could do without some treatment of group velocities, or words to that effect. Since this was the bit he did not understand and had been told to omit, that was entirely fair and above board.

I was asked, as usual, to name the prize-winners for maths that year. Another student had been given a mark of 100% for the standard exam in arithmetic— not even mathematics. [I think they were equal on the standard maths exams.] Michael had been given 99% for arithmetic. But whereas the other had done nothing else, Michael, had won national prizes— first prizes— for mathematical problem solving and mathematics projects and had, as before, done an additional, special exam which measured his advanced knowledge and, if that were not enough additional distinction, obtained an A level from London University at A grade. In addition, he had done to a very high standard, the same prelim in Analysis as the sixth formers, though still in fifth year. Of course I awarded the prize to Michael. The headmaster reversed my decision and the other student was awarded the prize instead. [This student obtained a first class degree like Michael but was unlikely to be a creative mathematician as he did not have the requisite outlook: closed instead of open. He depended upon being asked questions in a fixed syllabus and he viewed his own development as a paper chase, not as an intellectual voyage of adventure, in which he was continually asking his own questions. To the creative thinker, asking one's own questions is fundamental. This is why someone like Lord Kelvin was world famous when Parkinson, who beat him in the

---

[12] Maclaurin was born at Glendaruel, which is close to Bute, and became Professor of Maths at Edinburgh on Newton's say so.

[13] Maxwell used dp/dt, however, instead of del. Interestingly, Maxwell's pseudonym to his 3 mathematical friends, one of them William Thomson, Lord Kelvin, was the symbol dp/dt. There is a postcard from the former to the latter signed with this derivative!

[14] d/dt is the differential operator, nowadays indicated by the Greek letter Del.

[15] Professor of Mathematical Physics

Tripos exams, was never heard of again. Passing exams is not what education is about. Nor is it what a genuine intellectual is interested in. That is ideas, especially new ones. They are usually beautiful and also powerful, having great range of application, not necessarily immediately. This distinction was not understood, I think, by the staff, even by the head who was a trained maths teacher. This failure of understanding was responsible for the mistaken belief in some that the success in projects was tainted by the help received. And yet, even a research student receives a great deal of help from his supervisor. So the objection is invalid, worthless and even stupid.]

The best I could do [apart from writing a full page feature of protest in the Times Educational Supplement about it] was to award my own prizes. I gave Michael a prize of £20 out of my own pocket. Learning this, the official school prize-winner was awarded much more than usual.

That, then, is why Michael did not attempt a project in his sixth year. The school had let him down. Of course he got an A in each of all five Maths papers in the sixth year. A John Welsh Mathematical Bursary at Edinburgh University followed 2 or 3 years later. In a similar situation when Bertrand Russell failed narrowly to get top marks in an entrance scholarship to Trinity, Whitehead named Russell first and destroyed the papers. He knew which was the more original mind. He was right: Russell was not only a wrangler but phenomenally original, not just in mathematics but philosophy too and was awarded two Nobel prizes, one for literature, the other for peace.

The decisive argument for the validity of this method of teaching— inspiring young mathematicians to understand the upper reaches of the subject at an early age, would be a better description— was that I never did know or understand some of the most advanced things they had done. There is nothing unusual in this in the mathematical community. In 1868 there were 12 subjects and 38 sub categories in Mathematics . In 1979 there were 60 subjects and 3,400 sub categories.[16] How many are there now, nearly 30 years later? Probably about double! Change accelerates, is not proportional. No one in 1979 was master of all these subjects and subcategories. Hardly anyone was master of more than two or three. So, that the teacher might know less about something than his ablest students, is nothing new.

Jim McColm's project on Einstein's Gravitational Equation is another example. I am not sure whose idea it was to attempt this. It may have been his or mine. I think I gave him some books to study but I believe he found some others he preferred in a library. I answered a couple of questions about Tensor Calculus of a technical nature at the beginning but I never saw this project until it was finished. It used Tensors but went far beyond them. I read it one night and discussed it the next day before submitting it. It was new to me, I understood it myself quite well and I was satisfied that he did. He had probably explained things more clearly than the textbook, knowing I might challenge any line. It was awarded first prize for the sixth form category in the Scottish Mathematical Council's projects competition: the top prize then.

It is easily seen that this is a perfectly valid method of proceeding. The advantages to the students were immense. Gave them, not only the kudos of success, brought distinction to their school and inspired others by it to similar efforts but, most of all, it gave them the experience of investigation, of teaching themselves, of finding things out for themselves and the techniques acquired were highly advantageous when they met them again, years later, at the end of honours degree courses. Beyond even this, these very techniques and these

---

[16] *The Mathematical Experience* by Profs. Philip Davis and Reuben Hersh, [Both were awarded the Chauvenet Prize by the Mathematical Association of America] pub Birkhauser 1981. Appendix B p29,30. I reviewed this book for *The Mathematical Gazette*.

experiences of advanced work at such an early age were bound to make it far more likely that they really would discover something remarkable in that window of opportunity [all too short for most, so it is commonly believed: ten years or so] when their creative powers were at their height.

After a lecture I gave to the staff and students of the maths department at Edinburgh University, an objection was raised by one of the staff, Dr Mott, son-in-law of Professor Alexander Craig Aitken, whose lectures I had had the honour to attend in my own first year there. Aitken nearly failed his Phd, it was said, and almost broke down trying to deal with the subject which E.T. Whittaker, then the Professor, had set him. That subject just could not produce an answer. Conclusion: no student should ever be invited to work on a subject in which the tutor is not already an expert and knows can be resolved.

This is nonsense! Nothing original would ever be done if the teacher had to know it could be done by himself in advance of the student's effort. Of course young minds at the peak of their ability should be encouraged to take on the most apparently severe problems. Anyway, if they are any good, they will do so, with or without supervision. But what if they are going to fail the Phd? Take more time; do another subject. Any mind with originality ought to attempt things that are genuinely difficult. It is what such minds are for. Something worthy, even if it is less than a solution, will come out of it. The pursuit of knowledge is a thing far more important than chasing a degree which is only a piece of paper, after all. Rather cut one's teeth on a problem which has defied everybody's efforts for centuries— and fail— than produce some boring, useless, tract no one will read, just because it can be expected to produce an answer.

The idea of teaching maths using projects and the stimulus of ideas far beyond the expected level of the student was undoubtedly an excellent one, provided the teacher had the enthusiasm to bring it off and the knowledge systems to make understanding possible ie not merely understanding the ideas but having a way of conveying the steps in the logic. Using the history was always useful. What was Newton trying to do? Why did he need Calculus? Why does Godel's theorem matter? What is so exciting about Einstein's Theory? And so on. Understanding how these ideas worked became, for some students, a kind of holy grail, which had them teaching themselves and each other, at speed, so as to bring them closer to full comprehension. Every time I returned from a maths or science conference I would fling fresh clouds of ideas into the air and soon find they had taken root in some mind or other.

But this is a specialised activity. Not every teacher is capable of it. Teaching has to be viewed, not as a job, but as one of the most exciting things one does. The excitement does rub off and it enables students to proceed independently. The buzz word in this kind of teaching is IDEAS, not exams or courses, still less, passes or grades. It is about learning for its own sake. Of course the ideas are useful, you can get jobs from what you do, you can do useful things in the world with these ideas. You should be able to pass exams more easily. [Invariably true in my experience]. But the ideas themselves are primary. They are beautiful and powerful and wonderful and they lead to so many more questions that lead into strange worlds we might never have imagined. The advantage to the young mind of meeting advanced ideas early is in enabling him to focus on the essential idea that solves the problem. This is the essence of all creative thinking. There is a question and there are answers. Asking the one and learning to understand the other is an invaluable asset in the youthful mind in showing him how to do it himself. It is no accident that my own university teachers— the best of them— urged me to read the original papers. Then I would see how the great men thought. And went about resolving difficulties.

Because of his very familiarity with advanced ideas and notation, nothing is outside his reach, no act of will is necessary to overcome the shock of what he is dealing with. Instead, fortified by his experience, the youngster is able to approach really difficult work in a relaxed way and with a formidable confidence that he will understand the matter. The sooner the mind is capable of this the more likely that something really original will be discovered. There is a common belief among mathematicians that they are past it at thirty. If so, all the years beforehand should be used to advantage. That is one of the things this method does.

Question: 'Do you understand that difficult set of ideas that you have been investigating?' 'Not quite all of it.' 'How much is that?' 'About 90%. I can't quite grasp this particular idea.' 'That's fine! Some day soon, you will understand even this. For now, you have done very well to understand as much as you do. And if there is time and if I am good enough I will try to help you to understand this idea that still escapes you.' That is the spirit of this sort of teaching. The central motive is: understanding. Eg Can I understand the proof of Maxwell's Equations? Since these equations are wonderful— relationships between physical variables that are very surprising— they are worth understanding; not only an intellectual challenge.

Recognise, by the way, that once one does, one is able to understand a host of other things and solve a wide collection of difficult problems, at least in principle.

A fundamental feature of the teaching, not just by textbook but by projects, was the determination that nothing unworthy would be praised. What you put in your project, you understood; were honest about what you did not understand, for what you were in pursuit of was knowledge, the increased ability to understand complex ideas which matter. The satisfaction and the enjoyment. The course work that was introduced in my absence abroad—partly as a result of my doings and papers of mine in mathematical journals—and became part of the work for certificates, failed to work as an examination procedure because the task of assessing it was left to the teachers and they had too great a vested interest in the outcome to deal severely with cases of fraud. And so this method that I had found to be so productive in stimulating and developing young minds was quickly given up. There is a lesson here. When a new technique like this is working well, even if only in a single classroom, it should not be trashed just because it cannot work everywhere else. Teachers are not all able to do what the enthusiast like me can do. I would spend many hours a week dealing with advanced ideas in my spare time so that I could stimulate my pupils with them. A lot of teachers do not have time for this.

Efforts to improve education by 'raising standards' are derisory, since these have fallen drastically, year after year, over the last 25 years. The best of my students in 1976-84 had 5 A passes in Sixth Year studies and a near perfect score in Higher and A level as well as national prizes. There is nothing like this now. Some honours maths courses now do not include work that my best school pupils did routinely while still at school. Nor is the most important thing a fine building and a small number of pupils to every teacher. The teacher is king! He is the key! If he loves his subject and is not hindered from doing his best and if the parents support his efforts and if the pupils have some native aptitude, that is all you need. But the most important factor in education is the enthusiasm and ability of the teacher. Everything should be done to maximise his performance in front of the class, for that is where the magic lies. Not in 'work shops' when the teacher spends 2 minutes with each pupil. Only people who do not understand education think this is of value. It is a waste of time! The best teachers are highly educated, highly motivated people who are like missionaries selling their subject. And their success depends upon the frequency of their getting through. They operate best in front of many pupils, not few, for their purpose is to inspire, that above all and that is best done before an audience of many.

Lest anyone should imagine that my career, even at my best, was an unqualified success, I am happy to point out that it was very different: a constant battle, usually against mediocrity. My best students could easily have done O levels a year early, giving more time for other things but were not allowed to sit the exams. As we have seen, the school's head appeared to care[17] less about real excellence than the rather juvenile procedure for measuring it, based on standard prelim exams— which were incapable of revealing the phenomenal differences of ability and attainment of some pupils.

In one important way at least, my performance of the role of head of department was deficient. I never did any socialising— at least until my last year in the place and then only briefly and in the evenings. I worked nearly all the time, began around nine A.M. and carried straight on through lunch to around five o'clock or longer if the maths club were meeting. I often worked through the coffee break and rarely sat down in a staff room and then only alone to think. I did spend time writing articles for the Times Ed. Supp. and various journals as well as reviewing books and giving lectures at times at educational conferences. From these my views should have been known. Yet, the opinion of the school staff at large should have been something I was willing to influence far more than I did. It could only have been done by going around talking to people and the outcome would have been doing a lot less work, something I would have regretted. I believe I did circulate papers on occasion but this is never quite so effective as having a group of supporters one sees everyday and who will easily take one's side because they know where you are coming from. Even so, I simply did not fit in. When there was a strike of teachers I would never take part, would carry on as usual until the school was closed down around me, which the head was willing to do. I never thought of myself as doing the job for money and would often spend my own money on books [some of which I lent out to students] and materials as well as courses. Teaching was what I wanted to do and I got great personal satisfaction from it. The idea of withholding my labour for the sake of a slightly higher salary was anathema. Teaching, at that time in my life, was my vocation. But money was tight. I turned down the chance of a Phd part time in Mathematical Logic at this period, partly because of the cost; there were two others, one in Philosophy, the other in Mathematical Education. The fact that I was conscious of doing original things in education was a large part of the refusal. Any creative mind must always take the most creative line available.[18]

Another mistake was this. Eager to reward the ablest, I might say to them: you and I are the only people in this school who understand this: the Godel Theorem or whatever. The only people in the county, very often. The staff would not, I expect, like this very much. Yet since it was true, why not state the obvious? The staff should have been big enough to accept it. Passing the boards covered in complex equations, beyond their competence, of course they knew it was true. A more sensitive soul would have declined to make that reward, even though it was clear enough, for the sake of the amour proper of the staff.[19] A

---

[17] It may be that he was prevented by his superiors from allowing this. Even so, he should have resisted it, been bright enough to put real excellence first. Probably the resentment of others played its part in the decision.

[18] In Santa Fe, in 1987, I encountered Anthony Brooke, who should have been 4th Rajah of Sarawak. I knew a great deal about him, having researched and written a novel about that place and understood his value very well, as he could see. I was offered all his papers to write his official biography which he begged me to do. I turned it down. I was busy on a novel, a far more difficult task.

[19] If I were in the same situation today, I might act differently for the sake of the morale of the staff for that is a fundamental element in any school's success. However, there are cases where the morale of an individual, if unrealistic, must be diminished. One of my experienced teachers with a lot of self belief came to me and enquired if she might award 100% to separate students for a sixth form exam question when they had different answers. Investigating, I found that neither answer was correct and marked both students down. That

lot of resentment was directed at me because of the unusual things I was doing. Of course this did not help—but it did help my students. It gave them a fine sense of kudos to think that they and I were lonely members of an exclusive club.

Another nonsense in current educational practice is the idea of throwing money at education. It is not about money! It is about fostering that most elusive quality, inspiration, in the staff, trusting it, when it is present and supporting it in every conceivable way. I have known a few people like myself who were inspiring teachers. All of them are distinguished by one factor: they all left teaching early, usually because of illness following battles against idiot managers who frustrated efforts towards excellence. One, a teacher of English with a gift for textual criticism, poetry (he had been a poet), producing plays, as well as the usual phenomenal crop of excellent results in exams, fought against a headmaster whose school allocated a morning for English once a week, and a morning for maths etc. Only an idiot would try to impose such a stupid regime. If there is no contact every day, of course everything learned on Monday will be forgotten by the next Monday. One of the anomalies in my own last port of call was a headmaster who thought the tearaway who could not add and subtract should be taught in the same class as the Further Maths student, just because they were the same age. And was prepared to over-rule me on this. The frustration of the tearaway could only increase and hinder the progress of the scholar. But probably the worst aspect of education is the bureaucracy which controls it, issuing major quantities of paper to be filled up and discarded and which has no real understanding of the process of teaching. It takes ten years to make a good teacher. The bureaucrats rarely have such experience. If they were any good they would remain at the chalk face.

Everything that has occurred in education in the last two decades has conspired to reduce the morale of staff and their individual self confidence. They have in effect been disempowered, have no control over the pupils because it has been taken away from them and have been demeaned by many of the things, like form filling, which they are required to do. There is far too much testing and time wasted on persuading people like parents that every child has made progress, though the extent of it is not worth measuring.

In the very successful years as a teacher that I enjoyed, success was partly due to the power I had as head of a large department. A lot of this was not in the job but in myself, my determination and ambition to do my very best for the 1600 students in my care. I was able to do many things that would not go down well now. I exercised a lot of sheer force in dealing with recalcitrants and even in dealing with my superiors, because it was necessary. I remember that I did not engage in routine form filling very much, though I would spend hours writing up my report on the department's doings-detailing the deficiencies of my superiors when necessary ie when they had frustrated my efforts to produce excellence; or compiling the department's budget, for I was quartermaster and how money was spent was important: buying esoteric books was part of this, though I invariably paid for them myself. I did very little marking, [only at exams or mid term tests] chose instead to spend my time acquiring fresh ideas, sometimes having to overcome intellectual difficulties of understanding: stimulating my own mind[20] in order that I could convey what I learned to my students. So my preparation for teaching was as much a continuation of my own education as anything. I attended lectures right across country in the evenings, took an intense interest in science, and philosophy as well as maths and often interrupted the normal course of events in the classroom by disquisitions upon any subject that seemed relevant or especially interesting. I have given lessons on 'Poetry is Mathematics' and 'The Peloponnesian or

---

teacher soon gave up teaching that subject. There are intellectual standards that must never be offended. Everyone has to know this, staff and students alike.

[20] This was no hardship! Since I was fascinated by the things I studied, it was a joy.

Trojan War' or 'Stories about Sir Isaac Newton', performed sensational experiments in Psychology eg Conformity studies etc; and then, having done nothing in the course, told the class to go home and teach themselves the simple things that came next.

None of this would be possible in the culture of today, I expect. But that is what education should be like and how teachers should behave. The freedom for the teacher to develop himself as an intellectual, first and foremost, has been lost. That is where the enthusiasm for ideas which makes inspiring others possible, comes from. His time is taken up with trivial routines which, though demanded by the job, do not assist him to inspire his students. Inspiration is the key. Inspire the student and he will teach himself.

Note: most of the equations mentioned and some of the mathematics are in this book in a separate appendix at the very end.

Peter McPhail, Jim McColm, Michael Crawford, David Stevenson, Craig Dowers, David Henderson, Sandra Bryan, Julie Sillars, Mary Roberts, Ann Hall, John Cleland, Paul Thomson, Margaret? McLean, Fiona Manson, Kirsty Wark, Alistair McIntosh, are the names of just a few of those it was my privilege and pleasure to teach. Many others, some just as distinguished, have been erased by deterioration in a quarter century of honourable struggle of diverse kinds.

FROM p 206: Yes, the word 'muggle' in modern children's fiction comes from me! JK Rowling heard me use the word and later phoned me to ask if she might use my word 'muggle'. Of course I agreed. Around 1994 or 1995, at the SAW writers conference at Crieff Hydro, I met her while waiting to go into the SAW AGM. She was unsure if she would be allowed to attend the AGM as I do not think she had become a member by that time. 'Are you a writer?' I asked. She said she was. 'Then you have every right to attend,' I told her. I took her into the hall and we sat together and talked before the others arrived. Amusingly, it seems now, I was performing my duty as 'an established writer' in offering help and advice to a novice. 'What is your writing name?' I asked. 'JK Rowling,' she replied. I didn't think that was a very good idea. 'What is your main character's name? I asked. 'Harry Potter.' I didn't think that was very good idea either. I thought she should change both. Then, enquiring further, I learned that she thought her fictions 'real.' This argument, using, my idea of muggle-dorpel, was my response. I had taught philosophy, using this very argument, for years and had it off pat. She lost the argument. She might think now that she should have won it. I would still disagree. Fiction is still fiction, though it be world famous.

Disappointed at the court case about the origin of the word being fought at great unnecessary expense, for I could have settled it in an instant, I wrote to her publisher, since the acknowledgement would have been useful to me, might have attracted a publisher. And received a phone call from her asking if I needed anything. I said I was depressed and trying to write but would manage. Of course I needed many things, living on a pittance while working full time at my writing. She insisted I write down her phone number and I did so and that I should get in touch if I did need anything; but the piece of paper soon fell off the desk and joined a hundred others on the floor. In dire straits often, I regretted this. However, the use of my word is not much and I do not grudge it. She has brought much happiness to the world of children. I have learned to do without publishers and even money, for I have never made a profit from writing.

APPENDIX 2: Mathematics.

Maclaurin's Theorem. [Colin Maclaurin (1698-1746) was an Argyll son of the manse, brought up in Glendaruel, who became professor of Maths at Aberdeen aged 19[1] and later at Edinburgh on Newton's recommendation. He was a geometer, mainly]

This theorem tells us that in many cases a function can expressed as a power series: that is, a series of terms in x whose powers increase one at a time, $f(x) = a + bx + cx^2 + dx^3 + \ldots \ldots (1)$ where the letters a,b,c,.... represent numbers or constants.

Notice that the differential of any constant is zero. $f(x + h) - f(x)$ is zero because the function is the same at x and x+h if f(x) is constant.

If x=0, in (1), $f(0) = a + b.0 + c.0 + d.0 + \ldots = a + 0 + 0 + 0 \ldots = a$

Now differentiate f(x) and we get $f'(x) = b + 2cx + 3dx^2 + 4ex^3 \ldots$, (2)

So let x=0 $\qquad\qquad\qquad\qquad f'(0) = b$

We can now fill in two bits of the formula for f(x), for we know that a is f(0) and b is f'(0). So $f(x) = f(0) + f'(0)x + cx^2 + dx^3 + \ldots \ldots$

How can we get c? Differentiate (2): $f''(x) = 0 + 2c + 3.2dx + 4.3ex^2 + \ldots$

$\qquad\qquad\qquad\qquad$ So $f''(0) = 2c$

This means that $c = f''(0)/2$

So $f(x) = f(0) + f'(0) + f''(0)/2 + dx^3 + \ldots$

To get d, differentiate f''(x) and we get $f'''(x) = 3.2 d + 4.3.2ex + \ldots$

So letting x be zero again, $f'''(0) = 3.2.d + 0 \ldots$ which means $d = f'''(0)/ 3.2$.

And so $f(x) = f(0) + f'(0)x + f''(0)x^2/2 + f'''(0)x^3/3.2 + \ldots$

the next constant, e is easily seen to be $e = f''''(0)/4.3.2$ and so on.

What would the next constant be? $f'''''(0)/5.4.3.2$

$e^{i\pi} + 1 = 0$ is easy to show with the above theorem, given the derivatives of sinx, cosx and e^x. These are: cosx, -sinx and e^x. This equation is marvellous because of the simplicity of the relation between the 5 most remarkable numbers that there are. It was Newton who first[2] produced the series for these functions.

$$e^{ix} = 1 + \frac{ix}{1!} - \frac{x^2}{2!} - \frac{ix^3}{3!} + \frac{x^4}{4!} + \ldots = cosx + isinx$$

---

[1] p468, *History of Mathematics*, Carl Boyer, pub Wiley,1968.
[2] Westfall, *Never at Rest*, p205

Einstein-Lorentz Equations.

These are: $m = \dfrac{m_0}{\sqrt{1 - \dfrac{v^2}{c^2}}}$; $l = l_0 \sqrt{1 - \dfrac{v^2}{c^2}}$; $v = v_0 \sqrt{1 - \dfrac{v^2}{c^2}}$;

$t = \dfrac{t_0}{\sqrt{1 - \dfrac{v^2}{c^2}}}$ where m_0, l_0, v_0, t_0 are the mass, length, volume and

time of an observer and the others the mass, length, volume and time of the moving object relative to him at the speed v, where c is the speed of light ie approx 186,300 miles per second in a vacuum These results mean that a body travelling at near the speed of light experiences changes of mass, length, time and volume, as shown above, relative to an observer. At the speed of light, the mass becomes infinite, the length and volume become zero and time infinite. This is a good reason why travel at the speed of light is 'impossible'. Students aged 12 were easily able to understand the proofs of these. Imagine v approaching c and these conclusions are obvious.

Kelvin's 'Mathematician' Result. $\displaystyle\int_{-inf}^{inf} e^{-x^2}\, dx = \sqrt{\pi}$.

Lord Kelvin, (Baron Kelvin of Largs) Sir William Thomson [1824-1907] was the son of a Belfast maths teacher, and attended the universities of Glasgow and Cambridge. See p 1139, Life of Lord Kelvin by Sylvanus P. Thompson, where, in a footnote, Kelvin is reported to have interrupted a lecture to enquire: 'Do you know what a mathematician is?' He wrote down the above equation and said: 'A mathematician is one to whom *that* is as obvious as that twice two makes four is to you. Liouville was a mathematician.'
There are probably many people who regard themselves today with some justice as mathematicians to whom this is not as obvious as that. In Kelvin's day, the world of mathematics was greatly contracted. Nowadays, there are legitimate mathematical fields in which people operate as mathematicians who are entitled to have forgotten this result altogether. Still, once you can prove it and have dealt with it enough, of course it does become obvious, even if, perhaps, never quite as obvious

as Kelvin suggested. The ambition to understand this result— the proof of it— was an invaluable spur to my best students, some of whom did so by the age of 16.

I set out to provide a proof of this but have had to abandon the idea because of the amount of space needed. There is no point in dropping the type size or cramming the work just to make it fit the available space. And the matter would have to be amplified at every stage for the sake of the general reader of whom nothing could be taken for granted. What I have done below is show the main lines of a proof involving beta and gamma functions. Some lines are omitted which the enthusiast could obtain for himself. There is still merit in this procedure: it gives the general reader the idea of what the mathematics looks like. It may look complicated but is fairly simple; it is also interesting because it looks sophisticated and even beautiful. However it is utterly contrary to my style of teaching which was to include extra lines if it made the matter clearer, a practice I have had to abandon here.

What does the above integral mean?

That the area between the curve of the function and the x axis is $\sqrt{\pi}$.

This is a very surprising result for π is a very remarkable number because it is impossible to define it as a finite string of digits. It is 3.141592653..... And yet this beautiful curve produces an area exactly equal to this elementary function of π . It is not hard to draw. Give x some values and you will soon see what it looks like. [e=2.71828....; take it as 3]

It is, however worth noticing that if we divide both sides by $\sqrt{\pi}$ we get the value 1 on the right hand side of the above equation. This means that the function then within the integral can be used a probability function.

The maximum value of the function is unity and this is on the y axis. The rest of the curve decreases as we approach infinity in either direction. So the curve lies between 0 and 1, as all probability functions do.

Indeed, by introducing the mean μ and standard deviation, σ, a far more general function is obtained which is the normal distribution curve. This can be used to determine the probabilities of a very wide range of variables such as a person's height, his weight and IQ.

There are more elementary ways of doing this proof but the one I favoured with good students in a comprehensive school involved beta and gamma functions.

Define, the gamma function, $\Gamma(m) = \int_0^{inf} x^{m-1} e^{-x} \, dx$, m>0

then $\Gamma(2) = \int_0^{inf} xe^{-x}$, $\Gamma\left(\frac{1}{2}\right) = \int_0^{inf} x^{-\frac{1}{2}} e^{-x} \, dx$, $\Gamma(1) = \int_0^{inf} e^{-x} \, dx = 1$

Theorem: $\Gamma(m) = (m-1)\Gamma(m-1)$, m=1,2.... for using

$\int uv' \, dx = uv - \int u' v \, dx$, $\Gamma(m) = \left[x^{m-1}(-e^{-x}) \right]_0^{inf} -$

$\int_0^{inf} (m-1)x^{m-2}(-e^{-x}) \, dx = 0 + (m-1)\Gamma(m-1)$ So

$\Gamma(m) = (m-1)\Gamma(m-1) = (m-1)(m-2)\Gamma(m-2)$
$\qquad\qquad\qquad\qquad = (m-1)(m-2)(m-3)\Gamma(m-3)$

Thus, $\Gamma(m) = (m-1)(m-2)(m-3)(m-4) \quad ......1\Gamma(1) = (m-1)!\,\Gamma(1)$

$\qquad\qquad = (m-1)! \int_0^{inf} x^0 e^{-x} \, dx = (m-1)! \int_0^{inf} e^{-x} \, dx = (m-1)!$

$\left(\left[-e^{-x} \right]_0^{inf} = (m-1)! \right.$

Define the beta function, $B(m,n) = \int_0^1 x^{m-1}(1-x)^{n-1} \, dx$, where m,

n>0. Theorem: B(m,n) =B(n,m) for,

$B(m,n) = \int_1^0 (1-y)^{m-1} \left(y^{n-1} \right) (-dy)$, if 1-x=y which is

$\int_0^1 (1-y)^{m-1} y^{n-1} \, dy = \int_0^1 y^{n-1}(1-y)^{m-1} \, dy = \int_0^1 x^{n-1}(1-x)^{m-1} \, dx$,

changing y into x.

$$B(1/2,1/2) \;=\; \int_0^1 x^{-\frac{1}{2}}(1-x)^{-\frac{1}{2}}\, dx \text{ which is}$$

$$\int_{\frac{\pi}{2}}^{0}\left(\cos^2\phi\right)^{-\frac{1}{2}}\left(1-\cos^2\phi\right)^{-\frac{1}{2}}\cdot\left(-2\cos\phi\right)\sin\phi\, d\phi \;\;,\text{ with x}=\cos^2\phi \text{ giving}$$

$$-2\int_{\frac{\pi}{2}}^{0}\left(\cos\phi\right)^{-1}\left(\sin^2\phi\right)^{-\frac{1}{2}}\cos\phi\sin\phi\, d\phi = 2\int_{0}^{\frac{\pi}{2}} d\phi = \pi$$

$$\Gamma(m)\,\Gamma(n)=4\int_{0}^{inf} x^{2m-1} e^{(-x^2)}\, dx \int_{0}^{inf} y^{2n-1} e^{-y^2}\, dy \;,\;\; \text{using x}=y^2$$

which gives
$$4\int_{0}^{inf}\int_{0}^{inf} x^{2m-1}\, y^{2n-1}\, e^{-\left(x^2+y^2\right)}\, dxdy$$

$$=4\int_{0}^{\frac{\pi}{2}}\int_{0}^{inf}\left(r\cos\phi\right)^{2m-1}\left(r\sin\phi\right)^{2n-1} e^{-r^2}\, r\, drd\phi \;\; \text{using } x=r\cos\phi, y=r\sin\phi$$

$$=4\int_{0}^{\frac{\pi}{2}}\int_{0}^{inf} r^{2m+2n-1}\cos^{2m-1}\phi\sin^{2n-1}\phi\, e^{-r^2}\, drd\phi$$

$$=4\int_{0}^{inf} r^{2(m+n)-1} e^{-r^2}\, dr \int_{0}^{\frac{\pi}{2}}\sin^{2n-1}\phi\cos^{2m-1}\phi\, d\phi = 2\Gamma(m+n)\cdot\frac{B(m,n)}{2}\;,$$

where $x=r^2$ and $y=\sin^2\phi$

$$=\Gamma(m+n)\,B(m,n) \text{ Thus } B\left(\frac{1}{2},\frac{1}{2}\right)=\frac{\Gamma\left(\frac{1}{2}\right)\Gamma\left(\frac{1}{2}\right)}{\Gamma(1)}=\left(\Gamma\left(\frac{1}{2}\right)\right)^2$$

Since $B(1/2,1/2)=\pi = \left(\Gamma\left(\frac{1}{2}\right)\right)^2 = \left(\int_{0}^{inf} x^{-\frac{1}{2}} e^{-x}\, dx\right)^2$ which means that $\Gamma\left(\dfrac{1}{2}\right)=\sqrt{\pi}$ and putting $x=y^2$, $dx=2ydy$ we have

$$2\int_{o}^{inf} e^{-y^2}\,dy=\sqrt{\pi}\quad \text{Thus}\quad \int_{-inf}^{inf} e^{-y2}\,dy=\Gamma\left(\dfrac{1}{2}\right)=\sqrt{\pi}\ , \text{ the curve being}$$

symmetrical.

Maxwell's Equations: James Clerk Maxwell (1831-1879), was brought up at Glenlair, near Parton, Galloway and India St, Edinburgh, when he attended Edinburgh Academy. Like Kelvin, he was second in the Maths Tripos. He came from a distinguished family of lawyers and mathematicians. His grandfather, a sea captain, wrecked on the coast of India, swam ashore using the bag for his pipes as a float and then frightened off the Bengal tigers and cheered the survivors by playing them[3]. Once, aged 23 he walked home from Carlisle to Glenlair: 50 miles. Professor at Aberdeen, King's College, London and directed the Cavendish laboratory, Cambridge, where he held the chair of Experimental Physics. Not given much credit in his lifetime, even by Kelvin, a good friend. Einstein was one of the first to fully appreciate his achievement, though, in spite of a strong Scottish accent and a habit of chaotic expression, his genius was obvious to many contemporaries. Even so, he was made redundant at Aberdeen when the colleges combined. Years after his death, letters to Aberdeen University addressed to JC Maxwell were returned routinely: 'not known at this address.' The inability of universities to recognise excellence is normal. Einstein was placed last in his class and did his best work while working as a clerk in the patents office, the humblest of jobs, but the only one he could get. The equations can be written in many forms. My preference is for the del form but the software does not have the symbol. Div and curl are differential operators in 3 dimensions, the curl is a cross product and the div a dot product of vectors.

$$\text{curl}\ \underset{\sim}{E}=-\frac{\partial \underset{\sim}{B}}{\partial t}\ ;\ \text{curl}\ \underset{\sim}{H}=\underset{\sim}{J}+\frac{\partial \underset{\sim}{D}}{\partial t}\ ;\ \text{div}\ \underset{\sim}{D}=\rho\ ;\ \text{div}\ \underset{\sim}{B}=0\ ,$$

---

[3] Tolstoy's Biography, p11

where ρ is the real volume density, $\underset{\sim}{J}$ is the real current density, $\underset{\sim}{E}$ is the electric field, $\underset{\sim}{D}$, the electric displacement and $\underset{\sim}{B}$ is the magnetic inductance, with some variability of definition. Able students of 16 could understand these very well.

Einstein's Gravitational Equation: Einstein (1879-1955) was born at Ulm, was disruptive in class and expelled from the secondary school (Luitpold Gymnasium[4]). Aged 16, discovered a paradox by considering what would happen if travelling on a beam of light at the speed of light, an early gedanken experiment (thought experiment), as all his best subsequent works would be. Without a secondary school certificate he was not admitted to Zurich Polytechnic without the entrance exam which he failed, though admitted the next year, trained as a teacher and became 'one of the awkward scholars who might or might not graduate.[5]' Renounced his German citizenship, aged 17 and became stateless till 1901 when he became a Swiss. Noticed by Max Planck and transported to Berlin where he taught until persecuted by the Nazis when he left and eventually settled at Princeton's Institute for Advanced Study. An important figure in the decision to build an Atomic Bomb at Los Alamos. The first world famous scientific celebrity.

$R^{ij} - \dfrac{1}{2} g^{ij} R + \lambda g^{ij} = -kT^{ij}$ These unusual symbols are tensors.

Note: Newton's Gravitational Equation can be written:

$\underset{\sim}{F} = -Gm_1 \dfrac{m_2}{r^2} \underset{\sim}{r}$, **where r is a unit vector.**

Newton (1642-1725) dated his transformation as a scholar to the day he defeated the school bully at Grantham Grammar. Yet he 'lost his groats' in the oral exam at Trinity ie failed[6]. Most original moves made while Cambridge was closed during the plague year, his annus mirabilis, 1665-6. In 1975 or 6, I picked up a hitchhiker at Strathaven, probably because of his bags of books and took him to the M74. A sculptor, he had been seeking white granite for a commission for Unicef when his

---

[4] Ronald W Clark's biog, p35
[5] ibid p52
[6] Westfall, *Never at Rest*, p140

car and all his money had been stolen. His mentor, Dame Barbara
Hepworth that day had smoked her last cigarette in bed and he had to
attend the funeral in the south of England. Hence the lift. He had read
the latest work on the Philosophy of Art[7] as I quickly discovered during
the short journey, for I had been reading it myself. Taking his leave, he
said, 'By the way, my name is Newton.' 'No relation, I suppose,' I
replied. 'Yes, actually. I was brought up in the Manor House at
Woolsthorpe.' I drove off, gobsmacked; and then, tearfully, turned the
car as soon as possible to relocate him and empty the contents of my
wallet into his. By then, he had found another lift, alas. Since Newton's
father died before he was born and his mother married a clergyman
named Barnabas Smith, (B.A, Oxford, 1601) my passenger must have
come from his father's side of the family for the name to have
continued.
Newton was descended from an East Lothian, Scottish family, of no
intellectual distinction, one of whom accompanied James I to England.[8]
His father was illiterate and it was his mother's family, the Ayscoughs,
who educated him. Newton was famously absent minded. He was found
dragging a bridle unaware that the horse bolted. Once, when he had
acquired a cat, to stop it disturbing his work by scratching to get in or
out, he had a hole cut in the bottom of the door. When the cat had a
kitten he ordered a smaller hole made beside it. His appetite for
knowledge was phenomenal. It was said of him that he 'would kill
himself with work' and he eventually suffered a mental breakdown. He
worked at maths, physics, astronomy, alchemy and religion, principally;
and went from one to another until temporarily sated. He was secretive
and suspicious and inclined to hold back from publishing. *Principia*
appeared in 3 vols dating from 1684 and was funded by Edmund
Halley. It was written in Latin to discourage 'little smatterers' from
asking annoying questions. *Optics* was published in 1703. I read most of
it at 17 having chosen it as the book awarded as my maths prize at
Rothesay Academy. Newton fought with both Hooke and Leibniz about
priority, to his discredit but won because of his powerful personality.

---

[7] *Art and Its Objects*, Richard Wollheim
[8] Westfall, *Never at Rest*, p40, CUP. According to Newton in a conversation reported
with James Gregory.

Leibniz's notation for Calculus is far easier. Newton was a covert unitarian and had it been known he would have been forced to leave the university. He was its Member of Parliament, knighted, and left in 1696 to become Master of the Royal Mint. He was President of the Royal Society for many years, author of the Corpuscular Theory of Light. Principia is subtitled: A System of the World. Every major question in the physical world of the 17th century was explained by him or capable of explanation—so he and many others believed—because of the power of the mathematics he had produced. Late in his life, Johann Bernoulli set a couple of problems 'to the world' not expecting a solution and maybe, as a way of showing off. Newton answered them after a single evening's thought and when the solution arrived, without a signature, Bernoulli is supposed to have said: 'I recognise the lion by his paw print.' [9]

Newton's distinctive characteristic, shared with Einstein, was a total focus upon his work: constantly trying to solve the problems that naturally and continually arose in his mind. He was not a people person. Erwin Schrodinger and Richard Feynman were highly sociable and enjoyed many affairs, like Russell. Von Neumann was reported to have downed 16 martinis at a party. W.R. Hamilton, author of quaternions, who could speak 14 languages at 14, actually died of gout, probably due to exessive alcohol. Littlewood fathered 2 children by his mistress, a woman married to someone else; and GH Hardy was a practising homosexual. Ramanujan believed a Goddess, Namagiri, carved his new theorems every night on his tongue. Hardy reportedly thought Ramanujan the best mathematician in the world in 500 years. Why? Because every day they worked together (which they did 5 days a week for a few years) Ramanujan gave him new formulas for infinite series, partitions etc which, mostly, Hardy immediately knew were correct but struggled to prove. Most mathematicians discover one or two theorems in a lifetime, if they are lucky. Ramanujan died aged 33, no one understands why. An unusual diet, caused by esoteric religious beliefs, perhaps.

---

[9] Westfall, p582

OTHER BOOKS BY William Scott

The Bannockburn Years published by Luath Press, Edinburgh, 543/2 Castlehill, The Royal Mile, Edinburgh, £7.95 paperback.

'William Scott,..a brilliant storyteller.' Nigel Tranter.
'A stirring and thoroughly researched account.' Scotland on Sunday.
'Compulsively readable.' The Scotsman
'Strong Bute bond in Bannockburn book' The Buteman.

This novel, set in Bute in 1314, which won the Constable Trophy in 1997, was written to discover arguments to settle the question of Scottish Independence. Four arguments were found. The first insights about how the Battle of Bannockburn was fought and where, are in this book. Original material on Scottish archery and on the tactics of the Scots which led to the victories. The research exposed inadequacies in the current thinking in the Scottish History Community. The two books that followed were the result of a decade of full time investigation of the battle which answer all the questions about it. Though the research which followed was used to upgrade the novel without increasing the number of pages— a matter of some difficulty, time, effort, labour and skill—made at the invitation of the publisher and despite a contract which allowed for this, he declined to make the small but important alterations in the second edition. He put profit before the truth.

Bannockburn Revealed published by Elenkus, 2000.
ISBN 9780952191018. £25. Hardback; 505pp, including 70 pages of colour photos and maps of the battle area. Signed copies sent to individuals in the UK post free; £35 rest of the world.
This is a very original investigation of the battle using new procedures which demolished the false beliefs which have lasted centuries. Where exactly the battle was fought and how won is made clear here and shown for the first time. All the written reports of the time are translated and analysed within the book. The conclusions, drawn from a dozen sources, tabulated, are clear and established with overwhelming force.
There was no Scottish cavalry charge as everyone has believed for centuries. The Scots attacked the English on foot, penned them between the two streams in the Carse in which they had camped out of bowshot of Balquhiderock Wood, which was in Scottish hands. And when they got within 60 yds of the English cavalry (which had, expecting a foxhunt of rebels camped in the van) cutting down the available space to get up speed in

a charge, the Scots dug their pike butts into the soft ground (it had been raining torrentially just before) the English charged, were held and then pulled off their horses and killed. Unable to move forward due to the 15,000 Scots present, who filled the half mile between the streams, sideways because of the streams, (swollen with rain and the tide and muddied by an army camped beside them) and backwards because of the press of hangers on, trying to see, the English were unable to manoeuvre and were systematically slain. Unless you have a good map of the battle area, the battle cannot be understood. The map here, was made by excising every change since 1314 on Gen. Roy's map of 1750—a brilliant production for that time. This new map of 1314 took a year to make and involved hundreds of visits to the area. In future, history will have to be done this way: assembling all the sources in one book, analysing them, issue by issue, and tabulating the results. When all the relevant sources are consulted and they are in the book, there is nothing more to be said. The battle area is shown in about 70 coloured photographs.

The above work breaks new ground in the communication of history in other ways. Every issue is decided by facts, photographed and justified by the inclusion of the translated written sources and every relevant map.

The simplest reason for the site of the battle is that the English were camped in the Carse and the Scots attacked them there. That is why the battle-site is the Carse. When all the relevant sources are taken together, the evidence for this overwhelming. One source, The Brut y Tywysogyon, by a Welshman, probably an archer, definitely present at the battle, tells of the 'battle among the pools.' This is the Carse. Even today, after heavy rain, it is full of pools of water, the only place around like this. Some of the pools are 100yds long and a yard deep. The idea that the battle occurred on the Dryfield is ridiculous. It never has pools of water, being a rounded hill from which water runs off or is absorbed. No wonder it is called; 'Dry.' It always is dry. Only the MS 20 version of this source says this [there are two others, both useless]. One of the enduring wonders of this subject is the bad scholarship and stupidity of the academic historians involved who have not consulted all the sources, have laid smokescreens with sources that are irrelevant being written centuries later by folk who knew nothing—and show it because they say practically nothing but a phrase of 3 words—and have never taken the trouble to understand the ground of the battle area, so that their maps are utterly inadequate. If you cannot draw the Pelstream accurately (as Fiona Watson and Prof Barrow cannot), of course you do not realize its significance. If, like Professor Cowan, you cannot even draw Gillies Hill, Coxet hill and the burn correctly, (see recent article in the Scotsman where Gillies Hill is beside the burn and Coxet Hill is north of Gillies Hill instead of east of it) bad scholarship is all you reveal. I have offered to show them the battle area and always been rejected. They are content with their ignorance. Barrow admitted to me in writing that his book was written after a 2 day walk around the six square miles of the area, as if this were enough. Plainly from his errors, he has never stood in the gorge of the Pelstream and does not know where it is, despite its being 100yds wide and 100ft deep. It took me hundreds of visits to the area over a decade to understand its many mysteries. When these people can appreciate Euclid's proof of the infinity of primes, I will believe they might make headway with the idea of proof. This was one of Hardy's favourites, justly—yet simple. I know that they do not. Those who have read my work are continually amazed by the stupidity of the academics considered to know best because of their titles and supposed authority. They do our country a disservice by concealing the truth because of their arrogance, laziness, stupidity and vanity. The battle site is under threat because of this. Of course they try to bury my work because it exposes the mistakes in their own. The fact that has become clear is that academic historians do not understand the idea of proof. To this mathematician they seem like children. If only they understood the necessity for rigorous study of all the sources that would be something, the willingness to get their hands and feet dirty in all weathers—especially very wet weather when unusual things are learned—and assume nothing in advance. Prejudice governs all they do.

Bannockburn Proved published by Elenkus 2005 ISBN 9780952191094; comb bound, A4, 343 pp including 70 pages of maps and photographs and 6 loose A3 enclosures including copies of the OS Map of the area surveyed 1860; and Roy Maps joined in full colour (I was the first to join the two maps), Jefferies' map of 1746 (both of which confirm the existence of the Knoll in the Carse) and Pont's—all of the area of the battle plus about 30 other maps, all necessary for a full understanding. A very limited edition, cost £100, p&p £10 UK; £15 Rest of World.

This work provides formal proofs of the result that the battle was fought in the Carse of Balquhiderock and how it was fought in detail. There are 8 levels of proof from a sentence to a four-page proof which uses quotations from all the sources, an original and compelling technique. The best proof is the last one, where 3 simple propositions are established and these are overwhelming. Only someone very stupid or prejudiced could read this carefully and not be persuaded. Future discoveries in archaeology are shown to be irrelevant,
The maps in this work are different. They are triangulated and the finest ever seen. Errors in Roy's maps due to the lack of triangulation have been removed. A year and half full time, with many more investigations of the

entire area was spent on these new maps alone. These maps show the elevations, the woodland, the streams, slopes, buildings, roads and fords as they would have been in 1314 (there were no bridges then: the first bridge across the Bannock burn was not erected until 1516) with great accuracy. Without a good, <u>fully justified</u> map (every detail is explained in a 27,000 word appendix[21]), the battle cannot be understood. This is the first time that anyone made <u>a fully justified map</u> of this important area at the time. All other maps have been unjustified and full or errors that made the reported description as well as the place of battle, in many cases, nonsense.

REVIEWS:

'You should get a doctorate from every university in Scotland for this.
This book {*Bannockburn Proved*], like its predecessor, *Bannockburn Revealed*, is the result of dedicated, exhaustive and patient research and, for one reader at least, settles the vexed question of the site of the Battle of Bannockburn.' Irvine Smith, Advocate, Sheriff and Historian.

'William Scott's is the best piece of research on history—not just Bannockburn—of that period that I have ever encountered.' Roger Graham, The Greenock Telegraph.

'I found Mr Scott's account quite fascinating…As regards the site of the battle, he demonstrates conclusively that it must be the Carse of Balquhiderock….Indeed, he demonstrates that [the Dryfield] would have been impossible.' Review by Patrick Cadell, Historian, ex Keeper of The Records of Scotland. In *Scottish Local History*, Spring 2006.

'William Scott brings to this sequel to his previous book, Bannockburn Revealed… his further consideration of the subject, attacked with the thoroughness and cold logic one would associate with a consummate mathematician. As a classical scholar and student of Ancient History I particularly appreciate his evaluation of evidence, sifting the dross from the gold. He has challenged the historical establishment and in so doing ruffled many a feather. *I would put him on a par with the young Michael Ventris whose work on the decipherment of Linear B confounded the Classical establishment of his time.*

---

[21] 100 pages of *Bannockburn Revealed* are about the battle area: the topography, which determines the tactics and is such an important feature of the victory.

'Hopefully, William Scott will in the end gain the same acceptance.' Tom McCallum, MA Hons, St Andrews.

'There are two reasons why *Bannockburn Proved* is one of the great publications of the early 21st century. The first is the combination of historical scholarship and painstaking on the ground investigation which shows clearly the true site of the battle, and how the Scots achieved such a notable victory in 1314. The second is that the author has found himself, in a modern context, engaged with the same kind of opposition that faced King Robert, in the guise of a coalition of intellectuals and town councillors who now find their superiority challenged and overthrown by a man who understands the battleground.' Rev Jock Stein, Minister and Theology Publisher.

'Thank you for *Bannockburn Revealed*. It's quite a while since I felt overwhelmed by a book—especially non fiction. A whole week-end was wiped out for me—engrossed in reading and map referencing, with the occasional twenty-minute trip out in the car to check out this landmark or that. Perhaps it was the enthusiasm of the style; maybe the pace and very compelling argument. Certainly I found myself delighted by your invaluable met-analytical approach. It's a storming piece of work. Thank you.' Dr David Simpson, Stirling.

'The Starting point is a close consideration of the original sources, all of which are printed together, in full, for the first time. This gives you a full opportunity to read them all and form your own views. This in itself is sufficient justification for buying the book...you will learn that there were not four schiltroms but three and why...that there was no Scottish cavalry charge...because noe of them fought mounted. There was no heroic appearance by the Small Folk, waving their laundry...and even had they appeared where they are supposed to have done, no one on the battlefield would have seen them. And, most surprising of all, the basis on which the size of the Scottish army has been computed is wholly fallacious. Mr Scott has, I believe, definitively established that the main action took place in the Carse of Balquhiderock. He has reached this compelling conclusion as a result of an in=depth study of old maps and photos of the area, particularly map of 1750 by General Roy and a team of cartographers who went on to great distinction...All this is combined with an unrivalled knowledge of the ground. The many photos of the area will leave you in no doubt that the maps you have seen in other books are at best simplistic and underestimate its complexity. This is an excellent book which I whole-heartedly recommend.' Review by Chris Jackson, Principal Crown Prosecutor, in *Slingshot*, no 230.

"I do believe that the battle area lay undiscovered for nearly seven centuries until William Scott walked the ground, year in year out, for nearly a decade! He alone studied this ground in minute detail making many remarkable discoveries in the process and I am convinced no one else has ever done this. I believe that no one else has made such exhaustive studies of the eye witness accounts and other important works associated with this event. His book is quite unique in that he applied scientific principles in his endeavour to find out what really happened. This turns out to be <u>far more astounding</u> than the account I was taught at school. All the Scots, including King Robert Bruce, on the day of main battle, walked to their glory! Not one Scot was on horseback! They walked up to the English camp in the early morning, made their presence known and, as the song says, 'sent them home to think again.'

"How did they do this. All is made clear in *Bannockburn Revealed*, a book of truly amazing scholarship, the first 'scientific' history book I've ever come across. The facts, the evidence, are all presented with great clarity and one is compelled to accept that here is the truth and because everything fits into place and makes sense. Sadly, what is truly astonishing, is that this book has not been properly read, understood and accepted by any historians from the academic community. These so called guardians of our national heritage, either through apathy or arrogance, have undoubtedly put one of our greatest national monuments, the battlefield itself, at risk. Their lack of commitment towards upholding what has proved to be the truth is likely to lead to a desecration of the battle site for commercial gain."

Donald Morrison, 2004.

'The earlier work *Bannockburn Revealed* is such an outstanding work of scholarship that every single molecule relating to the event has been exposed. In *Bannockburn Proved* William Scott has taken the molecular level to the atomic. Every minute detail has been re-examined raising the status of this book to a scientifically tested proof for all time. The medieval battle maps alone are outstanding documents justified by exhaustive scientific investigation. This proof was obtained after nearly two decades of hard labour. No ivory towers here but an intense examination of every square inch of the battle ground. No odd reference to an ancient map but a close scrutiny of all maps ancient and modern. No sporadic quote from an occasional source but a thorough searching of all the sources. No skimming of a few works relating to this event. In the process every strand of evidence has been teased out. Having studied W. Scott's work for many years I have to conclude that unlike many discoveries in mathematics, physics, medicine, astronomy, genetics etc, this work is not a theory but is the absolute truth simply because no other facts will ever be discovered which will discredit this truth. What a wonderful challenge for all the academic historians from every Scottish university to dissect this work and try to find fault with it. They will find none and only conclude that W. Scott should be appropriately recognized and applauded for his achievement..

'My involvement with W. Scott's work led me to undertake the construction of a 3D model of the battle area based on the Roy maps. Mr Scott has been examining every line and mark on the maps for almost two decades and I am convinced that he is in a class of his own with regard to Roy's maps. I concluded that Mr Scott had confirmed, one hundred per cent, everything of importance on the ground by an exhaustive study of the Roy maps supported by other useful maps of the area and the ground itself.'

Donald Morrison, 2006, 118 Alexander St, Dunoon, PA237PY tel 01369703006

The Bute Witches published by Elenkus 2007. ISBN 9780952191070.
What caused the witch trials in Bute in 1662, after which six women were burnt, who were responsible and why did one who escaped return 12 years later to be executed then?

344 pages softback Royal Octavo, notched bound, £12, £15 including postage in the UK; £19 Rest of the World. A book which contains all the relevant historical records, analysed, together with a reconstruction of events in narrative form. Obtainable from www.elenkus.com or Elenkus, G/L 23 Argyle Place, Rothesay, Isle of Bute PA20 0BA, UK. Individuals may have signed copies on request.

'*A masterly piece of writing and a riveting story*, based on meticulous research, by award winning author, William Scott. This tale captures the reader and transports him back three an a half centuries to dark and dangerous days, with a compelling solution to the mystery of the witches of Bute.' David Torrie, an editior, D.C. Thomson Publications

'I must give you all praise for your imaginative interpretation and fleshing out of the account in the archives. I can't fault your logical explanation of the witches' "evidence" and the return of Jonet McNicoll. Your novel is *enthralling* and would stand alone as historical fiction.

Tom McCallum, MA Hons Classics, St Andrews

'A formidable benchmark.' Craig Borland, *The Buteman*.

'**An astonishing true story**,' Martin Tierney, *The Herald,* 22.9.07

Honour Killing in Argyll & Bute published by Elenkus 2008.
ISBN 9780952191056. A5 paperback.
Price £8.99 from www.elenkus.com or £11 post free, UK; £15, rest of world.

<u>This novel answers the question: What would you do to divert a suicide bomber from, blowing himself and innocents to fragments? The characters discover the answer.</u>

'**I loved it. Beautifully written**, There is no tame happy ending, but there is much happiness.'—Rev Jock Stein, Minister and Theology Publisher, Kincardine

'**A riveting read**, showing in a dramatic and exciting way, through the lives of two young people, how religious and cultural differences can be overcome and how the idea of paradise can change with different circumstances. **This engrossing story leaves the reader totally overwhelmed.** A gripping and inspiring tale.' —Christine Boyd, Primary School Teacher, Glasgow

'**Award winning author, William Scott, has reached new heights with this powerful novel that will hold the reader spellbound.** In a style reminiscent of John Buchan at his best, the author tackles head on the subject of honour killings, and produces a devastating ending which will shock the reader.'—David Torrie, an editor, DC Thomson Publications   Dundee.

'I finished this in two sessions. **I found it moving, profound and gripping; the best fiction I have read for some time**. Modern cultural and religious dilemmas are shown to be solvable in a fascinating way. I particularly liked the final chapter; the puzzle of the Russian femme fatale solved in a pleasing if gruesome way.'—Tom McCallum, MA, Classicist, Stromness

'Your book has been read by me at almost one sitting. I found it very interesting, easy to read, very enjoyable and **a book I did not want to put down**…Not only is William Scott a very talented, dedicated and engrossing writer of Scottish History, he is also an accomplished writer of fiction..' — Colonel Bruce Niven, MA, MBE, PPA, ex Chief of Staff, S.A.S., Geographer, writer, Everest climber, Gurkha Commander and Leadership Trainer, Singapore

'**A great read**, in which mathematical and philosophical insights are seamlessly intertwined within a fascinating study into the fallacy of known paradise.' —Gordon McConnell, BA, BSc, Principal Maths, Ayrshire.